The Heiress Hunt

Without thinking, he cupped her jaw and tilted her head back to see her face. The touch was unexpectedly intimate, their bodies alarmingly close, and when their eyes met, they both seemed to pause. The skin beneath his hand was soft, like the petals of a flower, and she smelled of the ocean and lavender. He could drown in the emerald fire of her gaze, familiar yet so mysterious. He wanted to learn every secret she kept buried, give her every little thing her heart desired.

The tip of her tongue darted out to wet her lips as her hooded stare focused on his mouth, and Harrison sucked in a breath. Did she want him to kiss her? He studied her lips and ached to know her taste. To delve inside and feel her slickness. Stroke her tongue with his own and swallow down her little whimpers.

Let me. Dear God, please let me.

"Maddie . . ." It came out as a whispered plea.

That seemed to snap her out of the moment. Blinking, she pulled away, and his arms dropped to his sides. She cleared her throat. "Forgive me. I grew dizzy for a moment."

Yes, so did I.

Also by Joanna Shupe

Uptown Girls
THE ROGUE OF FIFTH AVENUE
THE PRINCE OF BROADWAY
THE DEVIL OF DOWNTOWN

The Four Hundred series
A DARING ARRANGEMENT
A SCANDALOUS DEAL
A NOTORIOUS VOW

The Knickerbocker Club series
MAGNATE
BARON
MOGUL
TYCOON

The Heiress Hunt

⌒ The Fifth Avenue Rebels ⌒

Joanna Shupe

AVONBOOKS

An Imprint of HarperCollinsPublishers

THE HEIRESS HUNT. Copyright © 2021 by Joanna Shupe. All rights reserved. Printed in the United States of America. No part of this book may be used or reproduced in any manner whatsoever without written permission except in the case of brief quotations embodied in critical articles and reviews. For information, address Harper-Collins Publishers, 195 Broadway, New York, NY 10007.

First Avon Books mass market printing: March 2021

Print Edition ISBN: 978-0-06-304504-0
Digital Edition ISBN: 978-0-06-304400-5

Cover design by Guido Caroti
Cover illustration by Jon Paul Ferrara
Author photo by Kathryn Huang

Avon, Avon & logo, and Avon Books & logo are registered trademarks of HarperCollins Publishers in the United States of America and other countries.

HarperCollins is a registered trademark of HarperCollins Publishers in the United States of America and other countries.

FIRST EDITION

21 22 23 24 25   QGM   10 9 8 7 6 5 4 3 2 1

*To the badass ladies of the
2019 Rita Writers' Room.
Thanks for all the laughs, the
support, the Cavill thigh pics,
and for making
this year a little less awful.*

The Heiress Hunt

Chapter One

New York City, 1895

No one hated being poor more than a rich man.

Harrison Archer, dressed in his shabbiest suit, tapped his knee with two fingertips and struggled for calm. It was nearly impossible in this house, the place where he'd grown up, surrounded by a family who made vipers seem friendly.

Remember why you're here.

Indeed, everything he'd been working toward was close at hand.

Vengeance.

He'd been plotting for a long time. Three years, in fact. Three years of studying and scheming in Paris, doing everything he could to amass a fortune large enough for the right moment.

That moment was now.

The Archers were weak. Nearly broke. Their company's stock value was the lowest in twenty years. Through investigators, Harrison learned that his father, who'd died eight months ago, had been borrowing company funds to cover personal debts for a decade. Thomas Archer, Harrison's brother, apparently had the business sense of a lump of coal, because he'd only worsened the situation when he took over as company president.

All that suited Harrison just fine. The destruction of the Archers was under way.

They'll never see it coming, not from a son they consider nothing more than a wastrel and lackwit.

His mother sucked air through her teeth, her cold stare sweeping over her second son. "I cannot fathom why it has taken you this long to return home, Harrison. Your father died more than half a year ago."

Harrison smoothed the rough wool of his old trousers. "You mean the father who disowned me three years ago? Funny, but no one sent me passage home to attend the funeral."

"Why on earth would we send you a ticket?" She lifted her nose as if a foul odor had overtaken the room. "Between all the mistresses and parties we hear about, no doubt you can afford passage on a steamer."

He could afford damn near anything, but he wouldn't tell his family as much. They had to think him poor and shiftless, no threat whatsoever to their precious little world. "That hardly matters, as I am here now."

"And thank God for that." Thomas rocked in his chair behind the desk, acting like the king of the kingdom he was raised to become. The panic lurking in his blue gaze gave him away, however, and Harrison relished the hint of desperation in the room. He wanted to soak in their anxiety, savor it like a fine wine.

Thomas nodded once at him. "Just in the nick of time, I might add. I assume you received my telegram."

There had been six telegrams, actually, all asking the same thing, but no use quibbling. Instead, Harrison reached into his coat pocket and withdrew the last one. He tossed the paper on the desk. "I came to New York just to tell you no to your faces."

And bankrupt them, of course, but he couldn't play that card quite yet. Shares of Archer Industries stock were still being located and purchased.

But soon. So very soon.

Today's visit was merely to watch them squirm when he refused their request.

"You cannot say no." Thomas slapped the smooth top of the walnut desk. "We need you to marry an heiress—quickly."

"Why would I bother?"

"Is it not obvious?"

"Not to me."

"We will lose the family company if you don't. Our grandfather founded Archer Industries before the war. We cannot be responsible for losing it."

Harrison lifted a brow. "We?"

Their mother huffed and thumped her cane on the floor. "Harrison, for once in your godforsaken life, pay attention."

The barb stung, a reminder of his childhood and the misery of living in this house.

Why can't you be more like your brother?

Why can't you sit still?
Why can't you ever do as you're told?

As a boy, he'd been energetic and unable to focus his attention for long stretches of time. That seemed to annoy just about anyone he encountered, including his nanny and tutors. His mother dealt with it through ice-cold silence, while his father's approach had been to use a heavy hand. A *very* heavy hand. As they grew, Thomas took to ridiculing Harrison, riling him up at every turn and causing him to lash out, which made Harrison appear increasingly more ill-mannered, an embarrassment to the family. His father began focusing more and more on Thomas, the perfect brother, until Harrison became an afterthought.

Harrison stroked his jaw. "Oh, I have been paying attention. You think I care about saving a family who disinherited me."

"Disinherited or not, you are part of this family," Thomas said. "Our name won't be worth anything in this city if you don't help us. What of my wife and family?" Married eight years ago, he now had three children. "We will lose the house, the company, the cottage in Newport. The racehorses, the yacht—everything we own will disappear, Harrison. We'll be out on the street."

"I fail to see how that is my problem." He checked his pocket watch for the time, feigning boredom to annoy both of them. "Considering my access to those luxuries was cut off years ago."

"Well, now." Thomas had the grace to appear sheepish. "I am certain, after you marry, we can come to some sort of an agreement, after the family debts are settled."

"I can change my will," their mother added, "to give you half of my stock upon my death."

Harrison nearly laughed. He would acquire everything they owned in less than a month. "What you are proposing is ludicrous. Even if I had an heiress in mind, it would take time to court her and plan the wedding." He started to get up. "We're done here—"

"You could compromise her," his mother said.

Harrison's stomach churned with disgust at those words, a horrific reminder of what he'd witnessed his father doing three years ago. He'd tried to stop Winthrop's abuse of the housemaid, but in the end it hadn't mattered. The police had been paid off and Harrison disinherited.

Now his mother had the nerve to suggest he compromise a woman.

Christ, he could not wait to destroy these people.

Thomas slid a piece of paper forward on the desk, obviously misinterpreting Harrison's silence for acquiescence. "Here are the names of every heiress of marriageable age who is not yet promised."

"Including that girl," his mother said. "The mannish one you followed around as a boy."

Harrison reacted instantly. Violently. The muscles in his body clenched and his lungs constricted as his system locked in disbelief. Even the dust motes seemed to pause in midair.

Was it true?

She hadn't married?

Maddie Webster had been his closest childhood friend and the girl he'd planned to wed.

Until she broke his heart. He had tried to forget her in Paris, not even inquiring after her with their mutual friends. He assumed she'd married some boring swell and settled into an East Side town house by now.

So what happened?

Not a lack of suitors, surely. Maddie's smile could transform a room, drawing in everyone just to bask in her joy. All of New York adored her, the golden girl of high society with more friends than Harrison could count. She'd been his opposite in nearly every way, yet the two of them had been inseparable as children. Thick as Five Points thieves—until the day he'd left for Paris.

"Though there are rumors," Thomas said absently, tapping his pen on the desk. "They say the Duke of Lockwood is soon to propose. Perhaps I should cross Miss Webster off—"

"Leave her." The words were out of Harrison's mouth before he could stop them, the order cracking throughout the cavernous space.

That got everyone's attention. His mother's expression turned calculating. "Does this mean you'll do it?"

His mind spun with possibility and he resisted the old urge to fidget. Before he left, Maddie had thought of him as a brother . . . but three years was a long time. They were adults now. He was no longer the supposed lazy and privileged second son, but a wealthy, hardworking businessman with property and interests all over Europe. He'd proven himself. She would notice the difference, wouldn't she?

Perhaps she'd see him as a man now.

How could she not? After all, no one knew him better—and he would ensure the word *brotherly* never entered her mind during their interactions.

Moreover, *soon-to-be-engaged* was not *engaged*. There was still time. Just barely, it seemed, but he and Maddie had a special bond, one even a duke could never rival.

Reaching out, he snatched up his brother's list. Over the next few weeks, he could devote all his attention to winning Maddie while the plans for Archer Industries fell into place. By summer's end he could have everything he'd ever wanted.

Every. Single. Thing.

His heart thumped with a familiar rush of determination. He'd accomplished the impossible in Paris, building a fortune from almost nothing. He could triumph once again with Maddie.

He stood and buttoned his coat. "I'll find an heiress and marry her."

"Thank goodness," his mother declared. "Finally you're of use to this family."

"Which one?" Thomas pointed to the list.

As if Harrison would tell them. "I haven't decided yet," he lied, and started for the door. "But I know just the person to help me figure it out."

MADDIE TWIRLED A lawn tennis racket in her hand and studied her childhood friend from afar as he approached the court. *He was back.*

Three years had passed since she'd seen Harrison Archer, with no word from him in all that time, and now he'd written a vague note last night to request her help.

She wasn't certain how to feel about that. While she was happy to see him, part of her still bristled that he'd dismissed their friendship so easily. She wasn't accustomed to being forgotten by those whom she considered close friends.

Christopher "Kit" Ward, had tagged along with Harrison this morning, but Maddie hardly noticed him, her gaze remaining locked on Harrison. The morning sun framed his face, illuminating his sharp cheekbones and strong jaw. While full lips and a straight nose complemented his perfect face, it was his piercing blue eyes that had caused debutantes to swoon.

Maddie hadn't thought much of his appeal back then, they were friends for so long, but this Harrison was . . . different. He walked with more confidence, his back straight and proud. His frame was bulkier than the college boy she remembered, with wider shoulders and a broader chest, and thick thighs that pulled tight against his white trousers.

A spark caught deep in her belly, a flare of appreciation that was entirely new—and unwanted. *You shouldn't be ogling him in such a crass manner.*

Yet she couldn't stop.

Goodness, he'd become a fully grown man—and a beautiful one, at that.

Exhaling, she stared at her feet and pushed away any fascination with his appearance. There had never been anything resembling desire between them—and she would not embarrass herself by starting now.

After all, they had known each other forever.

She'd been an only child desperate for a friend and he'd been a boy eager to escape his family. They had explored, swum, ridden bicycles and played together each summer since she was ten and he was twelve, the two of them nearly inseparable.

Until he'd left without a word during her debut. He hadn't returned to college for his senior year, instead disappearing to Europe.

Soon, stories of his Parisian escapades began reaching her ears. Women, parties, friendships with artists and cabaret dancers . . . Then she stopped listening because she didn't recognize this reprobate, the one arrested by Parisian gendarmes for cavorting with anarchists. Oh, yes. She'd heard that one, too.

Meanwhile, life in New York had carried on. Maddie threw herself into her love for tennis and decided to craft a plan for her future:

Practice every day without fail.

Hire Valentine Livingston, the finest doubles player in America, to act as her coach.

Push off marriage for two years so she could play competitive tennis across the country.

Marry at the end of her third season, making the very best match possible.

Thank goodness her mother and father had agreed.

This past spring, three years of hard work and carefully laid plans had finally paid off. She had qualified for the All-Comers competition at the Philadelphia Cricket Club at the end of June, also known as the U.S. National Championships.

It was her ultimate dream to become the top women's tennis player in the country.

"About time you arrived," she said as the men walked up. "I was afraid I'd need to play alone."

"Good morning," Kit said, kissing her cheek. "Have we thrown off your precious schedule?"

"You know you have. My whole day is booked and I must get in my practice."

"Blame this one." Kit jerked a thumb in the other man's direction. "He made me wait forever."

"I had to dig out the tennis whites." Harrison's voice was a deep rumble that rolled through her chest. "It's been a while since I've played. Hello, Maddie."

"Hello, Harrison. I see you've returned from Paris."

"Just yesterday."

"Ah."

Silence stretched. There was knowledge in his blue eyes, all their shared conversations, the sly smiles. A hundred jokes, a thousand secrets. He was at once so familiar and yet a complete stranger. Her throat burned with questions and recriminations, as well as stories of what he'd missed while he was away. But that was for her old friend. She had no idea what to say to the man standing in front of her now.

She willed him to offer up something—an apology? An excuse? Anything to help her understand his absence—but he remained silent, watching her. Was he also taking in the changes since they'd last seen each other? Thinking of their past history and wondering what happened?

One thing was clear. Their friendship hadn't

meant as much to him as it had to her. He'd moved away without any warning, with no goodbye. He hadn't even written her a letter in all this time.

"Shall we play?" Kit pointed to the court.

She cleared her throat. "I'm ready if you are."

Harrison shoved his hands in his trouser pockets. "I'll pour some coffee and switch out with Kit in the second set."

"There's no need for that," she said. "I'll play you both."

Harrison blinked several times, and Kit slapped him on the back. "You've been gone a long time, pal. She's better than the two of us combined, trust me." He wandered off to select a racket, leaving Maddie and Harrison alone.

"You look well," he said.

"Thank you. I was sorry to hear about your father."

The edge of his mouth hitched because they both knew better. "Were you, really?"

"No. He was not a nice man. I daresay Hell is grateful to have him."

Harrison chuckled. This was familiar territory, with bits of her old friend showing through in his amused expression, and the knot between her shoulder blades eased somewhat. "Pick up a racket. Let's get started."

The three of them soon stood on the court, with Maddie on one end and the men on the other. "You may serve first," she told Kit. "I need to work on my return."

Kit hit a slow serve that Maddie sent up the line for a winner. Harrison whistled. "Excellent shot, Mads."

The forgotten nickname nearly caused her to trip. Only Harrison had ever called her Mads. She didn't respond, and there was no more discussion for the next twenty minutes as play went back and forth. She focused on her swing, perfecting the spin and angles that made lawn tennis so exciting.

"So, Maddie," Harrison said between points. "Tell me about this duke of yours."

The question surprised her, and she bounced the tennis ball several times while considering a response.

To be precise, Lockwood wasn't her duke—at least not yet. When the Duke of Lockwood took New York society by storm in March, Maddie's mother reminded her of their agreement—that it was time for Maddie to choose a husband. After all, a fourth season was practically unheard of, even if the reason for not settling down was justified. Everyone knew that an English duke was the most powerful aristocrat save the queen, so Lockwood became the catch of the season. The challenge excited her, with the title of duchess as the final prize. She wasn't alone, however; the matchmakers went into a tizzy to get their daughters near the duke.

Maddie angled to attend several dinners where the handsome Duke of Lockwood was a guest, and the two of them got on well together right from the start based on a shared love of the outdoors and sporting pursuits. Since then, their relationship had blossomed and they now went driving in the park every Monday at four o'clock. Rumors of a betrothal raced through Fifth Avenue receiving rooms, and Maddie had every confidence she would soon receive Lockwood's ring.

When that happened, she would become a duchess and go on her own grand adventure across the pond. What more could a girl in her position possibly ask for?

Still, she and Harrison had never discussed other women or men in a romantic sense. The topic had been avoided, though she'd always assumed he chased bosoms and bustles, as had every other young man of her acquaintance back then.

He left and slept with half of Paris. Why should you feel the least bit awkward in discussing your future husband?

"He's a bit of a bore," Kit said, sotto voce, when Maddie didn't speak up.

"He is nothing of the sort." Maddie lifted her chin as she readied to serve the ball. "His Grace is kind and intelligent, a good conversationalist. We share many of the same interests."

"He's a hunting and fishing sort of chap," Kit said to Harrison. "Probably has hounds that chase foxes."

He did, actually. Lockwood had explained the practice to her one afternoon. She served the ball, starting the point.

"Sounds awful," Harrison remarked and hit a return to the left side of the court.

Maddie's skin prickled with irritation and anger. No one had the right to disparage Lockwood, least of all Harrison, a former friend who'd dropped her like a roll straight from the oven when he left town.

Before she could stop herself, she sent the ball whizzing toward his head.

He dove for cover and hit the ground, his chest flat on the grass, as the ball sailed over. "Good God, Maddie. What on earth was that for?"

An apology burned on her tongue but she swallowed it. "You have no right to criticize me."

"I am not criticizing you." Harrison rose and put his palms out. "I was criticizing the duke."

"Whom you've never even met."

"That never stopped us from criticizing your mother's guests during her garden parties."

Though she tried to stop it, her lips twitched as she fought off a smile. That had been one of their favorite games, to hide in the bushes just off the lawn and watch the guests, then invent names and backstories for each of them. "Remember the time she caught us and made us come out so she could introduce us?"

He grinned while he brushed dirt and grass off his white suit. "You were the color of a tomato."

"As were you, Harrison Archer."

He laughed, and Maddie suddenly realized how much she'd missed the sound. How much she'd missed *him*. She started to tell him as much, but quickly closed her mouth.

He didn't miss you. He never even wrote. Stop thinking you matter to him.

The only reason he'd reached out to her now was for a favor. Perhaps it was time to get to the point of the morning's reunion. "Your note mentioned you needed something."

"Yes, I need your help." Harrison ambled to

the net. "I realize it is an imposition, but I am desperate."

"Then I promise to keep an open mind."

"Good. I need you to help me find a wife."

Her jaw fell open. Out of everything he could have asked, she hadn't expected *that*.

Questions whirled in her mind like a spinning ball, yet she fought to keep her voice even as she drew closer. "A wife?"

"Yes—and fast."

"Wait a minute." Kit joined them at the net and frowned at Harrison. "Why on earth would you need to marry?"

"Mother says she'll cut me off otherwise."

"Dash it," Kit muttered.

"Precisely." Harrison's expression sobered as he turned to her. "Will you help me? You're friends with everyone in town."

"I can give you a few names to call upon." Heiresses were like hansom cabs in New York City; there was one on nearly every corner.

He shook his head. "That will take too long. I need this to happen quickly. I want to return to Paris before the end of the summer."

"End of the summer?" She blinked, stunned at this news. The man she remembered had been impetuous, prone to acting rashly, but this was shocking, even for him. Had he thought this through? "Finding a wife is not something you should do off-the-cuff, Harrison, and courtships take time."

"Let me worry about that. Besides, it's not like I have a choice."

"Regardless, this is a busy time for me. I have an important tennis tournament at the end of June."

"Yes, the Nationals. Congratulations on that, by the way."

"Thank you. So you can see I haven't time to squire you around town and introduce you to my friends. I'm leaving to practice in Newport soon." It was cooler there, with fewer distractions than the city.

"That's perfect," Harrison said. "What about a house party over a long weekend? You could invite some friends."

"Good idea," Kit put in. "Beach, sun and champagne. You'll find a wife in no time."

"Exactly. What do you think, Maddie?"

She wiped a bead of sweat off her forehead. Strange to imagine Harrison getting married, but they weren't kids any longer. After all, she was nearly engaged. And the Archers were one of the oldest and wealthiest families in New York. Word of Harrison's return and interest in finding a bride would cause a minor sensation.

"Please, Mads," Harrison said. "You're the only one I trust to help me find a wife who won't make me miserable. You know me better than anyone else."

"That may have been true three years ago, perhaps, but not now."

"You're wrong. I am the exact same person who beat you at croquet all those years."

A surprised laugh tumbled out of her throat. "You lying liar! I beat *you* at croquet."

His blue eyes twinkled with familiar mischief, a look she recognized from years of their escapades. "I don't want to do this without you. Please, Maddie."

Warmth blossomed in her chest and her resentment toward him softened. *This is Harrison, your childhood friend. You've always helped each other.*

Like that time she fell and skinned her knee, and he carried her all the way home on his back . . .

Or when his father had been so drunk and angry that she hid Harrison in her room for an entire day . . .

And how he willingly went along with all of her schemes and games, never complaining once . . .

How could she possibly refuse him one weekend in Newport with her friends?

"All right. I'll speak with my mother and start forming a guest list."

Leaning over the net, Harrison pressed a quick kiss to her cheek. "You're the best. Thank you."

It was nothing he hadn't done a hundred times before, but Maddie's stomach flipped for some inexplicable reason. She ignored the reaction and pointed to the house. "If we are finished, then I'll go get cleaned up."

Harrison tucked the racket under his arm, appearing extremely pleased with himself. "We shall leave you to it, then. Until Newport, Maddie."

Chapter Two

Eleven Summers Ago

*E*ight weeks of freedom.

Soon. Very soon.

The carriage ride from the train station was excruciating, yet Harrison didn't dare speak. He tried to hold still and not give his mother any reason to shout at him—or worse, confine him to his room. A summer away from his family depended on his good behavior.

The early June Rhode Island air wafted through the carriage windows as they rode, carrying the familiar smells of salt and sand. Flowers and sea grass. The ache behind his eyes began to recede, anticipation building like a crescendo in his veins. This was what he lived for, what kept him sane the rest of the year, these few weeks he spent outside of tutors and classes. Where there were no responsibilities and he could slip away, unnoticed, to see the other children. Swimming, sailing, riding . . .

Newport was paradise compared to the grim confines of New York City.

As they turned along Bellevue Avenue, they passed the Websters' new cottage. Mother sniffed and fanned herself. "That family is obscene. Look at them flaunting themselves."

Harrison disagreed. The structure, completed just this year, looked like a castle, with its stone columns and massive iron gate. It had been named Chateau de Falaise, or Cliff Castle, because it overlooked the Cliff Walk. He couldn't wait to see the inside. There were probably all kinds of hiding places and secret rooms. Maddie would show them to him.

He tapped his fingers on his knee, wishing he could jump out of the conveyance right there. The Websters were their neighbors in the city, and their only daughter, Maddie, was his good friend. He hadn't seen her since she'd shown up at his house late one night in April, throwing pebbles at his window until he came out and talked to her.

There were lots of children hanging about in the Newport summers, but Maddie was his favorite. He didn't know why, exactly, except that she liked all the same things he did. Plus, she never backed down from a challenge and competed as fiercely as anyone else. Even though she was younger than the group of boys Harrison had befriended, they were all fairly terrified of her.

Harrison wasn't afraid of her, though. He thought she was the bravest, smartest and surest child he'd ever met. She listened to him, even when he complained about his family, and invited him to dinners with her parents, which sounded as if it would be awful but never was.

With Maddie around, the loneliness retreated. He felt accepted and understood. Normal. *Happy.*

One more turn and the carriage arrived at the Archer cottage. Harrison waited as patiently as possible while his mother descended, then he started to exit. Thomas pushed him back onto the seat. "Wait your turn, maggot," his older brother snapped, and stepped down.

The rudeness didn't bother Harrison, not today. He was about to escape anyone with the surname of Archer for eight weeks. They would see one another at the occasional dinner, when their mother wasn't busy with her social engagements. Otherwise, he and Maddie would explore and run and swim until they were exhausted.

His feet crunched on the gravel as he walked toward the house. No one looked at him or offered a comment. His family went inside while the staff busied themselves with the bags, and Harrison glanced over his shoulder. He could be at Maddie's new house in less than ten minutes, if he ran.

He was sprinting before his brain arrived at the decision.

His summer traveling suit chafed as he sprinted, but he didn't stop. If Maddie was already down at the water, he would look ridiculous wearing a light wool suit. But it was too late.

The massive gates were open, the drive lined with carriages. Was Mrs. Webster entertaining?

Hoping to go unnoticed, he slipped around the side of the house and around the back to peek. The view took his breath away. Blue as far as the eye could see, whitecaps flashing as the waves rolled toward shore. Sky that reached for miles, with clouds like cotton in the air. He stood and took it in, frozen.

"There you are!"

Blinking, he found her. *Maddie.* She was grinning from beneath a straw bonnet, the yellow ribbon tied under her chin. Freckles dotted her nose, proof that she'd already spent a fair amount of time outside. The restlessness in him quieted as he watched her approach, like a curtain coming down at the end of a play. Her presence meant he could finally relax. Finally *breathe.*

As if they'd seen each other yesterday, she grabbed his arm. "Come on. Mama is hosting a garden party and there is a cake with white icing that I have been dying to try."

He allowed her to tug him across the lawn toward a row of hedges. "She let you attend a garden party?"

"Of course not. I am supposed to be inside with the dancing instructor. So we must steal the cake."

They stopped behind the hedges and Maddie pointed. "Look at it. Tell me you don't want a piece."

Harrison peered through the branches and leaves and looked toward the dessert table. A three-tiered cake with strawberries on top lorded over the other desserts, its white icing gleaming in the sunlight. Two footmen hovered nearby, while tables of guests chatted under the enormous tent. Big silk hats layered with chiffon and ostrich feathers dotted the landscape.

The cake looked delicious and he was starving. He liked this idea. "I'll wait until the footmen are called away," he declared. "Then I will rush out there and take it."

"I have a better plan. I will create a diversion during which you'll steal the cake."

"You can't be seen out there. Your mother will be furious."

"She won't even notice. She's sitting on the opposite end of the lawn with her closest friends. They haven't stopped talking for five minutes."

"We still have to get the cake into the house, though."

"I have it all planned out. You are going to bring the cake behind those hedges." She pointed to bushes near the dessert table. "Then we'll put your coat in front as we carry it inside."

"Where we'll be discovered before we can eat it."

"Wrong. I have the perfect hiding place. No one will find us."

He trusted her. Maddie thought everything through down to the tiniest detail. "What is your diversion?"

"I will walk to the left of the two footmen at the table and then pretend to trip and fall—"

"And get hurt?" He imagined her with scraped palms and raw knees. "No. Untie your bonnet strings and then 'lose' your bonnet in the wind on the near side of the dessert table. The wind is blowing away from us, so it should carry your bonnet right past them and into the grass. They won't be able to resist helping."

"And when their backs are turned, you'll grab the cake."

"Yes. I'll come from the front, so the guests can't see what I am doing."

Two minutes later their plan was under way. Harrison waited until the footmen were chasing the bonnet before he hurried toward the dessert table. The cake was lighter than it looked and he carried it carefully, keeping his back to the crowd, until he was behind the hedges.

Placing the plate on the ground, he took off his coat. Maddie appeared, her breath labored from the chase. "Hurry. Give me your coat."

She used the garment to shield the cake, sort of like a Spanish matador with a bull, as they awkwardly walked to a side door. They made it inside without incident, but he knew this was only the beginning. A legion of staff was required to maintain a house this size, and there were always people about in the daytime. "Where now?" he asked.

"At the end of the back hall is a staircase to the lower level. Follow me."

The inside of the chateau was equally as grand as the outside. It was like a cathedral, with stone arches and buttresses, balconies and tapestries. But Harrison was too focused on not dropping the cake to get a decent look around. At thirteen, his limbs felt awkward and he found himself tripping all the time.

She will kill me if I lose this cake.

He gripped the plate tighter and concentrated on keeping it steady while she held open a door. "Down the stairs. Hurry."

"Miss Madeline," a deep voice called in the distance. Likely the dance instructor searching for his pupil.

"Go, go, go," Maddie urged in a whisper.

He ducked through the doorway and went down the stairs. Maddie was right behind him, closing the door softly, then following. "Turn right," she said.

When they reached the lower level, she led him to a large blue and orange tiled room where an indoor pool shimmered. An oasis in the summer heat. "Whoa."

"Daddy loves to swim." She edged around the side toward a door in the back.

"Where are we going?"

"To the changing room." She showed him into a tiny space with hooks along the tile and a wooden bench along one side.

He set the cake down and shook out his tired arms. He'd need to build up his strength if she had any more confectionary heists planned.

Then he frowned. "I hadn't thought to steal forks."

She produced two forks from the pockets of her dress. "I took them just before I lost my hat."

He grinned—his first genuine smile since seeing her in April. "You always think of everything."

"We'd better start eating it before it melts."

They both sat and took a bite. It was lemony

and delicious, so moist it melted on his tongue. "This is good."

"It's better than good. Thank you for helping me steal it." She nudged his shoulder with hers. "I'm so glad you're finally here."

Me too, he thought, and reached for more cake.

Chapter Three

✦

Chateau de Falaise, Newport
Eleven Summers Later

The heiresses descended in the morning.

Harrison and Kit watched from an upstairs window as carriage after carriage lined up at the chateau. The five-day house party began today, an event that would provide him with unfettered access to Maddie, the one woman he actually planned to marry. The trip was a waste of everyone else's time, but he couldn't worry about that. He would do whatever it took to win her, no matter what. All he needed was time.

Below, the Webster staff toted bags and tended to guests. Maddie was surely down there somewhere, overseeing it all, welcoming everyone and putting them at ease. It was what she did best and one of the reasons society loved her.

"Look at them." Kit motioned to the activity below. "Maddie said she merely had to whisper your name and heiresses were fighting for a spot at the house party."

Harrison said nothing. There was only one heiress he wanted. No one else mattered.

No one else had *ever* mattered. He'd followed Maddie around every summer since the age of twelve, then more often during college, when he made frequent trips to the city. From early-morning tennis matches and late-night walks, to rides in the park and swimming in the ocean, they had been together constantly.

Their relationship hadn't been romantic, though, at least not from her side. While he'd been in love with her, he planned to wait until her debut before declaring his feelings. The chance never arrived. At a ball one night, he overheard how she truly felt about him and he'd left early, setting forth a chain of events that would change his life.

Kit still appeared fascinated by whatever was happening on the ground. "I'm almost jealous. Look at some of these gorgeous ladies. How will you choose?"

Kit was one of Harrison's closest friends, along with Preston Clarke and Forrest Ripley. Four rebellious outcasts of society families who became like brothers in college. He clapped the other man on the shoulder. "Glad you're here, Kit."

"I wouldn't miss it. You, wooing a bride? That I must see firsthand."

"You have seen me woo plenty of women."

"Indeed, I have. What a grand time we had in Paris."

It had been fun—drinking, gambling and cavorting like men possessed. "We certainly did."

"God knows, after meeting Esmée I can understand why you never wanted to leave."

Esmée had been Harrison's mistress in Paris for almost two years. Vivacious and beautiful, Esmée had appetites that matched his own, and her sharp wit made her the perfect companion. There had been deep affection but no love between them. Whatever heart Harrison possessed had long been given over to Maddie, even if she didn't realize it. "She called you the American wolf," he said.

"She was not wrong," Kit said with a chuckle. "However, I still don't understand why your mother is anxious for you to marry."

Harrison decided on the truth. "They're broke."

"Who?"

"My family."

Kit's head swiveled, his expression disbelieving. "Are you joking?"

"I am not. My father lost everything after the Panic. Thomas can keep them afloat for just a few more months."

"And you must save them by marrying an heiress." Kit's gaze sharpened. "It's not like you to save them. What are you up to?"

"I plan on ruining them."

"Fucking hell. That's why you need an heiress."

Harrison didn't bother correcting his friend. Admitting he had money would lead to explaining why he needed this house party—and Harrison was not ready to tell anyone of his plans for Maddie.

"Does anyone know?" Kit asked.

"No."

"Not even Maddie?"

"I haven't spoken to her since we played tennis the other morning. She'd call a halt to the house party if she knew."

"Don't worry, I won't say anything. Jesus, no wonder you need an heiress quickly. Now I'm even more glad I came."

They both turned back to the window, lost in their own thoughts for a moment.

"Good God," Kit said suddenly. "Look at Red Dress down there. Bold thing, isn't she?"

A woman in a red silk day dress had emerged from a carriage, her face obscured by a wide hat. An older lady trailed her, wringing her hands and speaking, looking as if she were almost pleading with the younger woman. Red Dress waved off whatever was being said and turned to the footman attending to the luggage. Whatever the young woman said made the footman's face go up in flames.

"Well, well." Kit clapped Harrison on the shoulder. "I think we have our first contender."

"For a partner to warm your bed?"

"No, idiot. For your bride. That one is a bold mystery wrapped in delicate silk and lace."

"That is your type," Harrison said. "Not mine."

The door opened after a brief knock. Maddie's face appeared in the crack, her eyes narrowed to slits. "I knew I saw your shadows in the glass. Stop watching them. You are looming up here like a pair of unseemly specters."

"Boo." Kit waved his fingers dramatically.

"I am serious." Maddie came in, and the door snapped shut behind her. She wore a cream dress with blue stripes, and Harrison tried not to notice the way the cloth hugged her curves as she moved—more curves than she'd possessed three years ago. She put her hands on her hips. "This is terrible of you both, making assumptions about them based on how they look. Harrison must get to know their personalities for this to work."

"Which I will do over the next several days," he said.

"Who was the woman in red?" Kit asked. "The one who just arrived."

Maddie huffed in frustration. "This is exactly what I am talking about—and I am not telling you. Figure it out for yourselves."

"Oh, he will," Harrison murmured.

"You two are revolting. How would it feel if you were attending an important event and a pair of women were up here ogling you as you arrived?"

Harrison shrugged. "Wouldn't bother me."

"I'd like it," Kit said. "I'd preen a bit, give them a proper show."

"God, you are both hopeless." Grabbing their elbows, she dragged them away from the window. "My friends are not here to entertain you. This is very serious for them. A girl's worth in this world is determined by the match she makes. I won't have you mistreating them or causing them discomfort."

That comment gave Harrison pause. Was that why Maddie allowed the duke to court her, to prove her worth? It seemed unlikely, considering she was one of high society's most popular girls.

She could have her pick of any eligible man, title or not. He tried to appear apologetic. "We shall be on our best behavior."

"Don't make promises on my behalf," Kit said. "I am not the one looking to get married."

Maddie pointed at Kit. "Do not seduce any of them. Not one. They are off-limits, Christopher."

Harrison smothered a smile. Maddie was as fierce as ever, in command and unafraid. Some things never changed, he supposed.

She continued, "You two had best be kind to these ladies. This is serious, not a circus for your amusement. Have I made myself clear?"

"Clear as glass," Harrison said. "Should we come down?"

"No, stick with the original plan. My father will take you both sailing today while the heiresses settle in. Then you'll meet everyone before dinner during cocktails."

"All right." Harrison shoved his hands in his trouser pockets and tried not to think about how much he wanted to touch her. How much he wanted to test the softness of her skin, the silkiness of her hair. To make her sigh and moan.

Soon.

Maddie misinterpreted his reaction because she said, "Harrison, this will be fun. I know these women, and I swear you'll like them. Well, at least one or two."

Doubtful, not when he wanted only her. Still, she had gone to a tremendous amount of trouble on his behalf and he didn't want her annoyed with him any longer. "I promise not to embarrass you. I'll be on my best behavior."

She headed for the door. "Good. Now I must return downstairs. Daddy will meet you at the boat at eleven. Do not be late—and I expect you to keep your word." Maddie disappeared, the sound of her skirts rustling as she hurried down the corridor.

Kit wandered back toward the window. "Are you ready for this?"

Harrison stared at the spot where Maddie had been, the scent of her—lavender and sunshine—lingering in his nostrils. "Indeed, I have never been more ready."

MADDIE GLANCED AT the empty doorway for what seemed like the hundredth time. Where on earth was that dashed man? Everyone save Kit and Harrison was already there, even her father. The trio had gone sailing this afternoon, so she knew the boat hadn't capsized. What was the delay?

The heiresses were mingling and laughing in the salon. No one appeared to care about the late arrivals except for her. But only twenty minutes remained for conversing before dinner was served. Perhaps a visit to Harrison's room was in order to find out what was taking so long.

Mama appeared from nowhere to block Maddie's path. "Where are you going? We have a room full of guests."

"I want to move Harrison along. He is late and it is embarrassing."

"Nonsense. No one has even noticed." Mama gestured to the room of chattering guests. "You are just impatient, worried about your schedule.

Furthermore, you cannot go barreling into his room. You aren't children any longer. Now relax and have a glass of champagne."

"I would knock first—and he is being rude. We need to get this under way."

Mama sipped her drink. "He is not being rude. He is acting like a young man forced to marry so his family doesn't cut him off. For heaven's sake, give the boy a chance to breathe."

"You always took his side, even when we were younger."

"I admit, I have a soft spot for him. I never cared for his family."

Maddie, either. The Archers were truly the worst. Their parents had given Harrison's older brother, Thomas, every advantage. The best boarding schools, holidays traveling the globe, extravagant Christmas gifts. While Harrison had been tutored at home and given books and journals, things to make him "sit still," in his father's words.

His parents had done everything possible to crush his spirit. It hadn't worked. All their cruelty had accomplished was solidifying a deep-seated hatred for his family.

"Besides," her mother continued. "I always knew the person responsible for the trouble you two caused—and it wasn't him."

"I was a perfectly behaved child."

Mama snorted, somehow making it elegant. "That is what you'd like everyone to believe, I'm sure. Let's hope the duke never hears of your—"

Movement in the drawing room doorway caught Maddie's attention.

Finally.

Harrison and Kit stood there, overlooking the scene. "Excuse me," she said to her mother and rushed to greet them.

Tall and fit, the two men were quite handsome in their black evening clothes. Harrison had tamed his hair with a bit of oil, which made it appear darker, setting off his sun-kissed skin and rugged jaw. His mouth hitched in a half grin when he saw her approach, and her insides fluttered. She quashed the silly reaction.

Stop. It's just Harrison.

"About time," she said when she reached them. Then the smell of whiskey hit her nose. "Good God. You're drunk."

"Kit is drunk," Harrison corrected. "I am only half-drunk."

"It's your father's fault," Kit said. "We merely tried to keep up with him."

Irritation swept along the nape of her neck, burning her skin. They hadn't even begun and nothing was going according to plan. "This is hardly the ideal first impression for your future bride, Harrison. What will she think?"

"That I have a higher tolerance for spirits than Kit?"

Kit snickered but Maddie merely glared at Harrison, her annoyance multiplying. "You are not amusing."

His grin turned positively wicked. "Admit it, I am a tiny bit amusing."

"Are you even taking this seriously?"

"Of course I am. Lead on. Let's meet these friends of yours."

She took Harrison's arm. "Kit, stay out of trouble and remember what I said. These ladies are off-limits. Come along, Harrison."

They started across the room, and he dipped his head toward hers. "Don't be angry, Mads. I cannot stand when you're angry with me."

Her heart thumped and skipped in her chest, and she instantly wished to kick herself for the reaction. *He doesn't mean anything by it.* He hadn't given her a second thought after he left—and she couldn't forget that.

"Maddie, are you ill?" Her friend Lydia Hartwell touched her arm. "You look flushed."

The Hartwells owned most of Montana, and Lydia was good fun, with a solid head on her shoulders. Harrison could do a lot worse. Maddie quickly performed the introductions to Lydia and her mother.

Harrison bowed. "Miss Hartwell. Mrs. Hartwell. A pleasure."

"Mr. Archer," Lydia said. "It is nice to finally meet you. Maddie has told me so much about you."

"All of it good, I hope."

Lydia brought a hand up to partially cover her mouth, as if sharing a secret. "She said you are the one who taught her to ride without a sidesaddle."

"Indeed, I did. Do you ride?"

"I grew up in Montana. I could ride before I could walk."

Mrs. Hartwell stepped closer to Maddie, angling the two of them away from everyone else. "Tell it to me straight," the older woman said under her breath. "Is he diseased? Did he pick up the French pox over there?"

Maddie's mouth fell open. "I beg your pardon?"

"Is he broke? Divorced? Illegitimate? There has to be something wrong with him. What is it?"

Maddie should have known that some of the mothers would question the motives of a hasty marriage. Most were too polite to ask it outright, but Mrs. Hartwell never stood on ceremony—one of the many reasons Maddie liked the Hartwell women. "Nothing is wrong with him. He returned from Paris to find a wife and I decided to help him."

"Balderdash. I know something's afoot." Mrs. Hartwell tapped her nose. "I was raised on a farm and we know when we smell something off."

Maddie shook her head. "Why on earth would I invite you here to meet him if I did not believe he was a good man?"

"I have no idea, but my Lydia won't marry any bounder."

"We've been friends since childhood and I can firmly say that Harrison is not a bounder."

"Really? Because I'm told he fathered two bastards with his French mistress."

Pain lanced through Maddie's chest, making it hard to breathe. Mistress? Children? The room tilted, her mind reeling. It couldn't be true. Someone—Kit or Preston, at least—would have mentioned it to her. That was too big a secret to keep, wasn't it?

She fought to appear more dismissive than she felt. "Utterly untrue. I never heard that."

"Well, you are fortunate to have landed your duke," Mrs. Hartwell was saying. "And such a fine one, too."

"It is not yet official," Maddie mumbled, though her brain was still tumbling over the idea of Harrison fathering children with a mistress.

"Only a matter of time, from what I hear. You're very lucky. Lockwood was the finest prospect this season."

Precisely why Maddie had set her cap for him. She was not accustomed to settling for second-best in anything.

She smiled politely at the other woman. "I certainly thought so. Now, if you'll excuse me, I should probably continue the introductions."

"Doesn't appear necessary. Seems he's carried on without you."

Maddie glanced over her shoulder. Harrison and Kit were in the center of the room, surrounded by young women, with the mothers observing from a few feet away. The men were obviously telling a story, their hands moving, expressions quite animated, and the heiresses were rapt. "Indeed, it seems he has," she murmured.

Chapter Four

❧

Maddie sat next to Kit for dinner, but she covertly watched Harrison as he entertained the group at her mother's end. And it was working. The heiresses nearby—two banking and one railroad—made calf eyes at him, thoroughly entranced.

Maddie signaled to the footman for more wine.

"Something wrong?" Kit asked from her left side. She had purposely seated him next to her in the middle of the table.

"No. Why?"

"For starters, I've never seen you have more than one glass of wine at dinner."

"Perhaps I am taking up after you and Harrison." Though Kit hardly seemed inebriated any longer. He had been clear-eyed and steady since they'd arrived in the dining room. She lifted her now-full glass and swallowed a mouthful.

"Does this bother you?" Kit tilted his chin toward Harrison.

"What? Dinner?"

"Watching Harrison around other women."

"Of course not," she said instantly. "It is the entire reason for the house party." The question of Harrison's illegitimate children burned on her tongue, but it was hardly proper dinner conversation.

"Good. That would certainly complicate things, with your pending engagement and all."

Right. Lockwood. She was being ridiculous. Harrison would choose one of these women to marry and Maddie would sail off to England as a duchess.

Ignore what is happening at the end of the table.

She focused on Kit. "Have you discovered your lady in red?"

"No. Any chance you'll give me her identity?"

"None." She knew, of course, but it was too much fun to torture him.

"I think it's the blonde fourth down from Harrison."

He studied her face but she gave nothing away. "Interesting."

"Dash it, Maddie." The older woman on Kit's left gasped, and he quickly shifted to apologize for his language.

Stifling a laugh, Maddie glanced at the young woman on her right, a shy shipping heiress from Boston. "Are you enjoying yourself, Miss Lusk?"

"Indeed, I am," Alice Lusk said as she cut into a roasted parsnip. "Though I'm not very good at making conversation with men my age. You seem to excel at it."

"There is not much to it. Men are interested in

simple things. Food, sports, horses . . . and Mr. Archer likes all of those, if you find yourself at a loss for conversation."

Alice heaved out a sigh. "I almost didn't come, I was so anxious. But my mother insisted."

Maddie had never liked Mrs. Lusk, who took every opportunity to inform her daughter of her supposed faults. This was the precise reason Maddie had seated Mrs. Lusk away from Alice at tonight's dinner. "You'll do fine. Harrison is— was—my closest friend and he's a good man. No matter what happens here or in the coming months, you will end up with a wonderful husband who deserves you."

"I've had two seasons," Alice said, color staining her cheeks. "Mother says I may have to take what I can get."

"Nonsense."

"That is what I told her. No lady should have to settle. After all, you had three seasons before you landed a duke—and you are one of the most popular girls I know."

No lady should have to settle.

Maddie wanted to agree, but . . . were they not all settling? Every woman in this room would marry a man she did not love because that was what their world required. Matches were made for financial and societal gain, usually at the whim of their parents. Fortunately, Maddie liked the duke and knew they would get on well together. It was not love, however.

You had three years before you were forced to marry. Yes, she'd had more freedom than most. Now she was marrying the best catch in all of England and America, an honest-to-goodness duke. Really, how could she complain?

The rest of the meal passed slowly. Finally, Mama led the women into the salon for coffee, while the men stayed behind to smoke cigars. In the salon, a few of the heiresses pumped Maddie for information about Harrison, no doubt to get ahead of the competition. She tried to be fair and speak to everyone, but some didn't seem all that interested in Harrison or marriage. Like Kit's mysterious lady in red, Nellie Young.

A gorgeous auburn-haired woman, Nellie was a hair's breadth from scandal at every turn. Her mother died when Nellie was a small girl, and Nellie now ran roughshod over her financier father, a man who doted on his only daughter. There were rumors of gambling, lovers—even of visits to brothels. They had debuted together, and Nellie was probably Maddie's closest friend. Still, while Maddie adored Nellie, she'd never been able to keep up.

Seeing Nellie alone by the window, Maddie went over. "Already tired of mingling?"

Nellie's lips curved into a smile. "Merely gathering my strength for the night ahead."

"Should I be worried?"

"Never fear, Saint Maddie. I won't ruin your house party."

Maddie lowered herself down to the other end of the window seat. "Actually, I was surprised you came."

"Father's idea. I occasionally do as I'm told, you know."

"No you don't. Plus, there's a strange light in your eyes that is vaguely familiar."

Nellie chuckled. "Fine. A friend is staying up the shore a ways. I am meeting him later for a midnight swim."

"You are incorrigible."

"You sound just like a duchess." Nellie's gaze turned thoughtful. "Though I must say, I always suspected you and Harrison would end up together."

"Oh, we're merely friends."

"On your side, maybe. You know he has been in love with you forever, right?"

Maddie waved that off, though her heart did a tiny flip in her chest. "Harrison was not in love with me."

"Not was—*is*."

"You are talking gibberish. The sea air has gone to your brain."

Nellie's gaze narrowed on Maddie's face. "My God, you really don't know, do you? He watches you all the time, like he's obsessed with you."

Yes, so obsessed that he left for Paris without saying goodbye, possibly had a mistress there with whom he fathered an illegitimate child or two. "He's not, I promise."

"I always thought he was an empty-headed swell, like some of his friends, but he seems different after Paris. More mature. Confident. And, dare I say, handsomer?" She paused and studied Maddie's face. "Wouldn't you agree?"

Was Nellie fishing to see if Maddie's opinion

of him had changed? Well, Maddie had no intention of confessing her private thoughts, not even to a close friend. "I hadn't really noticed."

"Liar. Nothing slips your attention, which means you didn't want to be honest with me. I wonder why?" Nellie's attention wandered for a brief moment toward the door. "He's just walked in. If he comes directly over here, then you'll know I am right about his feelings for you."

"Hardly an empirical study, Nellie."

"There's no need for an empirical study when it comes to men. All the knowledge I require is right here." She tapped a fingertip to her temple.

"Hello, ladies." Harrison now stood there, glancing down at them. "I hope I am not interrupting."

Nellie shot Maddie a smug look before rising. "Of course not, Mr. Archer. Here, take my seat. I need to stretch my legs a bit." She moved away to join a small group of women near the fireplace.

Harrison sat at the other end of the window seat. "I hadn't thought she knew my name."

"All the ladies here know your name."

"I suppose that's true, but I haven't been introduced to that one yet."

"That's Nellie Young. You probably don't remember her."

"I don't, I'm afraid. Should I?"

She studied him from under her lashes, distracted by the transformation in him. Even Nellie had noticed it, apparently. He was thoroughly masculine, a grown man, with a thick, strong throat and rugged jaw. He still had adorably rumpled hair, though. And the same smile.

Why was she so fascinated by these changes? And why did they set her heart racing?

He was looking at her carefully, one brow raised in question, and her mouth started moving before she could stop it. "Did you father a child in Paris?"

THE QUESTION CAUGHT Harrison off-balance. His face slackened, his brows shooting high. Maddie must have been equally taken aback because she immediately put her hand over her mouth, her expression filled with pure horror.

Silence descended for a long moment before her cheeks turned a dusky rose. "Forgive me. I have no right to ask you such a thing. Forget I even brought it up."

Unlikely he could forget such an unexpected question. She and Kit had whispered all throughout dinner, so had his friend led her to believe Harrison had fathered a bastard in Paris? Kit was certainly capable of such troublemaking. "Who told you that?"

She carefully straightened the pleats of her skirt, not meeting his eye. "I won't say. Besides, your personal life is none of my concern."

He folded his arms across his chest, fighting a smile. Her discomfort was adorable. "Someone must have put the idea in your head. Who was it?"

"No one. I must have drunk too much wine."

"Yes, I noticed you had a second glass."

That made her look up, her brows pulled low. "Why would you notice such a thing?"

"Do not change the subject, Mads. I want a name."

"I won't tell you. So is it true?"

He studied her carefully. She seemed to be holding her breath, as if bracing for bad news, awaiting his answer. Was she worried he would say yes?

This was an interesting turn. Why would his answer matter? If she felt nothing for him, then she would not have pressed the issue. Was this jealousy?

Jealousy implied feelings. Deeper, non-brotherly feelings.

Was his plan working?

Spirits lifting considerably, he said, "I have no children, legitimate or otherwise."

Her shoulders relaxed, though her voice remained nonplussed. "Oh."

"*Oh?* That is all you have to say?"

"As I said, it's none of my business. I don't really care either way."

She was a terrible liar. She bit her lip and looked down each time she lied, just as she was doing now.

He decided to explore this idea of jealousy a bit more. Leaning in, he dropped his voice. "If you must know, I had a close longtime friend of the female variety while there, and we were diligent about preventing consequences."

She cleared her throat, and her hands curled into fists in her lap. "I see."

Harrison pressed his lips together to keep from grinning at this turn of events. It was like a door had opened, a new path revealed, one that led to a future with Maddie. And he had no intention of going backward.

But he knew she didn't like to be pushed, preferring to do the pushing instead. Therefore, he took pity on her and changed the subject. "Why did you wait until your third season to marry?"

"So I could play tennis."

"Married women play tennis, Maddie."

"I know, but I wanted to take time to really focus on my game, see if I could compete nationally. Mama agreed, thankfully."

"Probably for the best. The English are quite stuffy about their royalty, you know. They like to produce heirs and keep up appearances. I can't imagine Lockwood is keen on your tennis ambitions."

"Wrong. He is entirely supportive. In fact, he sends me flowers to wish me luck before every match."

Harrison nearly snorted. He knew dukes, and they all had a long string of boring names as well as ridiculous nicknames from Eton. They were, in short, insufferable prigs. "I met a few dukes during my time in Paris," he said. "Generally not the most enlightened bunch."

"Lockwood is not like that."

Harrison seethed, his teeth clenched at her defense of the precious duke. "Are you certain?"

Twin spots of color returned to her cheeks, this time accompanied by a flash of anger in her gaze. "Of course."

Kit arrived and frowned at them both. "Have you forgotten?" He jerked a thumb over his shoulder. "Heiresses? Marriage? Stop arguing and go circulate."

"We are not arguing," Maddie said when Harrison remained silent.

"Maybe, but the two of you are having an intense conversation in the corner while a roomful of eligible women are watching."

Sure enough, several sets of eyes were directed toward their corner.

"And," Kit said quietly to Maddie, "if you are serious about this endeavor, then you mustn't monopolize his time."

Maddie opened her mouth, likely to argue, but Kit lifted an arrogant brow, daring her to deny it.

"I came over first. It isn't Maddie's fault," Harrison said. Still, Kit was right. It was time to circulate.

Besides, he wouldn't win her after one conversation. This was a dance that required him to advance, then retreat, advance a bit more, then retreat. Like a hunter, he had to use intelligence and stealth to get what he wanted. He couldn't scare her with too much, too soon.

Standing, he crossed to the sideboard to get a drink. Lydia Hartwell was the first to approach him, asking, "Attend any races at Longchamp while you were in Paris?"

He picked up his crystal tumbler. "I did. At least two or three every season. Have you been?"

"No, though we went to Ascot two years ago. I love horse racing."

"Horse mad, are you?"

"Guilty." The edges of her mouth twisted in a self-deprecating smile. "I like to spend time outside. Sitting indoors, talking and sewing, bores me to tears."

"That must be why you and Miss Webster are friends, then. She's much the same way."

She laughed, the lines of her face softening. "I once asked her to teach me tennis. After that, I decided to stick with hunting and riding."

"She takes tennis very seriously. It's her competitive nature."

"I soon realized as much. She did not go easy on me, either. It was a thrashing."

Harrison shook his head and took a sip of bourbon. "If it's retaliation you're after, take her shooting. She cannot hit the widest of targets and she hates to lose."

"I like that." She clinked her glass coupe to his crystal tumbler. "You have a devious mind, sir."

He tried not to smirk. *You have no idea.*

Chapter Five

When Harrison left, Kit lowered himself onto the window seat. "I thought we were supposed to help him."

She smoothed the fabric of her skirts. "Whatever do you mean?"

"Maddie, you must encourage him to find a bride. All the guests were staring just now, wondering what is going on between the two of you."

He watches you all the time, like he's obsessed with you.

She pushed Nellie's words aside. "Nothing is going on." Other than her thoughts running away from her. Inappropriate thoughts of her childhood friend . . . which had to stop. She couldn't even claim surprise any longer, because she'd spent too much time in Harrison's presence today.

The plan is for him to find a wealthy wife. Your plan is to win Nationals and marry a duke.

How could she have forgotten?

"You're right," she told Kit. "We were catching up, but we'll do that later. At the moment, he needs to focus on the young ladies."

"Glad to hear you agree." He sipped his drink and gestured to the room. "Now, let's discuss said ladies and decide which prospect we like for Harrison."

"Should Harrison not decide for himself?"

"Yes, but that's hardly fun."

God knew, Kit was all about fun. Still, he was her conspirator in matching Harrison with a bride this weekend. Perhaps Kit could be of use. "The woman in the blue silk with blonde hair is Angelica Dent, a cousin to President Grant. Next to her is Alice Lusk. Her father is big in shipping."

"Met her mother earlier," Kit said. "Terrible person."

"Unfortunately, that is true. But Alice is smart and kind, the complete opposite. Now the group by the fireplace is Nellie Young, daughter of Cornelius Young. She's the auburn-haired one."

"I've heard of her."

"Most everyone has. She's quite the troublemaker." Kit's eyes gleamed with speculation, so Maddie snapped her gloved fingers in front of his face. "Off-limits, Christopher."

He waved his hand. "I remember. Keep going."

"Next to Miss Young in the cream silk is Louise Martin, and next to her is Martha Thorne. Both old money. Knickerbockers through and through."

"In other words, boring."

"That is a terrible thing to say."

"I'm right, though, aren't I?"

He was but she would never admit it. "Emily Mills and Katherine Delafield are on the sofa."

"Delafield, like the real estate family?"

"That's the one."

"Preston absolutely hates her father," Kit murmured. "Good thing he decided not to come."

Their friend Preston Clarke was currently buying up most of Manhattan to erect skyscrapers. Maddie was not surprised to hear that he was at odds with Mr. Delafield.

Kit nodded to where Harrison stood. "And the one talking with our man over there?"

"That's Lydia Hartwell. Her father owns most of the silver mines in Montana."

Kit whistled under his breath. "And pretty, too. They look cozy." He tipped his chin to where Harrison and Lydia stood at the sideboard. "This seems promising."

Was it? Harrison and Lydia had chatted before dinner as well, so perhaps this would work out for Harrison, after all.

And Maddie was happy about that. Really.

She decided to mention the rumor from earlier. "Someone told me he fathered two children in Paris."

Kit's eyes nearly bugged out of his skull. "Harrison?" When she nodded, he threw his head back and laughed. "I've never seen a person want children less than Harrison."

He didn't? She hadn't known that. They hadn't ever discussed having children, not until tonight when he'd mentioned his mistress and preventing "consequences." Information that had been, frankly, unnecessary.

Harrison had a longtime mistress in Paris.

It shouldn't have surprised or upset her, yet for some reason it did both. Hearing about his mistress had unsettled her stomach with a sickening weight that slid down to her toes.

"One can hardly blame him," Kit continued. "The Archers were not the most loving family. He said if it weren't for you and your parents, he never would have known what real familial affection looked like."

Warmth filled her, chest fluttering with memories of all their time spent together. What fun they'd had. "There were lots of children around, but Harrison quickly became a fixture here."

"Never a hint of anything romantic between you?" Kit looked away, studying the room as if memorizing every detail. "That is to say, a teenaged boy has one thing on his mind, and I cannot imagine Harrison was any different."

She remembered a sixteen-year-old Harrison, with his lanky limbs and shy smile. Not once had he ever hinted at feelings for her—or any other girl. "No, never."

A huff of laughter escaped Kit's mouth. "No wonder he was so unrestrained in Paris."

"What does that mean?"

"Nothing." He rose and pulled on his cuffs. "I see that your mother is throwing me a disapproving look. I sense she's about to reprimand me for not allowing you to circulate."

"I needn't circulate. That is Harrison's job."

"Well, I wouldn't wish to upset—"

"Mr. Ward," her mother said, interrupting. Mama's scowl could be fierce when she wanted, like when Maddie misbehaved. "Run along and let me speak with my daughter. Go charm one of the other girls."

"Yes, ma'am." Kit hurried away as if his life depended on it.

"I cannot understand why you dislike him so much," Maddie said to her mother. "He's been a good friend to me."

"Yes, a good friend who almost ruined your chances with a duke." Mama lowered herself into the seat. "I'll never forgive him for trying to discourage Lockwood, pretending you were spoken for."

"Mr. Ward thought he was protecting me from a fortune hunter."

"As if that is his right." Her mother's nose went into the air. "Fortune or not, we are honored by the duke's association with our family. You will be one of the most powerful women in England when Lockwood proposes."

"I know, which is why I sought him out in the first place."

"And I applaud your ambition. As I've said many times, the match a girl makes dictates the rest of her life. Marrying someone as powerful as the duke means you'll want for nothing."

Maddie reached over and patted her mother's hand. "You've been a wonderful mother and role model."

Her mother softened at those words. "I remember what it was like to starve and scrimp growing up, before I met your father. My parents worked themselves to an early grave. I don't wish that on anyone, let alone my daughter. You should be protected and pampered."

Years ago Mama had angled to meet Stephen Webster, already a wealthy man at twenty-five, in Detroit. The two had fallen in love, and Daddy had given Mama a leg up from her middle-class upbringing. It was a story Maddie had heard many times over. "And I will, should Lockwood ever propose."

"He will—though I do hope your tennis obsession is not giving him pause. Women participating in sports and sweating in public." She made a face. "Furthermore, I don't care for all those men hanging around the matches, trying to talk to you afterwards. It is unseemly, Madeline."

This was an old battle, one Maddie had no intention of caving on. She loved tennis and she was *good* at it. Why would she ever stop playing? "Then you shouldn't have allowed me to take lessons all those years ago."

Mama sniffed. "Your father allowed it—over my objections, I might add."

Daddy had always been a softer touch than her mother. They both looked at Maddie's father where he stood across the room, holding a glass of amber-colored liquid and talking to Kit. A boisterous sportsman, Daddy had inspired her love of all things outdoors. While at the chateau, he would play golf or tennis in the morning, then sail every afternoon. Her grandfather had made a fortune in steel and iron at the end of the war, and Daddy liked to brag that most every train in the nation ran on Webster rails.

"Come along," her mother said. "Let's help Harrison mingle. He is letting that Hartwell girl monopolize his time almost as badly as you did."

* * *

THE HOUSEHOLD HAD long settled for the night, yet Harrison couldn't sleep, his mind wide awake. So he'd donned a dressing gown and found his way onto the terrace overlooking the ocean. A three-quarter moon had transformed the back lawn into a deep glowing green, and waves churned onto the rocks below in a steady rhythm.

Today had been promising. He hadn't expected results this quickly, but her jealousy had both surprised and delighted him. He had to continue his campaign tomorrow, making sure to remind her of their shared history and interests. Perhaps pay her a compliment or two. He would flirt and make her laugh, turn on the charm when necessary. By the third day he might kiss her in a very non-brotherly way.

Leaning against the stone balustrade, he lit a cigar, turning it in the flame first to warm the leaves. He pulled smoke into his mouth, enjoying the rich, sweet taste before exhaling into the air. Standing in this particular spot, smoking, reminded him of the last time he'd been here, the night when everything changed . . .

"COME WITH ME."

Harrison glanced over at the voice and found his friend Preston at his elbow. "Why?"

Preston gestured to the Webster dance floor, where nearly all of society had gathered for this Newport ball. "Because, my friend, you are standing here gawking at her and it is approaching pathetic. Besides, I have cigarettes. Let's go out for a quick smoke."

Harrison took one more peek at Maddie. Stunningly turned out in an ivory ball gown, she was laughing at something her dance partner said. Every song had her dancing with someone else, which didn't surprise him considering she was one of the most sought-after debutantes that year.

No one knew, however, that she already belonged to Harrison.

He'd loved her since he was fifteen, yet it hadn't felt right to confess his feelings before she debuted, so he'd waited until they were here, back at the beach, to finally tell her. He had no idea whether she returned his affection . . . but they had grown up together. Were best friends. The first person each of them sought out in a crowd. Each other's keeper of secrets, the provider of unwavering support.

He couldn't wait any longer. Girls usually married at the end of their first season, sometimes second. There was no time to lose. He intended to get her alone after dinner, tell her how he felt and hopefully make plans for their future.

Nerves twisted in his belly, his throat drying out. Perhaps a small distraction in the form of a trip outside would relax him. "Fine," he told Preston. "But not too long."

The two of them dodged the crowd until they reached the terrace, which ran the entire back side of the chateau, similar to an Italian palazzo. Preston kept going, however, striding toward one of the sets of stone stairs that led down onto the lawn.

"Where are you going?" Harrison called to his friend's back.

"Out of sight. Kit and I have a bet to see who can go the longest without smoking. I don't want to lose."

"So you will cheat instead."

"Yes, without remorse."

Harrison chuckled under his breath. Preston was ruthless when the mood struck him. The two of them ended up in an alcove below the terrace. The moon, combined with the house lights, provided enough illumination for them to see. Preston flicked open a silver case, removed two cigarettes, then pocketed the case. After lighting them both, he handed one to Harrison. "Here."

He accepted the lit cigarette and brought it to his mouth. His lungs burned as the smoke entered, then his mind calmed, relaxed, and he leaned back against the stone as he exhaled. He didn't often smoke, but had enjoyed the occasional cigarette or cigar since attending college. Always with Preston, who was both a terrible influence and a great friend. "What is the bet for?"

"The one with Kit?" At Harrison's nod, Preston blew out a mouthful of smoke and said, "Fifty dollars."

"You can afford it."

"I know but I hate to lose. It's the principle of it."

"You're ridiculous."

"Says the man who's pined after the same woman for four years."

More like six, but Harrison didn't correct his friend. "Pining no longer, I hope, after tonight."

Preston's eyes grew round. "Tonight is the night? Are you serious?"

"Yes. I am telling her as soon as I can get her alone."

"About goddamn time. We're starting our senior year. You can finally live a little."

Harrison didn't need saloons and women. He only needed Maddie. "I plan to."

"Are you going to tell her how you feel straight off?"

"Not at first. I'll start by saying I plan to court her and then see how that goes."

"I'd wish you luck but I don't think you need it. I've never seen two people so perfect for one another."

Before Harrison could comment, noise drifted down from the terrace. That was the thing about Newport: private conversations were near impossible. Whether because of the water or the wind, sound carried for miles here.

He and Preston remained quiet, each puffing off a cigarette while they waited and listened.

Different high-pitched giggles, then the shuffle of slippers on stone . . .

A group of young girls, if Harrison had to guess. This was confirmed a second later when they began speaking.

". . . is really a terrible dancer. He stepped on my toes twice."

Maddie.

Harrison froze, his gaze catching with Preston's. His friend immediately understood, nodding once.

What was she doing out here? He thrust the

half-finished cigarette into the planter filled with sand, intent on going up there. Preston put a hand on his arm and shook his head. *Wait*, his friend mouthed.

Harrison wasn't keen on eavesdropping, but perhaps Maddie didn't need him interfering.

"At least he asked you to dance. I cannot get him to notice me." Another girl, a voice Harrison didn't recognize.

"Don't feel bad," a third and higher voice said. "Everyone notices Maddie."

"That is hardly true," Maddie said, humble as always.

"Of course it is," another girl said. "I wish I knew your secret."

Harrison smothered a snort. There was no secret or trick to Maddie's appeal. It was part of her, like her wide smile and sparkling eyes, or her boisterous laugh and generous wit. No other girl came close.

"Me too," the highest voice said. "I certainly wish Harrison Archer paid me as much attention as he does you, Maddie."

"Mr. Archer? Oh, we've been friends forever."

"Well, you know the old adage about friendships between men and women," the other girl said.

"What adage is that?"

"I cannot remember exactly, but something like it's impossible to remain strictly friends because one side or the other always wishes it was more."

"That is absurd," Maddie snapped. "I harbor absolutely no feelings for him whatsoever. He's like a brother to me."

Harrison frowned into the darkness. A brother? She thought of him as a brother . . .

The friend continued. "Come now, Maddie. All those years you've been friends and it's never been romantic? Not once?"

"Never. I cannot think of any man I am less attracted to, honestly."

Less. Attracted. To.

Harrison swayed on his feet and if not for Preston's steadying hand on his shoulder, he might have toppled over. He couldn't breathe, his body frozen in one spot, the pain ripping through his chest like it was splitting apart. Black dots swirled in his vision, his brain tripping, spinning, careening over this information, unable to take it in.

She didn't want him, not as a husband. All these years he'd thought to give her time, tried not to rush her, and it turned out he'd been kidding himself. Deluding himself with ideas of them together, married with a family, traveling between the city and Newport.

He bent over at the waist, hands on his knees, and struggled for breath.

"Do you mean it?" the girl asked. "I think he's handsome."

"Of course I mean it," Maddie answered. "To prove it, let's go inside and I'll introduce you to him. Then he'll ask you to dance."

"Oh, would you, Maddie? I'd be forever in your debt."

"No need for that. Seeing two of my friends fall in love would be gratitude enough. Come along. I think I saw him heading toward the card room about an hour ago."

Harrison straightened and stared out at the lawn, unseeing. He hadn't visited the card room tonight. Clearly, she hadn't watched him as carefully as he'd watched her.

And why would she? Maddie didn't want him, not like that. She was trying to introduce him to her friends, for God's sake. Pawn him off onto some other woman for the rest of his life.

He closed his eyes and tried not to break down and howl like a wounded animal. Fuck, why did this hurt so badly?

"They're gone," Preston said, his voice grave. "And I'm sorry, Harrison."

Harrison's mouth opened but no sound came out. What could he possibly say? He was empty. Utterly empty. There was nothing left inside him.

"Come. I'll walk with you back to your cottage."

Harrison's feet refused to move, his heart rebelling. No. Not Newport. He could not stay here one moment longer. Not here, where he'd chased and played with her. Spent so many days and nights surrounded by Maddie. He had to get away. "New York," he croaked. "I need to leave for New York."

"The trains aren't running until morning—" Preston broke off, presumably at something he saw in Harrison's expression. "I'll make a call," Preston said, putting his palms out. "Let's get you out of here first."

THAT NIGHT HAD changed the course of Harrison's life.

Arriving in New York, discovering his father,

the terrible row . . . then he'd been disinherited. Hours later he'd left for Paris, ready to drown himself in the renowned debauchery of the city. It had all happened quickly.

He'd tried hard to forget her, and it had seemed to work for a bit. But there were always reminders and memories haunting him. Now he could see it was because they were destined for each other.

Three years ago he'd run away, instead of pressing his case and trying to woo her. He would not repeat that mistake.

A figure emerged in the darkness, catching his attention. Someone was coming up the path from the beach, alone. Definitely a woman. Harrison puffed on the cigar and watched as she picked her way toward the house. Her feet were bare and the hem of her skirts was damp. She was singing to herself, her head swaying in the moonlight. She was too short to be Maddie, so who was it? Had one of the ladies gone for a midnight swim?

Another few feet and he saw it was Nancy— no, Nellie Young. The daughter of Cornelius Young, the well-known financier. Her auburn hair was piled on top of her head, a towel slung over her arm.

Though he wasn't properly dressed, he made no effort to hide or look away. He spoke when she climbed the steps. "Miss Young. You are certainly out late."

"Mr. Archer. Hello." She drew closer, unabashed about being caught. "Couldn't sleep?"

"No. You?"

"I met a friend for a swim."

A midnight assignation? He couldn't help but grin. "I see. How was the water?"

"Frigid."

"Everyone knows you can't get in before July."

She leaned on the balustrade and matched his posture. "Now, where is the fun in doing what everyone says?"

"A fellow rebel, I see. With your friend nearby, may I assume you are not here in the hopes of marrying me?"

"You assume correctly. May I?" She gestured to his cigar, so he handed it over. She took a deep inhale and blew the smoke out slowly before passing it back. "Cuban. Nice. Besides, you aren't interested in marrying any of us."

He stared at the expanse of dark lawn and willed his voice steady. "I'm not?"

"Of course not."

"The purpose of the party is no secret. So enlighten me as to how you are certain I don't wish to marry any of you, Miss Young."

"Nellie, please. May I call you Harrison?"

"I think we are beyond formality at this point." He gestured toward his dressing gown. "And you haven't answered my question."

"You don't want to marry any of us because you are clearly in love with Maddie."

The cigar fell out of his hand and dropped onto the stone terrace. He bent to pick it up, buying himself a few seconds of time to compose a response. "That's absurd," he said when he recovered. "We are friends."

"I have plenty of male friends, and I don't stare at them the way you and Maddie do when you think the other is not watching."

Maddie stared at him? *Interesting.* His mood lifted significantly. "Are you always this forthright?"

"Women who play by the rules do not get far in this life."

"A progressive, I see."

"I don't consider it an insult, if you're wondering. A progressive woman merely wishes to improve the lot for all women."

"I didn't mean it as an insult. I prefer bold women who know what they want."

"Yes, that much is obvious."

"I beg your pardon?"

Nellie smirked up at him. "Harrison, if you truly want one of these women to marry you, then you need to work a bit harder to conceal, you know . . . the other thing."

His feelings for Maddie. "I will try. Thank you, Nellie."

"*Oh.* Excuse me."

He turned at the familiar female voice and his pulse doubled, tripled, as blood rushed through his veins.

Maddie had stepped onto the terrace, also wrapped in a thin dressing gown. Her gaze bounced between Harrison and Nellie. "Am I interrupting?"

Chapter Six

⤎⤏

Harrison's tongue grew thick as his eyes focused on the curve of Maddie's bare ankles, now peeking out from below the hem of her dressing gown. She was absolutely gorgeous, every part of her.

Nellie broke the silence. "Don't be silly, Maddie. I must get changed, anyway. I'm freezing." She started for the house. "My thanks for the smoke, Harrison. Good night to you both."

Then they were alone—truly alone—for the first time since he'd returned from Paris.

Maddie drifted closer, the heavy silk swirling about her legs, and he tried not to think about how little they each wore at the moment. Rays of moonlight played off the angles of her cheeks and highlighted her delicate nose and full lips. He'd studied every inch of her face over the years, mapped her every expression and catalogued each of her smiles. She was stunning, like a burst of sunlight on the cold darkness blanketing his soul.

She leaned a hip against the balustrade. "That

seemed cozy. Sharing a smoke? And she called you Harrison. Have we found Mrs. Harrison Archer?"

He cleared his throat and tried to match her relaxed posture. "She met a man on the beach for a midnight swim. It's safe to say she's spoken for."

"Oh, I sense that's nothing serious. Furthermore, I think the two of you are well matched."

"She's good fun, I suppose, but I'd be gray before the age of thirty if I married that woman. She'll lead a husband to an early grave."

"Does that mean she has been eliminated?"

"Yes, on mutual agreement."

"That's progress, I suppose." They stood in silence. "What do you think of the other ladies thus far?"

That they pale in comparison to you.

Instead of the truth, he hedged. "Too soon to tell, really. They all seem nice enough."

"But you think Nellie is fun."

"Not as fun as you, of course. There was a reason why you were the most popular girl in Newport growing up."

"That's hardly true, but very sweet of you to say."

"We're all quite proud of you, you know."

"Who, and whatever for?"

"Me, Kit, Preston. You've poured your heart and soul into your tennis pursuits. Kit used to send me your clippings." Even though Harrison had repeatedly told Kit to stop.

"I had no idea."

"He never told you?"

"No," she said. "They never mentioned you at all."

Well, that stung. "Probably for the best. I'm not a rising tennis celebrity, after all."

"Not for a lack of skill. You always had a wicked backhand." She pointed to his hand. "May I try your cigar?"

"What?"

"Your cigar. May I smoke it?"

Maddie was not a smoker or a drinker. In fact, he'd never seen her impaired or inebriated. What was she up to? "Why?"

"It sounds fun. Plus, I like the way it smells. May I?"

Was she trying to prove something? "Maddie . . ."

"Harrison . . ." she replied in the same tone. "What happened to the boy who dared me to climb out onto the roof to see how far the ocean went? Not to mention that you let Nellie. Why not me?"

He held out the cigar to her. "Here. Draw the smoke into your mouth, not your lungs."

"So suck on the end but don't breathe it in?"

"Exactly."

Wrapping her lips around the outside, she drew in some smoke, her cheeks hollowing slightly.

Oh, sweet Christ.

Lust tore through his gut at the sight. His cigar in her mouth was erotic. Mesmerizing. Downright torture. He couldn't help but picture his cock between her lips as she sucked on him, an image his body liked very much, apparently, as all the blood rushed to his groin.

Briefly closing his eyelids, he took a deep breath and struggled for self-control.

Smoke teased his nostrils as she exhaled. "Hmm. I like that."

He took the cigar from her and immediately put the end to his mouth, putting his lips in the exact same spot her lips had just touched. Drawing in, he tasted the smoke and tried not to think about all the other things he'd like to taste at this moment. "Go easy."

She plucked the cigar from his fingers and took another puff, exhaling smoke. "Why?"

He swallowed, stared at her mouth and willed his body not to react further. "Smoking can cause nausea the first time if you aren't careful."

"No, I meant why did you leave without telling me?" She handed the cigar back.

Of course she wanted to know why he'd disappeared. Truthfully, there hadn't been any other choice. Adrift and alone, his heart shattered, disinherited from his family . . . What option had been left but to escape?

He couldn't tell her the real reasons, however. Not about overhearing her that night, and not about coming home to catch his father fucking a maid in the salon. Winthrop Archer had claimed the maid was willing, but that was nothing more than an egregious lie by a man who felt entitled to take advantage of a woman in his employ. Harrison called the police but his father had merely paid off the officers, with the maid unwilling to press charges. And who could have blamed her, with her livelihood on the line?

Winthrop had kicked Harrison out on the spot. *You are no longer welcome here. You are dead to me and to this family.*

After that, Harrison had only wanted to get away from everything—his family, Maddie and himself.

But he couldn't explain half of it without explaining the rest. The two events were linked, like dominoes, falling and changing the course of his life. While Maddie might be exhibiting a tiny bit of jealousy in regard to him, he couldn't risk total honesty . . . not until he knew how she felt about him.

It was better to dodge the question.

He took the cigar back. "You know I'm not one for sentimentality."

Surprise and hurt flashed over her face. Her brows lowered dangerously. "*That* is your answer? Are you joking?"

"I couldn't think of what to say. At the time, you were busy with your season and I assumed you'd marry and . . ." He shrugged. "It seemed best just to go."

"How about, 'Dear Maddie, leaving for Paris. Will be having too much fun to write. Enjoy your life'?"

"I wasn't thinking clearly."

"For *three years*?"

"I apologize, Mads. It was selfish of me."

"Exactly, and—" She began weaving on her feet. "Whoa."

Concerned, he reached to steady her. "Are you all right?"

Without thinking, he cupped her jaw and tilted her head back to see her face. The touch was unexpectedly intimate, their bodies alarmingly close, and when their eyes met, they both seemed to pause. The skin beneath his hand was soft, like the petals of a flower, and she smelled of the ocean and lavender. He could drown in the emerald fire of her gaze, familiar yet so mysterious. He wanted to learn every secret she kept buried, give her every little thing her heart desired.

The tip of her tongue darted out to wet her lips as her hooded stare focused on his mouth, and Harrison sucked in a breath. Did she want him to kiss her? He studied her lips and ached to know her taste. To delve inside and feel her slickness. Stroke her tongue with his own and swallow down her little whimpers.

Let me. Dear God, please let me.

"Maddie . . ." It came out as a whispered plea.

That seemed to snap her out of the moment. Blinking, she pulled away, and his arms dropped to his sides. She cleared her throat. "Forgive me. I grew dizzy for a moment."

Yes, so did I.

Disappointment crashed through him but he reminded himself of his plan. Advance, retreat, advance, retreat. He could not push her too quickly. For now, the flash of desire he'd seen on her face a moment ago was enough.

Maddie had wanted to *kiss* him.

When he was sure his voice was steady, he said, "I told you not to smoke too fast."

"So you did." She shifted on her feet and gave a short, strangled sort of laugh. "I must have been quite topsy-turvy for a second because it seemed . . ."

"What?"

"It seemed as if . . ." Trailing off, she looked out into the darkness rather than at him. "This may sound silly, but were you about to kiss me?"

THE QUESTION HUNG between them, with Harrison's expression registering his shock. Truth be told, Maddie couldn't believe she'd asked it. She wanted to blame the cigar, but Harrison's presence had set her off-kilter.

Something seemed different between them, her awareness of him heightened. The things she noticed about him had changed, such as the way the dressing gown molded to his lanky frame, and how his long bare feet were now so elegant and rugged. Her old friend was appealing and handsome . . . and her body was having a definite reaction to him.

Then he'd caressed her face. Like a lover. He'd stared at her so intently, wickedly, and her mouth had gone dry. Had he wanted to kiss her?

Worse, had she wanted him to?

You are being ridiculous. This is Harrison. He doesn't think of you in that manner.

Besides, she had mapped out her life already. Distractions were hardly beneficial toward achieving her goals. This party was about finding a bride for her old friend before she conquered Nationals and moved to England as a duchess.

Dream big, my girl, her father had always said. After all, he'd never let anything stop him from getting what he wanted.

And neither would she.

"Back to your leaving three years ago," she said, purposely changing the conversation away from kissing.

"This again?" Harrison rolled his eyes. "I never meant to upset you. Leaving was more . . . impulsive self-preservation. Starting over fresh somewhere else."

"You didn't drop Kit or Preston or Forrest in your fresh start. Only me."

"They're men, Maddie. It is different."

"That's ridiculous—and offensive. Plus, I've known you longer."

He leaned against the balustrade, tall and broad in the semidarkness. "Still, I am right."

"You couldn't even write?"

"My life in Paris did not lend itself to proper correspondence for a lady."

"Meaning I would have been scandalized."

"Yes."

A disbelieving noise erupted from her throat. It was like he'd forgotten everything about her. "You never worried about that before. Remember those letters you wrote while at college?" His letters used to have her howling with laughter. Stories about his classes and clubs, but mostly about his friends. He hadn't tempered them for her inexperienced ears, either.

"Paris was different."

"Why?"

"Because I was wilder there. Practically a reprobate. I didn't want you to know that person."

"I wouldn't have judged you."

The expression on his face said he believed otherwise. "I had to grow up, Maddie. Being here was . . . strangling me. I found myself in Paris."

"Oh." A lump formed in the back of her throat, an ache of disappointment brought on by his illuminating perspective. So New York and Maddie's friendship had strangled him, while Paris and mistresses had liberated him. How had she failed so miserably at being his friend? "I understand."

"No, you don't. You are just saying that while secretly blaming yourself."

She fought a smile and studied her feet. How did he know her so well after all this time?

"Because you still wear your emotions on your face," he answered, even though she hadn't voiced the question.

This time she did smile. "It's how you always knew when I was lying."

He pointed at her with his cigar. "Precisely. So don't try to get away with it now. Tell me why you blame yourself for my leaving."

"I must have been a terrible friend to you, if you couldn't be yourself here. Then you were gone and never wrote, like it was easy to forget about me."

"Maddie," he said, his voice quiet and solemn. "I never forgot about you. Never."

The earnest declaration rolled over her like a warm ocean wave, weakening her limbs. Anchoring herself with the railing, she tried to lighten the mood and squash these improper reactions. "That's a relief, because you still owe me five dollars from our bet when I was thirteen—"

"You would bring up that outrageous lie again." He gave a disbelieving chuckle. "You cheated because you couldn't stand to lose."

"I would never," she said haughtily, much like a spinster aunt. "You lost the bicycle race, Harrison."

"Because someone partially deflated my tires beforehand. I wonder who would have done such a thing . . . ?"

"As if I would stoop so low."

"Nearly a decade later and you still cannot admit the truth." He shook his head slowly, smirking as if disappointed in her. "You'll take that one to your grave, I suppose."

She would, but where was the fun in coming clean now?

"This is nice," she said, bumping his shoulder with hers. "Reminiscing and talking with you. I've missed you."

The skin around his eyes crinkled, little lines of amusement that transformed his face. Lord, he was a good-looking man. "We always had fun together."

"Yes," she said, "we certainly did."

"Do you love him? Your duke, I mean."

"He isn't my duke." *Not yet, anyway.*

"Fine, your rumored-to-be fiancé. Is there a romantic attachment between you?"

"We get along. Fond of the same pursuits, that sort of thing."

"He's a tennis player?"

"A bit, but the duke generally loves sports and the outdoors."

"Do you at least get to call him by his Christian name, or does he insist on formality in private, as well?"

Odd now that she considered it, but she actually didn't know Lockwood's Christian name. She called him either Lockwood or duke, as everyone did. "The title deserves respect."

"Does becoming a duchess mean that much to you?"

Oh, the stupidity of men sometimes. "Harrison, every girl dreams of being a duchess. Well, a princess, but princes are in short supply."

"So a duke will have to do?"

"Something like that."

They both knew how it worked with society marriages. A young woman had to make the very best match possible when it came time to marry. Maddie was fortunate in that her parents had allowed her to have a say in her husband. Most society parents arranged the marriage without a daughter's input.

And honestly, how could one do better than a duke?

"Allow me to guess?" Harrison reached over the balustrade to tap ash onto the grounds below. "A crumbling estate or two, needs the American dollars to shore them up."

"It's hardly unusual. Furthermore, it's not as if your circumstances are much different, considering your mother's threat."

"At least I didn't need to travel to another country to find a bride."

"No, you left to find a mistress." She clamped her lips shut, horrified.

Dipping to catch her eye, he cocked a brow. "Are you *jealous*? Because that sounded a lot like jealousy, Mads."

"Don't be absurd." The words came out strangled.

"Hmm. Does the thought of me with Esmée make you jealous?"

Esmée. Even her name was beautiful. Maddie pictured her: a witty and cosmopolitan French woman, draped in fabulous Worth gowns and drinking absinthe at a salon. Her belly cramped uncomfortably. Had he been in love with her? Was that why he hadn't come home?

Oh, God. She *was* jealous. Jealous of Harrison's mistress.

No, this could not be happening.

Harrison and his mistress and his stupid handsomeness could not distract from her purpose. He was a friend, nothing more. A friend who would marry someone else and disappear from her life as he'd done before.

Turning, she started for the house and waved over her shoulder. "I should find my bed. I have an early practice tomorrow with my coach. Good night."

"Maddie."

Halting at his sharp tone, she glanced over her shoulder. She'd never seen him appear so fierce, so focused, and it both scared and thrilled her. "Yes, Harrison?"

"The question you asked earlier, about me kissing you?" A wolflike grin slowly twisted his lips. "The answer was yes."

* * *

WHITE TENTS BLEW in the breeze on the chateau's east side, where the Webster staff was busy carrying provisions for the afternoon picnic. Harrison squinted in the bright sun, the harsh light burning his dry and tired eyes. The night had been a long one, with his mind continuing to spin long after he'd finished his cigar and left the terrace.

Things were progressing with Maddie faster than he could have dreamed. Two important developments had crystallized. First, she was attracted to him, as illustrated by the longing in her gaze and the way her tongue moistened her lips when he'd held her.

Second, she felt something deeper for him. Otherwise, why experience jealousy over his mistress? No, that reaction meant this wasn't one-sided. He wasn't chasing after a woman who did not return his regard.

He was close. Fueled by fierce determination, he would continue to scheme and plot, to use every available trick he knew in the limited time left to win her over.

Because only one man would marry Maddie—and that was *he*.

Kit suddenly appeared at Harrison's side. "Late night?"

He slowed his pace. "Not particularly. Why?"

"First, because you look absolutely terrible. Second, I went for a stroll last evening. Heard you and Maddie out on the terrace."

"Oh?"

Kit put a hand on Harrison's arm, bringing them both to a halt. "I saw you holding her face like you were about to kiss her. She wasn't exactly pushing you away, either."

Though Kit was his closest friend, it didn't feel right to talk about this. Not here, not now. "It's not what it looked like."

"Please. You've been in love with her forever. Still are. Had you thought no one noticed?"

Apparently Maddie hadn't. "And? What is your point?"

"I want to know what's going on. Are you really here to marry one of these women?"

"I am here to marry one woman," he hedged.

"A tennis-playing woman who is nearly betrothed to a duke?"

"Nearly betrothed is not betrothed."

A smile broke out on Kit's face. "Say no more. I get it. I tried to stop it, you know."

Harrison blinked. The discursive manner in which Kit's mind worked would test the patience of a saint. "Stop what?"

"Lockwood's pursuit of her. Did everything I could think of—short of seducing her—to throw him off the scent. But Maddie finally told me to cease interfering."

Harrison cast a glance toward the tent. "Well, there's nothing to worry about there. A boring duke hardly stands a chance of coming between Maddie and me."

"That's the spirit." Kit slapped Harrison's back. "It goes without saying that you have my support."

"Thank you. I was worried you would resent being dragged along under false pretenses."

"Are you kidding? False pretenses are my

very favorite pretenses. Come on, we're late." He started for the tent.

The two of them arrived at the tent together, where they found Maddie, Mrs. Webster and the guests drinking lemonade in the shade. Maddie didn't meet Harrison's eyes as they approached.

"There you are," Mrs. Webster called. "Join us, gentlemen." She beckoned them to her table, which was filled with mothers and chaperones. After a round of greetings, Kit drifted to the tables with Maddie and the heiresses, leaving Harrison behind.

"Mr. Archer," one of the chaperones said. "I happened to see your mother the day before we journeyed here. I was surprised to learn she had no idea about this house party."

Because I would rather swim back to France than have my mother involved in my life.

He tried to smile but likely failed. "I must have forgotten to mention it to her."

Mrs. Webster patted his arm but addressed the women. "I told his mother that I would help young Mr. Archer by hosting this house party. She is still in mourning for her late husband, of course."

"And do you plan to stay in New York indefinitely, Mr. Archer?" This was from another chaperone.

"I haven't decided." It was a lie. He planned to live in the city and oversee Archer Industries— but no one could know that yet.

"You should decide soon," a different woman said. "I don't like the idea of my daughter living in France."

"Me neither," someone at the table said. "It's pure hedonism over there."

"Have you bought a house in the city yet? I hear there are some nice properties on Ninety-Fifth Street."

"Oh, yes, you really must get a house, Mr. Archer. The West Side has some lovely brownstones for sale."

He couldn't keep track of who was speaking because the voices all came at once. Sending a longing glance toward the house behind him, he resisted the urge to pull at his collar.

"Excuse me, won't you?" Maddie arrived at his side and slipped her arm through his. "I must steal Mr. Archer for a moment. He will soon return." She towed him toward the dessert table, which was covered in small cakes and cookies. "You looked as if you needed rescuing."

"I did. Thank you." He selected two pistachio macarons, his favorites. "They had more questions than I was prepared to answer."

"You're welcome."

He stared down at her, but she was concentrating on the desserts, not looking directly at him. Was this because he'd confessed the desire to kiss her?

No matter what else happened in the next few days, he couldn't allow her to ignore him. "Something wrong, Miss Webster?"

"No, why?"

"Because you won't look at me."

Her head snapped up, a familiar defiant set to her chin. The reaction was so purely Maddie that he nearly laughed. "That's silly," she said. "I am looking at you right now. And besides, I assumed you were avoiding me."

"Why would I avoid you?"

"I couldn't say, but you skipped breakfast."

He had, but not because he didn't want to see her. It was because he'd wanted to see her *too much*. He couldn't stop thinking about her, about everything said last night. *Advance, retreat.* "I slept in. Had a hard time falling asleep."

"Me too."

She didn't elaborate, so he glanced at the offerings spread out on the table. "Are we serving anything harder than lemonade or . . . ?"

"Just lemonade, I'm afraid. Now, come chat up the ladies or we might have a revolt on our hands." She took his arm, and the two of them strolled toward the young women. "Oh, and I've organized an egg hunt this afternoon."

"What?" He tried to dig in his heels but she wouldn't allow it. "No. Maddie, I do not want to play ridiculous games—"

"You will do it and you will like it," she said in a low stern voice. "The girls must get to know you."

"They may get to know me at meals."

"That is not enough. And it'll be fun. Stop being grumpy and smile."

Arriving at the table full of unmarried women, he had no choice but to stop arguing. "Hello, ladies."

The young women all sat up a bit straighter, their smiles growing wider, as they greeted him.

Forcing a smile, he experienced a pang of guilt. After all, they were here only as a way for him to charm their hostess into marrying him.

Maddie patted his arm. "Mr. Archer has agreed to a game of—"

"Good afternoon," a clipped British voice announced from the edge of the tent.

Every head swiveled in that direction. A tall, well-dressed man stood there, his unwavering attention stuck on Maddie.

She jerked slightly against Harrison's side, then dropped his arm and hurried toward the newcomer. "Oh, my goodness, Your Grace! I had no idea you were coming. Welcome to Newport."

The man greeted Maddie warmly, bending to kiss her cheek, and pain lanced through Harrison's chest like a javelin. He looked down and stared at the tips of his shoes as he struggled to breathe, unable to watch the joyful reunion one second longer.

It seemed the Duke of Lockwood had arrived.

Chapter Seven

Lockwood was here. In Newport . . . at the house party.

Maddie could scarcely believe it as she made her way over to greet him. True, she had casually invited him the week before, but she hadn't expected the duke to actually accept.

But she was happy definitely happy—to have him here.

Tall and athletic, Lockwood was classically handsome in the way of old statues. He had strong, symmetrical features on a face that belonged stamped on coins. He was perfectly put together as usual, not a hair out of place, and wearing a light brown suit. Indeed, everything about him was perfect: his looks, his personality. Even his laugh. There wasn't one single thing to complain about.

Why then did she have the urge to glance over her shoulder at Harrison right now?

"Are you surprised?" Lockwood murmured as he kissed her cheek.

"Indeed, I am. A good surprised, however."

"Your Grace!" Mama rushed forward to greet the duke, nearly knocking Maddie over in her haste. "How honored we are by your presence here at our little gathering."

Lockwood bowed over Mama's hand. "Thank you for your hospitality, Mrs. Webster."

"It is our pleasure. Come, you must meet our guests."

Mama dragged Lockwood to the guests and introduced him. The duke was gracious and charming, quickly winning them over with his smile and posh accent. The young ladies, on the other hand, stared at Lockwood in pure fascination, as if he were a mythical creature come to life—except for Nellie, who was uncharacteristically stiff in her greeting. Maddie must remember to ask Nellie about it later.

Kit smirked as the women were presented, his eyes dancing with some hidden glee. Harrison, however, looked as if he'd sucked on a lemon. She tried to scowl at him before ushering the duke over. "Your Grace remembers my friend Mr. Ward, and this is Mr. Archer. Gentlemen, may I present the Duke of Lockwood?"

The duke extended a hand. "Nice to see you again, Ward. And Archer, you say? You must be the one from Paris. How do you do?"

Harrison's flat expression remained unchanged as the two men shook hands. "Lockwood."

The curt, one-word greeting was rude, even for Harrison. Maddie would have kicked him, had he been standing closer. "Would you care to sit?" she asked Lockwood. "I have an egg hunt planned, but you are probably tired from the trip."

Lockwood's brow quirked. "An egg hunt? I haven't done one of those in ages."

Did dukes participate in silly childish games? "You aren't obligated to participate, of course."

"Even still, I'd love to play. If you organized it, I know it'll be good fun."

Harrison snorted, but Maddie didn't spare him a glance. She would deal with his horrible attitude later.

"I agree," Kit called out. "Get us started, Miss Webster."

Maddie retrieved her egg hunt supplies, including slips of paper with numbers on them. Everyone selected a piece of paper from a hat and teams were quickly organized, with one chaperone agreeing to play so as to keep their number even.

Kit and Alice Lusk were paired up, while Lockwood matched with Nellie Young, who looked pale at the moment. Harrison's partner was Katherine Delafield, an extremely likable woman who had just returned from an extended stay in Spain. At least she and Harrison could chat about their recent European adventures. Perhaps the two would hit it off in grand style.

Maddie forced a brilliant smile. "Now that you've found your partners, it's time for the rules. This works much in the same way it does at Easter, except that I've hidden twenty blue eggs, eight green eggs and one yellow egg on the chateau grounds. Prizes will be awarded to the team that finds the most eggs, the most green eggs, and whichever team finds the yellow egg will go on a picnic with Mr. Archer tomorrow." She glanced at the mothers. "Chaperoned, of course."

"What are the prizes?" one of the ladies shouted.

"I thought you'd never ask." Maddie reached into her basket and pulled out two blue boxes. "Jewelry from Mr. Tiffany's store. I have a diamond bracelet and a diamond necklace for the winning ladies."

Any proper heiress loved diamonds and this group was no exception. Most drew closer to inspect the pieces, oohing and ahhing, before moving off to whisper with their partners. Plotting their strategy, most likely.

"You have one hour," Maddie announced. "Ready? Hunt!"

The guests hurried out of the tent except for Harrison and Katherine. He stared thoughtfully off into the distance, rubbing his jaw, while a seemingly confused Katherine waited at his side. Maddie drifted over. "Is there a problem, Mr. Archer?"

His lips twisted into a smug smirk. "I have an unfair advantage."

"Oh?"

"I could probably guess every hiding place without stepping outside this tent."

"Impossible."

"No, I'm absolutely certain of it." He turned to Katherine. "Which prize would you like?"

"The diamond necklace."

"Then you shall have it." He held out his arm. "See you in a moment, Miss Webster."

Maddie pursed her lips together as she watched them depart, certain Harrison was wrong. He didn't know everything about her, not any longer. She had changed in the last three years, grown up and matured. Decided on a future for herself and worked dashed hard to achieve it.

Just as he was not the same man—and not just physically. This Harrison was bolder, with sharper edges and more intensity. He'd even flirted with her last night. The Harrison from three years ago never would have crossed that line.

And the old Maddie wouldn't have enjoyed said line crossing this much, either.

His parting words would hardly leave her brain, her mind replaying them over and over. *The question you asked earlier, about me kissing you? The answer was yes.* She didn't know what to do with that bit of information.

Yes, you do. You wanted to kiss him back.

No, that was ridiculous. Absolutely out of the question. She was nearly engaged. Her focus should remain on Lockwood and no one else.

Dream big. Stick with your plan.

With Lockwood here, an engagement was likely forthcoming. Why else would he follow her from New York out to Newport if not to propose? He might as well have held her hand in public, for all the gossip this would start.

But the bigger question was, why wasn't she giddy at the prospect of an impending engagement?

"This is very exciting," Mama said quietly as they both stared after the guests. "The duke has taken you up on our invitation to attend. The other chaperones are positively green with envy."

"We don't know that he plans to propose."

"Poppycock. I bet the ducal betrothal ring is packed in his luggage."

"Nevertheless, we shouldn't assume."

Mama took Maddie's arm and maneuvered her until they were face-to-face. "Do I detect a lack of enthusiasm on your part? A week ago, you were studying a map of London so as to not get lost when you move there."

Had she been so transparent regarding her current confusion? Maddie lightened her tone. "I am merely staying practical. It is promising that he's here, of course, but there are plenty of other unmarried ladies here, as well."

"True. I was a bit concerned about his pairing with Miss Young in the hunt. She is reckless to a fault."

Maddie waved a hand. "Lockwood is not to Nellie's liking, believe me. She's tried to talk me out of marrying him on several occasions—and not because she has designs on him herself." Nellie said Lockwood would bore Maddie to tears, that the duke was too nice, too proper. That Maddie needed someone with more fire and passion, qualities that matched her personality.

Maddie had told her friend to stop interfering. After all, Nellie felt no pressure to marry and her father would certainly never insist on it. Cornelius Young positively doted on his only daughter.

"Indeed," her mother said, "I cannot see Lockwood tramping out to Newport if not for you. Still, it would be humiliating if he ended up choosing someone else at this point. We must do what we can to keep the two of you together as much as possible, away from the others."

Maddie's eyes trailed over to where Harrison had disappeared with Katherine. Her mother was right. Maddie must focus. *There could be no more late-night chats on the terrace. No more talk of mistresses and kissing.*

She had to concentrate on winning both Nationals and Lockwood. Anything—and anyone—else was a distraction.

HARRISON ADDED ANOTHER green egg to the pile in Miss Delafield's hat. Thus far, they had located eleven of the twenty-nine eggs. As he predicted, Maddie had used most of her old hiding spots

Miss Delafield's eyes grew wide as she struggled to hold all the eggs. "You were not joking when you claimed an unfair advantage."

He shrugged, took the hat full of eggs from her hands and started for the greenhouse. He knew at least one egg would be hidden inside. "Comes with years of experience."

Miss Delafield hurried to keep up. "You and Maddie have known one another a long time?"

"Since I was twelve. We met here in Newport, and her family lived close to mine in the city before they moved uptown."

"And you've remained close. That's sweet."

Sweet? It hadn't felt sweet. More like slow torture, always being denied something he desperately wanted.

All that waiting and agonizing would soon come to an end, however.

True, the duke's presence had added a wrinkle into Harrison's plan . . . but it wouldn't stop it. While Lockwood might have a title, Harrison had years of knowledge when it came to Maddie. He would use that information to his advantage, to maneuver around the duke and win her over.

It meant he must try harder, that was all. This wasn't England, where a fight remained polite and cordial while maintaining a stiff upper lip, old chap. This was America, and Americans were not opposed to getting down in the mud to come out ahead, no matter the cost.

That meant he would use every goddamn trick, scheme and ruse he could think of to marry that woman—and quickly.

"I debuted a year behind her," Miss Delafield said. "I suppose you were already in Paris by that time."

"I was, yes."

"Judging by your familiarity with these grounds, you must have spent a lot of time here."

"I did." He didn't bother to hide his smile. "More often than not I was at the chateau during the summer months. Maddie and I caused a lot of trouble together." Pointing to the gnarled oak tree on their right, he said, "I fell from that big branch one time. Nearly broke a rib. Maddie laughed for hours."

"That wasn't very compassionate."

"I put a slug in her shoe two days later, so we were even."

Miss Delafield chuckled. "You're awful!"

"She was just as terrible. Do not let that genteel demeanor fool you. A devil lurks underneath those dresses."

"A devil? I've known her for years and have never seen her act anything but kind."

"Then she's fooled you. For example, she convinced me *scrumtilious* was a word and I used it for two years before someone corrected me. There was the time she jumped out from behind a doorway to scare me when I was carrying a hot bowl of soup. Once she gave me an apple dipped in chocolate but it turned out to be an onion. My breath smelled horrid for a week."

Shoulders shaking, Miss Delafield covered her mouth. He nodded. "Go on, get it out. I know you want to."

She let out a chuckle. "An onion. Oh, that is clever."

"It was. We had a lot of fun together."

"So what happened?"

He steered her toward the greenhouse entrance. "What do you mean?"

"You moved away and she is nearly betrothed to a duke."

Yes, but I am back and she's not yet betrothed.

Cradling the egg hat with one hand, he opened the door, and Miss Delafield walked in ahead of him. He set the eggs on the bench. "Look under these pots. I can almost guarantee an egg will be here."

She began to search, lifting up the lid of each pot as he did the same. "You never wished to court her yourself?"

Of course he had. For six years he'd bided his

time, waiting to tell her of his intentions . . . until she called him brotherly.

But he'd rather not answer those kinds of questions at the moment. He wasn't ready for anyone to learn of his past, present or future feelings when it came to Maddie. "We may move on to other topics of conversation, you know. We needn't discuss Maddie the entire time."

"Oh, look! The yellow egg!" She picked it up. "That makes twelve. Shall we stop or keep going?"

"The odds that one team found more eggs than we did are incredibly low. Let's return and collect your prize. We might pick up one or two more on the way."

They left the greenhouse and headed for the tent. Miss Delafield held the yellow egg in her hands while he carried the rest in her bonnet. He got the feeling Miss Delafield was not altogether comfortable with silence, and he was proven right when she asked, "So are you going to tell her?"

He looked over. "Tell what to whom?"

"Maddie. Are you going to tell her that you love her?"

Harrison's entire body jolted and his grip on the bonnet slipped a fraction, allowing one of the hard eggs to slip free and crack on the ground. She scooped it up, then grinned at him. "Did you think I hadn't noticed?"

First Nellie, then Kit. Now Miss Delafield. Was everyone *but* Maddie aware of how he felt about her?

"Love her?" His voice sounded strangled. "I am attempting to find a bride at this house party."

"Yes, and she is yet unmarried."

"Lockwood's presence here does make that seem like a foregone conclusion."

"Oh, horse feathers. She got wrapped up in the competition for the duke's attention this spring. It became a point of pride for her, especially when there were whispers about why she took so long to marry. She had to prove that she could land a duke."

That did sound a bit like Maddie. She hated to lose.

A girl's worth in this world is determined by the match she makes.

It was clear there was no grand romance there. Maddie didn't desire Lockwood. She merely wished to marry a duke. "You don't think she would resent missing out on being a duchess?"

"Who, Maddie?" She made a noise in her throat. "More like she'd resent living in some remote little town in England, without her friends and family around."

He happened to agree, but said no more. Just before they entered the tent, Miss Delafield grabbed his arm. "Don't worry. I'll help you in any way I can, Mr. Archer."

Before he could ask what she meant, she disappeared into the tent.

They were the first team to return. The chaperones quieted as Harrison presented their bounty, which now held fourteen eggs, five of them green and one yellow.

Maddie's jaw fell. "I cannot believe it."

Harrison moved to the lemonade table and poured two glasses. "We were thirsty or else we would have found the remaining eggs." After handing Miss Delafield a lemonade, he toasted Maddie with his glass. "I warned you."

"You were lucky. I'll work harder next time."

"Next time? Are there more of these types of games?" Christ, he hoped not.

"Do not even think of complaining. You shall play and enjoy them, Harrison."

No, he dashed well wouldn't. Not unless Maddie played, too.

Instead of complaining, he lowered himself into an empty seat at Miss Delafield's table. The other teams trickled in but none matched Harrison and Miss Delafield's total, so they were declared the winners of both the picnic and the jewelry. Miss Delafield graciously gave the bracelet to the second place team, Kit and Miss Lusk.

"Thank you all for playing," Maddie announced to the group. "Mr. Archer and Miss Delafield will picnic tomorrow at noon. Then I have another activity at three in the afternoon. See you all at dinner this evening." She started toward the edge of the tent.

Wait, she was leaving?

The duke hurried after her, and Harrison gritted his teeth. He longed to be the one to chase her, then steal her away for an illicit afternoon in his bedroom.

Kit sat down. "What is your plan now that Lockwood is here?"

"The plan remains the same. He may be a duke but he doesn't know her like I do."

"I see. Well, be careful. I left my dueling pistols in the city."

"Do you own dueling pistols?"

"No," Kit said with an effortless shrug, "but I could probably locate a pair, if it comes to that."

"It won't come to that."

"Pardon me. Do you mind if I sit?"

The clipped British voice caught them both by surprise. Glancing up, Harrison found Lockwood aside the table, but he couldn't bring himself to speak. The last thing he wanted to do was make pals with Maddie's beau. Furthermore, why was the man out here instead of with Maddie?

"Of course," Kit answered when Harrison remained silent.

The duke lowered himself into the seat and removed a silver flask out of his inner jacket pocket. "Either of you whiskey drinkers?"

"I'm a whatever-is-on-hand drinker." Kit motioned for the flask. Lockwood handed it to Harrison first, who passed the flask straight on to Kit without drinking.

"When did you arrive?" Kit asked as the flask was returned.

"Just now. Took the train up first thing."

"Must be a perk of being a duke," Harrison couldn't help but say. "Showing up anywhere you like without an invitation."

"Miss Webster invited me, actually."

The comment dropped in Harrison's chest like a stone, a boulder-sized lump of jealousy that lodged under his ribs. He forced his shoulders to relax, unwilling to see Lockwood as a true threat. *It doesn't matter. She will end up with me in the end.*

"First time to Newport?" Kit asked the duke.

"It is. Lovely little town. Quite charming."

Harrison could barely smother a snort as the flask went around once more. God, the snobbery. "Charming" described a small English village, not a seaside beach resort where the wealthiest families in America spent eight weeks every summer.

"We like to think so," Kit said.

"Do you plan to stay long?" Harrison blurted, not caring if he sounded rude.

Lockwood angled his chair and crossed his legs, as if settling in for the duration. "I hadn't thought about it, actually. Suppose I'll see when I wear out my welcome."

"Then you should—" Harrison started but Kit talked right over him. "You'll enjoy it here," Kit said loudly. "The chateau is one of the finest properties in the country. Don't you agree, Harrison?"

"I've always loved it. But then, I spent my entire childhood here so I am likely biased."

Lockwood lifted a brow. "Ah, yes. From what I understand you're practically a member of the family."

It was an unwitting jibe, but one that hit a bit too close to old wounds. "Practically, but not quite." His smile was all teeth.

Lockwood took a sip from his flask. "So what do you fellows do around here for fun? I hear the Newport Casino is a roaring good time."

Kit rubbed his hands together. "Oh, it is. We could go tonight, once the household has settled after dinner."

"I'd like that," the duke said. "The three of us could make an evening of it."

Harrison would rather eat glass. However, if Kit took Lockwood out, then at least the duke wouldn't be spending time with Maddie. "I'll politely decline, but you two carry on without me."

"That's a shame," Lockwood said. "Maddie said you are quite the cardsharp."

It was true, and cards had been an easy way to make money in Paris, after he was disinherited. But he didn't like Lockwood knowing anything about him.

"Harrison's a corker with cards," Kit put in. "I wouldn't play against him, if I were you."

Harrison rose and straightened his clothing. "Indeed, that is good advice. Best be careful, Lockwood, or I'll take everything you have right out from under your nose." With that, he excused himself and sauntered toward the house.

Chapter Eight

Despite the lively conversation around her, Maddie was distracted at dinner. Tension hung in the room, an uncertainty compounded by the questioning glances she received from both her mother and Lockwood. Harrison sat across from her, though he hadn't contributed much to the discussion, either.

The afternoon hadn't gone as planned. Harrison won all the egg hunt prizes, including a picnic with Katherine tomorrow. Maddie should be happy for them both. Katherine was a good sort, nice and intelligent without a hint of scandal— yet the idea of their pairing caused Maddie's stomach to churn.

Would he make Katherine laugh during their outing? Would he charm her . . . then kiss her?

It's none of your concern, Maddie.

Indeed, she had other things to worry about— such as why she hadn't been thrilled to see the duke. Lockwood had traveled there to surprise her, yet she hadn't felt anything more than appreciation for his thoughtfulness. No burning giddiness to get him alone. No desire to touch or kiss him. No jealousy as he'd interacted with the other young ladies.

What was *wrong* with her? Lockwood was the catch of the season. She should have doted on him today instead of hiding in her room this afternoon. She made a desperate lunge for her wine.

"Are you all right?" Lockwood asked softly. "Is it your head again?"

She'd used a headache as an excuse for time alone earlier. "I am feeling much better, thank you. Is Your Grace having a pleasant time thus far?"

"Of course. You are here. What more could I want?"

The compliment warmed her. Lockwood really was a decent man. So why wasn't she swooning with giddiness? She'd plotted since March to gain his attention. Now she had it—and she was focusing on Harrison's outing with Katherine Delafield instead.

Get your head on straight. Remember your planning.

"Your Grace," Mama said from Lockwood's other side. "Tell us what exciting news you hear from London."

The duke wiped his mouth with a linen serviette. "I haven't any excitement to share, I'm afraid. Most of my news is from the House of Lords. It's quite boring."

"Yes, governing over the rabble," Harrison drawled. "How tedious."

Maddie gaped, astonished at her friend's rude

behavior. Lockwood, on the other hand, merely shrugged. "We do what we can to improve society. Leading is never an easy task."

Harrison opened his mouth, as if to cast another volley over the table, so she turned it around back on him. "What have you done to improve society while you were in Paris, Mr. Archer?"

"I was working, actually."

Maddie blinked, surprise robbing her of speech. So his time away had been about more than merely mistresses and champagne. Why did she find that reassuring?

Because you were jealous. She studied her plate, hoping no one noticed her reaction.

"And where did you work?" Mama asked.

"I had a position at the Compagnie Générale Transatlantique."

"Ah, the French shipping line," Lockwood said as he cut into his beef. "Interesting choice. A competitor to your family's company, if I am not mistaken."

"Are you intending to take a position at Archer Industries, then?" Mama signaled for more wine. "Now that your brother has taken over?"

"Perhaps." Harrison did not expound, but Maddie knew the answer. Harrison wanted nothing to do with his brother or Archer Industries. As soon as he found a bride, he planned to return to Paris.

The duke reached for his wineglass. "If I am able to offer any assistance, Archer, send me a cable. I have contacts all over the world, you know. My name can open almost any door."

A muscle jumped in Harrison's jaw as he stabbed a roasted potato with his fork. "Thank you."

Harrison's gaze locked on hers, and the emotion roiling in his midnight-blue eyes pinned her to the seat. She could not move, could not breathe. The look was intense and heated—a combination she had seen only one other time in all the years they'd known each other.

And that was when he'd nearly kissed her on the terrace last night.

Growing up, they had been able to communicate without words, their minds almost linked, but this new man perplexed her. What was going through his head? Why was he wearing such a fiery, greedy expression, as if he were contemplating leaping across the table to get to her?

A shiver worked down her spine.

Then he blinked, his face clearing, and the moment passed. With an exhale, she angled her head toward her lap. Had she imagined the entire encounter?

No, she hadn't. The certainty of what she'd seen sank into her bones. Hand shaking, she reached for her wine. What was happening between them? He'd invaded her mind, twisted her into knots ever since he'd returned. It was more than friendly flirting, too. Kit and Preston flirted with easy jokes and broad smiles. Harrison's attention lingered on her with steely purpose, communicating a new message she hadn't yet deciphered . . . but found intriguing.

They had always been drawn toward each other. She tried to tell herself this was merely another example of their natural ease and amiability, yet the tiny voice in her brain said this was *more*. Her heart was beating faster, her breath more rapid. A seductive warmth would spread in her lower half, her eyes searching for his whenever they were in proximity.

This connection between them felt dangerous and wicked, but exciting, as well.

Dinner continued until finally the ladies excused themselves to retire to the salon. Mama caught Maddie's arm as they entered and kept her voice low. "Whatever animosity is between the duke and Harrison must stop. We are trying to find that man a bride. He cannot be sniping at Lockwood at every turn."

There was no use pretending ignorance. "I will speak to him."

"If Harrison is jealous of Lockwood—"

"Harrison is not jealous. He's being protective of me because of our past friendship."

"Even so, we cannot have the other girls suspecting jealousy, else he'll never find a bride and Lockwood will never propose . . . unless that is your purpose?"

"What do you mean?"

"Madeline." Her mother stopped and let the other ladies go on ahead of them so they were alone. "I know you and Harrison were close all those years. He did seem particularly fond of you during your debut. I hope you are not seriously thinking of throwing over a duke for—"

"Absolutely not."

"Good, because your father and I want you to have the best. Someone powerful who will lay the world at your feet. Harrison is a nice boy but he is not a duke, with hundreds of years of lineage and history, pomp and circumstance. I never could have reached so high, but you, my girl, can have absolutely everything you desire once you become a duchess."

"I know, Mama. I am eager for Lockwood to propose."

"Good. To ensure it, you must fix this situation between the two men. If they spend time together, they'll come to like one another."

Maddie wasn't certain that would work, but she would try. "I'll invite them to play tennis tomorrow morning. Kit, too."

"Good idea." Mama continued to her favorite velvet sofa and addressed the room. "Ladies, let's enjoy our coffee in peace before the men join us."

Coffee, fruit and tiny cakes were passed about. Before Maddie could sit, Katherine waved her over to the window. "Maddie, a word."

She went over. "Yes?"

Katherine lowered her voice. "Will you come with me tomorrow?"

"Come with you . . . ?"

"On the picnic with Mr. Archer."

Maddie frowned, unsure what to say. "But that is your prize. Why would you want me there?"

Katherine's hands twisted, her eyes wild with panic. "I'd feel more comfortable with you there than my aunt. She will embarrass me to death."

"Oh." She had no idea what to say. It stood to reason that Katherine would prefer an outing without an elderly aunt looming the entire time, but Maddie wasn't certain how she felt about serving as a chaperone. To watch Harrison and Katherine laugh and smile at one another sounded positively awful. Yet who else could do it? "What if I sent a maid? Or one of the other ladies?"

"No, Maddie. It has to be you. Otherwise we'll just stare at the sea and search for topics of conversation. It'll be so awkward."

"I swear that Harrison is easy to talk to. Did you not have a good time hunting eggs today? What did you discuss?"

"You, mostly." Katherine took a breath, then pressed her case, reaching out to grab Maddie's hand. "I don't know him as well as you do. Please. Please say you'll come."

Maddie couldn't think of a good reason to refuse. "Fine. I'll come. May I bring the duke? That could be a fun outing, the four of us."

Katherine's face fell. "Oh, I thought . . . that is, it'll be more of a group outing then. Not a way for me to get to know Harrison."

That made sense. The winners had been promised a picnic with Harrison, not another man. "No, no. You're right. Just the three of us, then."

Katherine bounced on her toes and squealed. "You are a peach, Maddie. Thank you. I promise, we'll have a grand time."

Maddie sincerely doubted that.

DRESSED IN THEIR summer whites, Harrison and Kit traipsed through the chateau's quiet corridors until they reached the terrace. The morning sun was barely up in the sky and they'd already been summoned for lawn tennis.

White stripes outlined the court, the grass worn from Maddie's regular use. During their summers together, she and Harrison had played nearly every day. Back then, they'd been fairly evenly matched, but he was sorely out of practice. Three years of debauchery and an office job hadn't done much to improve his game.

He nearly tripped when he caught sight of Lockwood, clad in a white sweater and matching trousers, standing with Maddie. Damn it. He hadn't known the duke planned on joining them.

Harrison wanted her all to himself.

"I hope you have coffee," Kit shouted as they approached. "This is too early to be awake."

"You should go to bed earlier," she called back. "But yes, there is coffee." She pointed to a table set up alongside the court, where a silver carafe gleamed in the sunlight.

"Thank Christ. You may have first game," he told Harrison. "I need to sit down."

"I told you not to stay out all night at the casino."

"I won three hundred dollars, I'll have you know."

"As if you need the money."

"That's hardly the point," Kit grumbled as he shuffled off in search of coffee and a chair.

Harrison went over to where Maddie and the duke waited. "Any reason this could not have transpired at a normal hour?"

She bounced the strings of her racket against the palm of her free hand. "A very good morning to you, too. We are playing now because it's still cool out—and stop complaining. Everyone staying up late is not my fault."

Harrison had gone to bed at a reasonable time, leaving Kit to take Lockwood to the Newport Casino. Knowing that the duke was gambling instead of spending time with Maddie had allowed Harrison to actually get a decent night's sleep. "Who has first game?"

"I thought we'd play doubles," Maddie said. "You and Lockwood versus Kit and me."

A harsh refusal lodged in Harrison's throat. Before he could speak, Kit ambled over, a porcelain cup cradled in his hands. "Wait a moment. No offense to His Grace, but those matchups hardly seem fair. Harrison is woefully out of practice and we have no idea if the duke is even competent on the court."

"I am familiar with the game," Lockwood said. "I'll do just fine."

"When was the last time you played?" Harrison asked.

"Miss Webster and I played in New York a time or two."

Harrison ground his teeth together, trying very hard not to react. He hated the idea of Maddie playing lawn tennis with the duke, showing off her bright smiles and sweaty skin. Jealousy burned under his sternum. "Lockwood and Kit will partner up, with you and I on the other team."

"But I thought . . ." She trailed off, then sighed. "All right. Perhaps we'll switch it up after a few sets."

They decided on ends of the court and selected rackets. Harrison followed Maddie, watching her lightweight skirts swirl about her ankles, a jaunty spring in her step. She truly loved the game, a passion that always made him smile to witness.

He felt a bit jaunty himself, actually. Lockwood had spent the night out on the town instead of wooing his potential fiancée. Perhaps the duke was reconsidering his matrimonial prospects, being surrounded by all these eligible young ladies.

Not that it mattered to Harrison. His only concern was Maddie. Perhaps he should dig a little, see what he could find out. "Did you sleep well?"

She frowned at him over her shoulder. "I suppose, why?"

"I was surprised Lockwood went out with Kit instead of having a late-night rendezvous with you. Stealing kisses out in the gazebo or something."

"Do not be crass, Harrison. Lockwood is a duke, for God's sake."

"Dukes don't steal kisses?" He knew from observing years of debauchery in Paris that they dashed well did. "Have you checked that he's actually a duke?"

She grabbed his elbow and positioned them so their backs were to Lockwood and Kit. "Why don't you like him?"

He feigned ignorance. "What are you talking about?"

"You have been purposely rude to him since the moment he arrived. Do you have a problem with him?"

Yes. He wants you.

"Of course not. Why would I have a problem?"

"I haven't a clue." She poked him with the edge

of her racket. "Be nice to him. I would like for the two of you to get along for the remainder of the house party."

God, no. He didn't want to like Lockwood—or even *pretend* to like Lockwood. "Why?"

Her mouth fell open, as if the question took her aback. "Because it looks odd for you to be fighting with him when you should be finding a wife. What will the other guests think? There is no reason for you to be rude to such an important man."

An important man?

Harrison almost threw his racket down at that comment. Just because Lockwood had been born a duke did not make him top-drawer. Plenty of dukes were reprobates and spendthrifts, riddled with disease, with bastard children tucked away with mistresses. What was so illustrious about an aristocrat? "You're worried I'll appear jealous."

"Jealousy implies there is something romantic between you and me, and we both know that has never been the case."

His throat dried up, rending speech impossible, so he dropped a tennis ball into her hand and strode away. Maddie was wrong about the lack of romance between them. There had been heat in her gaze on the terrace, a new awareness that hadn't been there three years ago. She felt something for him . . . he just didn't know how deep it ran.

One thing for certain, he'd been playing it safe, moving slowly, but there was no more time for that. Not with Lockwood here, and not with the party ending in two days' time.

He had to make his intentions known.

The four of them began to warm up with gentle forehands and backhands. Lockwood obviously hadn't played much, evident when most of his shots landed in the net. For his part, Harrison was not as rusty as he'd feared. Years of wine and absinthe hadn't stolen his athletic ability, apparently.

The game started with Maddie serving first. Kit returned the serve to her and she smashed the ball just inside the sideline for a point. "Good shot, Miss Webster!" Lockwood called, and Harrison gripped his racket so tightly he thought the wood might snap.

The next return came his way, so he lined up and sent a blistering backhand straight toward the duke's crotch. Lockwood jumped out of the way, unable to get a racket on the ball.

"Ho!" Kit pointed his racket at Harrison. "Ease up, man. No one is looking to get hurt."

"Apologies." Harrison had to smother a grin. Perhaps this morning wouldn't be so terrible, after all.

And on it went. Harrison refused to go easy on Lockwood. There was a perverse pleasure in making the duke run all over the court, if only to watch the haughty aristocrat sweat.

Maddie encouraged Lockwood and cast dark looks at Harrison every time he won a point. Kit wasn't fooled, shaking his head at Harrison's antics, but said nothing.

"That's enough," Maddie announced when Lockwood's ball went wide to cost his team the game. "We should break for a bit."

"Not yet." Harrison retrieved the ball. "It's my serve."

Without waiting for anyone else to agree, Maddie walked off the court and went to the beverages. The duke followed, which left Harrison standing at the net. Kit ambled over. "Rather obvious, ain't you?"

Harrison bounced the ball and wouldn't meet Kit's knowing gaze. "No idea what you're talking about."

"Right. Bear in mind that making the duke look foolish won't endear you to her." Resting the racket over his shoulder, Kit strolled off toward the others, and Harrison had no choice but to follow.

Maddie avoided his eye over the rim of her lemonade glass. Finally, she put her glass down with a snap. "Come, Kit. Let's play one quick set before I break my racket over someone's head."

No need to ask whose head she contemplated bashing.

Harrison poured himself a cup of coffee and sat down. The duke did the same before dropping into the chair beside Harrison. Neither of them spoke as they watched Maddie and Kit play.

Though he should probably apologize for his behavior, he couldn't bring himself to do it. Liking Lockwood was out of the question. Harrison and Maddie had been close for almost a decade . . . and now Lockwood thought he would saunter over to Newport and snap her up? Absolutely fucking not.

In the end, Maddie would marry him, not the duke. Harrison alone knew how to make her happy. They'd always brought out the best in each other, and their marriage would be no different.

"She's quite good," Lockwood said, his eyes never leaving Maddie as she ran around the court.

"She's exceptional," Harrison corrected. The Devil suddenly lurked on his shoulder, whispering with the impulse to derail any matrimonial plans. "Has she told you she intends on competing for a few more years?"

"No, she didn't, but I am not surprised." The duke leaned back and folded his hands behind his head. "As long as it makes her happy, why not?"

"You're not appalled? Women sweating and competing in front of a crowd like that?"

"No, of course not. Are you?"

"Are you positive you're a real duke?" Harrison snapped.

Lockwood's expression eased, as if he'd finally solved a challenging puzzle. "Oh, I see. You assumed because of my title that I was some insufferable aristocrat, looking to lock her away in an ivory tower."

"I've met plenty of dukes. They are generally not known for their open-mindedness."

"True, but it's hard for me to care about any of that, not when my estates are in shambles. Nobility won't save me or those depending on my family."

"And for that you need money."

"I do, but look at her." Lockwood tilted his chin toward the court. "She's the most spectacular woman I've ever met. I would pursue her even if the money didn't matter."

This insight was hardly reassuring. Stomach churning, Harrison carefully set his porcelain cup down in the saucer. "You know, there are other unmarried ladies from wealthy families here this weekend. You could take your pick. Find one who has no interest in anything other than becoming a duchess."

Lockwood cocked a brow in Harrison's direction. "She said the two of you are merely friends, but I am detecting a definite tone in this conversation. Are you trying to warn me away from her?"

It nearly killed him, but Harrison forced a lie. "Of course not, but I don't think she'll be happy living on a remote estate somewhere in Boringshire, England."

"What about London?" Lockwood's expression was positively smug. "You've heard of it, I assume. Think she'll find enough to do whilst living there?"

The conversation was pointless. Lockwood was clearly determined, and no amount of arguing from Harrison would make a difference. And in the end, Maddie had to make up her own mind. Yes, years of friendship gave Harrison an advantage in pursuing her, but the decision on a marriage was ultimately hers.

He stood and straightened his coat. "I believe

I'll go find a proper breakfast. Nice game this morning, Lockwood."

The duke continued to watch the court. "I'll get in some practice and then we'll play again, Archer."

Not likely. Harrison smiled, though his words were anything but friendly. "I do so look forward to the competition."

Chapter Nine

 $\mathcal{L}$ ockwood waited at the bottom of the steps as Maddie descended the stairs. He'd requested a walk after tennis, so she had suggested a visit to the gardens. The flowers were in full bloom and there were benches if they decided to rest and talk. Even better, they would be completely alone there.

"You look lovely." Lifting her hand, he kissed her knuckles.

"Thank you. Shall we?" She gestured toward the back of the house.

He offered up his arm, his tone teasing. "No chaperone? You are quite the radical, Miss Webster."

"More like forgetful. I never think of it here at the beach because we're so much more relaxed." Rules were easier to bend in Newport when out from under the watchful eye of New York society—which probably explained why she liked spending time at the chateau.

"I am certainly not complaining, as I now have you all to myself."

Maddie forced a smile, unsure why she wasn't giddy with excitement. Lockwood had come to Newport and now asked to see her alone. She should feel *something*—a sense of anticipation, at least. Or satisfaction that her three-month-long quest might end in success.

Yet she had a strange sense of disquiet sitting on her shoulders, as if she wore an ill-fitting jacket.

The feeling will pass. This is what you've been working toward.

Of course, he liked to be outdoors as much as she did. Perhaps Lockwood merely wished to walk together in the morning sunshine.

Best not to examine whether it was relief or disappointment that coursed through her at the idea.

The sun was not quite directly overhead when they descended from the terrace onto the lawn. A warm breeze carried the scent of the ocean and gulls flew through the sky, dipping and swirling on their way to the beach. Turning her face to the sky, she took a deep breath and let the summer heat sink into her bones.

"Thank you for humoring me with a walk," Lockwood said. "You must be tired after your tennis practice this morning."

"Not at all. I try to play every day, even if I must hit against the wall in our cellar."

"Smart. Then you are not dependent on the weather."

"It keeps me physically fit for matches. Speaking of, did you enjoy the match today?"

"I enjoyed watching you. However, I'll need to work on my game before playing with you lot again."

She wouldn't subject Lockwood to another doubles match, not with Harrison. "It's not normally so competitive."

"It seemed Mr. Archer was trying to prove a point."

That he is an insensitive ass? Yes, point made.

She was still furious with Harrison—and he would have to explain his behavior just as soon as she could get him alone. "He is usually quite agreeable. You'll like him once you give him a chance."

"I have no issue with him, but it is clear he feels a bit . . . protective of you. Sort of like an older brother."

Maddie knew it was more than that. The look Harrison had given her on the terrace, when he'd held her face, had been anything but brotherly. Same for the emotion in his eyes at dinner last evening. Yet where was this coming from? She hadn't expected such fire and intensity from him, or discussions of kissing and jealousy. This version of Harrison was both reassuringly familiar and disturbingly different.

And the dichotomy in his personality was causing her head to spin.

Returning her attention to the duke, she said, "I will speak to him. He has no right to feel protective of me, considering he's been gone so long. He missed his chance to play at being an older brother."

"I don't mind. I hardly scare easily."

"No?" That was a relief, wasn't it?

He chuckled. "I once broke my lucky club during a round at St. Andrew's against the Duke of Argyll. We had three hundred pounds riding on that game. If that didn't scare me, nothing else could."

"Did you win?"

"By three strokes. Argyll was quite unhappy to lose that wager."

"I've always wanted to play there. It's unfair that men won't allow women to play the same courses."

"I agree, but they are convinced women shouldn't play." He gave a tiny shrug. "Minds will soon change, however. Look at you and lawn tennis. I daresay you could beat most anyone you challenged. You are quite talented."

"Thank you." Talent hadn't been enough, however. She'd put in hours and hours of hard work to hone her skills. Thankfully, nothing made her happier than spending time outside with a racket in her hand.

They entered the gardens, where the scent of roses was overpowering. They were Mama's favorites, and the cut flowers decorated nearly every room of the chateau in May and June. The fig and plum trees offered a tiny bit of shade on the perimeter, while a large copper beech sat in the far corner, near the fishpond. "Shall we sit on the bench?"

Nodding, he guided her toward the corner. When they were settled, he draped a long arm along the bench's back. "This is a peaceful spot. Do you come here to enjoy the fresh air?"

"I feed the fish every now and then. This is more my mother's spot than mine."

"Is that so? Well, perhaps now it may be ours." Slipping his hand into his coat pocket, he revealed a black ring box.

Her brain tripped over itself. *Oh. This is happening.*

Lockwood went down on one knee in front of her and held out the box. "I have already secured your father's blessing. Will you do me the honor of becoming my wife and my duchess, Miss Webster?"

She inhaled sharply. A gorgeous ring with a large emerald dazzled in the sunlight like green fire from inside the box. The stone was surrounded by smaller diamonds and finished with a platinum band. "It's stunning."

Lockwood removed the ring from the padding. "This belonged to my grandmother, then my mother. It is my hope that it will now belong to you."

A duchess. He wishes for you to be his duchess.

This was what she wanted, as well. All the parties she'd attended, the late-night dinners. Small talk over waltzes. Tea and cakes during calls. She had worked incredibly hard for this moment.

So why weren't the words coming out of her mouth already?

You are being ridiculous. You cannot make a better match than this.

She drew in a deep breath and let it out slowly. "I would be honored, Your Grace."

His mouth hitched. "Excellent."

He helped to remove her glove, then slipped

the band onto her left ring finger. She held the stones to the light, turning them every which way. The ring was . . . astounding. "You've caught me entirely by surprise."

"Surely not entirely, as I appeared on your doorstep yesterday without warning."

"Well, perhaps not entirely," she admitted. "Thank you, Lockwood."

"You are welcome." Gracefully rising, he retook his seat on the bench, grabbed her hand and lifted it to his mouth once again. "I shall endeavor to make you very happy, Madeline."

It was the first time he'd used her given name.

She blinked, a bit jarred to hear him say it . . . which was silly. She would marry this man. They would be intimate, share every life event together, like having children and growing old. Why should hearing him use her name surprise her?

Yet, it did. The way he said *Madeline*, in his clipped British accent, was so different than the way Har—

No. She would not think about Harrison at this moment. He had no right to intrude on her thoughts during this happy occasion. No right whatsoever.

Swallowing, she said, "And I you, Lockwood." *Does he insist on formality in private, as well?* Pushing that voice aside, she squeezed the duke's hand. "Or, is there another name I should use . . . ?"

"Andrew, but friends call me Stoker."

"Why?"

"One of those silly prep school nicknames, I'm afraid. It just stuck."

I met a few dukes during my time in Paris. Generally not the most enlightened bunch.

Dash it, why was she letting Harrison's comments ruin this moment? He didn't know Lockwood—Stoker—as well as she did. But the doubts were already seeded in her brain.

Would the duke truly try to prevent her from playing?

Best to begin how she meant to go on. "I do wish to continue competing for another few years, as long as my knees allow it." She braced herself, not knowing what her fiancé's response would be.

"Of course. Were you worried I'd object?" After studying her relieved expression, he grinned. "I see. Madeline, as a duchess, you may do and say nearly anything without fear of recrimination. Furthermore, you'll find that I am not planning to live in your pocket, as I assume you'll not live in mine once we're married."

That last bit should have reassured her, but it sounded . . . lonely. As if he were planning to live separate lives, where they would schedule dinners together through secretaries. She longed for a partner in all things, not a passing acquaintance. The sort of marriage her own parents had.

The duke is not American. They do things differently there.

Yes, she supposed that was true. These adjustments would merely take some time for her to get used to.

Not a cloud floated in the sky that afternoon as Maddie and Katherine Delafield walked along the gravel path. Brisk ocean winds blew their skirts, and Maddie was forced to hold on to her hat so the breeze didn't carry it away.

Mama had, of course, been thrilled about the engagement to Lockwood. She cried and told Maddie how lucky she was to have such an important husband, one that would elevate their family tree to practically royalty. *Your children will influence the course of history*, her mother had said. This was quite a lot of pressure for children who hadn't even been born, but Maddie kept that opinion to herself.

Now she was headed to the gazebo along with Katherine, though she longed to be anywhere else.

She had considered claiming a headache or monthly pains. An upset stomach or organ failure. Anything to get out of going on this blasted picnic. But she was not a coward. A promise of chaperone duties had been made, and Maddie couldn't desert Katherine, no matter her irritation with Harrison.

And she *was* irritated. His behavior toward Lockwood had been downright appalling. If this was Harrison's idea of protecting her, she would need to set him straight. He was about three years too late for that nonsense.

The gazebo rested near the edge of the property, almost at the cliff's edge, where one could watch the boats and the surf while sitting in the shade. She spotted Harrison there, his hands jammed in his pockets, gaze locked on the ocean. He wore no hat, the wind plastering a cream linen suit to his flat chest and long legs. Her insides jumped as if touched by an electric spark, then everything turned warm. Thank goodness for the cool breeze to chill her overheated skin.

You are betrothed. Stop ogling Harrison.

Katherine pulled Maddie to a stop. "Oh, rats. I realized I've forgotten something. I need to return to the house."

"What? No, wait—"

"It's important." Katherine leaned over and spoke from behind her hand. "Woman problems."

Maddie nodded, completely understanding. "I'll come with you."

"No, no. That's unnecessary. I'll go to the house, then come back." She pushed Maddie toward the gazebo. "You go on without me. See you later!"

Without waiting for a response, Katherine hurried in the direction from which they had just come. Maddie considered tagging along, but Katherine could surely find the way herself. Resigned, she resumed her trek to the gazebo. At least this would give her the opportunity to speak to Harrison alone about his deplorable behavior.

His brows lowered as she stepped inside the open wooden structure. "What happened to Miss Delafield?"

"She'll return. She needed to retrieve something from the house."

"I see." He rocked on his heels. "Turned out to be a bit windy. Are you certain we shouldn't move this outing—?"

"Why do you antagonize Lockwood at every turn?"

He had the grace to appear sheepish. "May we at least sit before you yell at me?"

"No. I am too angry." Her arms flopped use-
lessly at her sides, fury robbing her body of its
usual coordination. "I cannot understand. You
are acting like an ogre and he doesn't deserve it.
Frankly, neither do I."

He gestured to the picnic basket and blan-
ket on the wood floor. "Please, Maddie. It's too
windy. Sit down."

She complied, if only to move things along.
They arranged themselves on the floor, the sides
of the structure blocking most of the breeze, and
Maddie held herself stiffly. He opened the large
wicker basket and pulled out a bottle of champagne along with two coupes. As he popped the
cork, she removed her gloves. "I hardly feel like
celebrating with you."

His gaze flew to her ring finger, his entire body
growing very still. "What is *that*?"

Clearing her throat, she tried not to fidget.
"Lockwood has asked me to marry him."

Harrison sat there, unmoving, for a long moment. Then he filled one coupe to the brim with
champagne and downed the liquid in two swal-
lows. After that he poured more. "Would you
care for champagne?"

A clear head seemed wise at the moment. "No,
thank you."

Stretching his legs out in front of him, he
leaned back and sipped champagne, his expression blank, gaze fixed on the horizon. The gazebo
was intimate, not overly large, and they were
close enough for her to see the hint of stubble
on his jaw. The long lashes that framed his eyes.
Slashing brows and high cheekbones. It was a

face she knew well, though he remained enigmatic, a mystery since he'd returned from Paris.

The silence wore on and she strove for patience. He seemed in no hurry to answer for his obnoxious behavior—which only angered her further. Katherine would return soon, which meant there wasn't much time. "Are you going to explain yourself?"

The remaining champagne disappeared into his mouth, and the strong column of his throat moved as he swallowed. "I don't have to like him, Maddie."

"You never even gave him a chance before you started sniping at him."

Harrison reclined until he was flat on the wooden floor, his hands resting on his stomach. He said nothing, and she sighed in defeat. This was exhausting. If he couldn't be honest with her, then she was wasting her time.

She started to rise, but Harrison reached over and wrapped a hand around her wrist, stopping her. "Wait, stay."

"Why? Katherine will return soon. You don't need me."

"Do not go," he said, his voice low and harsh as he propped up on an elbow. "Not until I explain."

She folded her legs to one side, adjusted her dress and perched on her hip. "Then explain."

The wind whistled through the gazebo's top and created a small pocket of intimacy on the floor, a hidden place where only the two of them existed. A muscle in Harrison's jaw worked, his stare locked on where their bodies were touching. She hadn't realized he was still holding on to her. His thumb rubbed her skin, stroking, and her flesh sizzled under his fingers, the warmth spreading up her arm and to her breasts. Down between her legs. The touch felt possessive, not the least bit gentle.

So why wasn't she pulling free?

Without releasing her, he sat up and locked eyes with her. Blue flames licked in the depths of his irises, heat like she'd never seen before, and her mouth went dry. "I am jealous," he whispered. "I acted like an ass because I am consumed with jealousy, so much so that I cannot think straight, Mads."

Her heart thumped as wicked pleasure flooded her veins, a rush of unexpected emotion that rose up like a wave . . . until she remembered.

Betrothal. Lockwood

A chill went through her, chasing away any residual heat, and she jerked out of Harrison's grip. "You shouldn't say such things to me."

His brows shot up. "Why? You were jealous of Esmée. How is this different?"

"Because you are not marrying her. You are not betrothed to another woman. I have a future decided, whereas you do not."

"Your future is not yet decided, Maddie."

How could he say that? "As of two hours ago, it is. I am promised to the Duke of Lockwood."

"Who merely wants the dowry."

"You act as if that is an uncommon occurrence."

"True, but he doesn't *know* you. He didn't teach you to skip a rock or dig up clams. Or spend

hours with you on the back lawn catching fire-
flies, making each other laugh."

"We were children. That is what children do
together."

"The only person I did those things with was
you. And unlike your fiancé, I actually care about
you."

She blinked, mouth open, at a loss as to what
to say.

"I . . ." He blew out a long breath. "You asked
for the truth and I did not want to lie."

A part of her wished he had, that he'd kept this
to himself. The knowledge threatened to strangle
her, her chest tight with the ramifications of his
revelation. Her mother had been right: Harrison
was *jealous* of Lockwood. That implied Harrison
had feelings for her, feelings that went deeper
than friendship.

How was that possible? They had been out of
contact with each other for the last three years,
all by his design. Now he had returned and,
what, developed a crush on her? It didn't make
any sense. Was this why he'd nearly kissed her
on the terrace?

And why he'd stared at her so intently at dinner?

She rubbed her temples as if to stop her mind
from spinning. None of this mattered. Not one
bit. She was engaged to another man, a fact she
hadn't hidden from him.

So why was he doing this *now*?

"I have no choice, Mads," he said. "It has to be
now."

He always had an uncanny ability to see what
she was thinking. "Stop reading my thoughts."

"I can't help it, not when I know you so well."

"Your timing could not be worse, Harrison."

"I am aware."

"I am betrothed to the duke."

"Again, I am aware."

He was so calm it only agitated her further. "Three years! Three years you were away without a word. And now you've returned, storm into my life, and talk of jealousy and kissing? It makes no sense."

"Maddie—"

"Stop."

She slid on the wooden floor, putting distance between them, but he inched closer, as if reluctant to part from her. "Something is happening between us," he said quietly. Seductively. "After all these years, something has changed between us, even if you don't wish to admit it."

Oh, God. She covered her mouth with a hand, frightened of what she might say. Because he was right. From the instant he'd returned she'd noticed the changes in him, from his broad shoulders and thick thighs, to his flirtatious and intense manner. The confident way he moved and the determination burning in his gaze. Her stomach now fluttered the instant he walked into a room.

Far from offering comfort, however, the realization terrified her.

For as long as she could remember, he had been the impetuous one, cajoling her to join in his antics. She had been the steady presence, a calm voice of reason to keep him grounded. Like when he'd tried to take the skiff out in a thunderstorm and she'd stopped him, saying it was too dangerous.

This time the danger was right in front of her, so handsome and alluring. If she lost her head, her entire life would be ruined. Lockwood would be devastated, not to mention her parents, and the scandal would be horrific. She'd never be able to hold her head up on Fifth Avenue ever again.

Go, go, go. If nothing else she had to put distance between them.

Drawing in a fortifying lungful of ocean air, she pushed to her feet. "This was a bad idea. I regret I brought it up."

"In other words, you wish you did not know."

"I should return to the house." *Damn and blast.* Where on earth was Katherine? Maddie sent a longing glance toward the path, but there was no sign of her friend. "We shouldn't be alone."

Gracefully, he unfolded his limbs and stood. "There's no need to be afraid of me. I won't pounce on you."

She could hear the hurt in his voice, the contrition. No doubt he wished he hadn't been honest with her. She quickly decided the only thing to do was give him honesty in return.

"I am not afraid of you, Harrison. I am afraid of *myself.*"

Chapter Ten

$\mathcal{A}$ flat expanse of lawn stretched behind the tennis court, the ground a lush green in the afternoon sun. Carefully groomed boxwood bushes edged the grass on three sides. On the lawn, wickets were arranged, along with the stakes, in a familiar figure-eight pattern, while mallets and balls waited nearby.

Though he longed to be elsewhere, Harrison stood alone in the tent aside the court, waiting for the rest of the guests to arrive for a game of croquet. He'd left the gazebo a few minutes ago, having sat there long after Maddie hurried off and disappeared into the chateau.

Their outing hadn't gone well.

The engagement had thrown him off. Seeing that ring knocked him sideways, stealing his sense of reason and tossing it into the sea. He should have expected it, with Lockwood's sudden arrival and all, but the garish ring on Maddie's finger had flipped a switch inside him. Powered up his panic and electrified his desperation.

So, without much forethought, he confessed

his jealousy to see how she would react. The end result had been mixed, with her scurrying from the gazebo, unable to get away fast enough. However, her final comment gave him hope.

I am not afraid of you, Harrison. I am afraid of myself.

This meant she knew something was happening between them, something deeper than friendship. Of course, he'd had years to come to terms with how he felt about her, but it was a recent development for Maddie. What did she plan to do about it? He couldn't let her ignore him, or pretend the gazebo hadn't happened.

Your timing could not be worse.

He disagreed. In fact, there was not a moment to lose now that she was betrothed. He had to keep pressing, keep trying to convince her, otherwise she would be lost to him forever. It had taken every bit of his restraint to let her walk away, not to chase her and continue their discussion.

But such was not the way to convince her. Maddie had a tendency to dig in her heels and refuse to see logic. Like when she wouldn't swim in the ocean beyond where she could stand because she thought a fish would eat her. Harrison had finally coaxed her into deeper water by showing her ever-so-slowly that it was safe.

She needed gentle pressure to come around to reason . . . not a harsh shove. If he wasn't steady and methodical in his pursuit, he would scare her off. Even if the waiting was pure torture.

What if she actually marries Lockwood?

The possibility turned his blood cold.

For now, he had to believe that he could persuade her otherwise. Losing her to another man was not an option.

Suddenly Kit ambled across the lawn, looking far too pleased with himself. "A fine day for croquet."

Was that a love bite peeking out from under Kit's collar? "You're certainly in a good mood. Where have you been?"

"Visiting with a friend." The nature of said visit was obvious, considering the smug twist to Kit's mouth. "How was your picnic with the Delafield girl?"

"She never showed. Maddie did, though."

"And how did that go?" Kit asked.

"I'm not sure yet. Lockwood proposed."

"Oh, shit."

"Exactly."

"What will you do?"

"Split them up, obviously. I just need to figure out how."

The ladies and chaperones emerged then, converging on the lawn and preventing Kit from offering up a response. The Duke of Lockwood brought up the rear of the pack, and on his arm was Maddie's mother.

Maddie was nowhere to be found.

Harrison's stomach sank. Damn it. Was she not planning on joining them?

"Good afternoon, gentlemen," Mrs. Webster called. "It's nice to see both of you eager for an afternoon of croquet."

Hardly. But there was no way for him to back out now. The guests filtered under the tent, while

Lockwood escorted Mrs. Webster over to Harrison and Kit. "Is Maddie coming?" Harrison asked bluntly.

"She wasn't feeling well," her mother said, "so I told her to rest. His Grace has volunteered to help instead."

The duke's stare held a note of challenge when it turned on Harrison. "I quite enjoy croquet. Seemed like an excellent way to spend an afternoon."

Harrison ignored him. "How will this work?"

"Maddie said you should play in teams of two." Mrs. Webster waved her hand, as if the details hardly mattered. "You and the duke figure it out." She disappeared under the tent.

"Shall we choose partners?" Lockwood asked.

"I'll sit out. I've had enough exercise today," Kit said before he walked away.

Harrison and the duke decided on two teams of three each. They would play two rounds of croquet, mixing up the partners so all the ladies eventually had a turn.

The ladies drew sticks for teams, and Lockwood was paired with Martha Thorne, who was from an old New York family, and Emily Mills, the daughter of a Chicago industrialist. Harrison's sticks were chosen by Angelica Dent, a relation to President Grant, and Nellie Young. Before selecting mallets, they had to decide which team would go first.

"Shall we go by rank?" Lockwood sounded bored, but Harrison wasn't fooled by the casual suggestion. The duke clearly thought getting out in front gave him a tactical advantage.

Harrison didn't mind. He'd rather trail Lockwood and catch up than look over his shoulder the entire game. "By all means."

The group strolled out to the lawn. Lockwood, the picture of aristocratic entitlement with a mallet tucked under his arm, leaned toward Harrison. "I should warn you, old boy. You'll find I am a bit more skilled at croquet than lawn tennis."

Ah, so that was Lockwood's plan. Revenge for the morning's match. Harrison lifted a brow. "Then I look forward to playing against you. Old boy."

Lockwood's expression hardened, his lips flat. "She's not here for you to impress, you know. I wonder if you'll try as hard." Without awaiting a response, he strode ahead to the starting stake.

Harrison ground his back teeth together and followed at a slower pace. He burned with the need to steal Maddie away from that arrogant bastard, no matter the scandal.

Martha led off for Lockwood's team. It was clear she hadn't played much, as her swings were wild and uncoordinated, and her ball went off course. Angelica started for Harrison's team and her ball fared better than Martha's. The other two ladies followed, leaving Lockwood and Harrison as the final two players.

Lockwood sent his ball through the first two wickets easily, then continued on to the next set. Harrison had no interest in the wickets. He did, however, have an interest in sending the duke's ball flying off the course as much as possible.

When it was finally Harrison's turn, he easily

caught up to Lockwood's ball, staying a little behind on purpose.

The next round began, with the ladies focused on getting through the wickets as quickly as they could. Emily was a decent player for the other team, while both Angelica and Nellie were aggressive in their play. In the third round, Nellie bumped into Martha's ball, so she lined up the two balls, put her foot on her own ball, then sent Martha's ball rolling several feet away.

Lockwood caught Harrison's eye. "I assume we are respecting the boundaries. A gentleman's game, nothing out of bounds."

Resting his mallet head on the ground, Harrison leaned onto the handle with one hand and crossed his feet at the ankles. "I'm not afraid of chasing my ball a time or two. Are you?"

Lockwood said nothing, but when his turn came around, he took revenge on Angelica by sending her ball to the far side of the court. Nellie walked over to Harrison and whispered, "That's hardly sporting of him."

"Don't worry. He'll get his."

Nellie chuckled. "I'll make sure to stay out of your way, then."

Harrison stepped forward and cleared the fifth wicket. When he lined up his next shot, he didn't aim for the wicket, but sent his ball rolling into the duke's green ball. Fighting a grin, Harrison lined up the two balls, put his foot on his orange ball and brought the mallet down with a mighty crash. The orange ball didn't move, but the duke's ball went sailing through the bushes and into the brush below.

Lockwood said nothing, but a muscle in his jaw worked as his gaze tracked the ball's progress. Shoulders stiff, he tramped off into the greenery.

Nellie didn't bother hiding her laughter. "Nicely done, Mr. Archer."

The ladies carried on, the mood definitely lighter. They got into the spirit of it, smacking their balls against one another's, laughing and teasing. Lockwood finally returned, green ball in hand. A grass stain marred his otherwise immaculate white trousers, and the sight amused Harrison immensely.

The duke soon took revenge and aimed directly for the crowded spot where Harrison's ball rested. In an absolute stunner of a shot, he managed to nudge the orange ball. Harrison expected to see his ball smashed into the Atlantic, but the duke showed remarkable restraint. Lockwood sent the orange ball to the farthest corner of the lawn, where it stopped just inside the perimeter of the course.

The point was obvious: Lockwood was a gentleman and Harrison was not.

Except Harrison hadn't ever cared about being a gentleman. He didn't need anyone's approval or society's blessing. Only two things mattered to him now: taking everything away from his family and marrying Maddie.

When it was finally Harrison's turn, he walked by Lockwood to get to his ball. "You are wasting your time," Lockwood murmured under his breath. "She'll never want you, not as long as she has someone like me."

Harrison swallowed the angry retort burning

his tongue. While Maddie currently wore Lockwood's ring, Harrison would not go down without a fucking fight.

And, unlike the duke, he did not play fair.

FOR THE REST of the day, Maddie did her best to ignore Harrison. She skipped the afternoon's activities, remaining in her room instead, where she'd rehashed what was said in the gazebo.

Something is happening between us, even if you don't wish to admit it.

It was true, she was attracted to him. However, the connection was more than simple attraction. Simmering under the appreciation of his appearance was a certain fondness, a wish to never leave his side. To tell him everything and share whatever came ahead. The admission of those feelings came as a great relief, even if she could do nothing about it. She'd accepted Lockwood's offer of marriage, and that was that.

Undoubtedly this would pass. The distraction of her old friend was merely a tiny setback in her grand plan. As soon as Harrison entered into a betrothal of his own, Maddie could focus on Lockwood.

Yes, that was it. She must turn all her energies into matching Harrison with one of her friends. Any other course of action was now out of the question, as the engagement was public knowledge.

Before dinner, Maddie's friends gathered around her, admiring the betrothal ring and offering up congratulations. Lockwood smiled adoringly from across the room, while Maddie's mother beamed as if she'd just met the Queen of England. During this time, Maddie hadn't allowed herself a single glance at Harrison. She was afraid of what she might see.

It was futile—the path to a different outcome had closed. Maddie could not break the betrothal, not without causing a horrific scandal, nor could she act upon the emerging desire for her childhood friend. Her future was set.

And if her happiness felt forced in that moment, well . . . that was only temporary. Her enthusiasm would bloom in the days to come as she made plans for the wedding and starting her new life in England.

After an interminable meal in the dining room, the ladies finally adjourned to the salon. Nellie grabbed Maddie's arm and dragged her to the far side of the empty room. "You missed a hell of an outing this afternoon," her friend said quietly, eyes sparkling with mirth.

Maddie was instantly worried. "What do you mean?"

"No one told you?" When Maddie shook her head, Nellie continued. "Your men were at each other's throats the entire time."

Maddie's mouth fell open and she quickly sputtered a denial. "They are not my men." Nellie's expression remained dubious, so Maddie moved on. "What happened?"

"Harrison was out for blood. He sent the duke's ball flying clear into Connecticut. Twice."

That didn't surprise her. Harrison played aggressively, as did she. The two of them had been unbeatable at croquet. "What did Lockwood do?"

"It was clear the duke was taunting Harrison throughout the afternoon, whispering under his breath, not that Harrison ever reacted. But the duke sent Harrison's ball flying a few times. Ended up winning both games."

Harrison hated to lose, much as Maddie did, so that must have bothered him. "I should have been there."

"It's better that you weren't. You wouldn't have been pleased with either of them."

The rustle of skirts alerted them to another arrival. Katherine approached, her eyes sparkling. "Are you discussing the croquet match?"

Maddie narrowed her eyes. "What happened to you earlier? You never returned for your picnic."

Katherine and Nellie exchanged a knowing glance that set Maddie's teeth on edge. "Forgive me," Katherine said, not sounding all that apologetic. "Was Mr. Archer angry?"

I am consumed with jealousy.

She swallowed. "No."

"Did something happen in the gazebo?" Nellie asked. "Is that why you skipped croquet?"

Maddie studied the curtains and struggled with how to answer. Hardly anything happened in the gazebo, but those few minutes had turned her life upside down.

"Oh, my God," Nellie exclaimed softly, eyes going wide as her hand clamped onto Maddie's forearm. "Something happened, didn't it?"

"Of course not. You are being ridiculous. I am betrothed." She held up her gloved hand, where the ducal engagement ring rested under the cloth.

"I know something happened. Please, tell me. Was there kissing or groping? Rubbing in all the best places?" Nellie put her hands together in a pleading gesture. "I must know. *Please.*"

"Stop it." Maddie glanced around them. "I am engaged and this conversation is unseemly. Someone might overhear."

Katherine and Nellie sent each other a small smile, and Maddie huffed in exasperation before walking away. Let them speculate without her.

The door to the dining room opened and Harrison was the first to appear. His eyes landed on her and Maddie paused as if caught, his stare igniting flames in every part of her body. Tingles raced along her skin, her breasts swelling, and she grew light-headed, as if she'd played an eight-hour match in the hot August sun.

It was over in a blink. Someone nudged him from behind, and he dropped his head and continued into the room. She hurried to the sideboard and poured a glass of sherry, not caring if she was the only woman imbibing at the moment.

"My dear." Her father smiled down at her. "Have a moment to spare for your old papa? Your fiancé and I would like a word."

The conversation with Nellie fresh in her mind, Maddie's stomach twisted and dropped. Had someone been talking about her and Harrison to the duke? "What is this about?"

"Come along. I'll not spoil the surprise."

Her nape prickled as if she could feel the weight of Harrison's stare on her as she left the salon. Trailing her father, she went into his office, where Lockwood already waited, his mouth curved into a hint of welcome.

She looked between the two of them. "Is it bad news?" Her hands trembled, so she buried them in her skirts.

"No, not at all," Lockwood said. "I have a surprise and I wanted to tell you right away."

Daddy sat behind his desk and leaned back, saying nothing. It was clear he didn't wish to give her any hints, but at least he didn't seem angry. "Oh?"

The duke folded his hands behind his back, the pose emphasizing the white evening vest hugging his lean frame. "I reached out to Mr. Charles Robb at the All England Croquet and Lawn Tennis Club in Wimbledon. He is the instructor of—"

"Mrs. Hillyard." Maddie clasped her hands under her chin as her heart started to thump with excitement. Blanche Bingley Hillyard was one of the greatest tennis players in the world. She had won several championships in recent years, and Maddie admired her career from afar.

Lockwood's expression softened, as if relieved. "Yes, Mrs. Hillyard. Mr. Robb has agreed to come here, to Newport, in order to train with you this summer."

Elation weakened her knees and she let out a soft gasp. Mr. Robb, coaching *her*? It was absolutely surreal.

"I see she likes the idea, Lockwood," her father said with a chuckle.

She blinked up at the duke. "How . . . ?"

"Think of it as an engagement present."

"I am stunned. Thank you, Lockwood."

"I thought you might like it." Lockwood lifted her hand and kissed her knuckles. "He'll sail here as soon as the tournament finishes in mid-July."

She nearly vibrated with excitement. That meant she could train with Mr. Robb during all of August. Of course, there would be wedding planning to get under way. Perhaps Mama could do most of that without her.

"And one more surprise," the duke said. "I have requested plans to have a lawn tennis court put in at my country estate."

Goodness, Lockwood had been busy. "This is tremendous news. Again, thank you. I will tell Mother so she knows not to count on having me around in August."

"No need to keep it a secret," the duke said. "Please, tell everyone."

Had she detected a bite in the way he said *everyone*? Was this something to do with Harrison and the game of croquet today?

It was clear the duke was taunting Harrison throughout the game . . .

Had Lockwood sensed the attraction between Maddie and Harrison? It seemed improbable, considering the most damning moments had happened when they were alone. Yet Katherine and Nellie had inferred an attachment. There was a good chance Lockwood had, as well.

Her neck grew hot, embarrassment climbing toward her face. Without meaning to, had she cast flirtatious glances at Harrison in front of the others? Was she wearing her heart on her sleeve at all times? How mortifying.

She had to do better at hiding her feelings. No one must learn of her improper thoughts. And it went without saying that she and Harrison could not be alone ever again.

Chapter Eleven

"Is everyone ready?" Maddie stood at the front of the tent, wisps of brown hair whipping about her head, the hint of a smile on her face.

Harrison studied her from under his lashes, admiring the fine bone structure beneath the tanned skin from her outdoor pursuits. She was a fascinating amalgam of proper lady and rebellious upstart. A conventional beauty with a penchant for mischief.

It was the rebellious side of her that had drawn him in all those years ago, two moths seeking the same light. The attraction had compounded until he was starving for her, with a ferocity that should have scared him. He always assumed they would end up together, that their personalities were a perfect match. And as he got older, the craving for her grew worse until she broke his heart, when he realized his feelings were unrequited.

But unrequited no longer.

He drummed his fingers on the table, restless and edgy. She'd avoided him ever since the gazebo. He told himself this was a good thing, that her reaction meant he'd rattled her, but it was hard to see her smiles bestowed anywhere but him. Difficult to hear her laughter aimed at others while receiving none for himself. He was greedy when it came to her attention and she was depriving him of it, and the loss shredded his insides like a thousand tiny cuts.

His eyes moved to Lockwood, who stood talking to Kit in the corner of the tent. The duke was a decent enough sort, Harrison supposed, and if he weren't in love with Maddie he'd bless their marriage with his whole heart. But his heart was spoken for, given to Maddie all those years ago when they'd played in the surf and tramped across the chateau grounds. Watching fireworks and chasing butterflies, digging up clams and climbing trees.

The question was what Maddie wanted.

Betrothals were not easy to break, especially one as high profile as Maddie's, and calling it off would cause quite the scandal.

That possibility didn't scare him, however. In fact, he liked scandal. He'd created so many in both New York and Paris that no one even bothered discussing him anymore. One thing he'd learned was that money smoothed over most every faux pas, especially in America. Wealth mattered even when propriety did not—and the Websters had more money than almost anyone, save J. P. Morgan and Vanderbilt. They could weather any storm . . . even a broken betrothal to a duke.

"Ready?" she called, reclaiming his attention. The ladies all rose in unison.

Damn. What was happening?

"Weren't listening, were you?" Kit slid into the empty chair next to Harrison.

"No. What are we doing?"

"Oh, not *we*." Kit chuckled. "You."

"Go!" Maddie said—and every eye swung to Harrison.

He resisted the old urge to fidget. "What am I supposed to do?" he muttered to Kit.

"Sardines. You're to hide and the ladies will find you."

Harrison remembered the game from childhood. When each woman found his hiding spot, they would squeeze in with him, all of them cozily waiting until the last person found the group. An idea occurred. "I think Miss Webster should play, as well," he called out.

Everyone in the tent paused, looking to Maddie. Her brow wrinkled. "Why would I play?"

"You know all the best hiding places on the property. You should hide and I'll search along with the guests."

She flicked a glance toward the duke before looking back at Harrison. "You also know the best hiding places."

"Nonsense." He waved his hand. "It's been years since I played hide-and-seek here. I've forgotten them all." Kit covered his mouth with his hand as if he might laugh, but Harrison ignored him.

"I agree," Mrs. Webster said from the side of

the tent. "You always loved this game, Maddie. Enjoy yourself."

Lockwood stroked his chin, lips pursed in thought, as if he were trying to figure out Harrison's angle. Yet he offered up no protest, probably assuming Harrison would be occupied with the ladies.

The assumption was reasonable . . . but also untrue.

"Fine." She put her hands on her hips, still looking unconvinced. "I'll play, but why must I be the one to hide? It ruins the point of the game."

Harrison tried to cover his desperation under a bored expression. "The game will be over in two minutes if I hide. I'll be found behind that bush over there. You are the only one who can make this a challenge."

One thing he knew about Maddie, she was competitive. It was one of the qualities that made her such a fierce tennis player. And while she could refuse to participate, everything told him she wouldn't.

"That makes sense, I suppose," she said.

He pressed his case. "Also, I'm not certain the chaperones would like the idea of me and one of the ladies alone together for a stretch of time, separated from the others."

Maddie cast a nervous glance at the table full of chaperones. "Oh, right. Good point." She nodded once. "I'll be the one to hide, then. Now according to the rules, I may hide either inside the house or somewhere on the grounds. The last person to find the hiding place is the loser and will sit out tomorrow's sail on the yacht."

This was not a team game, so the ladies remained quiet, most likely plotting their strategy. The risk of being left out from a sail on the Webster yacht would motivate most anyone.

Except Harrison. He would find Maddie first, and it had nothing to do with tomorrow's outing.

Gesturing toward the occupants of the tent, he said, "We should put our heads down until Miss Webster is safely on her way to a hiding place."

"You certainly are taking this seriously." A deep crease formed between Maddie's brows as she studied him. "Fine. Everyone sit and close your eyes. Mama, give them the signal to begin when I've been gone long enough."

Harrison nearly rubbed his hands together. He hadn't forgotten anything about the chateau . . . or their games together. He knew exactly where she would go. He closed his eyes.

Kit kept his voice low. "Couldn't be more obvious if you tried, my friend. I hope you know what you are doing."

"Of course I do."

"How are you certain you'll find her first?"

"Because I know where she's planning to hide."

"Where?"

"The changing room by the indoor pool."

Kit heaved an exaggerated sigh. "I suppose I'll need to entertain her fiancé while you're seducing her in the dark."

"That would be dashed nice of you."

"Just do not say I didn't try to warn you when this all goes sideways."

MADDIE HURRIED TO her hiding place. For some reason Harrison had pushed her to participate in the game, although his reasoning made sense, she supposed. Being trapped with one young lady for a long stretch of time could lead Harrison into a hasty wedding.

Why did that thought unsettle her?

It shouldn't. You are betrothed.

The best outcome was for Harrison to marry one of her friends and return to Paris, away from Maddie. Then they could both get on with their lives and forget this momentary bit of madness. Surely it was the reminders of their past, the sound of the sea and the salty air, causing them to descend into this strange nostalgia for each other.

This is not nostalgia. You are attracted to him.

She was really coming to hate that internal voice of hers.

How had their relationship changed so dramatically? Before he went to Paris, he'd been a confidant and playmate, nothing more than a friend. Now a slightly older Harrison had returned, and her obsession switched from tennis to *him*. Never had she been attracted to a man like this, where thoughts of him instantly jumped to licking and biting, exploring and kissing . . .

Stop.

She gave herself a mental shake. This could not go on. Another day of this house party, then

Harrison would have his fiancée and Maddie would focus on tennis and the duke.

There was no other choice.

The east side of the house was quiet as she slipped through a side door and into the morning room. Giant fans slowly turned overhead, creating a glorious breeze that countered the June midday heat. Unfortunately, she couldn't stop here.

The point of the game was to find a small spot into which a group must squeeze itself, just like sardines in a tin. The first two floors of the chateau comprised large, open rooms, impractical for her purposes. There were closets and washrooms, but those were too obvious. The third floor contained staff quarters, and she would not dare to disrupt their private space with houseguests tramping through.

That left the basement, which contained the perfect hiding space: a small changing room tucked away beside the indoor pool. Three or four adults could fit inside comfortably, but seven or eight would be a tight squeeze. She had briefly pointed the room out to her friends during her tour on the first day of the house party. Time would tell if any of them remembered.

If no one found her in an hour, she'd come out and restart the game.

As she went to the stairs, she happened to pass the library. Quickly, she snatched a thick book off the shelf, not bothering to check the title. There was no time for dawdling. Hurrying on, she went downstairs.

The pool room was humid, due in part to the

underground heating system used to warm the water. The surface of the pool was like glass, undisturbed and completely still in the silence. Careful not to slip on the tiles, she walked around to the changing room. There was a moment of indecision as to whether to close the door behind her, and she decided to leave it cracked. The space would overheat without any air wafting in, and she could use the light coming in from the pool room by which to read.

Low wooden benches lined the walls of the tiny changing room. She sat and peered at the spine of the book in her hand. Disappointment weighed down her shoulders. *Soil Quality of the Western Plains.* This was one of her father's research books for railroad expansion. She tossed it aside. Not even utter boredom could get her interested in that subject matter.

Minutes later, a faint scuffle caught her attention. She held her breath and waited, listening. *Impossible.* A guest could not have found her this soon.

Another noise, closer this time. Holding perfectly still, she kept her eyes locked on the sliver of light at the door's opening. Seconds ticked by, and she began to wonder if the noises had been her imagination.

Then a large shadow cast the changing room into darkness and she tried not to gasp.

Harrison.

He slipped into the room, a satisfied smirk on his face. "I knew it."

"You lied. You said you forgot all the hiding places."

Not answering, he came in and closed the door. Darkness enveloped them both. Though she couldn't see him, she heard his clothes rustle as he settled on her left side. There was barely an inch of space between them, his body too close, too imposing. Too tempting.

Her heart kicked hard in her chest, anticipation buzzing in her veins like electricity. "What are you doing?"

"Sitting."

"*Harrison.*" She tried to put a healthy amount of extreme displeasure in her tone. "We should not be alone in here."

"I can't help it if I let it slip to a few of the ladies how you used to hide in the carriage house as a young girl."

"Which is a lie. *You* used to hide in the carriage house. I used to hide in here."

She couldn't see his face but she could hear the smile in his voice. "I know. Remember the time we stole a cake from your mother's garden party? We nearly ate ourselves sick in here."

Yes, she remembered. She remembered nearly all of their adventures. "We should open the door."

"Why?"

He was deliberately being obtuse. Could he not feel the heat jumping between them? "You know why."

"Is this about not trusting yourself with me again?"

Dashed man. Stood to reason he would bring up her words from the gazebo. She ducked her head, shame scalding her from the inside out. "I shouldn't have said that."

"I like when you are honest with me."

"If only you could do the same."

A rough finger brushed the top of her hand, stroking each of her knuckles, one by one. Sparks shot along her skin, an effervescence skipping along every nerve in her body, making her feel both light and heavy at the same time. Though she couldn't see him, he was all around her, the scent of him—the outdoors and a faint hint of cigar—surrounding her. The sound of his steady breathing echoed in the small space. By the time he reached her pinky, she had nearly melted on the bench.

He linked their fingers together. "I'll tell you anything you'd like to know," he said, his voice like silk.

There was really only one question to ask. "What do you want from me?"

"*Everything.*"

The single word fell between them like a perfectly placed drop shot over the net. She had no way of catching it, no hope of returning it. Worse, there was no avoiding the consequences. "I cannot break the betrothal."

"Others have done so and survived. You can, too."

"This is madness. You ask the impossible."

His hand held steady, their two fingers intertwined, anchoring her. She wasn't ready to pull away.

The air grew heavier as her lungs worked, her breath coming fast and shallow. They'd spent so much time alone together over the years, but this was different. Even their interactions on the terrace and in the gazebo hadn't felt like this, like he was air and water, food and shelter. Absolutely essential, as if they were tethered to each other in some elemental way.

"Tell me what you are thinking," he said.

Though he couldn't see her, she shook her head, not ready to share the emotions roiling inside her just yet. "You are supposed to marry one of the ladies here."

"I don't want one of those ladies. I want you."

Her lower body clenched at the declaration, arousal pulsing between her legs in time with her heartbeat. *I shouldn't, but I want him, too.*

She dragged in a deep breath and attempted to remain logical. "You had years to declare an intention. Never once have you hinted at more between us until now, when it is too late."

"If I ask you a question, do you promise to answer it honestly?"

"Of course."

"Forget your betrothal. Do you want to kiss me right now?"

She swallowed, her mouth suddenly dry. "Why would you ask me that?"

"Because your answer is all that matters."

"Hardly. There are other people to consider, as well."

"No one else is here. It's just the two of us at the moment. So tell me. Do you want to kiss me?"

"You ask the impossible."

"That is not an answer, Mads."

The truth lodged in her throat, the words unable to break free. Saying them would change everything, create a scandal and harm those she cared about. How could she act so selfishly?

He must have sensed her hesitation because she heard him shift a brief instant before a large hand settled on her thigh. The heat of his skin scorched her through the layers of cloth between them. It was far more intimate than any other touch they had shared, and the air turned thick, charged with a portentous energy, like right before a thunderstorm rolled in.

The moment stretched, each second crawling by as every nerve in her body concentrated on his hand. Strong fingers moved ever so slightly, testing, teasing. Caressing. Maddie's own fingers curled into her palms and she trembled, goose bumps racing all along her arms. She wanted to lean into him and beg for more. The idea was madness, but her rational half had clearly fallen back to allow her emotional side to take charge.

"Shall I remove my hand?"

She should have answered affirmatively. The touch was personal and possessive . . . in a place only a husband should access. And yet . . .

"No," she whispered.

His fingers tightened as if he'd expected a different answer. Without missing a beat, his other hand found her jaw and cupped her face, the touch confident and calming. She grew light-headed, the floor shifting below her while the world fell away, but he held her tethered, safe in a familiar, yet totally unexpected, way. Her fingers wrapped around his wrist, the tips pressing into his flesh, and she held very still, unwilling to break the moment by breathing or talking.

His forehead met her temple, his humid breath gusting over her cheek as he whispered, "Do you want to kiss me?"

Unable to stop herself, she nodded . . . and he sucked in air, a gasp of surprise that she felt all the way to her toes.

Just then, the door swung open, casting light into the room and blinding her. She instantly jumped apart from Harrison and shielded her eyes.

"Aha! We found her!"

Chapter Twelve

❦

The ladies trickled into the changing room over the next thirty minutes. The air in the tiny room soon grew stifling from the outside heat and number of bodies. By Harrison's count, they had two more guests to go before a loser was declared and they could return upstairs. Nellie Young and Alice Lusk were still searching the chateau grounds for Maddie's hiding place.

During the wait, he was polite, responding when prompted, but his focus remained fixated on the woman next to him in the dark, her sweet curves pressed tight to his right side.

Maddie wanted him.

Victory had streaked through him at her admission, making him dizzy. His body responded swiftly, his cock thickening in his trousers and hunger slithering through his veins. He suspected they would have kissed, if not for the inopportune intrusion.

Soon.

On his other side was Lydia Hartwell, a young woman who spoke her mind, unafraid of expressing her opinions. Much like Maddie, which probably explained why the two were friends. Also, Miss Hartwell was unapologetically interested in unconventional pursuits, similar to Maddie's love of tennis.

"I cannot believe you've never hunted," Miss Hartwell was saying.

Killing other creatures had never been high on Harrison's list of relaxing endeavors. Bordellos, salons and cafes were his preferred methods to unwind, at least in the last few years. "I am a city boy, through and through, I suppose. We went to the Adirondacks and Newport, but that was mostly about swimming and sailing."

He felt Maddie move closer. "Harrison doesn't even enjoy fishing," she chimed in. "He insists on throwing his catch back in the water."

"So do you," he pointed out.

"Goodness," Miss Hartwell said. "You are both hopeless. Come to Montana and we'll go fly fishing. Then we'll cook what we catch on an open fire."

That sounded like a punishment, not a vacation. Nevertheless, he said politely, "Thank you. Perhaps one day—"

A gentle brush on his right knee caught him by surprise. He froze, his words dying in his throat as every muscle in his body went on alert.

The fingertips returned, bolder this time as they deliberately slid over his leg. Someone was touching him, *groping* him, with light fingers. He blinked in the darkness, uncertain what to do. Who would dare? Was Maddie responsible?

The women around him talked as if nothing

was amiss. Yet someone was dragging her fingers along his leg, feeling his thigh through his trousers. Maddie must have been responsible. She was the closest, other than Miss Hartwell, who did not seem the type to act so boldly with a stranger. Not to mention it would require her to reach over him, which was not as easily done.

Then, just for an instant, the hard edge of a metal prong, like the ones on a large stone setting, brushed his leg.

The ducal betrothal ring.

Those fingers belonged to Maddie. He was absolutely certain of it.

A light sweat broke out on his skin, heat rushing through his entire body as her exploration continued. He allowed it, reveling in the knowledge that she wished to caress him. Hell, he'd encourage her. In fact, she could keep going until she reached his cock, which was growing stiff and eager for the attention.

"Is something wrong?" Maddie whispered.

"Not a dashed thing," he said quietly. "Keep going."

The touch was delicate but it seemed as if every nerve in his body was centered in that one place. His chest heaved, nostrils flaring as he pulled in air, the rest of him perfectly still while the fingers lingered and bedeviled him. Teased and tested the shape of his thigh.

"You are worrying me," she said. "Is everything all right?"

How could she not know?

Leaning over, he put his lips near the shell of her ear. "Higher."

The fingers skimmed upward, onto his inner thigh.

Fuck.

His head dropped back, thumping against the wall, and he struggled not to move, not to roll his hips or push into that seeking hand. His skin crawled with anticipation, turning both hot and cold at the same time, desire burning him alive. Was she enjoying this, too? Because he might actually break down and cry if she pulled her hand away.

Miss Hartwell began speaking to him again, asking about his time in Paris. Had he been to the restaurant inside the Eiffel Tower? Had he met many artists and writers? What was the Folies-Bergère like? Harrison answered as best he could, each sentence a trek through quicksand. Mostly he grunted one- or two-word responses, praying that was enough to avoid drawing any attention to his lower half.

Higher and higher went the swirling, tempting fingertips, doing everything possible to drive him out of his mind. A tempest raged inside him, this burning need for Maddie that he'd tried to control for years, and with her fingers creeping ever so closer to his groin, he feared he might lose his grip on his restraint. Would she stop? Or would she stroke him, feel the hard ridges of his cock and soft weight of his balls through his clothing?

He groaned and tried to cover it with a cough.

"What is going on?" Maddie hissed.

He hadn't known her to be a clever liar, but those questioning fingers had to belong to her.

He felt it deep in his bones. There was no other plausible explanation. If he believed another guest was responsible, he would have put a stop to it from the start.

No, this was most assuredly Maddie, and he craved her caresses like his next breath.

The lack of stimulating conversation must have frustrated Miss Hartwell because she turned to the young woman on her other side and struck up a chat. The fingers on his thigh stilled, unsure, and he waited, blood rushing in his ears, while time slowed to a halt.

Her lips hovered near the shell of his right ear. "Shall I remove my hand?"

Fuck. His words from earlier.

He angled toward her, close enough so that only Maddie could hear. "Don't you dare."

The touch grew bolder, a voyage of discovery. Attention was paid to the crease of his thigh, the fingers ever so lightly smoothing the cloth there. He gripped the edge of the bench, and his nails dug into the wood like a man hanging on to his sanity. *God, yes. Keep going. Just a bit to the left.*

Then she danced away, moving closer to his knee again, and he slumped in the seat, disappointed. He couldn't help but offer instruction. "Wrong direction," he crooned in her ear. "Tease me, Mads."

Her fingers flattened along his thigh and slid upward, lighter than he preferred but somehow perfect because it was *Maddie.* His balls ached and his groin was heavy with need, every cell in his body straining to remain still and quiet. Would she stroke his cock? If she did, he might spend in his trousers.

The door flew open, startling everyone, and Harrison blinked into the light. The hand had already disappeared from his thigh by the time he saw Kit in the entryway.

"There's been a slight mishap," Kit announced. "Miss Lusk has turned her ankle, so we're calling an end to the game."

The ladies each expressed their sympathy for Miss Lusk, talking among themselves as they filed out the door. Harrison remained seated, rude as it was, in an effort to hide the erection in his trousers. When Maddie rose and started to follow everyone to the exit, he clasped her wrist, stopping her.

She cast a frown down at him. Her skin was flushed, but he wasn't sure if it was from touching him or the heat inside the room. She said, "I must go and check on Alice."

Was she serious?

"Wait a moment." The last of the guests departed and the two of them were alone. "What about just now?"

She huffed in annoyance, her eyes shooting daggers at him. "Harrison, I don't have time for this."

Fair enough. He would rather have her alone for this discussion, anyway. "Meet me in the gazebo at half past midnight."

She started to open her mouth—to protest, no doubt—so he held up a hand and came to his feet.

"Tonight, Maddie. Be there." He moved closer and dipped his head. "Or else I'll come find you."

FLUSTERED FROM THE changing room, Maddie stepped outside and slipped her hat on her head. What had come over her in there? It was like his presence in that tiny room had stolen her reason, scattered her thoughts. She'd been brazen. Daring. A selfish woman who'd behaved recklessly, with little regard to the serious consequences that could result.

Now everything was different, like the heavens had been flipped upside down. The sun felt cold on her skin, the soft breeze like needles.

Yet she couldn't begin to stop and contemplate what it all meant, not when one of her friends had been injured.

Kit gave her a secretive glance, one that said he was aware of what had transpired in that tiny room, but that was impossible. No one could have any idea because Maddie wasn't certain herself.

The tent was quiet, with everyone huddled in one corner around a woman in a chair. "What happened?" Maddie asked.

Alice was seated, her foot propped on another chair. "Forgive me for ruining the game, Miss Webster." Misery shone in her troubled gaze. "There was a hole in the grass and I overlooked it. My ankle's turned."

"No apologies necessary." Maddie clasped Alice's hand. "I feel awful that you've been hurt."

"It appears to be a mild twist," Daddy said. "We sent for the doctor just to be sure."

"Thank you, Mr. Webster," Alice's mother said,

her lips thin and white with anger. "We are sorry for the inconvenience. Alice is too clumsy for her own good."

Before Maddie could stick up for Alice, Nellie spoke. "Clumsy had nothing to do with it, Mrs. Lusk. There was a giant hole in the lawn. Anyone might have stepped in it."

"Rotten gophers," Daddy muttered. "I'll speak to my gardeners."

Mama sidled up to Maddie and cast Alice a sympathetic glance. "Poor thing. We should make Miss Lusk comfortable upstairs, don't you think?"

Mrs. Lusk moved closer to her daughter, a challenging gleam in her eye. "No one should move her until the doctor arrives."

"Nonsense." Harrison pointed at the chair. "If we gents take a side, we can lift her and get her upstairs."

"Ah. We used to do that in college," Kit said. "Like a litter."

"Surely that is not safe," Mrs. Lusk said. "Or proper."

"We'll not drop her, I promise." Harrison put a hand over his heart. "But I think she'd prefer to be out of the midst of all the attention."

The normally shy Alice beamed at him, relief flooding her expression. "I would be very grateful, Mr. Archer."

The ladies stepped back as Kit, Harrison and the duke removed their coats and arranged themselves at the sides of the chair. Maddie and her mother cleared a path for them to maneuver. When the three men lifted the chair, Alice grasped the wood to hold herself steady. The pace was slow and careful, with Mrs. Lusk hovering nearby to give unnecessary commentary and directions.

Maddie started to follow, but her mother stopped her. "I'll go with Miss Lusk. You stay here with the other guests."

"Are you certain?" She watched the strong muscles of Harrison's shoulders shift as he moved toward the house. Goodness, he was very fit.

Meet me in the gazebo at half past midnight.

Under no circumstances could she meet him. Not alone, not after this afternoon.

Though . . . would he really come to her bedroom if she didn't?

Her stomach fluttered, everything in her lower half clenching. No, no, no. That idea should absolutely *not* appeal to her. If she was dreaming of any man in her bed, it should have been her fiancé.

God, what was she going to do?

When she looked up, nearly everyone had left the tent. Nellie was the only one left. "Want to walk a bit?"

Had her friend been waiting to get her alone? Maddie went over. "I'd like that. The path by the cliffs?"

Nellie nodded and the two of them picked their way down the stone stairs to reach the Cliff Walk. Maddie was breathing hard by the time they found the narrow stretch of path that ran between the great cottages along the shoreline and the water. Every year the homeowners made the walk longer and safer to traverse.

"I apologize for Alice's accident," Nellie said as they started along the path. The sea churned below, the foamy waves lapping at the rocks and sand. "It was my fault she was hurt."

"You didn't force the gopher to dig a hole in our lawn, Nellie."

"Yes, but I did drag her across the grass in the first place. She preferred the path but I convinced her my way was shorter."

"Accidents happen. Do not worry about it. She'll recover."

"Even so, I should be declared the loser. Don't let Alice miss out on the boat excursion due to my selfishness."

Right, the winning prize. A day on the water with Harrison and the unattached ladies sounded like absolute torture to Maddie at the moment. "Perhaps I should cancel in light of recent events."

Nellie appeared horrified at the idea. "No, don't cancel. They're all looking forward to it."

"They, but not you."

Nellie lifted a shoulder and turned her face toward the water, but not before Maddie saw her small smile. "I admit, I would rather spend my afternoon elsewhere."

"Are you going to tell me the identity of this mystery man?"

"No. He's nothing serious. Regardless, a few hours trapped with a bunch of girls mooning after Harrison Archer is not my idea of fun."

Nor Maddie's—not any longer.

Nellie smirked when she caught Maddie's miserable expression. "It's obviously not your idea of fun, either. Why are you doing this to yourself?"

"Doing what? Hosting a house party?"

"You know what I mean. Watching Harrison cozy up to these other women."

"I am engaged. There's nothing to be said."

"Engagements are broken all the time. What is it gaining you to play by their rules? A miserable marriage?"

"We're not all as rebellious as you, Nellie."

The other woman stopped and took Maddie's arm. "There's nothing stopping you. Look out there." She gestured toward the endless expanse of water, glistening in the distance. "A whole world awaits us, one not bound by conventions or the dictates of society, and women are told not to want it because it isn't proper. But this is our *life*, Maddie. Our only chance for true happiness. I am not about to waste it. Are you?"

Maddie sighed. "You make it sound so easy."

"It's not. Being a woman is like swimming against the tide to survive—yet you fought for the right to play tennis. What happened when that tennis club owner tried to bar women from hosting a tournament last year?"

A grin tugged at the corners of Maddie's mouth. "I challenged him to a game."

"Which you won. After that, he allowed women to host a tournament."

"This is different. There are other lives that would be affected."

"If you mean the duke, I think three of the guests and a few chaperones would propose marriage to him on the spot if you cried off."

"I get the sense you don't care much for Lockwood."

"Oh. Well, I hardly know him, do I? Seems a bit stiff, but that goes with the ducal territory, I suppose." She linked their arms, and the two of them started along the path once again. "I only ask that you think about it. The man is hopelessly in love with you."

"The duke?"

Nellie chuckled. "You know perfectly well who I mean."

Chapter Thirteen

At twelve-thirty that night, Harrison paced in the gazebo, restless energy coursing through him like a locomotive. Waves crashed on the beach, while the night air tasted of salt and smelled of roses. The quarter moon overhead offered little illumination, but he didn't need it. In fact, the darkness might benefit them, as it had in the changing room.

The thought of those sweet fingertips—exploring, caressing his thigh until he'd been hard as stone—had caused him to break out in a sweat all evening.

Her bold touch had caught him unaware. Maddie was careful, the person who thoughtfully considered every outcome before deciding on a course of action. In other words, Harrison's complete opposite. So whatever was happening between them must have overridden her proclivity for caution while they were in the changing room.

And thank God for that, because he had no reason, no caution when it came to her, especially now. Every moment that passed brought him closer to the end of this house party and her future as the next Duchess of Lockwood. He could not lose her, not this time.

Shoving his hands in his trouser pockets, he stared out into the blackness and forced himself to relax. There was every chance she wouldn't show. She might decide not to risk it, that her marriage to Lockwood was more important. But Harrison didn't think so. Maddie wouldn't like the unanswered questions, the uncertainty of their feelings. She would come looking for answers. For resolution.

He was prepared to give her whatever she needed, if it convinced her to marry him instead of the duke.

A rustle of cloth caught his attention. Spinning, he saw her creeping toward the gazebo, and all the breath left his lungs.

She came.

He said nothing as she approached, merely watched while heat scalded the underside of his skin. Judging by her expression, she was nervous and he didn't wish to scare her further.

When she stepped in, she avoided his eye. "I shouldn't be here."

"No one needs to know, Maddie. Whatever happens is between us."

"You know that isn't true." She crossed to the wooden bench, sat and arranged her skirts. Her hands were bare and that damn betrothal ring glinted in the dim light.

The breeze carried a chill in the air and he saw her shiver. Removing his coat, he strode over and placed it around her shoulders. "You should've remembered how cold it can get at night."

"Yes, well. I wasn't thinking clearly when I left my bedchamber, obviously."

He lowered himself onto the bench. "I'll not force you to stay."

"I couldn't risk that you'd sneak into my bedroom."

His excitement dimmed slightly. He preferred that she came to him of her own free will, but he wouldn't apologize for the threat, especially seeing as how it had worked. Instead of dancing around the subject, he blurted out what was on his mind. "You cannot marry him, not with things between us uncertain."

"They are merely uncertain because you keep pushing me."

"Hardly. You've admitted your attraction to me—without much prompting, I might add."

"I never should have said that, not while I'm engaged to Lockwood."

"Then there is what happened in the changing room."

"Another mistake," she said. "A momentary fit of insanity."

"Wrong. It's called desire and you are dancing around the obvious. I'll not allow you to pretend any longer."

"Oh, you'll not allow?" She pushed off the bench, her movements stiff with anger. "You'll not *allow*? Harrison, I am not free to declare my regard for another man. You have nothing standing in your way, no pressure to remain silent. Such a luxury does not exist for me."

She was still denying her feelings for him, which irritated him beyond measure. Shooting to his feet, he stalked toward her, his soles thumping on the wooden floor. "Lockwood does not deserve you. He is completely wrong for you and will bring you nothing but loneliness and misery."

Uncertainty flashed over her face before she masked it, but she did not back down. Instead, her spine straightened as she watched him draw closer. "You have no way of knowing that."

"Please. I am familiar with the way your mind works. You need someone who will stand up to you, who will excite you. Otherwise, you'll grow bored and unhappy."

"What are you talking about?"

"The other children did whatever you said, no questions asked. You were like a brigadier general here, organizing and cajoling. I was the only one who challenged and questioned you. That was why you liked me best, why we became such good friends."

She made a scoffing sound. "That is hardly true. We enjoyed causing mischief together."

"No, I enjoyed causing mischief. You enjoyed planning said mischief." He folded his arms and gave her a sly smile. "You never wanted a devoted acolyte . . . you wanted a partner in crime."

"Perhaps, but that was a long time ago. We are not children any longer."

"We haven't changed all that much," he said. "Not on the inside, which is how I am certain Lockwood will make you unhappy. Because you will run roughshod over him and become bored within a week."

"I'll have my tennis, our children. Life as a duchess."

A life without him.

Children that were not his.

The idea of it made Harrison want to howl. He threaded his fingers through his hair and pulled on the strands, struggling for calm. "You are settling, Maddie."

"To become a duchess?" Her voice rose several octaves. "You actually believe becoming a duchess is somehow settling?"

"When it comes to your happiness, yes I do," he shot back. "I want you more than that arrogant duke ever could."

She rocked back on her heels, seemingly stunned at his admission. "Why now? What has changed?"

He certainly did not want to travel this path, not yet. If he told her of his longstanding feelings, she'd likely go dashing back into the house. "Does that matter? Can you not just accept the fact that it has?"

If he thought that would appease her, he was wrong. Her eyes flashed green fire, as if his evasiveness angered her. "You're right—it doesn't matter because I cannot break this betrothal. The die has been cast."

The hell it had.

He didn't stop until he was directly in front of her, the tips of his shoes brushing her skirts. She had to crane her neck to meet his eyes but she didn't move. A lovely flush worked its way over her cheeks, and he could see the pulse pounding on the creamy slope of her throat. The air grew heavy around them, as if it were weighted with anticipation and longing, and the tops of her breasts heaved as her chest expanded. His fingers itched with the need to finally touch her . . . but he wouldn't do it. Not yet.

"Nothing has been settled until you walk down the aisle and recite vows. And I will not stop pushing when I am certain you are making a mistake."

She licked her lips before whispering, "You cannot possibly know that."

"You'd be surprised at what I know." He leaned down, allowing his breath to tease her skin, and put his lips near her ear. "I know the two of you treat one another like strangers, when all the while you have been thinking of kissing me. Not trusting yourself alone with me. Nearly stroking my erection in the changing room."

She sucked in a ragged breath, her body trembling. "Harrison . . ." The sound was faint, but he heard the plea, the yearning in the way she said his name.

Sensing victory, he pressed on. "I want to give you everything. All you have to do is ask."

"Oh, God. This is wrong."

Thunder rumbled overhead, as if the heavens agreed with her. He didn't care. Nothing would keep him from her, not Lockwood or a betrothal. Not her family or society's ridiculous conventions. Not the fucking Devil himself . . .

The only person who could stop him was Maddie.

"Do you want me?" He pitched his voice low, his body still angled over hers. "You may have as little or as much as you want tonight. I am yours for the taking."

"I shouldn't."

They were both breathing hard, nearly panting. Need chewed its way through his lower body, his cock hard and ready. He knew he should take it easy on her, not pursue her so relentlessly. But *Jesus* . . . nearly everything he'd ever wanted stood in front of him.

"That is not an answer. It's just the two of us here right now. No one else. But you must decide."

Her teeth sank into her bottom lip, her eyes shifting to his mouth. The restraint nearly killed him, but she must come to him willingly, without coercion. Without guilt.

Without regrets.

It seemed like an eternity before she spoke. "Kiss me. Please, Harrison. Just kiss me."

Triumph flooded him, causing his muscles to tighten in expectation, yet he didn't move. "Take off his ring."

A crease formed between her brows as she met his gaze. "Why?"

"Because tonight you belong to me."

He held out his palm and waited. More thunder shook the sky, a portentous rumbling under their feet that made him crave her compliance— her acceptance—all the more.

With shaky fingers, she removed the large emerald and diamond ring from her finger and placed it in his hand. He slipped the ducal piece, the sign of another man's ownership, into the pocket of his coat, which she still wore. Lifting his hands, he cradled her face, holding her like the most precious antique as he merely stared down at her. She wrapped her fingers around his wrists, holding on to him, linking them to each other.

"Just for tonight," she breathed before pushing up on her toes and capturing his mouth with her own.

Distracted by the feel of her soft lips, he didn't bother correcting her. He couldn't stop, not even if every houseguest suddenly surrounded the gazebo to gawk at them. Because finally—*finally*—he had her pressed against him, their lips moving together, her soft sighs falling into his mouth as they kissed.

It started sweet, as they learned and explored, but the kiss quickly became something else entirely. The backs of his thighs sizzled, lust careening through his belly as their mouths worked hungrily. Her fingertips dug into his skin, and he deepened the kiss, his tongue slipping past the seam of her lips, inside the wet haven of her mouth. She stroked him with her own tongue, meeting him, driving him insane with swirls and flicks, making him contemplate laying her down on the gazebo floor so he could kiss every inch of her. Lick between her thighs. Feast on her until she begged for mercy.

Never had he felt so out of control, so wild to dive beneath a set of skirts. He knew it was the woman, this gorgeous and maddening creature he had loved for years. The one who had been a summertime playmate and friend, confidant and champion. He'd never felt lonely in those months.

His family had treated him with disdain, but Maddie's kindness and acceptance had mended his soul, even for a short amount of time.

And he was going to give her the world in return.

He'd been a fool to think he could ever forget her, that he could shed the memory of her from his blood. Nothing had worked, and the fever had only increased the instant he set eyes on her again.

Mine.

The word echoed through his skull like the toll of a bell. Chest heaving, he broke off from her mouth to run his lips over her jaw. He sank his teeth into her perfect skin, then soothed the sting with his tongue. A moan worked its way out of her throat, the most perfect sound he'd ever heard, and he kept going, down along the column of her neck, nipping and licking, until she yanked on his head, pulling him up to meet with her lips once again.

It wasn't enough. He slid his hands to her hips, jerking her flush to his body as they kissed. She gasped and wrapped her arms around his neck, delicate fingers threading through his hair. If she was bothered by the erection digging into her stomach, she gave no sign of it. Instead, she wriggled closer, like she needed more contact, not less.

Just as he started to move them to the bench, the heavens opened up and water poured from the sky.

WITH A GASP, Maddie shoved away from Harrison, horrified. She was engaged and had kissed another man. Not only that, she had asked for it. Had enjoyed it. What did that say about her? Shame dulled the edges of her desire, much like the dark clouds that had rolled in with the storm.

Rain sluiced from the sky around them, an angry torrent of relentless water. She watched it fall outside the gazebo, half wishing to bathe herself in it, as if to somehow rid herself of this guilt. Pressing a hand to her mouth, she could still feel the delicious press of Harrison's lips to her own.

My God, what had she done?

"Maddie," he said gently, lifting her hand away from her face. "Stop berating yourself. You are not yet married."

"That doesn't matter, as we both know." She took several steps back and his arm dropped to his side.

"You have broken no vow. We merely kissed."

There was nothing *mere* about that kiss. It had shaken her to the core, with more passion and longing than she'd ever thought possible. Harrison's kisses had been perfection, sin and salvation at once.

Still, it had been wrong. A betrayal. She had given a promise to marry Lockwood. She had been disloyal to the duke, dishonored him by kissing another man. If anyone found out, the scandal would ruin her.

Tears stung the backs of her lids. Engaged for not even two days and she'd failed. All her scheming and planning completely destroyed in a few short days. How could she ever face Lockwood again?

How could she ever face *anyone* again?

She wrapped her arms around her middle, her knees knocking in the cold. Or perhaps it was from the weight of her transgression. Harrison's coat had fallen to the ground, pushed off her shoulders during their kiss, so he bent to retrieve it. When he tried to give her the coat again, she put up her hands. He frowned. "You'd rather freeze than accept my coat?"

"Yes." His coat smelled like him, warm from where it had touched his body. Wearing it might drive her to kiss him again. Indeed, she deserved the misery.

He didn't bother putting the garment on, merely held it in his hands. "You cannot marry him, Mads. Not after that kiss."

Rubbing her temples, she tried to think clearly. Impossible, considering her lips still stung from the force of Harrison's mouth, her fingers tingling from touching his soft hair. Blood coursed through her limbs, between her legs, in a demanding and distracting urge. She had to get away from him. Regain her equilibrium and decide how to handle this. "We should go in."

Without waiting for a response, she stepped onto the lawn. Water hit her in fat drops, soaking her from head to toe within a few steps. She pushed onward, her shoes squelching in the mud.

Fingers wrapped around her wrist, pulling her to a halt. Harrison stood in the rain behind her, his white shirt quickly molding to his strong shoulders and arms in the downpour. His blue eyes blazed as he shouted over the storm. "Tell me you will break the engagement."

"I . . ." She couldn't bring herself to say the

words. How could she act so selfishly? It wasn't fair to Lockwood—or to her parents. They had enabled her tennis pursuits and shown remarkable patience during the last three years. A scandal would embarrass and horrify them, as well.

No, she needed to come up with a plan instead of rushing into a decision she might regret.

"I must have time," she said.

The sharp angles of Harrison's face twisted in displeasure. "Why? This is not a difficult decision."

"I cannot beg off, not right now. This must be handled carefully and thoughtfully."

"There is no reason to wait." Water ran down his cheeks, his nose, over his gorgeous mouth. His wet hair lay in dark streaks of midnight against his forehead. "You are only prolonging the inevitable."

Regret burned in her stomach. Watching all the scandals over the years, the girls who had been compromised or ruined, Maddie hadn't understood. She'd played by the rules, had taken a chaperone everywhere in public after her debut. Charted her life so carefully. Temptation had seemed so absurd, so impossible.

And yet, a few days spent in Harrison's company and she had done the unthinkable.

"Maddie," he growled, his eyes narrowing on her. "You must break it off."

"You must let me think!" she shouted. "Unlike you, I cannot make a rash decision. For God's sake, you have turned my life upside down in a matter of days. I must catch my breath for a minute."

"I won't let you marry him."

"It is not up to you. Stop being selfish."

"Hardly selfish when I have your best interests in mind. He only wants your money. I only want *you*."

Her heart soaked up the declaration, but this was not the time to let that traitorous organ rule her life. She had to remain logical about what came next. "I need time."

"There is no time."

"It cannot be helped. This is not a decision to be made lightly—"

"Wrong." The word came out in a thick plume of brittle air. "Every minute you wait is another minute wasted. Lockwood won't care, I promise you. The scandal will fade, and your mother will get over her disappointment."

"You are so certain of that, but I am not."

He stepped closer. "I am certain you are the only woman I want—now, tomorrow and ten years into the future. If you want me as well, then nothing else matters."

Lord, her stupid heart again. It skipped in her chest as if this solved everything . . . but it wasn't so simple.

Jerking away, she shook her head, water flying everywhere. "Do not push me for an answer tonight. I won't give it."

Water ran in rivulets down the planes of his face, droplets sticking to his long eyelashes. "Tomorrow, then."

With a growl of frustration, she turned and started toward the terrace. Her clothing was soaked, making it hard to walk in the heavy skirts. She was going to make a mess inside the house, but it couldn't be helped. He made no attempt to catch up or help her, but she felt his presence behind her keenly, as if he were still pressed against her.

There was no running from what had happened tonight. No pretending the kiss didn't happen. She had instigated it, willingly participated, even enjoyed it.

And she would probably do it again, if given the chance.

That was the worst part. The knowledge that she was not strong enough to resist this. That whatever she felt for Harrison was more powerful than her sense of duty, her sense of right and wrong. All her plans, destroyed in an instant. She was a horrible daughter and an even worse fiancée.

She drew in a deep breath and tried to compose herself. Running through the house in tears, soaked to the bone, even at this hour, could attract unwanted attention. As soon as she was warm and changed, alone in her room, she could think about what happened tonight and what she would do.

Water ran down her back, into her bodice, and her skirts were caked with mud and grass. Her thin slippers sloshed with every step, and she wished she'd worn her short boots instead. Teeth chattering, she started up the stone steps toward the back entrance—and her foot slipped out from underneath her.

Before she could tumble on the stairs, strong arms pulled her upright. "Don't worry," he said in her ear. "I have you. I'll always have you."

The flat plane of his chest was warm and comforting against her, but she could not allow herself to enjoy it. "Let me go," she said. He obeyed and she went up the stairs stiffly, holding on to the side to keep from falling again.

She stepped into the house, her body shaking, and he was right behind her. A puddle immediately formed on the parquet floor underneath her feet, so she hurried for the stairs. All she could think about was being dry and alone.

He grabbed her arm, bringing her to a halt. "Please, just a moment."

"Harrison, I cannot talk about this. Not here, not now."

A tempest swirled in his eyes, a whirlpool of emotion hidden underneath his calm exterior. He reached into his coat pocket and withdrew Lockwood's betrothal ring. Maddie stared at the piece, stunned she'd forgotten about it. He pressed the ring into her hand. "Soon, Maddie. Good night."

She wrapped her fingers around the emerald and diamonds, emotion lodged in her throat. Even if she'd been capable of speaking, there was nothing to say. She closed her eyes, unable to look at him just then, and she felt the soft brush of his mouth over hers and then he was gone.

What am I going to do?

Pressing two fingers to her lips, she took a step toward the main stairs—and abruptly stopped. Mrs. Lusk was in the entrance to the library, book in hand, her sharp gaze firmly locked on Maddie. The older woman said nothing, but her disapproving stare spoke volumes. How much had she seen?

Maddie's stomach clenched while goose bumps raced along the nape of her neck. Still, though she quaked on the inside, she did not cower. She and Harrison had been quiet and he hadn't lingered, so perhaps there was no need for panic.

Gesturing to her sopping wet form, she tried to make light of it. "I was out walking when it started to rain."

"Yes, I can see that." Cradling her book, Mrs. Lusk moved toward the stairs without another word, and Maddie was left with a burning sense of dread in her chest.

Chapter Fourteen

Sleep proved elusive for Maddie that night. Thoughts of Harrison, worries over her future and a sense of impending doom kept her pacing until dawn. She canceled her early-morning tennis practice, even though Nationals was just three weeks away. The idea of being around people right now terrified her.

Perhaps if she stayed in her room, she could avoid her problems.

Now you're being childish.

Shaking her head, she flopped on her bed and stared at the ceiling. There was no way around it: she had to tell Lockwood about kissing Harrison.

It was the honorable thing to do, though the duke could very well call off the wedding as a result. Her mother would be devastated if that happened. Daddy, too. Maddie hated the idea of disappointing anyone.

Why had she gone to the gazebo last night?

Because you wanted to. Because you needed to see if these feelings for Harrison were real.

She'd gotten her answer, at least. Whatever was between her and Harrison was very real. The realization only compounded her problems, however.

A knock sounded, and she blinked into the bleary sunlight pouring through her windows. Had she fallen asleep? The clock on her nightstand read shortly after nine o'clock.

"Maddie, are you awake?"

That was Nellie's voice. Maddie was instantly out of bed, throwing on a dressing gown and rushing to the door. "What happened?"

Nellie entered and shut the door behind her. "Alice's mother asked to speak with your father this morning. Then they called for the duke. Something is going on. You need to get dressed."

Oh, no. Mrs. Lusk was telling her father about last night. There was no other explanation. *Dash it all.*

"I have to hurry."

"Yes, you do." Nellie summoned Maddie's maid while Maddie rushed into the washroom.

Nellie spoke through the door. "Would you like some advice? I do have a bit of experience with handling fathers, you know."

There was no reason to keep it from Nellie. Her friend was no stranger to scandal, after all. "I kissed Harrison last night in the gazebo," Maddie said. "We got caught in the rain and Mrs. Lusk may have seen us come in together."

"Oh, shit."

"Exactly."

"What are you going to do?"

"I haven't a clue." The backs of Maddie's eyelids began to burn and she blinked rapidly, hoping to stave off the tears.

"Look on the bright side," Nellie said. "This may have happened for a reason. Remember, this is your life, Maddie, not anyone else's. Do what makes you happy."

"Will you still speak to me if I am ruined?"

"As if you need to ask me such a ridiculous question. And if you're ruined from this, then I am the worst jezebel New York has ever seen."

"We'll be ruined together, I suppose."

"Stop talking nonsense and hurry up in there. No matter what happens we'll always be friends."

Fifteen minutes later, Maddie's hair was in a simple knot at her nape, and she wore a light pink morning gown. A footman arrived just as Maddie put on her gloves. "Miss, your father would like to see you in his office."

It felt like her stomach had suddenly lodged in her throat. "Thank you, Robbie. Please tell him I am on my way." She exchanged a worried glance with Nellie. "Walk me down."

They descended the staircase, their slippers whispering over the carpet, and Maddie tried to focus on not tripping as she hurried to her father's office. Nellie squeezed Maddie's hand, then let her go, and Maddie pushed on the heavy wooden door.

The room was quiet. Harrison stood at the window, staring out at the lawn, while Daddy and Lockwood were both seated at the desk. Mrs. Lusk wasn't anywhere to be found.

"Madeline, close the door."

Her lungs constricted at hearing her full name,

but she approached the desk and tried to read their faces, looking for some hint as to what was to come, but there was nothing. Lockwood appeared perfectly put together and calm, as always, and Daddy seemed impatient but not angry. Harrison didn't look her way, just continued to stare at the lawn.

"What is this about?"

"Sit, please." Once she was seated, her father said, "I had an interesting visit this morning."

"Oh?" She clasped her fingers together to stop her hands from trembling.

"Mrs. Lusk asked to speak with Lockwood and me this morning. Apparently, she was up late last night and noted some inappropriate activities in the house."

She couldn't speak, couldn't breathe. The air in the room was stifling, heavy with foreboding and thick with anxiety. Her father's gaze narrowed when she remained silent, his brows dipping. "She claims to have seen you and Mr. Archer come through the terrace doors well after midnight, soaked to the bone." He paused. "She also said that Mr. Archer returned your engagement ring and kissed you before he went upstairs."

Maddie's mouth had gone dry, so she licked her lips in a desperate attempt to unglue her tongue from the roof of her mouth. It was everything she had feared. "That is certainly a tale. Are we sure she hadn't been drinking?"

"Madeline Jane." Her father's voice was sharp with disapproval. "Were you outside with Mr. Archer last night?"

She glanced at Lockwood, who was watching her carefully, the flat set of his lips an indication of his unhappiness. She owed him the truth. "Yes."

Lockwood frowned and let out the breath he'd apparently been holding, and her guilt compounded. A decent man, he had been so kind to her. He did not deserve to be humiliated like this.

Daddy rubbed his eyes vigorously, as if trying to make this all go away. "So it's true?"

She didn't dare look at Lockwood or Harrison. "It is."

The disappointment in her father's expression nearly cut her in two. It was so rare, so upsetting to see him anything but proud and supportive, that tears threatened once again. He sighed and regarded the duke. "Lockwood, I'll write you a check with enough zeroes that perhaps we might keep this quiet for a bit."

"Of course, Webster. I am sorry this didn't work out."

"I feel the same. You have my deepest apologies."

They were so polite, as if they were discussing the weather. "What do you plan—"

"Not another word, young lady," her father said, his voice low and harsh. "Sit and do not speak until I am ready for you."

Her mouth fell open, the command so unlike him. Before she could argue, he swiveled his chair toward the window and addressed the silent man in the corner. "Well, Archer. Are you prepared to do the right thing?"

Harrison didn't move. "Of course."

"We need to make this right as quickly and quietly as possible."

Harrison nodded once.

What was happening here? Panic caused her to blurt, "Wait, what does that mean?"

"It means you have been compromised, Madeline," her father said, his jaw tight with anger. "It means you will marry Mr. Archer. Immediately."

Oh, my God.

She flew to her feet and put her palms out, as if to calm everyone down. "That's hardly necessary. I haven't been compromised. I went for a walk last night and Mr. Archer found me and assisted me inside."

"Mrs. Lusk saw you both and remarked—quite loudly, I might say—about the intimacy of what she observed. Not to mention you had taken off your engagement ring and given it to Mr. Archer at some point."

"Oh, speaking of the ring," the duke said, his tone even. "If you don't mind, Miss Webster."

Dropping her head, she removed her glove, slipped the heavy piece off her finger and placed it carefully on her father's desk. The duke picked up the ring and smoothly dropped it in his coat pocket. If not for the patch of red skin above his collar, she might have thought him unaffected.

You've humiliated him. Of course he is affected.

She hated the idea that she'd hurt him in any way. This was not the place to explain or apologize, however. She'd seek him out once they were done.

For now, she had to convince her father this was nothing to worry about. "Daddy, Mrs. Lusk has leapt to conclusions."

"Perhaps, but she is one of the biggest gossips on the East Coast. I won't have your name associated with a scandal, and the duke asked to be released from the betrothal if the story proved true. You will marry Mr. Archer and that is final."

She and Harrison . . . *married*. Her eyes flew to where he stood, now facing her, the morning sun forming a ring of golden light around him. His expression revealed nothing, his emotions locked up, even in this moment of upheaval. That angered her, considering much of the blame for this lay at his feet. He'd pushed and pushed until he'd broken her engagement.

Lockwood rose and extended a hand toward her father. "Good luck, Webster."

Daddy stood and shook the duke's hand. "And you, as well, Your Grace. Thank you for your discretion."

Then Lockwood gave her a grim smile. "Miss Webster, I wish you the very best."

The moment was surreal, and she half expected to discover it was all a bad dream. "The best to you, as well, Your Grace."

"Thank you." Focusing on Harrison, the duke said, "Under any other circumstances, I'd offer to shake your hand, Archer."

"And under different circumstances, I might accept," Harrison returned, his tone colder than the Atlantic in March.

The duke spun on his heel and quit the room,

his shoulders straight and proud. The silence that followed was awful, and mortification crawled over her skin like thousands of ants. She didn't wish to leave things like this with Lockwood, with him believing the worst of her—and she owed him an apology. He must absolutely hate her for embarrassing him like this.

Guilt gnawed at her stomach. She needed to set this right—or as right as she could, considering how badly she'd blundered. Rising, she gestured toward the office door. "I should speak with him."

"Go on, then." Her father waved her out. "I need to discuss things with your fiancé, anyway. You and I will talk later."

Fiancé, meaning Harrison.

This was all happening too fast. "Is there any chance I might change your mind?"

Daddy's expression hardened, his tone the one he used for discussing business. "Absolutely none. You two will be married as soon as I can drag a reverend here, Madeline."

HARRISON STRUGGLED TO keep from grinning like a madman as Maddie dashed from her father's office.

She would soon be his *wife*.

It was too perfect. Her betrothal broken, she would now be forced to marry him. No, he hadn't planned on winning her this way, but he couldn't dredge up an ounce of regret over it.

Things were shaping up nicely. Once they were married, he could return to New York and to the business of ruining his family. At last count, there were fewer than five thousand shares of Archer Industries stock to recover.

Yes, things were shaping up nicely, indeed.

"I suppose you best sit down," Webster said. "Then I won't need to crane my neck the entire time."

Harrison lowered himself into the chair opposite the desk. "I am sorry about all of this."

Webster cocked his head, his gaze turning thoughtful. "Are you?"

"Not really."

Maddie's father rubbed his forehead with the tips of three fingers, slow frustrated sweeps across his wrinkled brow. "I want honesty from you, Archer, and I'll only ask this once. As a gentleman, have you compromised my daughter under my roof?"

"Does it matter?"

"It matters to your future father-in-law."

"Perhaps, but still I'll not answer it. Whatever happened between Maddie and me remains private."

Webster leaned back in his chair, rocking slightly and causing the wood underneath him to creak. "I should hate you for that response, yet I cannot help but respect it." He sighed heavily, his chest deflating. "And it leaves me no choice but to force a marriage between you."

Undoubtedly the Websters would much prefer an aristocratic son-in-law, but that was too damn bad. Harrison was on the verge of having Maddie as his wife . . . and nothing would stop a wedding at this point. "That is your right."

"It is. Also within my right is to not offer you

the same betrothal agreement I gave Lockwood, considering the circumstances."

"I don't need your money." Harrison shrugged. "I made my own money in France."

"Your inheritance, you mean."

"No, I was cut off from my trust fund when I left and my mother subsequently spent it."

That got Webster's attention. He sat forward in his chair, shaking his head as if to clear it. "Cut off?"

"My father's doing. It was part of why I went to Paris."

"I don't understand. I always assumed you were . . ." The older man cleared his throat. "Well, second son and all."

"A layabout is probably the term you were searching for. A do-nothing. Ne'er-do-well. Wastrel. I've heard them all over the years." Usually from a member of his family.

"So how did you survive over there?"

"Cards, at first. We wastrels use our skills where we can, you know." He gave a grim smile. "Then the Paris Stock Exchange, which is just gambling on a larger stage. After that, I started working for Compagnie Générale Transatlantique. I helped them design cruises for upscale American passengers, recommending amenities and food that would appeal to travelers of a certain sensibility. For a cut of the profits, of course. Thus far, the cruises have been wildly successful."

Webster's jaw had fallen open midway through Harrison's speech. He closed his mouth and finally said, "That's quite clever."

"Thank you. Though I don't need money, I could use your help with another matter." Harrison crossed his legs and smoothed the fine wool of his trousers. "It's not been made public but my father lost everything in the Panic a few years ago. The Archers are broke."

Webster blinked a few times. "Broke?"

"Indeed. They've been borrowing money from the business, which has suffered under poor leadership the last decade or so. But I plan to change all that when I take over Archer Industries in a few weeks."

"You plan to take over your family's company? Why not try and help them save it?"

"The reasons are my own, but they do not deserve my help. No, I plan to take it all away—in a hostile takeover, if necessary. That is where I need your assistance."

"With?"

"Speaking to members of the board, if it comes to that. Many of them are close in age to you and there's a good chance you know many of them personally. Additionally, I am hoping, as my father-in-law, that you will also serve on the board once I restructure it."

Keen understanding shone in the older man's gaze as he nodded once. "Anything in my daughter's best interests going forward, you may count on my lending support. I never had much affinity for your father or brother, anyway. Does Madeline know any of this?"

"No, no one does. The stock price will plummet if word gets out and the company will fold before I can acquire it."

Webster stroked his jaw, staring across the desk as if trying to figure Harrison out. Maddie's father was a shrewd businessman, who'd doubled his family's steel empire after the war, and he did not suffer fools gladly. There was a reason the Websters owned nearly the largest house in both Manhattan and Newport—and it was the intelligence and drive of the man sitting in front of him.

"I always thought you were frivolous and not very ambitious," Webster finally said. "I can see I was wrong, and I have to say that comes as a goddamn relief. The last thing I want is for my only child to marry an empty-headed bounder who will spend my money on women and booze."

"You have my word I will not. I love your daughter."

"See that it stays that way. Does this mean you are staying in New York?"

"It does."

"Indeed, I am happy to hear it. I was not looking forward to sending her off to another country." Webster pushed back from the desk and stood. "I'll provide you with half of what I originally promised Lockwood. A half million in cash and one million in stock. You'll have it after the ceremony."

"It's not necessary, but thank you. I'll have a portion put into trusts for Maddie and our children." Harrison rose and shook the other man's hand. "I appreciate this."

"Never forget I am doing this for her."

"Of course."

Maddie's father checked his pocket watch. "When did you first know?"

"Know what?"

"That you wanted to marry my daughter."

Harrison's mouth hitched. "When I was fifteen."

Webster shook his head and he pinned Harrison with a hard stare. "You could have returned from Paris sooner and saved us the trouble."

True, but until a few days ago Maddie hadn't thought of him in a romantic way. "I could have, but where would have been the fun in that?"

"I daresay it won't be easy earning Maddie's forgiveness. She's been working on this match with Lockwood since March. Between that and tennis, it's all she's talked about for months. You know how much she hates to be taken by surprise."

"I do." Harrison remembered how annoyed Maddie became whenever he didn't follow her schemes to the letter. "And if you don't mind, I'd like to find her now, start working on that forgiveness."

"Go on, then. I need to find my wife. I'll let you know what time to show up for the ceremony."

Chapter Fifteen

𝒩ellie was lingering in the corridor when Maddie left her father's office. She followed Maddie toward the stairs and hissed, "What happened?"

"It's a disaster. I need to find Lockwood."

"He went up the steps and asked the butler to send up his valet. Then he said he'd need a carriage to take him to the train station."

Maddie paused on the bottom stair. Oh, God. Lockwood was leaving.

Of course he is leaving. You humiliated him.

"Come with me." Nellie grabbed Maddie's arm and dragged her toward the empty drawing room. Maddie followed blindly, her mind still tripping over all that had happened.

When they were alone, Nellie folded her arms across her chest. "Spill."

"Mrs. Lusk told my father everything and Lockwood has begged off. Harrison and I are being married this afternoon."

Nellie's eyes rounded. "Goodness gracious. When you decide to go bad, you really take the three-tiered cake, don't you?"

That hardly made Maddie feel better. "Nellie!"

"I'm teasing. Listen, you kissed a man and got caught. It's not the end of the world."

"It feels as if it is. Lockwood despises me, and my mother is no doubt reaching for the smelling salts."

"Perhaps, but so what?" Nellie gave her a smile full of affection and understanding. "I am aware of your desire for everyone to like you best, but no one is perfect, Maddie. Not even you."

"I don't need for everyone to like me best"— she ignored Nellie's disbelieving expression—"but I do not like hurting people. Or embarrassing them."

"I understand, but have you considered that maybe you were meant to be with Harrison all along?"

"No, I haven't."

"Someday, you will—and you will thank Aunt Nellie for all the great advice she gave you these past few days."

Maddie threw her arms around the other woman. "After this party, you might be my only friend left."

"Stop." Nellie patted Maddie's back. "Society has a short memory. Time heals all scandals, as they say."

No one said that, but Maddie didn't quibble. She let Nellie go. "I need to find Lockwood and apologize. I feel absolutely awful."

"Don't feel too awful. The duke would have made you a terrible husband."

Her friend said it with such certainty that Maddie cocked her head. "Why?"

A look passed over Nellie's face before she could mask it. "Because he isn't Harrison. Now go."

Maddie had the sense the other woman was not telling the whole truth but there was no time to dig into that pile. Best to leave it for later. "Thank you for attempting to make me feel better."

"You are welcome," Nellie called as Maddie dashed out of the room.

At the top of the staircase, she spotted Lockwood striding along the corridor, headed right toward her. He walked briskly, as if desperate to leave. Swallowing, she drew in a deep breath and prepared to grovel. "May I speak with you?"

"Of course," he replied easily. "Shall we continue this outside? The carriage is waiting."

He held out his arm, ever the gentleman. The consideration was more than she deserved. Placing her hand atop his forearm, she let him lead her down the main stairs, through the vestibule, and out the door. In the drive, footmen were securing the duke's things to the top of a carriage.

Folding his hands behind his back, Lockwood stared off into the distance. The angles of his handsome face were harsher, less welcoming than they'd been yesterday. Her stomach roiled with self-loathing and regret as she considered what to say. "Please accept my heartfelt apology. I never meant for this to happen."

He cleared his throat. "I assumed as much. If I had thought your attentions were engaged elsewhere, I never would have pursued you."

"They weren't. There is no explanation for what happened."

"I'd say Harrison Archer happened," he said, wryly.

"Nevertheless, I have no excuse for my dishonorable behavior. I feel terrible for treating you this way."

His jaw tightened, lips thinning into the hint of a grimace. "If you are hoping for absolution, I'm incapable of providing it at the moment. Honestly, it is quite humiliating to be thrown over like this. I hadn't expected it, especially considering how well we got on together."

A duke was a position of great power and responsibility, and she could imagine losing was a bitter pill for him to swallow. A tear slipped from out of the corner of her eye and rolled down her cheek. Then the other eye followed suit. "I understand, and I regret causing you any embarrassment. Someday, I hope you will be able to forgive me."

He gave a short nod but didn't reply. A man, she assumed the duke's valet, approached. "Your Grace, the bags are packed and secured. We may depart whenever you are ready."

Lockwood nodded once. "A moment, Wilkins." The valet climbed into the carriage to wait.

Maddie clenched her hands together tightly, more tears leaking, unsure what more she could say. "Do you plan to return to England?"

"No, I'll return to New York first." His gaze darted over her head and his expression hardened. He grunted, the noise sounding full of derision. "I suppose he's come to gloat."

She didn't need to turn around to know who stood there. "Perhaps he wishes to apologize."

A grim smile twisted the duke's lips. "He isn't sorry, not one bit." He pulled on his cuffs. "I wish you luck, Miss Webster."

Lockwood disappeared into the carriage and a groom set the step, then the carriage rolled down the drive. Maddie watched, her mind spinning as the emotion of the day settled on her shoulders, weighing her down. She'd caused so much damage, all from a single moment of passion.

How could she ever forgive herself?

By THE TIME Harrison discerned Maddie's whereabouts, she was already engaged in conversation outside with the duke. Lockwood stood stiffly beside a carriage, while Maddie talked quite animatedly at his side. Crossing his arms, Harrison leaned against the doorjamb and openly watched. A better man would probably give the former couple privacy . . . but Harrison was not that man.

Instead, he didn't move, just waited patiently for the conversation to end. Anticipation throbbed in his veins, a constant drumbeat of victory, reverberating with the knowledge that he and Maddie would be married by day's end.

Married.

Fuck, he could not wait.

Lockwood's gaze flicked toward Harrison, and the duke frowned when their eyes met. Harrison allowed a smug half smile to twist his lips. *You lost, Your Grace. Do run along.*

Lockwood murmured something to Maddie, then inclined his head before disappearing into the carriage. She stepped back and appeared to swipe at her cheeks.

Dash it, he hadn't thought she'd *cry*. Shout and carry on, yes. But he hadn't prepared himself for tears.

He hated when she cried. The last time he could recall was when she stepped on a jellyfish one summer. He'd carried her, nearly running, up the beach to the chateau where they could rinse her foot in vinegar.

He stroked his jaw as the carriage rolled down the drive, taking the duke to wherever dukes went when they lost their fiancée to another man. Harrison felt a touch guilty, but Lockwood would be fine. There were hundreds of wealthy women in America who would undoubtedly leap at the chance to become a duchess.

When the carriage disappeared, Maddie turned and her eyes locked defiantly with his, her chin thrust high. She had indeed been crying, and the sight tore at the inside of Harrison's chest, stinging as if he'd been flayed open with a sharp instrument.

They stood there, not speaking, while the staff drifted away to other duties. She was normally easy to read, her feelings right on her face, but he had no idea what she was thinking at the moment. Was she distraught? Angry? Resentful?

"You've been crying," he said, commenting on the obvious as he drifted closer.

"Yes, Harrison." Sparks glittered in her green gaze, which was a relief. Anger he could handle. "That is what generally happens when I hurt those I care about."

Like the duke. "Lockwood's a sore loser, I suppose."

"This is not a game."

Lifting a hand, he brushed the backs of his knuckles along her jaw. "Wrong. This was most definitely a game and you were the greatest prize."

She stepped back, her lips pressed flat. "You should have spoken up in my father's office. You should have said you did not compromise me. Then we wouldn't be forced to marry."

"Why on earth would I have done such a thing?"

"To spare me, not to mention my parents, the humiliation. And Lockwood, for that matter. The list is endless, Harrison."

"While I wouldn't have chosen a scandal as the backdrop for our marriage, I cannot regret it, either. I told you I wanted you."

Maddie closed her eyes and pinched the bridge of her nose with two fingers. "That was a momentary fit of passion. We became overzealous in the gazebo. It was the rain and the darkness, a temporary insanity. Neither of us knew what we wanted."

"Wrong. I told you earlier yesterday that I wanted everything from you. I meant marriage and children, laughter and tears, a lifetime of having you by my side."

"And when did you arrive at this momentous decision? When you were in Paris, entertaining can-can dancers and sipping absinthe?"

"Long before, actually." The truth slipped out, but he didn't hide from the astonishment in her expression. He owed her honesty, at least about this.

"What do you mean, long before?"

He held up his hands. "I promise to explain everything tonight. Right now, I must stroll over to the Archer cottage and get the place prepared."

"For what?"

His couldn't help but grin. "Our wedding night."

"No." Her back straightened. "This is no traditional marriage with an ordinary wedding night. I am far too angry with you to even contemplate it."

He lowered his voice seductively. "I promise you, there will be nothing ordinary about our wedding night."

"Now you make *jokes*?" She threw her hands up and let them fall. "This has upended my life, Harrison. This is hardly a time for levity."

He sobered. "I apologize. It was insensitive of me. But look at it this way: I saved you from a dull marriage to a dull man who would have undoubtedly given you dull children."

"Oh, so I should be grateful to you. Is that it?"

He clamped his lips shut. They were going round and round, getting nowhere. She was still too angry and he was too dashed happy. This conversation was better had tonight, once they were married and alone. He could explain everything then, and she would have no choice but to listen.

But for now, he had to give her a choice. Maddie preferred logic and reason to make a decision. He couldn't forget that all this had taken her by surprise.

Reaching out, he took her hand, relieved not to see the ducal betrothal ring any longer. Softening his tone, he said, "I know this is happening quickly, and you haven't had much control over the last few hours, but please believe me when I say I want nothing more in this world than to marry you. Every minute of my life, every breath I take will be spent making you happy. Please, marry me, Mads."

Tears pooled against her lids. "I have no choice. The scandal will be all over New York by dinnertime."

"There is always a choice. You could move to Rome or Barcelona, live abroad for a year or two. The scandal will eventually blow over."

"Not for my parents. And what of my plans to be the best lawn tennis player in America? I cannot leave."

"Some girls travel West. Change their name. No one ever need know what happened here."

Her brows drew together. "And never see my family or friends again? I don't want to start a new life like some sort of confidence man on the run from the law."

"Then I'm afraid you're stuck with me."

"You're stuck with me, as well." She pulled free of his grip. "And I am still angry with you for pushing me when I asked for more time."

"That's fine." She'd forgive him . . . eventually. Hopefully once she understood his feelings for her. "I suppose I'll see you later at the ceremony, then."

"I am serious about the wedding night, Harrison. Do not even think about it."

Impossible. He could do almost nothing *but* think about it.

He thrust his hands in his pockets and started walking toward the street. "I suppose we'll see, my soon-to-be wife."

THE CEREMONY TOOK hardly any time at all.

In a furious daze, Maddie recited the words that would bind her to Harrison for the rest of her life. He did the same, his voice clear and strong in the near-empty salon, the hint of a smile on his face.

This was most definitely a game and you were the greatest prize.

She ground her back teeth together. He hadn't bothered to woo her or confide in her. This had been a challenge to him, to steal her away from Lockwood, and in one weak moment, she'd succumbed. Not that she could entirely blame Harrison, either. There had been two of them in the gazebo, and she'd willingly allowed him to lead her down the path to ruin. Had asked for it, even.

Now everything had changed.

He placed a ghost of a kiss on her lips when it was all over. Then the small group still remaining at the house—her parents, Nellie, Kit, Maddie and Harrison—toasted with champagne and sat through a short celebratory dinner Maddie would never remember. When it was time for them to depart, Maddie disappeared upstairs, desperate for a moment alone.

"Slow down," Nellie called from the stairs. "My legs aren't as long as yours."

She hadn't realized her friend was following, so she paused on the landing until Nellie caught up. "Was that as awful as I imagined?"

"Not for me," Nellie said. "Kind of nice seeing someone else embroiled in a scandal for a change."

"I have new sympathy for you."

"Oh, don't feel sorry for me. The whispers and snubs hardly bother me anymore."

"I suppose I better get used to it. Hardly anyone said goodbye to me before they left today." The chaperones had packed up the young ladies in a blink after the news broke, worried that an association with such a scandal might harm future marriage prospects.

"It'll all blow over, I promise," Nellie said, her voice filled with confidence.

Maddie wasn't so certain.

When they arrived at her room, Maddie closed the door and leaned against it, sighing. "Is it too late to swim for Cuba?"

Nellie chuckled. "Yes, so cheer up. It won't be that bad."

"Which part? Tonight, or my marriage?"

"Both." Nellie took in Maddie's disbelieving expression. "I cannot help with the marriage part, but I can answer questions you have about the wedding night. Has your mother told you what to expect?"

"No, of course not. She won't even discuss my monthly. But it doesn't matter because I am not speaking to Harrison. I'm furious with him."

"Maddie." Nellie sounded disappointed. "You were in the gazebo, too. Unless he forced you, then you share the blame."

"I know, and I am angry with myself, as well. But he pushed and pushed, then didn't even try to protect my reputation. He said nothing and let me bear the brunt of our mistake."

"That is because Harrison isn't sorry."

"Precisely what Lockwood said. Goodness, what a blasted mess."

Nellie's brows shot up as she sat on the edge of the bed. "Did you honestly wish to move to England and live in some drafty old manor house? So far away from your family and friends? And what about lawn tennis? Really, Maddie."

"It wouldn't have been so bad."

"Please. In England, you would have withered and died like wisteria in winter. If you ask me, you are lucky. You've married a man who is head over heels in love with you."

"After only a few days? Impossible. He told me himself this was a game and I was the prize."

"Because he wanted you. And believe me, it's always better if a man wants you more than you want him."

"So I don't get my heart broken?"

"No." Nellie patted the empty mattress beside her. "Sit down and let Aunt Nellie tell you all about men."

"Goodness, you are smug when you know something I don't."

"Because all you care about is tennis."

"That is not true. I intended to spend my engagement gathering knowledge about what happens in the bedroom. Then I would have been prepared."

Nellie shook her head. "This is not a campaign to be waged or an exam for which to study. I'll tell you everything you want to know about the basics. The rest is simple biology and physical attraction."

Maddie lowered herself to the bed. "The point is moot. We will not consummate the marriage tonight."

Nellie looked horrified. "Why not?"

"I don't feel ready. I hardly know this new version of Harrison. Moreover, I don't like the way we married."

"Maddie," her friend said on a sigh. "Men are good for very few things in this life. Sexual congress is one of them. Don't pass up one of the things you'll actually enjoy in a marriage."

"Will it hurt?"

"It shouldn't but it might pinch if he doesn't prepare you."

"Prepare me?"

"Widen you. Stretch you. With his fingers." Nellie wiggled her index and middle fingers. "Maybe you'll get really lucky and he'll lick between your legs."

Maddie buried her face in her hands. "Oh, my God."

"Is that embarrassment or revulsion?"

There was no denying Maddie was attracted to Harrison, that her body crawled with tension whenever she was in his presence. And that kiss . . . it had nearly scorched her. "Embarrassment."

"That's what I thought." Nellie bumped her shoulder against Maddie's. "You never would have kissed him if you weren't attracted to him. I think Harrison is going to treat you well. All those skills he picked up in Paris? They must be of good use to some woman—and she might as well be you."

"I'm still mad at him."

"Understandable, but take your frustrations out on his body tonight. Trust me, you will feel better."

"I don't even know what that means."

"It was a joke." Nellie reached to grab Maddie's hand. "As someone who has experience in this area, believe me, you have nothing to worry about."

"Are you sure?"

"Absolutely positive. Enjoy yourself. You cannot do anything wrong. Just ask questions if you're unsure what to do. Pretend it's a tennis match and you have to learn everything you can about your opponent."

Hmm, that explanation actually made sense to her. Discovering strengths and weaknesses, using them to her advantage. If Harrison thought this was a game, then she would prove a worthy opponent.

Still, she was furious with him—and herself. It had all happened so quickly, and their rashness had hurt others. Burned into her mind was the embarrassment on Lockwood's face, the disappointment radiating from her father. Then there were her mother's tears, accompanied by a list of everything Maddie had lost out on because of this scandal.

Harrison had upended her life, twisted her carefully laid plans, in a matter of days. How could she play the dutiful, loving wife tonight when all she wanted was to be alone? "Do I have to sleep with him?"

"No, but you should. It's fun. Rather, it should be fun. Why do you think there are so many babies in the world?"

Maddie groaned. "Why did you have to mention babies?"

"Just have him pull out before he finishes. If he doesn't spend inside you, then you won't find yourself with child."

All of this talk of babies and fingers was giving Maddie a headache. She turned the topic onto Nellie instead. "You know a lot about this business. Why have we never had this talk before?"

"I didn't wish to corrupt you. Now, shall we get you changed?"

Chapter Sixteen

$\mathcal{U}$nable to stand still, Harrison paced near the entryway. He was anxious to get this wedding night under way. Finally, noise on the landing caught his attention. Nellie came down the stairs first, a knowing smirk on her face, then his wife followed.

His *wife*.

Jesus, he would never tire of saying that. Maddie was all he'd wanted, the only woman he'd ever loved, and she was his. Forever.

She avoided his gaze as she said goodbye to her parents. Then she wrapped her fingers around Harrison's arm and tugged him out the door. "Let's go."

Once at the carriage, he helped her up. "I assume you are still mad at me."

"Perceptive of you." She settled on the seat and stared out the window.

The Archer cottage was barely five minutes away from the chateau. There wasn't much time for a protracted conversation, which he would initiate once they were at the house. However, he did want a bit of his old Maddie back, the girl with the sunny disposition and loud laugh.

Before anything else happened, he had to coax some of the anger out of her. Slipping off his gloves, he shoved them in his coat pocket and snatched her hand. She tried to pull away, but he wouldn't relent. "What are you doing?" she asked.

"Worshipping you, if you'll let me."

The answer seemed to stupefy her so he took advantage by pressing his mouth to the bare skin of her arm, just at the edge of her glove. She gave another tug, weaker this time, and sucked in a gulp of air. He kissed her again, his tongue flicking the tender skin, and goose bumps erupted on her flesh. Feeling victorious, he began unbuttoning the glove, the tiny pearl beads slipping through the holes one after another. Each small bit of her skin received attention from his mouth, moving higher and higher, toward her hand, until he nibbled on the delicate underside of her wrist.

Her soft pants filled the carriage as they drove through the quiet town. Working steadily, he loosened the thin cloth until he was able to pull each finger free. When he finished, he pressed a deep kiss to her palm. "I always liked your hands. They're strong and capable, not delicate."

"It's from tennis. I try to soften them with ointment," she whispered, her gaze locked on their hands. "Nothing works."

"You don't need to soften anything for me, Mads. I like every rough edge and hard spot. You are perfect."

He heard her swallow thickly. "I am hardly perfect."

"You are perfect to me. You always have been."

"Even when I was covered in sand and seaweed that one time? You called me The Colossal Sea Creature for the rest of the summer and said you were going to write to Mr. Barnum about hiring me."

"Even then." He flipped her hand over and kissed the back. "Especially then, because you never failed to make me smile at a time in my life when I desperately needed it."

The carriage slowed as the wheels turned into the drive of his family's cottage, and he reluctantly released her. The dark mansion was cold and brutal, with its boxy front and looming chimneys. Squat and forbidding, with no flowers or hint of welcoming, so very much like his family. He'd been trained to be quiet here, to walk instead of run, to hide his thoughts and never let anyone know what he was feeling.

Soon the property would belong to him and he would refashion it into whatever Maddie wished. Maybe he'd tear the structure down and start over, build something entirely new. Then they could forge happy memories here, with no remnants of his past.

The front door opened and Evans, the butler, began directing the footmen to help with the trunks. "Mr. Archer," he said as Harrison descended. "Welcome back."

"Hello, Evans." He turned and helped Maddie out of the carriage. "May I present my wife, Mrs. Archer?" Maddie stiffened, likely surprised at hearing the words for the first time, so he put his hand at the small of her back and guided her forward.

"Mrs. Archer." Evans bowed. "It is a pleasure. Please accept my congratulations on behalf of the staff."

"Thank you." Maddie's face softened at the older man, one she'd met often during their childhood. "I see you haven't changed a bit since the last time I visited."

Evans puffed up, obviously pleased from the compliment. "Kind of you to say, ma'am, but the knees are a bit creakier. I can always tell when rain is coming."

"I'll send you some of the liniment I use on my sore muscles," she said. "It helps after tennis practice. I got the recipe from one of the pitchers for the Brooklyn Bridegrooms."

Harrison frowned as they moved inside. "A baseball player?"

"Yes. He's a friend of my coach, Valentine Livingston."

Jealousy curled through his belly, but he stifled the growl rising in his throat. Of course she'd made friends and gone out during these past three years—he had done the same in Paris—yet he was greedy to reclaim every minute of the time they were apart. He wanted her all to himself.

You are the one who left. You can hardly blame her for carrying on here.

True. Someday he would learn of all that he'd missed, the adventures she'd undertaken without him. Tonight, however, had a very different purpose. And it wasn't talking.

He tugged her toward the back of the house, in the direction of his surprise. "Evans, as soon as everything is settled with our bags, you and the rest of the staff may have the night off."

"Thank you, sir."

"And please pass on my thanks for all you and the staff have accomplished today."

The staff had moved mountains to do as Harrison had asked. His father had accepted their obedience as his due, acting as if every employee and staff member owed him absolutely everything—including their bodies, if he so desired. He had been an abusive employer, and Harrison had to prove to the staff that he would not act in the same barbaric manner.

Shaking off those memories, he clutched Maddie's hand tighter and led her outside. He was ready to let go of the past and embrace their future together.

Once they reached the back lawn, she asked, "Where are we going?"

"It's a surprise."

She tried to dig in her heels as they neared the stables. Not far was the carriage house, its wooden doors closed. "Harrison, I have experienced enough surprises today. If you don't mind, I'd like to be alone in a bath."

Turning, he scooped her into his arms. "I swear, you'll like this one."

With her arms wrapped lightly around his shoulders, she remained quiet the rest of the way to the carriage house. The feel of her against him was dizzying, like he'd sipped absinthe for hours. He'd thought of this night so often, had imagined it over and over, that he almost couldn't believe he'd finally done it.

She's my wife. Mine, forever.

Tonight, he was going to show her exactly what that meant.

He set her on the ground and pulled the carriage house doors open. Inside, everything was arranged exactly as he'd asked. The structure had been emptied, the vehicle and equipment replaced by a tiny round table, two chairs and a divan. Lights were strung across the ceiling, the bare bulbs casting a gentle yellow glow over the interior, and plush carpets covered the floor. An array of sweets and fruit littered a side table, while a bottle of champagne chilled in a bucket next to the table.

Her head swiveled as she took it all in. "What is this? I don't understand."

He took a deep breath. Even if what he said scared her, it was time for honesty. He owed her that much. How could they ever move forward if he didn't tell her why he'd come to Newport?

He closed the door and slowly approached her. Shoving his hands in his trouser pockets, he tried to slow his pounding heartbeat. "You know I used to hide out here during the summers. That house, Mads . . ." Grimacing, he gestured behind them to the cottage. "It holds no pleasant memories. None at all. I was miserable there. But here, I was free. I used to lie in the closed carriage or up in the loft, anywhere I couldn't be seen. Do you know what I used to think about when I was here?"

A crease formed between her brows. "No."

"You. I went over every word you uttered, every smile you bestowed. I imagined what our future might look like, if we were together. I wondered if you could ever want me as much as I wanted you. And do you want to know what else?"

Her eyes were wide and steady. "What?"

Stepping forward, he took her hand and threaded their fingers together. "I thought about kissing you."

"Really?"

"All the time. So it seemed fitting to bring you here tonight in the hopes of sharing our first kiss as man and wife."

"You kissed me after the wedding ceremony."

He shook his head. "That was not a kiss. I mean a proper kiss, one that will steal your breath and soak your drawers."

She gave a startled laugh. "I see." Then her head cocked to the side as she studied him. "You wanted me, even then?"

"I did." He lifted his free hand and placed it on her cheek. "I still do."

"You are making it very hard to stay mad at you."

"Then you had best brace yourself for what I am about to say next." His thumb stroked the soft skin of her face. "I came to Newport for you. I never had any interest in those other women. The house party was a ruse just to be close to you."

Her jaw fell open. "You are joking."

"Not even a little. From the moment I heard you hadn't married, I decided I would beg, borrow and steal to win you. Fate had handed me one more chance and I was not going to waste it this time."

"What do you mean, this time?"

"That I wasn't going to give up so easily."

"You are the most confusing and infuriating man, Harrison Archer."

"At least I'll never bore you."

She put a hand on his shoulder, putting space between them. "Wait, you asked me to host a house party for you, to invite my unmatched friends, merely as a way to spend time with me?" She asked the question flatly, without a hint of emotion, and he wondered if he'd erred by telling her.

You had to tell her. Lies merely breed more lies.

"Yes."

Understanding dawned on her face. "Nellie insisted you had no interest in any of the other women. And this explains why Katherine never returned to the gazebo."

"Your friends told you?"

"Not all of them." She fingered one of his collar studs absently, but he was very aware of her touch, each tiny movement sending waves of heat through his veins. He held perfectly still, desperate for the innocent fondling to continue. She shook her head. "I cannot decide whether to be angry or flattered."

"I am hoping the latter, obviously, but I probably deserve the anger, too. You went to a lot of trouble on my account."

"Yes, I did, and all of my friends attended in good faith." She paused. "What if it hadn't succeeded with me? Would you have pursued one of those other women?"

The answer came swiftly. "Absolutely not."

"So you would have let your mother cut you off?"

"I don't wish to discuss my mother—now or ever." He pushed a lock of silken hair behind her ear. "Just know that this right here was all that mattered—you and me, together."

She softened, warmth darkening the emerald of her eyes to more of a moss green, and she slid her arms around his shoulders. He held his breath, not wanting to push her, letting her take the lead. For now.

She toyed with the hair at his nape. "I have so many questions. My head is spinning."

"I'll address all of them in due time, I promise." He slid his hands onto her hips. "And I'd like to think more than questions are making your head spin."

She licked her lips, her chest rising and falling more rapidly, their hips almost touching. "You owe my friends an apology."

He stared at her mouth. Those full, wet lips were begging to be kissed, to cushion his mouth as he told her without words all that she meant to him. "I'll send them each dozens of flowers if it means you'll forgive me."

"That will be a start. And you owe Lockwood an apology, as well. He did not deserve to be humiliated like this. I will find my own way to make amends to him, and you must do the same."

"I will, I promise." He arched a brow at her. "Does that mean we may proceed with more interesting pursuits?"

"Like kissing?"

"That will be a start," he echoed. Bending closer, he lowered his voice. "Kiss me, please, Maddie. Make that young boy's dreams come true."

"I'd rather make the man's fantasies come true."

Lust streaked along his spine and settled in his groin. "Are you certain? Because the man has quite a number of fantasies and some are shockingly creative."

"You should know by now that I am always up for a challenge."

Goddamn, he loved this woman.

He pulled her close, leaving just a sliver of space between their bodies. "Then we best get started."

MADDIE HELD ON, her mind reeling from Harrison's proximity and words. She knew she should be furious that the house party had been a ruse—and she was definitely angry on behalf of her friends, who'd attended in good faith—but part of her was flattered.

I decided I would beg, borrow and steal to win you.

She wasn't used to this ruthless, ambitious version of Harrison Archer. But at least that explained why he'd pushed her, why he hadn't liked Lockwood.

Unfortunately, the lust crawling over her skin was scrambling her reason, dulling the questions she knew she should be asking. Numbing the anger and masking the bewilderment. Everything faded as Harrison continued to stare down at her.

It was a face she knew well, from the tiny lines around his eyes to the way his hair curled near his collar. But this was new between them, new and thrilling. She never dreamed he'd stare at her with such fierce longing and intense devotion, as if she was absolutely everything.

Just know that this right here was all that mattered— you and me, together.

Answers and apologies could wait.

"I don't want to rush you." He searched her eyes, his fingers tightening on her hips ever so slightly, as if he struggled to hold on to his self-control. "Would you like champagne first?"

She thought back to the changing room, to the gazebo, where the connection between them had proven untamed and irrefutable. Every part of her craved that wildness, the passionate frenzy she'd experienced only with him. "Champagne can wait."

She rose up on her toes and closed the distance between them, her mouth meeting his in a less-than-perfect effort. He didn't seem to notice, though, and instantly moved to meld his lips with hers. His mouth was coaxing and gentle but he gave no respite, stealing her breath and her wits. Soon she was dizzy and desperate, her fingertips digging into his scalp to hold on.

Closer. More. Please.

As if she'd spoken the words aloud, Harrison parted his mouth and flicked his tongue against her lips. She opened for him with an urgency that would have shocked her a week ago. His mouth was warm and slick, and the kiss deepened, their breathing harsh as they each struggled for air. It was as if they were still in the gazebo, picking up exactly where they left off last night.

His hands slid to cup her backside and he pulled her flush to his front, her hips crashing into his, and she could feel his erection, hard and impatient, against her. It was impossible to remain still. She was feverish, burning alive, with every part of her growing more frustrated and needy as the kiss wore on.

He broke off to press openmouthed kisses along her jaw, her throat. He sucked hard on the sensitive skin at her pulse point, and pleasure arrowed straight between her legs. Releasing her, he murmured, "I want to mark you, even though I shouldn't. Make it so that everyone knows you are mine."

The idea appealed far more than it should have, considering she had been engaged to another man this morning. "Only if I may mark you in return."

"God, I would love nothing more." He nipped at her bottom lip, and the delicious sting of his teeth caused her to shiver. "But it's hardly necessary. I have always been yours."

Speech proved impossible after a declaration like that, so she kissed him instead, slower this time, and he let her, his hands holding her steady as she explored his mouth. Her tongue swept over his plump lips, then she nibbled and sucked until his breathing hitched, and then he was diving into her mouth, taking over with bold strokes and deep kisses until she whimpered. Everything in her strained toward him, her pulse pounding in her ears like a drumbeat.

Why had she never known it would be like this between them? So necessary, so utterly perfect. Desire clawed and scratched inside her, more forceful than she'd ever experienced during her own explorations. His hands were everywhere, coasting over the places within reach. When he palmed her breast, she arched into him, eager for more, but all this clothing . . .

"Shall we go to the house," he panted against her mouth, "where I may do all manner of wicked things to you in a proper bed?"

She thought about the house, with its impersonal coldness and disapproving shadows. A place he hated, one that held no kindness or hospitality. It hardly seemed fair of her to contemplate staying there, and besides, they were here, in the spot where he'd dreamed of her. Dreamed of them together. "No. We should stay."

"But . . ." He cast a quick glance at the divan, as if weighing the tiny piece of furniture against all the things he longed to do to her. "Are you sure?"

She'd never been more certain. "I don't need a bed, but I will need help out of this gown."

The side of his mouth hitched. "That I can do."

Spinning her away from him, he set to work on the tiny buttons at her nape, unfastening them with brisk efficiency. The air in the carriage house was warm and filled with the songs of crickets and cicadas from outside, a familiar and fitting backdrop to their wedding night. He said nothing as his fingers plucked and moved, both of them breathing hard. She started to unfasten the buttons at her wrist, though her progress was slow and unwieldy.

"Goddamn it," he muttered. "So many buttons."

Finally, he loosened the dress enough to slide his hands inside, around her corseted waist and up to her chest, where he covered her breasts. When her back met his front, his erection nestled into her backside and she inhaled sharply. He surrounded her, sensation everywhere, and she pressed closer, rocking her pelvis into his.

Harrison hissed, his fingers tightening on her chest before turning her around, where she saw the raw need on his face, the flush to his skin. There was a wildness in his eyes that hadn't been there a moment ago, but a vulnerability, too. "I don't know if I can be gentle with you," he whispered. "I've wanted you for so long."

"I am not fragile." She held up her wrist in a silent plea for help.

The buttons on her wrists were quickly undone and he lowered the gown to the floor. She untied her petticoats, letting them fall, as well.

Then she stood in her corset, shift and drawers in the middle of the floor, and though nerves bubbled in her stomach, she made no attempt to hide herself. If this had been anyone else, she'd likely be terrified. But she wasn't shy with Harrison, never had been.

He took his time looking her over, his hands gliding over the curves still hidden by whalebone and cloth. "My God, you are gorgeous." Stepping behind her, he plucked at the corset strings, loosening them, until the heavy piece could be removed. Her breasts were average-sized, but right now they were full with longing, the nipples tight points behind her thin shift. When he took the flesh in his strong hands, shaping and caressing her, she let her head fall back onto his chest, her lids drifting closed, as the pleasure sizzled along her spine and down between her legs.

Her shift came off and his hands caressed the bare skin of her breasts, shooting a jolt of electricity to her core. His touch turned rougher, his hot breath in her ear, and he squeezed with delicious pressure. Then his fingers went to the tips where he teased her nipples, pinching them, and she gasped. "*Harrison.*"

With a growl, he dug his hard shaft into her backside. "I have waited a lifetime to hear you say my name like that." His palm traveled south until he reached the juncture of her thighs. "Hmm, your drawers are soaked."

"I guess that means you've kissed me properly." She raised her arms and twined them around his neck, curving her body to his. She felt so comfortable with him, as if nothing she could do would shock or disappoint him.

His fingers delved inside the cloth until he found her center, where she was swollen and slick. No hand but her own had ever explored here, and she loved the feel of his calloused fingertips as he traced every part of her, from the outer lips to the entrance.

"You're so perfectly wet," he murmured against her neck. "I cannot wait to taste you."

He continued to pet her, avoiding the one place that ached the most, and she could hardly stand the teasing. "Please," she heard herself say as if from a distance.

"Get on the divan."

Though his voice was steady, his breathing was not, and his reaction emboldened her. She walked to the divan, knowing he watched, knowing the heels of her short boots angled her backside higher. When she turned and perched on the divan's edge, bare from the waist up, his gaze was bright and hot, hungry and full of adoration. She felt even more powerful than she did on the tennis court. Deep down, she knew that Harrison, her closest confidant for most of her life, would always protect her.

I wondered if you could ever want me as much as I wanted you.

At the moment, the answer was unequivocally yes.

Never taking his eyes off her, he shrugged out of his black evening coat and dropped it to the floor. He yanked on his bowtie, unfastened his vest. Collar and cuff links were next before he removed his dress shoes. In just suspenders, shirt and trousers, he stalked toward her, hair askew from her hands and lips swollen from their kisses. "Lie back."

Was this it? Was he going to prepare her, then mount her? Nellie had assured Maddie she would enjoy it, and she knew Harrison would never knowingly hurt her. Unsure, she reclined and forced her limbs to relax.

Instead of climbing onto the divan, Harrison

knelt on the floor by her legs. He lifted her foot, unlaced her shoe and removed it. Then he did the same with the other boot, leaving her in stockinged feet. Slipping his hands under her backside, he jerked her to the edge of the divan, putting her at a slight angle. "Open your legs."

This was unexpected. "Why?"

"Like I said, I can't wait to taste you."

Maybe you'll get really lucky and he'll lick between your legs.

Was this what Nellie had meant?

Biting her lip, Maddie fought a wave of self-consciousness and parted her thighs. Air washed over the hot skin, and he stared down at the bare flesh exposed by the slit in her drawers as if fascinated by it, his face alarmingly close to her quim. Just as she started to grow nervous, he bent his head and his warm breath ghosted over her, then his tongue touched her center. "*Oh,*" she said, the intimacy and pleasure of it shocking her.

Bolder, he pressed kisses to her flesh as he explored, nuzzling and caressing her, before he dragged the flat of his tongue through her folds, licking every bit of her. She trembled, her lids falling closed, and he moaned, the long rumble vibrating against her skin. "*Christ.* I have died and gone to heaven."

It felt like the other way around, as if eternal bliss resided in that swollen, wet place and he'd unlocked it. With a few swipes of his tongue, he'd caused her entire body to shiver in ecstasy. What would happen if he continued? Would she combust?

He laved at her, tasting the wetness gathered

at her entrance, then working his way to the tiny bundle of nerves atop her sex. Lust rolled over her in waves, building, doubling and tripling, until she was panting, her head thrashing on the divan. It was both too much and not enough. Then he sucked the bud into his mouth, nursing and flicking it with his tongue, and her body drew as tight as a wire, her blood thrumming with indescribable sensation.

Her nails clawed at the fabric, muscles clenching as he pushed her higher, his mouth unrelenting, giving and giving until the crest was upon her. The climax ripped through her lower half, her mouth hanging open as a long moan escaped her throat. It went on and on, an explosion of white sparks that popped and shimmered under her skin.

When she finally came down the other side, he eased up, still gently licking as if savoring her. His eyes traveled the length of her body, until he met her gaze, his blue depths bright with lust. "Did you like that?" he murmured.

She nodded, unsure she could form words just yet.

"Good. Then let me do it again."

Chapter Seventeen

$\mathcal{H}$arrison could not believe his excellent fortune. The woman he'd wanted forever—now his wife—was here, nearly naked before him, the taste of her arousal bursting on his tongue. Even failing to ruin his family, he could die a happy man.

The woman was gorgeous. Long limbs toned from exercise, soft skin and high round breasts that begged for his mouth and hands. She hadn't been shy, either. It was clear she hadn't much experience, but she didn't hide from him. Trusted him to show her pleasure. She was a goddamn gift, one he would never take for granted.

He continued to taste her, reveling in her body's response to his mouth. She had climaxed quickly, beautifully, leaving her limp and her cunt wet, and he couldn't wait to repeat it.

"Again?" she breathed, coming up on her elbows. Her gaze was slightly unfocused and he had to bite back a smile.

"Yes, my delicious wife. Again."

She shuddered, her chest heaving as she

watched his mouth and tongue lick and suck, nip and kiss between her legs. It was his very favorite part of a woman's body, so delicious and ripe, so full of secrets. He hoped Maddie never tired of allowing him to give her orgasms with his mouth.

Her clitoris was swollen and sensitive from her last climax, so he concentrated on her entrance and her lips, lapping gently. Taking one finger, he slid it partway inside her channel, nearly groaning at the feel of the tight warm clasp. His cock was painfully hard, and it jumped at the idea of sinking into all that snug heat.

Not yet. He wanted her ready. More than ready. Begging, actually. And it didn't need to happen tonight. While he was dying to get inside her, they had years of fucking ahead of them. Months and days and hours of teasing each other, exploring, playing . . . just being together. If she needed time to come to terms with the physical side of their relationship, he didn't mind. Eventually, she would crave this as much as he did.

"Oh, God. *Harrison.*"

She rocked her hips, pushing his finger in deeper, and he groaned into her skin. There was every chance he might spend in his trousers, like a lad, if she kept that up.

He left his finger inside, letting her adjust to the feeling, while he lightly circled her clitoris with his tongue. One of her hands found its way onto his head, holding him in place as he teased her. It didn't take long until she was writhing beneath him, and he increased the pressure of his mouth just before inserting a second finger. A tight squeeze, but she accepted the added width after two pumps of his hand.

"I'm ready," she breathed, her nails digging into his scalp. "Please, Harrison. I'm ready."

He said nothing, just continued to work his fingers in and out of her channel as he laved at her. When her thighs began to quiver, he nursed on the bud of her sex, determined to drive her over the edge once more.

She jerked on his hair and he lifted his head. Wild eyes stared at him. "Now, please. I need you now."

"We don't need to do more than this tonight. Relax and let me make you feel good."

That got her attention. "You don't want to do more than this?"

"Of course I do." He was so hard, the skin of his cock stretched so tight that it was actually painful. "But I can wait until you are ready."

"I just told you I was ready."

He laid his head on her thigh and smiled at her, his fingers continuing to work in and out of her body. "You're not ready, sweetheart."

A flash of annoyance crossed her face before she blinked at him. "What?"

"Mads, as of twenty minutes ago, you implied you would strangle me if I touched you tonight. Trust me, you are not ready."

"But you're touching me now."

He bent to suck on her clitoris, and she gasped in the most appealing fashion. He smiled. "I am most definitely touching you."

"You are being deliberately obtuse."

"And if you can still speak in complete sentences, then I am not performing my husbandly duties properly." He curled his fingers inside her, rubbing the spongy tissue on the upper wall of her vagina. Maddie's entire body twitched and she let out a hoarse cry. He gave her a long lick in appreciation.

"Harrison, stop. Get undressed. I need you now."

So commanding. He loved it. Still, he ignored her. Instead, he tried another finger, rewarded when her body accommodated the thickness. How many orgasms could he give her tonight? Four?

All of a sudden, she pushed his head away and struggled to sit up. He frowned at her. "Where are you going?"

"You are not listening to me." She yanked one suspender off his shoulder, then reached for the other. "Clothes off."

Chuckling, he stilled her hand. "I love your enthusiasm but—"

"Stop laughing. This isn't a game."

He softened his tone. "There is no rush. We have a lifetime to enjoy one another."

"Now there is no rush?" Her lips flattened, eyes flashing. "You infuriating man. Hurry up. I want a real wedding night."

That caught him by surprise. "You do?"

"Yes, I do." She shoved the other suspender down, then began unbuttoning his trousers.

My God. She was serious. His erection throbbed, desperate for her, and he found himself standing and quickly shedding his clothes before he even realized what was happening. While he removed his shirt, she opened the placket of his trousers and slid her hand inside. Warm pressure closed over his cock and his knees buckled as lust exploded in his groin. Cursing, he closed his eyes.

"I don't know, Harrison," she cooed. "You don't feel quite ready to me."

A strangled sound left his throat as he removed her hand. "If I am any more ready, I will spend before we even begin. Take off your drawers."

She did as he asked, untying and sliding off her drawers and stockings as he removed his union suit and socks. When he was naked, he let her look her fill.

Her gaze lingered on his erection. "Are you sure you used enough fingers?"

Cool air kissed the heated skin of his cock and he couldn't resist stroking it. Each pass of his hand was excruciating bliss and delicious torture. "No, probably not. But we may do all manner of other things besides fucking."

Delicate brows shot up at the word. "You have a wicked mouth, Harrison Archer."

"I think you like it. In fact"—he tipped his chin toward her cunt—"I *know* you like it."

She reclined on the divan, all feminine grace and supple skin, and he hardly knew where to start. He wanted to touch and kiss her everywhere. When she parted her thighs, he could hardly draw air into his lungs.

He hoped this wasn't something he'd regret

later, but he was starving for her. And she wanted a proper wedding night. He had to make this as comfortable for her as possible.

Slipping his hands under her back and behind her knees, he lifted her just enough to slide underneath her body. Then he twisted her so she straddled him, her core on top of his shaft. She was hot and wet, and the proximity to that tight heaven was almost too much to bear.

She put her hands on his stomach. "I don't understand. Won't it be harder for you to take my virginity this way?"

"It's not mine to take, it's yours to give." With a hand on her hip, he raised her slightly and placed his tip at her entrance. "Lower yourself down at whatever pace you need. It'll hurt less this way." He didn't actually know this as fact, as he'd never fucked a virgin before, but the general physics of it made sense.

"Oh." Biting her lip, she wriggled a bit, and Harrison actually thought he might die as the fat head of his cock worked its way inside her channel. This was so much better than he'd imagined . . . and he'd imagined it plenty over the years. Impossible to think he would last.

He ground his teeth together, struggling to hold out. "And if you change your mind, we can stop."

"I won't change my mind."

She sounded determined, but the first time was more difficult for women. Licking his thumb, he pressed it to her clitoris and began rubbing her, hoping to relax and excite her. "You're so beautiful," he whispered, moving his other hand to her breast. "I loved putting my mouth between your legs."

Moaning, she slid down, taking more of him inside. He continued to talk to her, praising her, and it went on like this for several long moments, her pussy squeezing his cock like a fist the entire time. He performed square root calculations in his head so as to not come too quickly.

"It feels good," she said, her voice full of wonder, as if the fact surprised her.

He clenched his muscles, trying not to thrust upward until she was ready. "I'm glad, sweetheart." His thumb kept working the nub atop her sex, his other fingers teasing her nipple, and she rocked her hips, chasing the pleasure.

Inch by torturous inch he tunneled deeper, her body sucking him inside. Her arousal coated his cock, the most provocative sight he'd ever seen. When she bottomed out on his erection, she was panting, her eyes wide. "Now what?"

"Now you move."

THERE HADN'T BEEN pain. Maddie could hardly believe it. Pressure, and perhaps a slight pinch, but that was all. And now Harrison was seated inside her body, the two of them joined in the most basic and elemental way, her first and only lover. Her husband. The way he stared at her, as if she were the moon and stars and peppermint ice cream all rolled into one, made her relax.

And what he was doing with his hands had her squirming for more.

"Move, Mads," he said again. "Do what feels good."

"All of it feels good."

He let out a rough laugh. "I am dying for friction. Please, have mercy."

Ah. She lifted up, until he was barely inside, and then sank back down. Harrison's eyes screwed shut, his face carved in torturous angles. "That's it," he groaned.

She continued to roll her hips, Harrison stretched out beneath her, his arms clenched at his sides as if struggling for control. He was absolutely gorgeous, from the hollow at the base of his throat to the strong chest with its light dusting of dark hair and flat nipples. Muscles and sinew sculpted his frame, one that had filled out since college. She hadn't seen him shirtless in years, but she'd never dreamed he would look this appealing as a grown man.

He grabbed her hips with both hands and began rocking her, pressing her down into his pelvis. Her clitoris dragged over his pubic bone and sparks shot down her legs, through her womb, on every pass. Pleasure built as her muscles tightened, and she began helping him, grinding down, moving faster, chasing the peak just out of reach. He shoved up on an elbow and wrapped his lips around her nipple, sucking hard, laving with his tongue, and she could feel the answering tug between her legs. Bliss crashed over her, the orgasm swift and slightly less intense than before, but no less enjoyable. She cried out, her nails digging into his stomach as he rode it out with her.

"Oh, God. Hurry, Maddie."

His plea sounded far away, her brain still spinning and sparkling. Then, before she'd stopped twitching, he angled her higher, brought his knees up and began thrusting from below. She held on, her breasts bouncing with every rough slap of his body, watching his handsome face as it twisted, grimaced, snarled . . . until he quickly moved her aside, his hand flying over his shaft as he pumped and squeezed. Jets of spend erupted from the tip and onto his stomach as the carriage house echoed with his shouts.

When he slowed, she collapsed at his side, partially draped atop him as she tried to catch her breath. He released his shaft and closed his eyes, his chest heaving. There was no hint of his thoughts on his face. Was he regretting that she'd talked him into this?

"I'm not sorry," she said.

He blinked a few times before meeting her gaze. "What would you be sorry about?"

"About demanding a wedding night."

The edges of his mouth curled up. "I am not complaining. I just need some time to recover."

She took in his lithe limbs, the softening penis between his legs. The area between her own legs pulsed with swollen contentment. "I hadn't expected you to be so proficient at this."

"Only because it's you. It's not always like this."

"It's not?"

He let out a strangled sound. "No, never. It's usually good but . . ."

"But?"

Pushing a lock of hair behind her ear, he said quietly, "It's amazing because it's you and me. Together."

Warmth bloomed in her chest and wrapped

around her heart like vines. She wasn't used to this tender and honest side of him. "You're very sweet for a man who put slugs in my shoe as a boy."

A slow grin spread across his face. "Once. I did that once. And you deserved it."

Sitting up, he reached for his undergarment, then used it as a cloth to wipe away the traces of his orgasm. "Too bad we aren't at the chateau. We could go swim in the ocean to clean off."

The idea appealed, but she wondered over the inspiration. "Was that something you did in France? Nude bathing in the Seine?"

"No. I'd be too afraid of what's floating in there."

He didn't elaborate and her curiosity got the better of her. "I want to hear about your life in Paris."

"I'll tell you anything you wish to know once I have you in the bath. Shall we go in now?"

His frown made it clear that he dreaded walking back into the Archer house. "I think we should sleep out here."

He shook his head. "Don't be ridiculous. We don't have blankets or pillows, let alone running water. You'll be miserable."

"I don't want to force you to spend the night in there."

Bending, he pressed a soft kiss to her lips. "You're not forcing me to do anything. Help me make new memories in there to replace the old ones."

It was impossible to argue with that logic. They gathered their clothing, donning only what was necessary for a mad dash back to the cottage. Harrison also grabbed the cold champagne bottle before dousing the lights in the carriage house.

He took her hand and led her through the house, which smelled of lemon polish. The cottage must have been closed before Harrison had it opened for their wedding night. She wondered if his mother planned to come out for the summer this year. Maddie did not anticipate sharing meals and holidays with her new mother-in-law.

Perhaps she and Harrison would move to Paris, far away from the Archers. Hadn't he said he wished to return?

Another matter we must discuss.

Though it was empty, the mood in the house was somber, with its dark woods and lack of personal touches. No flowers or family paintings. No silhouettes or photographs. When his father had been alive, anyone in the house had to walk softly and speak in whispers so as to not disturb him. It had been a depressing place to visit.

They ended up in Harrison's smaller chambers. Thomas had been given the bigger room between the boys, but Harrison claimed not to mind. His room had a large oak tree near the window, with a branch he'd used as a means of escape.

He dropped her hand but continued to the washroom. The water started running as she wandered around the bedchamber, curious to see if bits of the old Harrison were still here. The wardrobe held the clothing the staff had just unpacked and the mantel was bare, with no books or knickknacks. There was a side table by the bed with a single drawer. She peeked inside and saw a handful of items stuffed in there . . . including a very specific old coin. It was the one she found on the beach years ago and gave to Harrison for his sixteenth birthday.

He'd kept it all this time.

Smiling, she picked up the small metal piece and carried it into the washroom. He was fiddling with the taps on the claw-foot tub, but turned at her approach. "Water's taking forever to get hot."

She held out the coin. "You saved it."

"Of course I did. Best birthday present I ever received."

"I didn't think you even liked it."

"Maddie, a sixteen-year-old boy cannot show a girl how much she means to him. It would be embarrassing."

"Is this back to you wanting me even then?"

"Yes. Does that make you uncomfortable?"

"No, but I can't believe I never knew. Why didn't you say anything at the time?"

He scratched his jaw, then busied himself with the water. The temperature must have been to his liking because he stood and started removing the little clothing he had on. "Let's get clean and we'll talk. All right?"

"So you'll bathe first?"

A devious smile twisted his lips. "We'll bathe together."

"In that tiny tub?"

"You'll see. Just get undressed, Mads."

He sank down into the water, causing some to

slosh out of the tub and onto the tile floor. As she stripped off her things, he watched her avidly, not even pretending to give her privacy. So strange to have a husband now, a man who had seen her naked. Had been inside her body. Had licked and kissed her everywhere. Her life had changed in an instant . . . and yet this felt right.

She went to the opposite end of the tub and started to get in. He waved her toward him. "Down here, beautiful." Sitting up, he spread his thighs.

"Oh. I see." She climbed in and sat between his legs, her back to his chest. It was surprisingly comfortable. "You must think I'm foolish."

"Why would I think that?" He settled them together and wrapped an arm around her front. "Because you've never taken a bath with a man before?"

"That, and everything else. I feel like these past three years have changed both of us. Except for what the gossip columns reported, there's this missing hunk of time, starting with when you left New York."

He smoothed her hair back, pushing a damp strand behind her ear. "My time in Paris wasn't half as exciting as the rumors made it sound."

"Still, I'd like to know about it. That, and why you left."

A long exhale rumbled in his chest. "There were two reasons I left. Do you remember the ball during your debut, the one at the chateau?"

"Yes. My mother insisted on hosting the ball in Newport rather than the city."

He cupped water in his hand and dribbled

it over her breasts, causing her to shiver. "Late in the evening that night, I went outside with Preston. He had cigarettes and convinced me to smoke one with him. So we were outside, shivering in the spring air, smoking in an alcove below the terrace where no one would see us."

"How rebellious of you."

"Preston always could talk me into doing stupid things. Anyway, you came outside with a few girls and I heard one of them ask you about me. About whether we would marry."

She searched her brain for the memory but came up empty. "What was my answer?"

He paused and put his hands on the sides of the tub. "You said you could never be interested in marrying me, that you thought of me like a brother." A harsh laugh followed. "Preston got me out of there immediately. He didn't even ask, just piled me in his carriage and took me home."

"I don't understand."

"I was devastated, Maddie. I had waited years for you to debut, patiently biding my time until I could properly court you. Hadn't you wondered why either my friends or I were at every event that first year? We were trying to keep the others away from you."

"Kit, Preston and Forrest all knew?"

"Yes. Jesus, they teased me about it mercilessly."

"Because you wished to court me."

"Again, yes."

This was surreal. All this time and she never had a clue. It was true that she'd thought of Harrison as a brother back then. However, that didn't mean her opinion of him couldn't change. She'd definitely appreciated his looks from time to time while they were growing up, and there had been moments of jealousy when he paid attention to other women at the society events. So perhaps the idea of *more* between them had been brewing for a while.

Why hadn't he ever said anything?

"If you wished to court me, then why didn't you?"

"I think the answer was fairly clear when you said I was like your brother," he said, dryly.

"That caused you to leave New York? To leave the *country*?" Her voice went up a few octaves, anger shaking her and the water around them. He hadn't even given her a chance to explain, to reconsider. Just disappeared from her life for three years without a word. "Why didn't you talk to me about it?"

"Are we having our first fight as a married couple?" he teased in her ear. "Because I hear the best part is making up afterwards."

Chapter Eighteen

Harrison's attempt at lightening the mood clearly fell flat because Maddie turned and pinned him with a hard stare. "This is serious. You left for three years without a word and only returned when your father died. If we want this marriage to work, then we must be honest with one another."

Though she was gorgeous when she was angry, and his cock had definitely taken notice, he nodded once. "You're right. Forgive me." He settled her on his chest again, kissing the top of her head.

"You should have talked to me about it. I might have changed my mind. Indeed, I did change my mind." She indicated the two of them sitting in the tub.

"But only after some time apart. Who knows? Maybe we both needed it, to grow up, then reconnect. When I left, I honestly never thought I had a chance with you."

"Nevertheless, between leaving three years ago and scheming for this house party, it feels as if you are making decisions without consulting me."

Fair point, though at the time, it seemed he had no choice. "I'll try to be better."

"I am serious, Harrison. You know how I hate to be surprised."

"I am well aware. You have my word it won't happen again."

She relaxed. "You said there were two reasons why you left."

"Ah. The second reason was my father." He stroked her arms with his fingertips, enjoying the goose bumps that pebbled on her skin following his touch. "I came home early that night, much earlier than expected. Mother and Thomas were still at the ball, but Winthrop had stayed here. When I rushed in, looking for the most expensive bottle of spirits I could find, I discovered my father taking advantage of a maid on the sofa." Harrison could still see his father's pale backside and the maid's pinched expression, as if she were in pain but daren't say anything.

Maddie gasped, a hand coming up to cover her mouth. "That's terrible. I had no idea he was mistreating your staff like that."

"Neither did I." He swallowed thickly. "When I confronted him, he told me to mind my own business, that no one was being hurt. I can only assume he convinced himself that the maids somehow enjoyed it. But then, he never could admit wrongdoing, so why would this be any different?"

"What a horrible man." She grabbed his right hand and threaded their fingers together. "Those poor girls."

"Exactly. I had to do something, so the next

morning I contacted the police. They came, spoke to my father alone and left. As far as I know, they never talked to the maids."

"No doubt he scared the girls into not talking or reporting it. He probably paid off the officers who came to investigate, too."

"Yes, that's what I assumed as well." He exhaled and shook his head. "As soon as the police left, he started in on me. Told me I was a disgrace, a wastrel, and he never wanted to see me again. There was no reason to stay after that."

"I'm sorry. You deserved a better father."

He squeezed her in gratitude. "The maids deserved a better employer. Believe me, I had a long talk with the housekeeper before I went."

"Did she know?"

"She claimed not to be aware of what my father was doing. Anyway, I wrote a note of warning and asked her to show it to all the female employees, present and future. I've always wished I could have done more."

"Do you think your mother or brother had any idea?"

"I've always wondered. Mother never stood up to Winthrop over anything and Thomas was the golden boy, the heir apparent and all that. If Thomas did know, there's every chance he'd stay quiet to protect his interests."

Which was why Harrison felt no remorse whatsoever about ruining every member of his family. He would take everything they had, from the house to the company. And it would happen in a matter of weeks.

He hadn't told Maddie about his plans. She

was light and sunshine, kindness and generosity. The Archers were the complete opposite of her, himself included. No matter what, he had to shield her from his family and their destructive influence. He would deal with them on his own, swiftly and completely, and Maddie could focus on her tournament.

The last thing he wanted was for her to worry or get distracted right before Nationals. He'd already upended her life. How could he compound it by bringing his family troubles to her doorstep just as she was about to compete in the biggest tournament of her life?

He'd spare her anything, if possible. He loved Maddie beyond measure, beyond reason. While she'd never love him as deeply in return, he hoped she developed feelings for him someday, feelings beyond lust and desire. He wanted to mean more to her than a childhood friend, the man who'd compromised her into marriage.

He wanted to mean everything.

She swished her feet in the water, regaining his attention. "I hate the idea of any woman who suffered his attentions still living in your family's house, even though he is gone. I can only imagine how traumatic it must be for them."

Harrison frowned. He hadn't considered that. Furthermore, he hadn't thought about the future of the staff once the Archers were bankrupted. "I was thinking of renting a house in the city. We could offer them a change of employment, if they wish."

She angled away to see his face. "I thought you wanted to return to Paris."

"We could live in both places."

"You wish to reside in the same city as your family? I thought the whole point was to live far away from them."

No use addressing it now, but the Archers wouldn't be able to afford New York much longer. Furthermore, he needed to remain in the city to complete the takeover of Archer Industries.

He dropped a kiss on the back of her head. "We may live wherever you like, but I'll need to go back and forth to Manhattan for some business matters. You could stay here and concentrate on your tennis while I'm gone."

"I don't care for your making these decisions without me. You haven't asked me what I'd like to do."

"What would you like to do?"

"Come with you."

How could he complain? He'd have access to her almost anytime he liked while he bankrupted his family. "As soon as I rent a place, I'll send for you."

"No need for that. We can stay at my parents' house, at least until Nationals. They'll remain here for the summer, so the house is just sitting empty."

"Good idea."

Done with talking, he let his hand slip below the water, his fingers sliding into her folds. She inhaled sharply and threw her head back, conveniently exposing her neck for his mouth. He tasted her smooth skin with his lips and tongue, certain he'd never get enough. She squirmed against his groin and his cock swelled, the stupid organ not realizing she would be too sore to go again tonight.

That was perfect, though, because he wanted to feel her climax on his tongue one more time.

He stood and lifted her out of the tub, water cascading all around them. "I like this compromise, this give-and-take in our marriage. And right now, wife, I'm in the mood to *give*."

New York City
Eighty-Second Street and Fifth Avenue

MADDIE WAS UNPACKING in her room when Preston and Kit were announced. She wasn't surprised that Harrison's friends had shown up this afternoon. They were likely worried she'd followed through on her threat to strangle her new husband last night after the wedding.

The impulse hadn't lasted long. He'd quickly rid her of her anger . . . and her clothes.

Her lower half gave a sore but satisfied squeeze at the reminder.

After her tennis practice this morning, they had bid farewell to Maddie's parents and returned to the city. Harrison was anxious to settle some "business matters" here, though he hadn't explained them other than to say it was about his trust fund. Fortunately, Maddie's tennis coach was amenable to coming back as well, so her practices would continue uninterrupted. With Nationals just weeks away, there wasn't a moment to lose.

By the time she made it downstairs, the three men were in the smoking room, a cloud of cigar smoke hanging in the air.

"There she is," Kit said, putting down his cigar and rising. "You let your husband live, I see."

"The day is still young." She let him kiss her cheek, then turned to their other friend. "Hello, Preston. We missed you in Newport."

If Kit was the life of every party, Preston Clarke was the organizer of said party. He was a planner and a builder, a force of nature. Using money he inherited from his grandmother, Preston was currently reshaping the Manhattan skyline, much to his parents' disapproval.

Tall with coal-black hair, Preston towered over her as he kissed her cheek. "If I had known there was going to be a wedding, I would have found the time. I hear it was quite the weekend up there, Mrs. Archer."

Harrison took her hand and pulled her close. "You have no idea. There were games, Preston. *Games.*"

"As I recall you enjoyed some of those games." She poked his arm.

Kit pointed at them, his gaze turning speculative as he retook his seat. "I knew something happened in that changing room."

Maddie could feel heat working its way under her skin, along the back of her neck. "I'll never tell."

Preston motioned to the lit cigar in the crystal ashtray. "Will this bother you?"

"No," she answered. "Besides, I don't plan on staying long. I have some errands to run."

Kit cleared his throat and exchanged a strange look with Harrison. "Like visiting friends?"

She frowned. "I need to order a few things

from Lord and Taylor's, if you must know. But now I have to wonder why you are asking."

The mood in the room shifted, growing serious, and Kit and Preston turned to Harrison, as if waiting for him to explain. Her husband grimaced. "Probably best if you wait a few weeks before going out on social calls, Mads."

A sinking feeling settled in her stomach. "Why?"

"The last few days have caused a bit of a brouhaha."

The duke. The scandal. How could she have forgotten? She had been living in a bubble of unexpected happiness when the rest of the city was agog at her shocking behavior. She slumped in her chair. "Oh."

"It's not so bad," Kit rushed to say. "You know how these old biddies get."

Preston blew out a stream of smoke. "Exactly. Don't give it a second thought, Maddie."

As if that was possible. "Was it mentioned in the morning papers?"

No one spoke for a long, terrifying moment, which was an answer in itself. She looked at her husband. "Have you seen it? What did they say?"

"You shouldn't worry over it. Focus on tennis and getting settled here for the next few weeks."

Wrong answer.

Without waiting for anyone to give her the truth, she went to the bell and rang.

"Maddie, please," Harrison called after her. "Why do you care what anyone thinks?"

She ignored him and waited at the door. A footman appeared seconds later. "William, please bring me the morning papers."

The footman cast a nervous glance across the room at Harrison. Had her husband given orders to keep the papers away from her? She moved to block the footman's view of the room. "William, the papers. Now, please."

When she returned to her seat, the men were watching her warily. "Perhaps we should go," Preston said cautiously to Kit, "and leave the two lovebirds alone."

"Stay where you are," Maddie ordered. "If anyone is leaving, it's me."

"Since when do you pay attention to the gossip columns?" Harrison asked. "New York society means nothing outside these twenty or thirty blocks on the island."

Not true—and he knew it. Otherwise, why try and hide the papers from her?

William returned with an armful of newsprint. He handed the stack to Maddie, then gave Harrison a glance that looked suspiciously like an apology. Maddie couldn't worry about her husband's high-handedness at the moment. She had bigger worries, like what was being said about her all over town.

She flipped to the "Town Talk" column, assuming it would be the worst of the lot.

NEWPORT SURPRISE WEDDING

A popular heiress has married the youngest Mr. A_____ last evening in a private ceremony at the bride's parents' home. This comes as quite the surprise, as she made no secret of her pursuit of a certain duke this past spring, finally landing His Grace's attentions and dashing hopes up and down Fifth Avenue.

From all reports, the future bride and groom spent their time on long walks and swims alone at night, forgetting, one supposes, that she had accepted the duke's proposal just hours before. Perhaps this second son of a venerable Manhattan family tired of trying to earn a fortune and decided to marry one instead. We only hope this tainted brush does not paint an unflattering picture of New York's girls across the pond.

Mortification roasted her from the inside. Of course the column painted her as a floozy, skulking about the Newport evenings with Harrison and flaunting an affair under the duke's nose. A "tainted brush." Was that how everyone saw her now, as tainted?

You knew this would happen. Why are you even surprised?

Because the reality was far worse than her imagining. Her stomach cramped and she couldn't move, hardly able to breathe. There was no point in running errands or paying social calls, going out to dinner or seeing a play. Until the next scandal came along, Maddie would be discussed and dissected from Thirty-Fourth to Eighty-Eighth streets. A cautionary tale mothers would tell their daughters for the next ten years.

Don't be like that Webster girl, the one who was compromised and lost a duke.

"Fellows, if you'll excuse us." Harrison stubbed out his cigar and looked at his friends pointedly.

Kit and Preston offered hasty farewells and strode from the room. Maddie hardly noticed. She kept thinking about Harrison's words in the gazebo, the prophetic promise he made about her and Lockwood.

I won't let you marry him.

Why hadn't she heeded those words? If she had, this could have been handled with more delicacy, quietly. But no, she allowed herself to be compromised and humiliated.

Suddenly, she was lifted up in strong arms, carried to the sofa and placed on Harrison's lap as he sat. The warmth of his body surrounded her as he nestled her into the cradle of his arms, and she pressed her face to his throat. He smelled like cigars and leather. "I am not sorry we are married," he whispered into her hair. "But I am sorry that anyone would dare speak ill of you because of it."

Sighing, she closed her eyes. "I've never been at the center of a scandal before. It feels awful, like I've disappointed everyone." Lockwood, her parents, her friends . . . the guilt was threatening to crush her at the moment. "I wish I'd let you hide the papers from me."

"I'll always try to spare you any pain, if possible."

She stared at the cold hearth, the unfairness of their world pressing down on her. "Men never suffer for their indiscretions. Society looks the other way, allowing them their mistresses and chorus girls. You are barely mentioned in that column and Lockwood is the poor man caught up in my schemes. I, on the other hand, am the jezebel. None of my friends will speak to me for a long time, let alone invite me anywhere, after this."

He kissed the top of her head and squeezed her. "I'm sorry, Mads. I don't know what else to say."

"Why did you stay away so long?" If he'd come home sooner, then all of this might have been avoided.

"Because I wanted you too much, even when I thought there was no chance. It tore my heart out every day. I couldn't be around you and not have you."

"Harrison . . ." It was hard to remain upset with him when he confessed like that. "Stop being sweet when I am annoyed with you."

A slight chuckle ruffled her hair. "I cannot help it. I've always hated to see you sad."

"I hate being sad."

"Just remember—they will move on in time. Another scandal will take the place of ours. This won't last long. And it'll be worth it in the end."

"It will?"

"Of course. You'll still be married to me."

She rolled her eyes, even though he couldn't see it. "You have a healthy opinion of yourself."

"Hmm. As I recall, you were calling me a god this morning."

Ignoring that comment, she put a hand on his

shoulder and leaned back. "Aren't you upset about the column, too? They practically labeled you a fortune hunter."

"They can write whatever they wish, but that doesn't mean it's true. Unlike Lockwood, I don't need your money."

"Yes, but your mother was going to cut you off if you didn't marry."

"Hmm."

A sinking feeling settled into her chest, below her ribs. Deep into her bones. This wasn't adding up. What was he withholding from her? "Harrison?"

His chest expanded and fell as he exhaled. "I'm not broke . . . but the Archers are."

Chapter Nineteen

The words tumbled from Harrison's mouth but he wouldn't take them back. He'd intended to tell her the truth after her tennis tournament, but she deserved to know that he wasn't a fortune hunter. That he'd married her because he wanted her, period.

Maddie stiffened then jumped off his lap to stand in front of him. "Explain."

"I have my own money."

"And the other part, about your family?"

He folded his arms across his chest and lifted a shoulder. "They're broke."

Her mouth fell open but she quickly recovered, her lips pressing flat. "You lied to me."

"Well . . ." He could feel the ground tilting, shifting, under his feet in the face of her disapproval. But he'd started this so there was no choice but to finish it. Carefully. "Not entirely. I said my mother had threatened to cut me off if I didn't marry, but the reality is my father cut me off years ago."

"Wait." Closing her eyes, Maddie put her hands

together under her chin, as if she were praying. He knew she often did this when struggling for calm. "Start at the very beginning, Harrison."

So he began talking. He told her of being disinherited and how he'd made his own fortune in Paris. The telegrams from his brother, which had prompted Harrison to hire an investigator into the Archer company finances. Then his efforts to buy up company stock over the next few months.

"You plan to save the company for them?"

"No," he said. "I plan to take the company from them."

"You want to buy Archer Industries for yourself."

"Yes, but I want more than that. I aim to bankrupt them."

"Your family?" After he nodded, she stumbled to an armchair and dropped heavily into it. "When were you going to tell me all of this?"

He sat forward and reached for her hand, clasping her fingers tightly. "I was not keeping secrets from you. I hoped to spare you from my family's drama, especially before Nationals. The Archers have caused enough destruction already."

"Wrong. That explanation is sensible for a petty squabble, not when you are planning to wage war on them. Do you understand the difference?"

"I suppose, though I will try to protect you from any ugliness if it is in my power to do so. Specifically in regard to my family."

She jerked her hand out of his grip. "By lying to me? There shouldn't be any secrets between us. We're *married*."

"I am aware." As if he'd ever forget. "And I didn't exactly lie."

"Semantics. I don't like being surprised like this, feeling as though you are keeping things from me."

"Maddie, if someone finds out what I am doing, the stock price will be affected."

She slapped her thighs and stood. "Oh, well. We cannot affect the precious stock price." Putting her hands on her hips, she looked at him sharply. "Stock prices, bankruptcies, French mistresses . . . Who are you?"

How could she even ask such a question? No one knew him better than Maddie. He rose and took a step toward her. "I am the same man you've known since you were ten. Nothing has changed."

"Not from what I can see. It's like the kind yet impulsive boy I knew has grown into this other secretive person, one obsessed with revenge and ambition."

"And you. Don't forget I am also obsessed with *you*."

"That doesn't make me any less angry about the rest of it." She paced away a few steps, then faced him. "You're rich."

"Very."

"Yet you led me to believe you still relied on your family's money."

"I didn't think it mattered to you whether I had my own money or not."

"It doesn't but I would like the truth. I want a partnership, Harrison, one where we play on the same side. Ours."

Ours. He liked the sound of that.

And she was wrong. They had a partnership. He was on her side no matter what, indefinitely. Once he bankrupted his family, Maddie would be his first and only priority.

He didn't want her to doubt it—ever.

Swiftly, he closed the distance between them. She watched him warily but didn't retreat. When he was within reach, he slipped his hand around the side of her neck, his thumb resting on her jaw. His other hand found her hip as he pressed their foreheads together. "We are partners," he whispered. "We always have been, since the very first moment I met you. It's why no one would team up against us in croquet or acting charades. Why I sought you out every time something terrible happened at home. Why I need you by my side until I draw my last breath. It is you and me, Mads. No one else."

She drew in a shaky breath as her fingers hooked into the waistband of his trousers. "Then act like it. That means not keeping things from me anymore."

"I won't. I promise." He kissed her brow. "Are we done fighting?"

"No." She kissed his throat, right above his collar. "I am still mad."

"Shall we go upstairs? I'll spend the rest of the afternoon apologizing in bed."

She stepped away and put distance between them. "I won't settle for a mediocre apology."

He gave her a smile full of wicked promise. "Who said anything about mediocre?"

"Don't be cute. Not all of our problems can be solved in bed."

They couldn't? "Then where should we solve them?"

"I don't know, Harrison," she said, her tone full of exasperation. "But 'Let's go upstairs' is not the answer after you've lied to me about almost everything. Do better." With a heavy sigh, she lifted her skirts and started for the door.

"Wait, where are you going?"

"To get changed. I feel like hitting tennis balls right now and pretending they are your head."

Ouch. "I could change and play with you."

She paused on the threshold. "No, thank you. I'd like to be alone."

"Maddie . . ." Frustrated, he ran his fingers through his hair. He'd bungled this. One day of marriage and he'd already caused a rift between them. He had to find a way to mend it.

Years of experience had taught him to give her space, yet everything in him fought against that instinct. He wanted the laughter and the easy camaraderie, the way she smiled at him. And yes, he wanted to take her upstairs and pleasure her until she screamed his name.

It would kill him to stay away . . . but he couldn't chase her. Couldn't push her into forgiving and forgetting.

He slipped his hands in his trouser pockets, grinding his back teeth together as she disappeared into the house.

"Do better, Harrison," she called.

He had to find a way to apologize, to make things right, but in a way that meant something to her. Only he had no idea where to begin.

* * *

THE BELL SOUNDED, echoing through the still house and startling Maddie. No one had so much as dropped a card or sent a telegram since the wedding. Had someone come to pay her a visit?

In the past, she would have hurried to the door and greeted the caller herself. Now she paused just inside the library, nervously waiting to hear who was there.

Coward.

It was true. She hardly recognized herself, hiding out in the house and feeling sorry for herself. It was unlike her. Harrison seemed concerned, as well, watching her carefully while they had dinner last night. She was still angry at him for lying, and he hadn't joined her in bed afterward. A relief really, as she was still sore.

Liar. You weren't relieved. You were disappointed.

Yes, she had been disappointed. However, she didn't want to start their marriage off with lies and half-truths. He needed to be honest with her about everything. She didn't like being caught unawares . . . and it seemed as if Harrison had done nothing but surprise her since returning from Paris.

A familiar voice sounded in the entryway. Hiding place forgotten, Maddie darted toward the front door, beyond relieved to have a friend with whom to talk.

Nellie's eyes went round when she saw Maddie hurrying toward her. "My, someone is antsy today."

"I am happy to see you." She threw her arms around Nellie.

After requesting tea from the kitchen, she led

her friend into the sitting room. "How did you know I was in New York?"

"Your husband. He cabled me this morning and asked me to pay you a visit." Nellie unpinned her hat. "How have you been holding up?"

Maddie blew out a frustrated breath. "Miserable. Please, entertain me."

Nellie paused in the midst of lowering herself onto the sofa. "May I rest for a moment and perhaps eat a cookie first?"

"Of course. Forgive me."

"Forgiven. Now, why are you miserable? Aren't you and Harrison getting along?"

"I suppose."

Nellie's brows rose. "You suppose? You've been married almost three days. Did you get along on your wedding night? And every night since?"

Ah. She should have known her friend would ask about this. It was Nellie, after all. "Yes, there's no problem with *getting along*."

"Good. I knew Harrison picked up a trick or two in Paris. I'm happy for you, Maddie."

"I should thank you for what you said before the wedding night. It helped."

"Good. Women don't talk about these things often enough. We rely on men to tell us—and you know how informative they can be. There should be some kind of guidebook or something."

"You should write one," Maddie suggested. "I would buy it."

"I'm no writer. I think all that typing would drive me mad, not to mention all the euphemisms I'd be forced to use. Can you imagine? 'When you lavish attention on his manly pole . . .'"

"'Be prepared to receive it in your feminine hole.'" They both burst into peals of laughter.

"Terrible. Absolutely terrible. Never take up poetry over lawn tennis." Nellie's gaze turned serious. "Though I am glad to see you smile."

"It's been rough."

"Why? I thought you said you and Harrison were *getting along*."

"Have you not read the papers? Everyone in the city is talking about me."

Frowning, Nellie sat back. "This city is much bigger than Fifth Avenue and high society. And you must ignore the small-minded people with nothing better to do than gossip."

Harrison had said the same, but it was hard, especially when she hadn't faced this sort of thing before. "I'll try."

Nellie pursed her lips, her gaze thoughtful. "Was this why I was summoned? Because you are hiding out in the house?"

Maddie grimaced. "I'm not exactly hiding. I am trying to let the scandal blow over before I venture out."

Sighing, Nellie stood. "Let's go. I am getting you out of here."

"I can't leave."

"That's ridiculous. Of course you may leave. Come on, we'll go together."

"No. I don't want to face them."

"We're not paying a call to Caroline Astor's house, Maddie. We are going to Graham's Ice Cream Parlor."

"I'm supposed to be on my honeymoon."

"Yet your husband is no doubt traipsing about

around town. Why are you not allowed to do the same?"

That was a good point—not that Harrison had asked her to stay inside. She'd hidden of her own volition once the story of the broken engagement and compromise hit the newspapers.

"So it's settled," Nellie announced. "Move your backside off that chair. You need to get out."

It was tempting. Graham's was close, just a few blocks away. The ice cream parlor was patronized by the masses, not only members of society, most of whom were in Newport at this time of year, anyway. So while Graham's might be busy, there was little chance she'd see anyone she knew. "I'll go if you promise two things. One, you won't leave my side, and two, that we'll leave should we find it crowded."

"I solemnly swear." Nellie waved her hand impatiently. "Get moving."

Ten minutes later they entered the ice cream parlor. The walk had been uneventful, and Maddie breathed a sigh of relief when the shop was empty. They found a table and sat in the small iron chairs.

"See?" Nellie opened her menu. "No society matrons chasing you with pitchforks."

"Yet, anyway," Maddie murmured as she flipped through the menu pages.

They placed their orders and relaxed. It was rude to dump her marital troubles on her friend, but Maddie had always been close to Nellie. "Harrison finally confessed the reason for the house party."

"To get time with you in order to convince you to marry him?"

"How did you know?"

"Maddie, please. Most everyone there was aware of it. He did a poor job of hiding his feelings for you."

"Well, were you aware that he was cut off from his family and made a fortune in Paris?"

"No, but it's reassuring he's not a layabout like most of these society gents. There's nothing more boring than a spoiled, entitled man."

Maddie drummed her fingers on the table. "How are you so sanguine in the face of everything?"

"Must be due to losing my mother at an early age." Nellie lifted a shoulder. "Life is fleeting. We have to enjoy it while we're here."

Reaching out, Maddie clasped her friend's hand. "That makes perfect sense."

Nellie smiled and squeezed Maddie's hand in return. When they pulled apart, she asked, "So you and Harrison have been fighting?"

"Yes. It turns out he's full of surprises."

"Good surprises or bad surprises?"

"Both?"

"Ah, I see what's going on here." Nellie's gaze turned shrewd. "Someone is annoyed that her best friend went off and grew wings without her."

"That is ridiculous. I am annoyed that he lied about it."

"Fine, but you expect to catch up on three years of separate lives in one day? That's not realistic, Maddie."

"You're saying to forgive him."

"Nellie!"

They both turned at the sound of the familiar voice. Katherine Delafield stopped beside their table, a wide grin on her face. "And Maddie. Hello to you both. Fancy seeing you here."

"Hello, Kat," Nellie said.

"Katherine," Maddie greeted with relief. Another friend who hadn't snubbed her. "It's so nice to see you."

"You too. How is—"

Katherine's aunt walked up, a deep scowl on her face, and the conversation died. Maddie's throat dried out in the presence of the matronly disapproval raining down on her like a thunder cloud. "Good afternoon, Mrs. Delafield," she automatically said.

Katherine's aunt did not acknowledge Maddie's words. She lifted her chin and pushed gently on Katherine's shoulder. "Come along. We must find a table far away from anyone who is considered a bad influence."

"But Aunt Dahlia—"

"Move, Katherine."

I'm sorry, Katherine mouthed as her aunt tugged her toward the back of the shop.

"Welcome to the bad influence club," Nellie said with an attempt at levity in her voice, but it rang hollow.

A stone settled in Maddie's stomach as she watched the older woman march away from the table. This outing had been a mistake. "Nellie, I'm not hungry. I should return home."

"No, stay," Nellie said. "The ice cream—"

"Really, I should go." She pushed her chair back and stood. "Thank you for coming to see me. We'll catch up later."

Though the urge to flee burned through her muscles, she forced herself to take reasonable, unhurried steps to the door. As soon as she was outside, she dragged in a bracing lungful of warm city air. The backs of her lids tingled with tears as she walked, but she held them off. Crying wouldn't do her any good.

As her mother liked to sometimes say, the milk had been spilled. One could only clean it up and move on.

Chapter Twenty

Maddie was restringing a tennis racket the next morning when her husband appeared. Eyeing the length of him through her lashes, she had to admit he looked quite dashing today, in a cream-colored summer suit and beige vest. Had any man ever worn clothing better?

Though he was spectacular out of clothing, as well.

She bit her lip and tried to ignore the heat suddenly coursing through her. He hadn't joined her in bed last night again, either, and she'd missed him—and not merely as a means to cure her lust. She missed the physical closeness, the connection they shared. The way he made her laugh, his kisses.

He'd pushed so hard during the house party. Why was he backing off now?

Because he's already won you. He doesn't have to try any longer.

That was a depressing thought.

His mouth curved into a half smile as he lowered himself into the chair beside her. "Do you have time for me today?"

"When?"

"Now. I'd like to take a walk and show you something."

She glanced at the racket in her hands. "I have no interest in going out, Harrison." This shouldn't come as a surprise, seeing as how she'd informed him of the ice cream outing during dinner last night.

"It's close by and I won't take no for an answer."

"How close?"

"Three blocks."

She hedged. That wasn't far, but she didn't care to risk running into anyone on the street.

"I've just been out and no one is walking this early. Please, let me show you something. You'll like it, I swear."

"Fine."

He stood and held out his hand. "Come along, wife. Let's have some fun."

Minutes later, they were walking north on Fifth Avenue. One of her arms was linked with his, and she used her free hand to hold up a parasol to block the midmorning sun. Thankfully, he was right about the lack of morning traffic. The sidewalks were empty, with only the occasional wagon or cart in the street.

At Eighty-Fifth Street, he stopped in front of the Xavier house and tilted his head toward the massive property. "Gorgeous, isn't it?"

A sprawling Romanesque structure, the speckled-brick house had been built four years ago on a grand scale, with balconies, turrets and gables. She'd been inside a few times for various events, and had even watched a lawn tennis match in the gardens during her debut. "It is. I've always liked this house."

"I know. I remember you going on and on about it three years ago. You loved the lawn tennis court in the back."

He remembered that conversation? "I did. The Xaviers are lovely people, as well."

"Her health is failing. Did you know?"

Maddie shook her head. "I didn't. How awful. I wonder if my mother is aware." Mama and Mrs. Xavier had chaired a flower show together years back.

"I think they are keeping it quiet. He's moved her to St. Augustine."

"Florida?"

"Yes." He reached into his coat pocket and withdrew a set of keys. "Would you like to look around?"

Her jaw fell and she stared at his hands. "You have their keys?"

"I do." Dipping his head under the brim of her hat, he kissed her nose. "Come on."

Taking her hand, he led her up the bluestone walk and under the portico. She stumbled along at his side, dumbfounded. "Wait, are you serious? How on earth did you steal their keys?"

"Stop asking so many questions and play along. This will be fun."

"Harrison, this is not like sneaking into the larder for cherry pie when we were kids. This is serious. We could be arrested."

At the door, he fit the key in the lock. "I am absolutely certain we will not be arrested. Now, after you." He opened the door and swept out his hand.

She went in, positive they would be turned away at any minute. Except the entryway was empty, the lights off. The air had a stillness about it, as if the house had been shuttered a while. "Where is the staff?"

"On holiday since the Xaviers left. We're alone." He suddenly pinched her left buttock through her skirts, as if to prove it.

She yelped and pushed his shoulder. "You're a scoundrel, Mr. Archer."

Grabbing her around the waist, he pulled her close. "I am *your* scoundrel, Mrs. Archer." After exchanging a leisurely kiss, he took her hand. "Let's explore."

The house was open and airy, big rooms meant to impress. The architectural details were stunning, with intricate carvings and mammoth fireplaces, not to mention a stained-glass ceiling over the ballroom. Mr. Xavier had been an avid collector of art, and there was no shortage of classic paintings hanging on the walls.

They walked the four floors, quietly commenting to each other on the things they liked. She was most impressed by the indoor pool and the conservatory. Harrison liked the master bedroom and oak-paneled library. Their footsteps echoed on the tiled floors, and she began to suspect why he'd brought her here.

He had mentioned renting a house for the summer, but this was more square footage than they required. She'd imagined a town house on the Upper East Side, not a thirty-room mansion. Even though she did love this house, this seemed excessive.

They continued to the back of the house, finally reaching the terrace that overlooked the gardens. Outlines of a lawn tennis court could still be seen, though the grass had become unruly. "That poor court," she murmured. "It was gorgeous a few years ago."

"It could be gorgeous again." Harrison leaned a hip against the balustrade and faced her. "With your help."

"You want to rent this house."

He shook his head, a small smile playing at his lips. "I want to *buy* this house."

"*Buy it?*"

"Wouldn't you like to stay close to your parents?"

"It's an awfully big house."

Stepping behind her, he wrapped his arms around her tightly. "I only want it if you agree. It's a great location and there is already a lawn tennis court." He kissed her cheek. "And this terrace reminds me of the chateau. Perfect for sharing cigars with you."

She relaxed into his chest, the memories heating her skin. "You almost kissed me that night."

Shifting, he cupped her jaw in his palm. His expression was filled with affection as he lowered his head. "I wanted nothing more in that moment."

She whispered, "I wanted it, as well," just before he kissed her. Gently, he nipped at her lips, delicate sweeps of his mouth that had her clinging to him within seconds. Their breath mingled in the quiet morning, with the birds as their only audience, and the entire world narrowed to just his hands, his lips and his tongue.

She was panting by the time they broke apart. He adjusted her hat, which had become askew during their kiss. "What do you think? Should we buy it?"

"Can we afford it?"

"I thought we covered this the other day, but yes, we can afford it. Would you like to live here with me?"

She could picture their lives here—with children one day, perhaps. They would make many happy memories together within these walls. It felt right. "Yes, I think I would."

"Excellent." He gave her one swift kiss, then led her back inside. "I'll have the real estate agent start on the paperwork."

By the time he locked up, more carriages were in the street, and the steady clip of hooves rang in her ears as she and Harrison crossed the street. "You found this house for us because you remembered how much I liked it," she said. "I'm impressed."

"I am trying to do better at the request of my wife."

"You don't have to buy us a house to earn my forgiveness."

"I realize that, but how could I pass up the chance to see you smile? Besides, someone else will buy this house if we don't."

"Do you have any other surprises, Harrison Archer?"

He squeezed her forearm. "Perhaps."

"Like what—"

"Harrison! Ho!"

A brougham jerked to the curb and a man jumped down to the walk. It was Thomas Archer, Harrison's brother.

"Shit," Harrison muttered under his breath, his body tensing.

Thomas didn't spare her a glance, directing his attention to his brother. "Why haven't you been answering me?"

Her husband offered no apology. "I've been busy."

"Yes, well." Thomas looked over his shoulder, as if to ensure they wouldn't be overheard. "That situation we discussed is quite urgent—"

"You remember my *wife*?" Harrison's voice was cold and brittle, a lash of reprimand.

Thomas winced and bowed in Maddie's direction. "Of course. Mrs. Archer, how nice to see you."

"Mr. Archer."

She'd never liked Harrison's brother. He was spoiled and supercilious. When they were younger, Thomas had purposely teased Harrison to elicit a reaction—one that invariably landed Harrison in trouble. It was as if Thomas tried to make himself look better at his brother's expense.

"We won't keep you from your errand," Harrison said to his brother. "Good afternoon."

"Hold up. When will you come by? We are quite anxious to see you."

"I am still on my honeymoon, Thomas. I'll deal with you in my own time."

"But—"

"Not another word," Harrison snapped. "Or that situation to which you referred will no longer be my concern." Without awaiting a response, Harrison practically dragged Maddie away, not that she could blame him. He'd suffered enough at the hands of his family.

"He still thinks you are going to save them."

"Yes, and his messages are growing desperate."

"You're allowing Thomas and your mother to boil in the stew a little longer."

His lips twisted, his eyes alight with sinister amusement. "Of course. That's half the fun."

"How close are you?"

"Close."

That was cryptic. "What about Thomas's wife and children?"

Harrison shrugged. "He'll need to find employment, I suppose, to support them."

"You have turned very hard-hearted."

"With everyone but you, Mads. Everyone but you."

"WHERE ARE YOU taking me?"

Harrison smiled at his wife, though her blindfold prevented her from seeing it. "You'll see."

Two days had passed since the ice cream parlor incident, and Maddie remained mostly quiet, subdued, which was entirely out of character for her. He hated that people were gossiping about them, crushing his wife's spirit and causing her to hide out.

The word is called guilt.

Yes, he felt guilty for what happened at the house party—not that he regretted it. She was his wife, and he'd suffer a thousand scandals to marry her.

Which was easy for him to say, he realized. Society was much harsher on women. She'd suffered these last few days, unused to being an outcast. Harrison, however, had been an outcast almost from the day he was born. Perhaps he could give her some tips.

Regardless, he longed to ease her troubles and rebuild the closeness between them. Staying away from her bed for the past three nights had been absolute torture.

"Let's go upstairs" is not the answer after you've lied to me about almost everything. Do better.

He was trying.

Morning sun warmed his skin as they stepped behind the house. Taking up nearly an entire city block, the sprawling grounds behind the Webster home contained a swimming pool and, of course, a lawn tennis court. This morning, thanks to clever subterfuge on Harrison's part, Maddie's tennis coach had canceled their session, claiming he was too ill to leave the house. And when Maddie changed into her tennis clothes, off to practice alone, Harrison had waylaid her with a blindfold.

"Harrison, I really don't have time for this. Nationals is right around the corner."

"Patience, Mads. Patience."

She huffed in annoyance and he tried not to laugh. Holding her elbow, he led her deeper into the gardens, toward the tennis court.

"I know we are outside," she said, as if that explained everything. "And if I step in something and ruin my shoes, then you will be sorry."

He couldn't hold in the chuckle. "I'll buy you new shoes if you ruin them."

"Shoes I'll need to break in before Nationals. Not to mention these are my lucky shoes."

"You don't need luck. You have talent."

They approached the court, where a man waited. He was dressed in white, performing some stretches while holding a racket in one hand.

"I know we're near the court. I can smell the roses."

He said nothing, just brought her to the edge of the short grass. Reaching, he removed her blindfold and let her blink a few times. "Maddie, I'd like you to meet—"

"Frederick Hovey," she blurted and rushed toward the other man, thrusting her hand out. "Goodness, I cannot believe it. What are you doing here?"

A rangy man with a bushy mustache, Fred had gone to Harvard Law School, a connection that had assisted in Harrison getting him here. That, and the promise of a seat on the Archer Industries board.

Fred's mouth kicked up as he shook her hand. "Mrs. Archer. You know who I am."

"Of course. I saw you play Mr. Wrenn in the '93 championships and again last year when you won your doubles championship. Your backhand cross-court return was a thing of beauty."

Harrison smiled at her proudly. This was what made Maddie such a fierce competitor. Not only did she work hard on the court, she studied off the court, as well. "He's also currently the top-ranked player in the country."

"For now," Fred qualified in an obvious attempt at humility.

"I am looking forward to seeing you at the men's singles championship in August," Maddie told him. "I think this is your year to win."

"We'll see. I assume Wrenn will be at his best, as well. He won't be easy to beat." Swinging his racket a few times, he said, "Shall we get to it?"

"Get to what?" She looked at Harrison. "I don't understand."

"Fred is here to train with you today."

The muscles in her face slackened. "Is that a joke?"

"No, absolutely not."

"I'd be honored, Mrs. Archer," Fred said. "I saw you play in Cincinnati last summer."

Another man approached the court. Maddie's coach, Valentine Livingston. A member of a prominent East Coast family, Vallie had been an outstanding doubles player before retiring from tennis the year before. He'd agreed to help Maddie train, no doubt due to pressure from her father.

"Vallie," she called, blinking in the sun. "I thought you were under the weather."

"You didn't think I would miss this, did you?" Vallie shook Fred's hand. "Hovey, a pleasure to see you again."

"Valentine." Fred pumped the other man's hand. "Came to ensure I don't undo any of your hard work, I see."

"Indeed," Vallie said with a light laugh. "We've been working on her serve for six months. I can't have you changing anything before Nationals."

"Fair enough." Fred pointed to the court. "Shall we, Mrs. Archer?"

Maddie bounced on her toes, excitement shining on her face, and Harrison's shoulders relaxed slightly. This had worked. At least for a few moments, he'd cheered her up.

She grabbed his arm and kissed his cheek. "This is the best surprise ever. Thank you."

"You are welcome. Have fun."

He waved to the two gents and went back inside. Not even nine o'clock in the morning and he already had one victory. Not too bad for a layabout wastrel.

Now, on to tackling his other problem.

The takeover of Archer Industries was close at hand, but he could not rush it. This was a game of chess, with each move strategic and careful, focused on trapping his opponents. Leaving them no choice but to surrender in the end.

And the end would be very soon.

As he walked back inside the Webster home, the butler found him. "Sir, a message was delivered for you."

Harrison took the card off the silver tray. "Thank you. Is Mr. Innis here yet?"

"He is in Mr. Webster's office, sir."

With a nod, he started for the office. "Thank you, Farley."

He glanced at the note in his hand and sneered, recognizing the stationery. The note was from either his mother or his brother, no doubt asking when their money was due to arrive. Harrison crumpled the paper in his fist without reading it. *Let them worry.*

William Innis was waiting in Webster's office. A young Black man, William was only a few years older than Harrison, and had graduated from Delaware State College with a degree in finance. While still in Paris, Harrison had hired William to oversee the takeover here in the States, and Harrison had instantly liked the other man's forthright manner and the capable way he tackled problems. William had proven indispensable in the takeover of Archer Industries the last four months.

Harrison shut the door and walked toward the desk. "Morning, William. Thank you for meeting uptown today." Since Harrison's return to the city, they had worked in William's office near Wall Street.

The other man adjusted the round glasses on his face. "I don't mind. I live directly on the other side of the park."

"I remember. Amsterdam near Eighty-Seventh, isn't it? Well, we might work up here a bit more until the takeover is finished." He wanted to remain close to Maddie in the hope that she'd soon forgive him. Not sleeping with her was driving him mad, like he was being deprived of food and water. The very air he needed to survive.

William removed a stack of papers. "Also, I've made progress on the other list, if you'd like to see it now. We acquired the last two big blocks of shares yesterday."

"Excellent. All that's left is to get the family shares."

"We talked about making your brother an offer through an anonymous company. Then he wouldn't know it was you."

"Thomas won't ever knowingly sell them. They're practically all he has left."

"Then I cannot see how to get controlling interest away from your family."

Harrison grabbed for a pencil. "I might have an idea. Let's see what we can do."

Chapter Twenty-One

$\mathcal{E}$ven Vallie was impressed with the way Maddie played against Fred Hovey—and her coach was a hard man to impress. She invited both of them to stay for lemonade, but they declined, so she shook Fred's hand vigorously. "This has been a treat. Thank you."

"As I said, it was my pleasure," Fred said as he toweled off his face. "You are fierce out there on the court, Maddie."

"I just hope I'm good enough to win at Nationals."

"Never doubt yourself. Always believe that you can do it," he said.

"Exactly what I keep telling her," Vallie said. "That, and to rush the net more often."

Fred laughed. "A player must go with his or her own instincts on that one. Vallie was always too aggressive for his own good at the net."

"Lies." Vallie shook Maddie's hand. "Great job today. I'll see you in the morning. Get some rest."

The men departed around the side of the house and Maddie nearly floated inside. She was exhausted, but it was the best kind of exhaustion, her mind happy and light. And she had her husband to thank for it.

This morning's gesture touched her, a gift utterly perfect and one that only Harrison could have pulled off. How had he arranged this? It couldn't have been easy.

I am trying to do better at the request of my wife.

No one knew her as well as he did, and he'd shown her time and time again how much he cared for her. Their wedding hadn't been perfect, true. Her dreams of a big affair at St. Thomas's Episcopal Church were dashed and she would have preferred to avoid a scandal. While none of this had been in her plans a month ago, she could not change the past.

Life is fleeting. We have to enjoy it while we're here.

Nellie was right. Did Maddie really wish to keep Harrison at a distance forever?

No, of course not. Though they'd shared dinner together the past three nights, she missed the rest of it. She wanted more of what happened during their wedding night, like the breathlessness and the anticipation. The hot kisses and the slide of his hands across her skin.

The feel of him inside her body.

Goodness, she craved that. Just thinking about that night in the carriage house melted her insides, her skin turning tight and hot, the need for him burning in her blood. Never had she imagined a man could give her so much pleasure—and she suspected it was their connection, their friendship that made it possible.

She had to see him. *Now.* Though she was

coated in perspiration and tired, she had to thank him for this surprise. Perhaps she could also distract him from whatever he was doing at the moment. A stolen hour or two where she could touch and kiss him, feel his strong shoulders and firm chest. Rub against him and hear him moan in her ear—

She nearly bumped into a footman in the corridor. "Oh, I'm sorry, Joseph." Could he see the wicked thoughts on her face?

"My apologies, madam." The young man started to go around her.

"Do you know where Mr. Archer is at the moment? Has he gone out?"

"I believe he is seeing Mr. Innis out, madam."

Perfect.

Heart pounding, she hurried toward the entryway, desperation and lust making her lightheaded. She was practically panting, nearly sweating with her need for him, the area between her legs thumping with desire. Coming around the corner, she spotted his wide shoulders in his beige coat, the long legs and the back of his head with his thick hair. The sheer handsomeness caused butterflies in her stomach.

The front door closed and Harrison turned around. Whatever he saw on her face sent his brows arching high. "Hello. Have a nice practice?"

No one else was around and she couldn't wait a second longer to get her hands on him. Not bothering to answer his question, she put her palms on his chest and pushed him toward the coat closet.

"Wait, what is happening?" He chuckled softly as she manhandled him, not resisting in the least.

Opening the closet door, she shoved him inside. He stumbled, getting tangled up in the few coats stored there. She shut them in, plunging them into semidarkness, and the light coming in under the door offered just enough illumination to make out the confusion on his face.

"Are we hiding from someone—or are we playing another game?"

She didn't want to talk. She launched herself at him, her arms wrapping around his shoulders like a mink stole while she captured his mouth. After a split second of surprise, he joined in, kissing her back feverishly. Had he been thinking about this, too? Had he needed her just as badly?

He tasted familiar, like coffee and mint, and she pressed closer, curling her fingers into his hair as their tongues worked. Their breathing echoed through the tiny space, mouths working in tandem, competing for dominance. Then he kissed her harder, his lips unforgiving against hers, relentlessly seeking her pleasure as his hands wandered.

"Upstairs." He dropped kisses along her jaw. "Let's go upstairs."

Her mind rejected the idea of leaving. *Now. Right here.*

While she wasn't keen on being surprised, she liked the idea of surprising Harrison. It was reminiscent of the changing room, a quiet, secret place where they could do all manner of wickedness together, where her inexperience and clumsy attempts at seduction wouldn't be quite

so humiliating. She'd enjoyed catching him unawares that day, hearing his breath catch and feel
his body tremble as her fingers explored him.

Also, there was something she'd been dying to
try, but hadn't worked up the nerve during their
wedding night. Here in the near dark seemed
like the perfect opportunity to make her first attempt.

Taking a small step back, she lifted her
skirts . . . and sank to her knees.

The ground was hard and unforgiving under
her bones but she hardly cared. Her face was directly in front of his groin, where the most entic-
ing erection tented her husband's trousers.

"Oh, God," he wheezed. "What are you doing?"

She reached for the fastenings, intent on getting to his skin as quickly as possible. He stayed
her hands. "Does this have to do with my surprise this morning? Because you needn't do this
to thank me."

Meeting his gaze, she pushed his hands away.
"I am doing this because I want to, and because I
hope you'll like it."

His arms hung loosely at his sides as she
started unbuttoning his clothing. When the
placket of his trousers hung open, she reached
in to unfasten his suspenders, first one side, then
the other. The trousers slithered to the floor, wool
gathering at his ankles.

"Mads, what if Farley needs to retrieve a coat?
Or someone comes to the door?"

Though it seemed highly improbable, the idea
they might get caught sent lust streaking up her

thighs and through her sex. "Then I guess you must be quick."

"Oh, shit," he breathed, his voice thick and rough.

She focused on the tiny buttons of his undergarment, pausing after a few to drag her palm over the stiff length of him. He groaned and grabbed on to the wooden rod holding up the coats. "Faster. Before I spill in my clothes."

After loosening enough buttons, she took him out and admired the thick shaft. Her fingers didn't quite meet as she circled the base, the skin so smooth and warm in her palm. Leaning in, she pressed a kiss to the tip, tasting the salty fluid gathered there. Then she licked him, and his hips shot forward as his body jerked.

"Take me in your mouth, she-devil," he growled.

Suppressing a smile at the nickname, she did as instructed, sliding the length of him past her lips and onto her tongue. It was not what she'd expected. His penis was hard and soft at the same time, like velvet stretched over bedrock, but sweet, like Harrison.

He gasped. "Look at me."

She tilted her face up, and the intensity that blazed down at her sent sparks along her spine. He stared at her mouth as if mesmerized. *He likes to watch me do this.* Not looking away, she repeated the motion two or three times, loving the way his breathing hitched on every pass. Then she swirled her tongue over the crown, noting how he hissed a curse when she paid attention to the underside.

Pretend it's a tennis match and you have to learn everything you can about your opponent.

She filed his reactions away, what worked and what didn't. She would become proficient at this, no matter what.

His thighs began to shake. "Suck hard. Take me deep."

She brought him to the back of her mouth while still watching him, and his chest heaved, his hooded gaze locked on her mouth. "That's it, beautiful. Faster now."

Holding the base with one hand, she moved quicker, setting a steady pace. His hips began to rock and she tried to bring him deeper each time. It was a challenge to see how much she could take. He didn't look away, barely blinking, and she dedicated herself to the task, determined to see and hear him unravel.

He began grunting softly with each thrust, and one hand found its way into her hair, cupping her head gently. "Oh, God. Oh, Christ. Oh, *fuck*. I am close . . . so goddamn close."

Her rebellious Fifth Avenue husband had a dirty mouth.

She hummed her approval, and the vibration must have sent him over the edge because he snapped, "Now. Fuck, I'm coming *now*."

There was a hint of warning in his voice but she wasn't sure why. Instead, she kept at it, and seconds later the muscles in his thighs tensed, his entire body locking in place. He threw his head back, moaning, and his erection swelled between her lips just before spend landed on her tongue. He trembled, jerking with each pulse, before it finally ended. She released him and swallowed the salty fluid.

Still panting, he yanked her up and lunged for her mouth, pressing his tongue inside, tasting her and him mingled together. Again and again his lips slanted over hers and she whimpered, already excited from using her mouth on him. She could feel the slickness between her thighs, the swollen tissues begging for his touch.

After a long moment, he rested his forehead on her temple, sucking in gulps of air. "That was the most arousing thing I've ever experienced in my entire life. Jesus, Maddie. I am wrecked."

"I'm glad."

He kissed her as his hands buttoned up his undergarment. "I am going to take you upstairs and reciprocate just as soon as I put myself to rights."

Tingles skated along her skin at his promise, the walls of her sex clenching. She wanted that so very much, but she hadn't cleaned up after her lesson. "I should bathe first."

"There's no time for that, and besides, I want you just like this. Go upstairs and get out of your clothing." He was already lifting his trousers and adjusting his suspenders. "I want to find you naked on my bed, wife."

Who was she to argue?

Leaning in, she decided to tease him. "I may have to get started without you."

Unbelievably, he began moving faster but his fingers turned clumsy. He struggled to fasten his trousers. "Goddamn it, Madeline."

Laughing, she slipped out of the closet and dashed for his bedroom.

MADDIE SNUGGLED AGAINST her husband's naked body, his arm wrapped around her back. Sweat still cooled on their skin as the afternoon light bathed the bedroom in a golden yellow. They had been in here for hours, pleasuring each other, ever since she accosted him in the closet.

Her cheeks warmed. Had that brazen woman really been she?

Harrison had seemed to enjoy it, so she pushed aside her embarrassment. And, really . . . this was still her oldest friend, the person who knew her better than anyone. He'd never once judged her or made her feel small. Indeed, he always encouraged and supported her.

This right here was all that mattered—you and me, together.

She bit her lip as emotions warred inside her. There had been so much she hadn't known, like his family's financial troubles and his reasons for leaving. His feelings for her. Hard to reconcile this secretive man with the boy who'd once shared everything with her.

He's not a boy any longer, Maddie.

Yes, that much was evident, as her gaze swept his muscular chest with its light dusting of dark hair. Perhaps he was right, that they had needed the time apart before coming together again. Had he stayed, would she ever have viewed him as anything but a friend, the brother she never had?

Or would she have dedicated herself so completely to lawn tennis, determined to become the best?

Furthermore, would Harrison have made his own fortune, then come back as ambitious and obsessed?

She suspected the answer to all those questions was no.

Like it or not, the events of that fateful night, the one before he left for Paris, had changed their lives. But every decision, every moment in the past, had led them here, married and bound until death. It felt right. It felt like . . . destiny.

Sighing, she dragged her palm over his sternum and ribs, mapping him with her fingers. This was all so new, but familiar, too. As if somewhere in the back of her mind she always knew they'd end up here.

Her chest expanded, her heart nearly bursting. She'd never been happier. *Am I in love with him?* She froze as the question echoed in her mind. It seemed too soon for love, especially since they'd just made up after he'd lied to her. Again.

Indeed, she cared for him, but love was hearts and flowers, rainbows and poems—not arguments and deceptions. Love required trust and mutual respect. A sense of partnership. Harrison hadn't even been completely honest with her until three days ago. Someday love might blossom between them, but she suspected this swelling inside her chest was just the lingering effects of lust combined with affection.

"What are you thinking about so seriously?" he asked quietly.

You. "Nothing. Merely enjoying the moment."

He huffed a laugh. "You have never once in your life slowed down enough to enjoy a moment. Your mind never stops planning what you are doing next."

"Says the man who never stops to plan, period."

"Touché. Though I will say I've spent a fair amount of time plotting these past three years."

"Speaking of, why did you work from here today instead of downtown?"

"I wanted to stay close to you."

There went her chest, ballooning once more. She relaxed against him and listened to the sounds from the back gardens coming in through the window. Gardeners clipped bushes and rolled carts over gravel. Insects were buzzing and birds chirped from the surrounding trees. It was a perfect moment, full of peace and quiescence.

He stroked the side of her breast with his fingertips, causing her to shiver. "What came over you today after practice? Not that I'm complaining, mind you. Merely curious."

"I missed you."

"I see."

She could hear the smile in his voice so she pushed up onto her elbow to see his face. "Do not gloat, Harrison Archer."

"I wouldn't dream of it." Sliding a hand behind her head, he pulled her down to his mouth. "And," he whispered against her lips, "I missed you, too." Then he kissed her, long and deep, with his lips moving against her own as if starved for the taste of her. Their tongues twined and danced, until she was breathless, light-headed, and she finally had to pull away to gulp air into her lungs.

He trailed tiny kisses along her jaw. "Are you still angry with me?"

"No." She looked down at him and searched his midnight-blue eyes. "Just . . . do not keep anything from me again. Please."

He cupped her cheek in his large palm. "You have my word that I won't."

Satisfied that he meant it, she nodded once. "Good."

"In the interest of full disclosure, then, I should tell you that I've come up with a way to acquire the remaining stock tomorrow morning."

"Oh? How?"

"It might not work, but I'm going to visit my family."

That sounded ominous. "Anything else you'd like to share in the interest of full disclosure?"

He rolled her onto her back, where he loomed over her, a wicked smile on his face. A lock of dark hair fell over his brow. "Yes. I plan to fuck you one more time before dinner. So would you like a bath now or later?"

Chapter Twenty-Two

The house looked much the same from the outside, still cold and forbidding. No flowers on the stoop, paint peeling on several shutters. Not so much disrepair as . . . neglect.

Harrison felt nothing as he stared up at the place in which he'd spent most his life. No warm nostalgia, no yearnings for simpler times. Those were horrible years, his misery alleviated only when he was in Newport with Maddie. In fact, the entire place could burn and he would not shed a single tear.

After ringing the bell, he entered the vestibule and removed his hat, but kept hold of the satchel he carried. He was shown to the smaller sitting room, the one used for immediate family. He strode inside, anticipation jumping in his veins, and found his mother seated on the sofa while Thomas sprawled in an armchair, looking petulant. As if his brother was annoyed to have been kept waiting.

"You're late," Thomas snapped. "We've been waiting nearly a quarter of an hour."

Harrison folded himself into an empty armchair and ignored the criticism. Far more important matters were at hand than tardiness.

"Why in heaven's name must we hear about your marriage from the papers?" his mother asked. "The very least you could have done was cable us with the news to alleviate our worry."

"My wife and I wished to enjoy a brief honeymoon before we dealt with the family's financial matters." He crossed his legs and smoothed his trousers. "Now, what is it you need from me?"

Thomas huffed, the sound loaded with impatience. "I should think that is obvious."

"Not entirely," Harrison said. "You wished for me to marry an heiress and I have done so. Now what?"

His mother and brother exchanged a look. "Now we discuss the family debts and how we are to keep the Archer assets from being seized by creditors."

"Oh, I don't care about any of that."

His mother's skin paled as she stiffened. "Excuse me?"

He spoke slowly, carefully, to get his point across. "I do not care. About any of that."

"What on earth does that mean?" Thomas's eyes nearly bulged out of his skull. "As a member of this family, you must care. Our finances are the whole reason for your marriage."

"Convenient I am a member of the family only when it suits you both."

"You have always been a member of this family, Harrison," his mother said, looking down her nose at him.

"And yet I never received one word from either of you while I was in Paris. Not a cable or a letter. Not even a message in a bottle. Thomas was there two years ago and never bothered to look me up."

The skin above Thomas's collar turned a dull red. "I was attending to business."

"Yet you found time to visit Le Chabanais. Twice." The famous French brothel was known to host many dignitaries and aristocrats, many of whom Harrison had become friendly with. It hadn't taken long for word of Thomas's visits to reach Harrison's ears.

"This is absurd." His mother sat forward. "We are not here to coddle your hurt feelings. This family needs the Webster money and you will turn it over, as a dutiful son should do."

He folded his hands and cocked his head. "I am not a dutiful son—and you will get no money from me."

The other two gasped, and his mother grabbed on to the edge of the sofa until her knuckles turned white. "What did you say?"

He knew there was nothing wrong with his mother's hearing so he didn't answer, merely let them sit with the news.

His mother's face twisted into the ugliness he remembered so well from his childhood. "Why, you ungrateful little—"

"Harrison, please." Thomas leaned forward, his gaze wild with panic. "My family . . ."

Harrison said nothing, allowing desperation to permeate the air, rolling and thickening, until he could nearly taste it. This moment was even better than he'd anticipated. It was sweet, a balm to the soul of an eight-year-old boy who'd craved his family's approval.

As he grew older, he'd realized that approval wouldn't come. That he was forever branded as the tarnished second son, the one who merely achieved at failing.

His mother lashed out once more. "You never could do as you were told. We should have known you wouldn't help us, that you would remain selfish. You are a disgrace to the Archer name."

Unbothered, Harrison allowed her vitriol to wash over him. The moment was too perfect, too precious to ruin by giving her words any power over him. The time for that had long passed.

"Mother, please," Thomas barked, then turned to Harrison, his eyes beseeching. "What do you want? To see me beg?"

Now they were arriving at a solution. Good.

"I want my ten percent back."

His brother blinked a few times. "Of Archer Industries?"

"Correct. I want you to sign over ten percent of the stock back to me. It's what I had before Winthrop disowned me."

Thomas owned fifteen percent of the stock, while his mother controlled forty percent. Ten percent should mean nothing to them.

"What do we get in exchange?" his mother asked, obviously the shrewder negotiator of the two.

Harrison gestured to the room. "This house, plus an allowance." No use informing them how small that allowance would be, at least not yet.

"That is insulting," his brother said. "I demand that you pay off all our debts, as well."

"No. Ten percent of the stock and I'll pay off the mortgage on this house. That is my final offer."

Silence descended as the weight of what he'd said settled in the room. Finally, his brother shifted toward his mother. "It's what he had before and controlling interest wouldn't leave the family. We'll still have the business, the stock dividends, plus this house will be out of debt. I think it's a good deal."

Christ, his brother was a terrible businessman. No wonder they were on the verge of losing everything.

"You cannot have a seat on the board," his mother said to Harrison. "Ten percent and the last name of Archer doesn't entitle you to that." When he said nothing, she dipped her chin toward the leather satchel at his feet. "And I suppose the necessary paperwork is in your satchel."

Harrison withdrew the legal transfer form and placed it on the tea table between them, along with a pen. "Sign at the bottom."

"Now?" Thomas frowned.

"Yes, now." He would not put it past his family to renege on their bargain once they concluded this conversation.

As Thomas read the document, Harrison and his mother sat in silence, her gaze shooting daggers at him. Because he knew from experience that it annoyed her, he offered no outward reaction of any kind, his face impassive, as if they were strangers. Her disappointment and hatred bounced off him like one of Maddie's tennis balls.

Apparently satisfied, Thomas signed with a flourish and handed the papers back to Harrison. "There."

Trying not to grin, Harrison put the papers away. "I should tell you what this means, both for the business and for you personally."

"What are you talking about?" Thomas asked.

Harrison put his elbows on the armrests and steepled his fingers. "With that ten percent you just signed over—my rightful ten percent, I might add—I now possess controlling interest in Archer Industries."

Thomas's brow furrowed. "That is impossible."

"I promise you, it isn't. I have spent the past few months making tender offers to the largest shareholders. To my surprise, most were willing to sell their shares to me for an inflated price. I now own fifty-one percent of the stock."

"How was I not informed of this?" his brother asked.

Harrison gave him a small smile. "You'd be surprised the silence a few greenbacks can buy in this town. Any guesses as to what I'll do next?"

Thomas began breathing hard and sweat broke out on his forehead. "The board . . ."

"Will do whatever I say," Harrison finished. "Including remove you as president, just as soon as I am able to call a board meeting."

"You cannot do that!" his mother shouted. "This is your father's company."

"Wrong." Elation surged in his veins, the

victory making him dizzy, as he grabbed his satchel and rose. "It's my company now."

His brother leapt to his feet, his face turning a deep crimson. "We won't let you do this. That company is my legacy, my children's legacy. You cannot just take it over."

"Simple arithmetic and the shares of stock I hold say that I can, actually." He started for the door. This meeting was over.

"And what of your wife?"

Harrison paused. The menace in his brother's question hadn't been lost on him. "What of my wife?"

"She's about to compete in the ladies' Nationals tennis tournament, is she not?"

"And what concern is it of yours?"

Thomas studied Harrison's face, and his brother must have sensed a weakness because he pushed. "I heard she was devastated by the recent scandal, how she can hardly hold her head up in public. Would be a shame if another scandal distracted her from the biggest match of her life."

"Or if she tripped and had to withdraw from the tournament," his mother added. "You know how clumsy young girls can be."

Hands curling into fists, Harrison took a step closer. "Are you *threatening* her?"

"No, of course not," Thomas said, though his tone conveyed otherwise. "We know how much she means to you."

"More than anything else in the world, I'd say," his mother put in.

Horror robbed him of speech for a long second. How was he related to these people? Did they care nothing for decency and principle?

You know the answer to that question.

There was no bottom, no limit to how low they would go to maintain their privilege. He could not allow Maddie to get dragged into the gutter with them. If she was unable to play in this tournament because of his family, he would never forgive himself.

Hardening his voice, he stared them both down. "Let me be perfectly clear so there are no misunderstandings. If harm should befall her in any way, if she sheds one tear over anything to do with this family, I will burn your entire world to ashes."

"We are only asking for what is fair," his brother said.

"Oh, I think you are getting exactly what you deserve." Spinning on his heel, he marched out of the room and right out of the house.

Kit lifted his half-empty glass in another toast. "Let us toast to Harrison. May the rest of us get every single thing we desire in the span of a few weeks, as well."

"Hear, hear!" Preston called loudly.

Harrison grinned at his friends. Upon returning from the meeting with his family, he'd learned that Maddie was still training with her coach. Not wishing to disturb her, he sent for Kit and Preston to help him celebrate today's victory over the Archers, and the three of them had been holed up in the smoking room, drinking his father-in-law's best scotch, for the better part of an hour.

"It hasn't been easy," Harrison said.

"Are you saying marriage to Maddie is a hardship, then?" Preston asked. "Because I won't believe it."

Not a hardship, but the start had been rocky—which had been entirely his fault. He didn't wish to discuss the details of his marriage with his friends, even as close as they were. So he shrugged. "There was a moment or two where I worried she wouldn't break it off with Lockwood."

"To be fair, she didn't," Kit said. "Thank God for nosy busybodies taking late-night walks."

Yes, Harrison owed quite a debt to Mrs. Lusk.

Thankfully, Maddie had forgiven him and they'd spent last night in his bed, continuing to explore each other. She was the perfect match for him, adventurous and responsive, passionate and demanding. He relished every minute. No matter what else happened, he'd never take for granted that he could touch and hold her, sleep next to her each night.

He was desperately in love with her. The words were on the tip of his tongue whenever they were together, a burning need to confess everything in his heart. Only she didn't feel the same . . . and he wasn't certain she ever would. Not once had she uttered any tender declaration or hinted at stronger feelings for him, other than the way she clung to him in bed.

And why would she? He had bamboozled her into this marriage, stolen her away from the man she'd actually *wanted* to marry. If not for Harrison, she would be a duchess, one of the most powerful women in England. Would she always harbor a small amount of resentment toward him for preventing that? His heart twisted, agony spreading in his chest.

I'd rather make the man's fantasies come true.

He'd never forget those words as long as he lived. And yes, he knew she cared about him and enjoyed their time in bed. Yet it wasn't enough. He wanted it all—her body *and* her heart.

Unfortunately, it seemed dashed unlikely.

Preston leaned forward to refill his glass. "Any of the shareholders give you trouble?"

"No. The stock price has been steadily falling ever since Thomas took over. They were happy to make a substantial amount of money by selling their shares to me."

Kit sighed dramatically. "I wish I could have seen your mother's face—Thomas's, too. That room must have been colder than a February blizzard in Maine."

Harrison swallowed a mouthful of scotch, feeling the smoky burn all the way to his stomach. "They were surprised. Angry. Horrified. Exactly what you'd expect." It had been immensely satisfying, a moment he was unlikely to ever forget.

"I can't believe you were able to pull it off so quietly," Preston said. "Normally these takeovers are long public battles, like when Vanderbilt tried to get his hands on Erie Railroad."

"No one was paying attention," Harrison said. "Thomas was busy traveling and spending money, and he didn't stop to notice what was happening with the company."

"He's a nincompoop," Preston said, direct and to the point as usual. "Always has been."

"While that is undoubtedly true," Harrison said, "that nincompoop threatened Maddie today." Harrison shook his head. "My mother, too."

Kit froze, his glass halfway to his mouth. *"What?"*

"Wait, what do you mean, they threatened her?" Preston's face darkened, the expression one that had sent many a man scurrying away in fear.

Harrison told his friends about the offhanded comments made by his family. "They said she's the most important thing in the world to me."

"They aren't wrong," Kit said, "but it is beyond low to threaten a man's wife." He looked at Preston. "Remember when Thomas held that young boy under the waves until he almost drowned?"

Preston nodded. "The Newbold son, wasn't it? The one who moved out West."

Harrison recalled that afternoon, when Thomas had picked on the skinnier, younger boy. "I was blamed for it, incidentally." At his friends' surprised expression, he elaborated. "Mrs. Newbold marched to the cottage and gave my mother an earful. Thomas denied his involvement, saying I was responsible instead. I couldn't sit for two days."

"Jesus," Preston muttered. "And here I'd always wished for a brother."

"My brother and I used to get into terrible fights," Kit said. "Still do, actually."

Preston pointed at Harrison. "You must be careful. Keep a close eye on her until the tournament. I can give you the names of men you could hire to watch over her."

"I don't think that's necessary," Harrison said. "Probably just bluster. A trapped animal lashing out."

Kit frowned. "I wouldn't give your family the benefit of the doubt. Ever."

"I agree," Preston said. "Maybe warn your wife, so she is aware of the threat."

"No." Harrison's voice was sharp and loud in the cavernous room. "Absolutely not. She's about to play in the biggest tournament of her life. I cannot let my family distract her in any way."

Preston's brow wrinkled in concern, but he raised his glass. "To our families. May they all rot in hell."

"Indeed." Kit toasted with his tumbler, as well. "To a friend in the morning!"

"And a mistress at night," Preston continued.

"To fill us with pleasure and blissful delight." Harrison finished their favorite toast and tapped his glass to the others. Then all three men drank.

"Speaking of friends," Harrison said. "How is Forrest? Anyone heard from him lately?" The four of them were like brothers, and it felt strange not to have Forrest here.

"In Chicago, last I heard." Kit shook his head. "Saw him in April for dinner. He was blind drunk before we even finished the first course. Had to get a waiter to help me carry him out to the carriage."

"He's always drunk," Preston told Harrison, his voice low and serious. "Worse than before."

"Christ." Forrest had always loved to drink, but this seemed excessive. Harrison grimaced. "Should we try to help him?"

"I've tried," Kit said. "He won't hear it, doesn't care."

"I took him to the Adirondacks to try and dry him out," Preston said. "He slipped out of a window when I wasn't looking and disappeared on me. That's the last I saw of him."

"When was that?"

"Early May."

"How do you know he's in Chicago?" Harrison asked.

"I hired a Pinkerton," Kit admitted. "He's been keeping a tab on Forrest for me."

Unease swept across Harrison's nape, pressing down on his shoulders. He'd been gone for three years and hadn't given much thought to those he left behind. Forrest . . . Maddie. Even Kit and Preston had been a distant memory until they came to visit him. "I am sorry. I should have paid better attention."

"Should have paid better attention to what?"

Silk rustled as Maddie sauntered into the room. Harrison's heart clenched in his chest, a visceral reaction that occurred every time he saw her. As if the organ belonged to her and only her, and needed to prove it.

Now out of her tennis whites, she'd changed into a dark green day dress that hugged all his favorite curves. Christ almighty, he couldn't wait to get his hands on her again.

The men rose and Harrison went to kiss her cheek. "Hello, wife."

After greeting Kit and Preston, she settled in a chair. "This looks cozy. Drinking at noon? Are we celebrating?"

"We are. I've just come from calling on my family."

"I assume that went well, considering." She swept her hand over the tumblers of scotch and half-lit cigars.

"Indeed, it did." He gave her a wide grin. "For me, anyway."

"Congratulations. I assume the takeover is complete."

"Not quite, but I have controlling interest and I'll remove my brother as president just as soon as I can call a board meeting."

"We should be going," Preston said, finishing his drink and stabbing out his cigar. "And leave the bride and groom to continue enjoying their honeymoon."

"Agreed." Kit rose, then bent to kiss Maddie's cheek. "Not sure if I can make the tournament, so give 'em hell, Maddie."

"I always do."

Preston kissed her cheek, as well. "I wouldn't miss it. I'll be the one shouting himself hoarse in the crowd."

Their friends left, then Harrison reached for his wife and pulled her onto his lap. He tucked a piece of hair behind her ear. "How was practice this morning?"

"Exhausting, but Vallie said he'll ease up in the days before we leave."

"You're going to win."

"I hope so." She rested her cheek against his shoulder. "If I weren't so tired I'd suggest going upstairs and celebrating your victory."

"Good idea. Let's celebrate with a nap."

She chuckled. "You are extremely transparent. That means getting undressed, which will lead to other strenuous activity."

"Perhaps . . . or perhaps it means merely resting together." He rose out of the chair, keeping her cradled in his arms. "Let's go and find out."

Chapter Twenty-Three

Maddie smothered a yawn as she stepped out onto the back lawn. Her husband had kept her up late last night as they celebrated his victory over the Archers. When she left their bed thirty minutes ago, he was still sprawled on his stomach, snoring softly. She added *sometimes snores* to the list of things she'd discovered about him since they married.

She would've loved to sleep in as well, but practice awaited. Valentine, her coach, was probably already here, setting up for their session. After the tournament, however, she swore she wouldn't rise before noon for an entire month.

Approaching the court, she was surprised to see Vallie holding a shovel. He was scooping something off the court, which he then threw into the brush several yards away. It had looked like a large gray animal of some kind.

"What was that?" she asked when she arrived.

Vallie put the shovel down and dusted off his hands. "An opossum. Another animal must have killed it and left the carcass on the court. I asked the gardeners for a shovel so I might spare you the grisly details."

"Thank you. Was it awful?"

"Let's just say that I am glad I possess a hardy stomach. Now, how do you feel this morning?" He clapped his hands together. "Ready to take me on in a match?"

This was new. Normally, he ordered her to repeat the same drills over and over. "No instruction today?"

"We'll talk about where to improve after. I thought playing a full match would help build up your endurance. Then we'll ease up from here on out."

She grinned, anticipation making her bounce on her toes. "I won't go easy on you and your sore knee."

He laughed. "The knee's feeling pretty good this week. I think we can keep up with you."

"We'll just have to see, I suppose." She went to find her favorite racket, then strolled onto the court. They stretched and took the time to properly warm up before starting the match.

She played well, but Vallie showed no mercy. Maddie ended up losing, but just barely. Though she was competitive, she preferred playing against tough opponents. They made her better. It was one of the reasons she liked playing with Harrison growing up, because he never coddled her or eased up because she was a girl.

Her coach wiped his face with a cloth. "The backhand continues to be your weakness. Your hips are not rotating enough into the movement. Any decent opponent will take advantage of it."

Maddie sighed and quickly drank a glass of lemonade. "We've been working on it since April. Before that, probably. I don't know what else to do."

"We'll figure it out," Vallie said. When she started to argue, he held up a hand. "I know you strive for perfection, which is good, but you have to be patient. Conversely, your short game is much improved and most male players couldn't return your forehand winner. Does that make you feel better?"

"A little."

"Good. It also helps that I know your weaknesses and look to exploit them as much as possible. A real opponent won't do that to you."

That made sense. "Then I am glad I won't be facing you in Philadelphia."

Vallie shifted, then winced as he wobbled. Maddie grabbed his arm to steady him. "You should come inside and rest your knee. I can fetch ice from the kitchens."

"No, but thank you. When I get home I'll have my valet rub it with that liniment Bill uses," he said, referring to his friend, "Roaring" Bill Kennedy, a pitcher for the Bridegrooms. "As you know, it works wonders on aches and pains."

"At least come through the house instead of going all the way around. It's shorter."

Vallie agreed, and they slowly walked up the terrace steps and into the back of the house. She sent a footman to hail a hack and they continued through the corridor toward the entryway. Resting on a table near the front door was a huge arrangement of deep crimson, nearly black, roses.

"Has someone died?" Vallie asked.

"Not that I know of."

Farley materialized from the shadows. "Those were just delivered for you, madam. There is a card there on the table."

"That arrangement is ominous, to say the least," Vallie said.

Maddie walked to the table and picked up the card.

BEST OF LUCK IN YOUR UPCOMING
TOURNAMENT.

Best of luck? But these were . . . dark and morose. Not the sort of thing that accompanied a message of well wishes. And there was no signature. Who would send these?

None of this made sense.

She tapped the card with her fingers. "Perhaps the flower shop made a mistake. We should throw them out."

"No, you need to show them to your husband," Vallie said.

"Who happens to be right here."

Maddie spun to see Harrison coming down the stairs. He wore a light gray suit and a black vest, his dark hair oiled and swept back. The style highlighted his midnight-blue eyes, which were currently locked on the flower arrangement. When he reached the table, he looked to Maddie. "Was there a card?"

She held it out, and watched his expression turn thunderous as he read the words. Then, in an instant, his face cleared. "I'll speak to the flower shop about it. This has to be a mistake," he announced, and put the card in his coat pocket.

"That's what I assumed," she said. "No doubt the flowers were supposed to be a brighter color." It still didn't answer who they were from. Was someone trying to make it appear as if she'd been unfaithful to Harrison?

"Farley, have these disposed of." Harrison motioned to the flowers. Then he struck out his hand toward Vallie and the two men shook. "Livingston, always a pleasure. If you'll both excuse me, I must travel downtown for a meeting."

Without another word, Harrison was out the door and into a waiting carriage. "Sir," Farley said to Vallie. "A carriage is here for you, as well."

"Thank you. Maddie, I'll see you tomorrow morning, bright and early. Get some rest."

"You too, Vallie. Stay off that knee."

When her coach left, she stood there, staring at the flowers, wondering. Farley closed the front door, then motioned to a footman to carry the arrangement belowstairs. "There, madam. It's as if it never happened."

"Have you ever seen an arrangement like it, Farley?"

"No, madam. I definitely have not. Couldn't have been easy, finding flowers that dark."

Maddie agreed. A bouquet such as that couldn't have been easy to procure . . . or cheap. So why had it been sent with such a cheerful note?

IT TOOK HARRISON just two stops to locate his brother.

The Archer home on Fifth Avenue was empty, so Harrison had hurried to the Archer Industries offices downtown. He had Preston in tow, since his friend had pulled up to the Websters' house just as Harrison set to depart. The arrival was fortuitous, as no one intimidated others better than Preston.

During the ride south, Harrison's blood boiled with the need to choke his brother, to shake Thomas until he understood that Maddie was to be left alone. How *dare* his family try and rattle her?

Finally, they arrived at the seventh floor where the executive offices were located. The staff watched Harrison's progress with wide, curious eyes as he marched the long space toward the president's office. Preston followed, remaining silent, also angry over the flower delivery.

Though the door to the president's office was closed, Harrison didn't stop his approach. The secretary chased after him, saying that Mr. Archer was in an important meeting and could not be disturbed, but Harrison didn't even slow down. He threw open the door, flinging it against the wall, and stepped inside.

His brother shot to his feet. "What on earth are you doing here?"

Harrison left Preston to deal with the secretary while he advanced on his brother. "Get out," he snapped at the stranger sitting in the armchair, gaping at him like a carp.

Within seconds, the man scurried from the office, leaving the three of them alone.

Thomas had nowhere to go, so Harrison caught him easily, grabbing his brother's throat and slamming his back against the wall. It suddenly became clear how much Harrison had grown in the last three years, because he now had several inches and at least twenty pounds over his brother. "You goddamn bastard," Harrison growled in Thomas's face, thumping his brother's head into the wall again. "I told you to leave my wife alone."

Thomas had the nerve to lift his chin. "I don't know what you are talking about."

"Liar. You are trying to intimidate her, distract her right before the tournament, just as you threatened."

"I've done nothing of the sort."

Harrison squeezed, pressing on the sides of his brother's throat. "You took me for a fool, Thomas. When I said I would bury you if you harmed Maddie, you didn't believe me and tried it, anyway. Now I get to make good on my promise."

Abruptly, he released his brother and stepped back, taking several deep breaths to get a grip on his chaotic emotions. He slipped into the abandoned armchair and smoothed his trousers. "Please sit," he told his brother, gesturing to the chair behind the desk.

Thomas's gaze grew wary, but he adjusted his clothing and sat down. "This is family business. Why is he here?" He jerked his chin toward Preston, who stood glowering near the door, his arms folded across his chest.

"He's here to make sure I don't kill you."

Preston gave a toothy smile that had caused men to piss themselves in the past. Harrison had witnessed it firsthand.

"This is ridiculous," Thomas said. "I haven't done anything wrong."

Harrison continued, ignoring his brother's denial. "Here's what is going to happen. I am selling the Fifth Avenue house, as is my right considering I now hold the deed. I expect you to vacate before the end of the week."

Thomas gasped. "You cannot do that—"

"Furthermore, I have called for an emergency board meeting in"—he checked his pocket watch—"one hour, during which the board will pass a no-confidence vote in you as president and install me as the new president."

The color drained from his brother's face. "Harrison, don't do this. It's not fair to me or my family. Where will we live? Think of my wife, my children. Mother. That is our *home*."

"You should have thought of that before you sent those flowers to my wife."

"Let us have the Newport house, then," Thomas said. "It is the least you can do."

"The least I can do?" Harrison's lip curled. "I don't owe you a damn thing. What about all those times when we were boys and you caused trouble, only to blame it on me? Was that the *least* you could do, Thomas?"

His brother's throat worked as he swallowed. "That's not true."

"We both know it is. You found it easier if father's wrath was aimed at me, not you. It was easier for you to be the perfect brother and leave me as the evil one. So do not presume to tell me what I should do. I owe you nothing."

"We will take you to court, if necessary."

"Please do." Harrison steepled his fingers, giving Thomas a smug smile. "Because I would love to tell everyone about how our dear father used to abuse the female staff . . . and how you knew and did nothing about it. What do you think the papers would say about that?"

Thomas shook his head. "I would deny it and you would look like a petty second son."

So Thomas had known. *Christ, the dark, twisted history of this family.* Harrison wanted nothing more to do with them. Rising, he straightened his cuffs. "See you in an hour, brother." Turning, he started for the door.

"Harrison, listen," Thomas called from behind him. "I am begging you. Not for myself, but for my family. My wife and children, who will have nowhere to go if you carry this out."

Harrison stopped and glared over his shoulder at his brother. "You have your stock dividends. Your wife has relatives. Be resourceful, man. Or do what I did when I went to Paris: *get a job.*"

"You're a bastard, Harrison," Thomas spat hastily. "You are just as devious and hard-hearted as our father. We're from the same stock, you and I. So do not presume to act like you're better than me."

"Wrong. I am nothing like the rest of you." He gestured to the interior of the office. "I'd pack up, were I you. Once I take over today, I'll have you arrested if you step a foot inside this building again."

Preston opened the door and the two of them walked out. Harrison nodded at Thomas's secretary. "Mr. Archer has a board meeting in an hour.

See that he's all packed up by then, if you please." The secretary said nothing, merely stared up at him with wide eyes.

When Harrison and Preston were alone in the elevator, Preston said, "I've never seen your brother so scared." He chuckled. "'Get a job.' I thought his head was going to pop off when you said that."

Harrison was not yet in a laughing mood. His muscles were clenched tight, rage coursing through his system. The thought of anyone hurting Maddie or distracting her before this tournament made him want to tear down the city, brick by brick. No matter what else happened, he could not let the Archers destroy her chances of winning in Philadelphia. He'd never forgive himself if something happened.

Looking at Preston, he said, "I want the names of the men you mentioned, the ones who guard for hire."

Preston sobered. "You think she's in that much danger?"

"I won't risk it. He has nothing to lose now. It makes him dangerous."

"It certainly can't hurt, as long as Maddie agrees to being shadowed."

Harrison frowned. "I don't want her to know. I convinced her the flowers were a mistake this morning. The tournament is too close and she shouldn't be worried about her safety. She needs to focus on winning."

The elevator opened onto the bottom floor and they started for the exit. "Harrison, I'm not sure that's a good idea. After everything you've hidden from her, are you sure you want to do this?"

His temples throbbing, Harrison contemplated Preston's words. Not telling her might make her angry later, but there was a good chance she'd never know. And informing her of a threat might prevent her from performing well at the tournament.

No, he wouldn't tell her. He would keep her safe throughout the tournament, then reassess the need for security. More than likely, it wouldn't be necessary.

"Just give me the names. I'll hire them to stay out of her sight until after the tournament is over."

Chapter Twenty-Four

❧

$\mathcal{A}$ knock sounded on Maddie's bedroom door. She'd just finished packing for her journey to Philadelphia tonight and her body buzzed with anticipation and nerves. She'd likely spend the rest of the afternoon prowling around the house and avoiding thoughts of tennis.

It was not an easy thing, considering this was the most important tournament to which she'd ever been invited. Every top female player would be there, all vying for the championship.

Dragging in a deep breath, she called, "Come in."

Her husband appeared, a giant box in his arms. "Hello, wife. Have you finished packing?"

"Yes, just now. What's that?"

"A gift. To bring you luck, I hope." He placed the box on the bed and kissed her cheek. "Go on. Open it up."

Lips curving into a small smile, she reached for the card affixed to the top of the box. The logo of her favorite sporting goods company was embossed on the front. Harrison's handwriting filled the back.

My Dearest Maddie,

Win or lose, I couldn't be prouder of you.
See you in Philadelphia.

All my love,
Harrison

The sentiment sent warmth cascading through her body, a rush of longing and affection that only Harrison could elicit in her. He hadn't spoken of love, however, not until now. Did he love her? The past few nights had been utter bliss, and she wished he was coming with her to Philadelphia tonight instead of waiting a few days.

Shaking off her musings, she tugged at the strings on the box and opened it. Inside was a new lawn tennis racket, four balls and a pair of white tennis shoes. Like her existing shoes, these were completely flat with a rubber sole.

"I wasn't sure what you needed, so I bought a bit of everything," her husband said.

Turning, she wrapped her arms around his shoulders and pressed up against him, soaking in his strength and fortitude. "Thank you, Harrison. This was very sweet of you."

He kissed her softly, a gentle but thorough meeting of their mouths, almost as if he were trying to reassure her or imprint her lips with his. She needed the distraction, the mind-numbing desire that swamped her every time he pulled her close. The kiss settled and relaxed her, and she felt herself leaning heavily against him after a few minutes.

When they pulled apart, he stared down at her, his expression soft. "There. Between that kiss and waking up with you this morning, that should hold me over until I see you in a few days."

She bit her lip. He had awoken her with his mouth between her legs, and she found her release twice before he finally crawled over her body and entered her. "I'll still miss you."

"I wish I could go now, but the takeover . . ."

He'd been consumed by Archer Industries since replacing his brother as president. And she understood his desire to achieve, perhaps better than most. Harrison wanted to prove to the world that he was capable, not the layabout second son as his family had claimed. "I know. You'll be there for the games, and that's all that matters."

"I wouldn't miss them," he said, and swept a lock of hair behind her ear. "I'll be the proudest man there, cheering you on from the gallery."

"I might lose. It depends on the seeding and who I play in the first round."

"Sweetheart, losing is for people who never try. You've made it this far, which is remarkable in itself, and I know you'll play your heart out."

She exhaled the breath she'd been holding. "Thank you. I needed to hear that."

"Good." He kissed her nose and let her go. "I need to go downtown, so cable when you're safe at the hotel."

"I will." He'd already instructed her to do this today. Twice.

"And do not leave Vallie's side at the club."

Again, she'd already promised this. "I won't.

You don't need to worry so much, Harrison. These events are completely safe."

A strange look passed over his face before he said, "You are the most important thing in my life, Madeline Jane Archer. Do not take your safety lightly."

"The same goes for you, Harrison Archer. Be careful."

"I will." He shot her a grin. "I love you, Mads."

She froze, her brain shutting off like a light switch as she struggled to comprehend what he'd said so casually. He . . . *loved* her. Hadn't she just been wondering over his feelings? And now he'd tossed the words out like he'd said them a hundred times. Like they weren't a surprise.

Like they wouldn't send her reeling.

Her mouth fell open, her tongue thick, and the moment stretched. The happiness in his bright blue gaze dimmed as he studied her face, and finally he straightened his shoulders. "Travel safely," he said, his voice rough, like pebbles were caught in his throat. Then he disappeared into the corridor, shutting the door behind him.

Oh, God. Pressing a fist to her chest, she realized she'd hurt him. He had clearly wanted her to return the sentiment . . . and she'd stood there like a dolt, gaping at him.

But he'd caught her unawares. She hadn't expected him to throw out those three important words as he was leaving her room. Shouldn't there have been a buildup or a warning, at least? A chance for her to compose a reply?

And what would you have said in return?

Did she love him?

Certainly, he was all she could think about, even while playing tennis. She never wanted to leave his side, desperate for his smiles and his laughter—not to mention his touch. Of course, their marriage had been an adjustment. During his three-year absence, she'd carved a perfect life for herself, one she'd planned carefully. Then he'd returned and upended everything, shifting her priorities and rearranging her future.

Yet, she was happy. Happier than she'd ever imagined, in fact.

There was no better man, no better match for her. They were like caviar and champagne, or oysters and a wedge of lemon. A tennis racket and strings. One complemented the other, making each significantly improved.

Was that love?

Yes, she believed it was.

Recalling the hurt on his face sent a spear of regret through her chest. She hated that he'd left, assuming the worst because she hadn't immediately repeated the words back. The urge to tell him now, before he departed, galvanized her toward the door.

She hurried downstairs, lifting her skirts to avoid tripping. From a distance she heard the front door close, so she flew down the main stairs to catch him.

In the entryway, she found her parents removing their gloves and hats. "Hello, Mama, Daddy. I didn't know you were coming back today."

"I had a few errands to run before we joined you in Philadelphia—Madeline!" her mother exclaimed as Maddie pushed by to open the front door. "Wherever are you going?"

"I wanted to catch Harrison before he left." She stared out onto the street, but the only vehicle in sight was the hack carrying her parents' luggage from the train.

"You've just missed him," her father said. "He was pulling out as we pulled in."

"Oh." Her shoulders deflated in disappointment as she came back inside.

"Send him a cable, if it's so important," Mama said, smoothing her hair in the hall mirror. "There's no reason to give yourself wrinkles over it."

"It's fine. I'll tell him when I see him in Philadelphia." She took her father's arm and began dragging him to the sitting room. "Now, please. Both of you come sit with me and catch up before I leave in a few hours."

Six lawn tennis courts were outlined inside the Philadelphia Cricket Club, and each would hold three matches over the course of the first day. This morning, spectators were dispersed among the various courts to observe matches already in progress. Harrison had studied the schedule, discovering that Maddie's first match was in the second half of first-round matches, which should get under way in thirty minutes.

Exhausted, he slipped his hands in his trouser pockets and stared unseeingly out at the crowd. He hadn't slept well in four nights, not since Maddie left.

I love you, Mads.

Why had he said it? He knew she didn't feel the same, yet the words had slipped out of his mouth. And the horrified expression she wore upon hearing the declaration was now stuck in his brain forever.

She doesn't love you. How could she?

He'd pressured her into this marriage, maneuvered the pieces on the board until he got what he wanted. But marriage to Maddie without love was a lonely, heart-wrenching endeavor, one he hadn't exactly thought through when putting these wheels into motion. The reality of loving a woman who didn't love him back—again—hadn't occurred until it smacked him in the face.

Not that he would let her go.

Patience, he reminded himself. Perhaps in time she would come to care for him a fraction of what he felt for her. And that would be enough.

It had to be.

A hand clapped his shoulder, startling him.

"There you are." Preston stood beside him. "Thought I'd see you at the hotel last night."

Socializing hadn't occurred to Harrison. He'd brooded in his room with a bottle of bourbon. "Didn't you bring Arabella?" Preston had said earlier he was bringing his mistress on the trip. "I assumed you'd be busy."

"Yes, but I do come up for air every few hours or so, you know. We could've had a drink together."

"Maybe tonight."

"I'd like that. You look terrible, by the way."

There went his hope not to draw attention to his mood. "I'm fine."

"Are you worried about your lawn tennis champion? I've been watching the matches today and I think she'll do just fine."

"No, I'm not worried about that."

"But you're worried about something else."

Harrison sighed. Preston was like a dog with a bone when he sensed a problem. "It's nothing."

"I'll get it out of you sooner or later, you know. You might as well tell me now."

This conversation was not one that Harrison wanted to have here, at the tennis tournament. "Tonight, all right? We'll talk tonight."

"Fair enough. Let's go get a good spot over at her court."

The current match on Maddie's court was nearly over, so they waited until the crowd began to shift before finding a spot at the edge of the netting right up front. He was surprised at the large number of people there to watch the matches. Harrison hadn't been to a tennis tournament of this size before; Maddie had started competing on this level only after he left for Paris. It seemed daunting, all these strangers observing and commenting as one played. Was she nervous? Would the attention bother her?

He doubted it. She was the bravest, most competitive person he knew. And she had already won several smaller tournaments this year, so she must be used to a public setting like this. He meant what he had said on the card. Regardless of how she played, he was damn proud of her.

Movement near the clubhouse caught Harrison's attention . . . and his body tightened when his wife emerged. The entire world paused and his vision tunneled to just her.

"You get that look on your face every time you see her," Preston said, amusement lacing his words. "You poor bastard."

"Fuck off," Harrison muttered—and the stranger next to him gasped before edging away, horrified.

"Nice fucking manners, Archer," Preston murmured.

"It's your fucking fault," Harrison shot back, a smile tugging at his lips while his gaze remained locked on Maddie. He and his friends hadn't ever played by the rules of polite society, so no use pretending now.

Maddie and Valentine Livingston descended the stairs, followed by another woman holding a racket and an older man. Maddie's expression was calm and resolute as she listened to whatever her coach was telling her. Last-minute advice of some kind, no doubt. Farther behind lingered two men, the guards Harrison had hired, following Maddie discreetly, keeping her safe.

"I told you they were good," Preston said, tilting his chin toward the guards. "She'll have no idea they're even here."

Excellent. Harrison was having his brother watched, as well, and he'd been informed that Thomas was still in New York. Hiring guards for Maddie might prove unnecessary, but Harrison wouldn't relax until the tournament ended.

He watched her stride smoothly toward the court and soaked in every bit of her appearance, from the cap to keep the sun out of her eyes, to her white shirtwaist and skirt. There was purpose and confidence in her gait. She was here to win, no doubt about it.

The players readied themselves and the judge climbed into the high chair. The two guards edged to the front of the opposite side of the court, well within reach of Maddie. Vallie walked over to their side, so Harrison lowered the netting for him to climb over.

Vallie straightened and shook Harrison's hand. "Good to see you, Archer. Fine day for tennis, isn't it?"

"Indeed, it is." He introduced Preston, then asked Vallie, "Think she'll win?"

The other man smirked. "Of course I do."

"How are you so calm?"

"Because I am her coach, not her husband. Don't worry, Archer. Your wife plays better than any woman I've encountered. She's aggressive and hits hard. You'll see."

The judge announced the players, and the crowd applauded. Hearing the words "Madeline Webster Archer" made Harrison grin, despite his morose mood. *She's mine. No matter what else happens, she's mine.*

After a quick warm-up, the match started. Soon, Harrison understood what Vallie meant about Maddie's style of play. The other woman lobbed the ball, hitting mostly up, like badminton, instead of forward, which slowed the game down. Maddie hit only forward, with spin and accuracy, the way she always did, her feet moving quickly. Her opponent couldn't keep pace.

The crowd clapped and cheered as she continued to dominate. If Maddie heard the surrounding noise, she gave no indication of it. Her focus was entirely on the game and her opponent. She hadn't even looked in Harrison's direction.

In the end, Maddie won it handily in two sets, 6–1 and 6–2. Harrison clapped loudly while Preston put his fingers in his mouth and whistled.

Vallie nudged him on the shoulder. "See what I mean?"

"I never noticed it before."

"Because you're used to the way she plays."

True. "Do the other women here play the same way?"

"One or two. She'll meet them in the later rounds."

Maddie came rushing over and threw herself at him, wrapping her arms around his neck. "Oh, my goodness. I won!"

He buried his face in her hair, relieved to be holding her again. "Of course you did, sweetheart. Congratulations."

She stepped over to speak to Vallie, and Preston quickly congratulated her as well. Harrison had never seen her look happier. "I can't believe it. That was so easy," she said.

"They won't all be that easy," Vallie said. "But enjoy your victory tonight. You were outstanding."

"We'll go to dinner to celebrate," Harrison said. "All of us."

"I already have plans," Vallie said. "But thank you for the offer. Just make certain she's in bed at a reasonable hour, Archer."

"Valentine!" Maddie's cheeks grew more flushed than when she was playing.

"I will," Harrison said and kissed her hand. "Don't worry."

Vallie hopped over the netting once more and onto the court. "I'll take her back to the clubhouse, and then go observe some of the other matches. I want to see the competition."

Harrison nodded and told Maddie, "I'll wait for you by the door."

Maddie and her coach departed for the clubhouse, where Maddie would change and store her equipment. The guards followed at a reasonable distance and Harrison exhaled in relief.

The crowd had now dispersed, and Maddie's mother and father soon found them.

"Hello, Mrs. Webster, Mr. Webster," Harrison said, pumping the older man's hand. "She was outstanding today, wasn't she?"

"Best she has ever played," her father said, a broad smile overtaking his face.

Even Maddie's mother looked pleased from under the shade of her parasol. "I cannot understand the appeal of the sport, but she certainly seemed in command of the game."

"Match, dear," Mr. Webster said, patting his wife's hand. "Game, set, match."

"We're taking her out tonight to celebrate," Harrison said to the Websters as they started for the clubhouse. "I hope you'll both join us."

"We'd like that," Mr. Webster said. "It'll be nice

to see how you and our daughter are settling into marriage."

The undercurrent was not lost on Harrison. They were still unhappy over the circumstances of their daughter's marriage, not that Harrison could blame them. Compromising her and forcing a marriage hadn't been his intention, either. However, once they saw him and Maddie together, he knew they would come around.

They all strolled toward the clubhouse. A large crowd was gathered out front, so their group waited in the back, off to the side. He relaxed, knowing he would spot her as soon as she came outside.

Chapter Twenty-Five

Maddie's heart continued to race long after she changed out of her tennis clothes and into an afternoon dress. Playing in a tournament was exhilarating—and winning was even better.

After her maid, Siobhan, helped her dress, she chatted a few minutes with Vallie. Then a reporter asked for a few moments of her time to comment on the match, so Vallie left to watch the other players. When the interview ended, Maddie and Siobhan went outside.

A crowd of people loitered in the shade directly in the front of the clubhouse. She twisted and turned, sliding between bodies to get through, accepting congratulations on her win as she went. She didn't stop to chat, however. Harrison, Preston and her parents were here somewhere, and hopefully they hadn't gone far.

She'd loved having Harrison at the match. He'd cheered the loudest, his whistles deafening. She had played hard, wanting to make him proud. A fluttering began in her chest, the burning need to tell him of her feelings.

Soon. They'd be alone in the hotel soon and she would tell him.

As she pushed through a large cluster of spectators, strong fingers pinched the skin of her hip, almost on her bottom. She gasped, surprised. That was no accident. Rather, it had been an intentional grope.

Her head whipped around, searching for the man responsible. He stood there, a few feet away, giving her a slick smile. A black wool suit hung loose on his frame, his collar soaked with sweat. A sense of wrongness came over her like an icy wind. She shivered with the need to get away, to put distance between herself and this stranger.

Unfortunately, with people all around her, she couldn't quickly step back as the man drew closer. She lifted her chin and pulled one of her hat pins from her hair. "Do not come any closer."

As if he didn't hear her, the man leaned in, using his size to intimidate her. "There's no need for that." He pointed to the hat pin in her hand and chuckled. "All I want is to see you smile, pretty lady."

Alarm bells were ringing in her head. She tried to slip through the people standing behind her, but met only with resistance. "I don't feel like smiling right now—and you need to move back."

He reached out to touch her again, this stranger who thought he could take liberties with her person. She didn't wait for rescue. Instead, she shoved the hat pin into his stomach. *Hard.*

Yelping, he doubled over, his hands covering where she'd stabbed him. People in the vicinity stopped talking, their gazes curious as they formed a wide circle around her and the other man. Siobhan arrived alongside, her eyes wide with concern. "Are you all right, madam?"

"I'm fine," Maddie said, watching the man who'd pinched her. She didn't trust him not to run off and escape, where he'd likely grope another young woman in the crowd.

Suddenly, there were shouts and the crowd instantly parted. Two men she'd never seen before each took one of her elbows and practically lifted her off the ground, towing her back the way she came. "Stop! Let me go!" She struggled in their grip, but it did no good. "Help! I am being kidnapped."

"Please, Mrs. Archer," one of them said. "You're safe now."

Safe? She was being dragged against her will by two large men she'd never met. "Help me!" She kept trying to twist away, to escape their strong hands, but it was no use. They didn't release her until they were in one of the small rooms inside the clubhouse.

"Who are you?" She rubbed her trembling arms and backed away from these strangers. "How did you know my name?"

The door flew open and Harrison rushed into the room. His hair was rumpled, his eyes wild with panic before they landed on her. He reached her in three steps and pulled her against his chest. "Christ. Are you hurt, Mads?" His voice shook as he held her close, his fingers digging into her flesh through her clothing. As if he never intended to let her go. She rested her cheek against his shirt and necktie, the familiar scent of him soaking into her muscles, easing the fear and anxiety from moments earlier.

"I've got you, honey," he murmured into her hair. "I've always got you."

Her parents entered the room, as well, their faces laced with concern. "What happened?" her father asked. "We heard a shout and a man was on the ground."

"I'm fine," she told everyone. "A man in the crowd pinched me. I used my hat pin to defend myself."

"A man pinched you?" Harrison let her go and rounded on the two strangers, his expression carved in fury. "You were supposed to keep her safe!"

Keep her safe?

"We apologize, Mr. Archer," one of the men was saying. "She disappeared into the crowd for a minute. We only lost sight of her for a few seconds."

"A few seconds is all it takes," Harrison snarled. "She could have been harmed."

"Wait." She put a hand on Harrison's arm. "Who are these men? Do you know them?"

"We beg your pardon, Mrs. Archer," the other man said, wringing his cap in his fists. "We won't let it happen tomorrow."

"Tomorrow?" She looked at Harrison. "What are they talking about?"

Preston came in, dragging the man who'd pinched her in his wake. "I brought the man responsible inside while we await the police."

"Good," Harrison snapped. "We will be pressing charges."

"We don't need the police," the man said, twisting in Preston's hold. "It was an accident."

"Goddamn mashers," Preston muttered. "We'll have him arrested, Maddie. Don't worry."

Harrison closed in on the man, his hands curling into fists. "How much did Thomas pay you?"

"I don't know any Thomas. She's lying," the man said, pointing at her. "Whatever she told you, she's lying."

Thomas? Why was Harrison asking this man about his brother?

None of this made sense.

Harrison lifted the man up by his necktie and shook him. "You're a liar. I know he put you up to this."

The man's face turned purple and he made choking sounds. Was her husband going to strangle this man, right here? "Harrison! Stop and tell me what is going on. Right now."

He dropped the other man and dragged a hand through his hair. "Everyone, may I have a moment alone with my wife?"

Maddie cocked her head and studied her husband. He was acting strangely, avoiding her eyes, his movements jittery. Her stomach twisted, a portentous feeling settling inside her like a stone.

"I'll keep him in another room with the police until you're ready," Preston said before departing with the masher. Everyone else quickly filed out and the door was closed.

She didn't waste any time. "What is going on?"

"Let's return to the hotel and discuss it there."

"I'd rather discuss it here. Who were those men who dragged me back to the clubhouse?"

He folded his arms across his chest. "Guards I hired to keep you safe."

"What?" She gaped at him. "You hired guards for me? Without telling me? Why?"

"My brother and mother threatened you last week, during the takeover. They knew you were the only leverage they had over me."

She dropped heavily into a chair. "They threatened me . . . and you didn't tell me?"

"I didn't want you to worry before the tournament." Striding to where she sat, he lowered onto his haunches and stared into her eyes. "I know how much winning this means to you. I didn't want them to distract or upset you. I wanted to protect you."

Her head was spinning from all this information and she needed space. Standing, she walked around him to the other side of the room. "Let me see if I have this straight. Your family threatened me and so you went out and hired guards. Without informing me. To protect me."

"Yes."

"Did you honestly think Thomas would hire someone to accost me in a crowd?"

"I put nothing past him, not after he sent you those flowers."

"The flowers were from Thomas?"

"Yes."

Her skin burned with outrage and hopelessness. God, this was too much. Harrison hadn't shared any of this information with her—*after* he'd promised never to keep secrets again. "Considering what happened right after our marriage, I would have expected you to discuss these things with me."

"Maddie, I didn't want to upset you. The Archers have caused enough damage. I needed to keep you safe."

"So what I want doesn't matter. Is that what you are saying?" She let out a bitter, brittle laugh. "You are not listening to me. You never have, even after I begged you not to keep anything from me again."

"We are talking about your safety. If I feel you are in danger and need protection, I won't hesitate to do it, whether you agree or not."

Her throat tightened with anger and resentment but she forced the words out. "Oh, I see. You'll hide it from me. Again. Is this how our marriage is destined to be for the rest of our lives?"

"It's hardly the same as what happened before. I know you are furious, but looking after your welfare is my responsibility as your husband."

"Not while disregarding my opinion. This is a marriage, not a dictatorship. If you wanted a society wife who allowed her husband to run roughshod over her, you married the wrong woman, Harrison."

He dragged a hand through his hair and tugged on the long strands as if trying to rip them out of his head. "I don't want a society wife. I want *you* . . . and only you. But I need you safe, Maddie. This is about nothing more than that— and a good thing the guards were there today, even if they were too late. Who knows what else might have happened?"

Frustration burned in her chest, making it hard to breathe. "That is not the point. You cannot make decisions about my life without consulting me. You, of all people, should know how much I hate surprises. To feel powerless in my own life."

"Maddie—"

"Stop. You cannot treat me like a thing, a possession without a voice. We've known each other for far too long for that. And you promised you wouldn't keep another secret."

"I couldn't let my family ruin this for you. I had to keep you safe."

"You broke your promise to me after only a few days. You have no intention of confiding in me, of trusting me. Of letting me be an equal partner in this marriage." She dragged in air, filling her lungs as best she could. "I don't know what happened to you during these last three years, but the man I used to know told me everything. He never hid things from me."

"That man was not your husband," he said, his voice hardening. "That man was not responsible for your well-being."

Tears threatened as the hopelessness of their situation washed over her. The same argument and he still didn't see her side.

And it was quite clear he never would.

Since he returned, he'd run roughshod over her life. Coerced her into marriage, even after she'd asked for more time. Hadn't told her about his plans to destroy his family, or the reasons he'd left. He was still dictating their terms, still telling her how this was going to work. Hiding what he deemed necessary instead of sharing with her.

The certainty of it sank into her bones like a lead weight. This marriage was a lost cause. She and Harrison had been compatible as friends, inseparable and synchronous, but that had been ages ago. A relationship required communication and compromise. Honesty and respect. He'd given her little of that, even after he'd promised to.

She wanted a partner, not an overbearing tyrant. Because, over time, such high-handedness would strangle whatever affection she held for him. She'd come to resent him, far more than she did at this moment, and that resentment would transform into loathing.

Clearly, their friendship hadn't carried over into something more meaningful, as perhaps they'd both hoped. Childhood friendship and physical attraction alone did not make for a happy marriage, and they would only hurt each other far worse if this continued any longer. Because she deserved better than being lied to and kept in the dark regarding decisions that affected her life.

This had all been a terrible mistake.

She had to clear her throat to get it out, but the words needed to be said. "I think we should separate."

HARRISON'S ENTIRE BODY seized, every muscle and tendon locked in surreal horror.

We should separate.

No, he refused to believe it. This was Maddie, and he knew her better than anyone on earth. She couldn't truly wish to give up on them so soon.

He'd hired guards to keep her safe. True, he

hadn't told her, but how was that a reason to walk away from their marriage?

Dragging in a deep breath, he let it out slowly. "You cannot mean that."

Her gaze was filled with unhappiness and resolve. "I do. This is not working, Harrison. *We* are not working. And if we don't separate, we'll only come to resent one another. I don't want that for either of us."

Resent her? Never. Not in a million years. "I love you. I don't ever want to be apart from you."

"You don't love me." She stared at the window blankly. "If you did, you would take my wishes into account. You'd keep the promises you made."

"Wrong. I love every bit of you, from your fierce competitiveness to your stubbornness." He stepped closer, intending to touch or hold her. Kiss her. Anything to stop this avalanche of panic compounding in his chest. "Your drive and determination, your smile and your laugh . . . there isn't any part of you that I don't love."

"I don't believe you." She dropped back a step, out of his reach. "Because if you did, you would *listen* to me."

"Fine. I'll fire the guards and protect you myself. Is that what you want to hear?"

"It's more than the guards. From the time you returned home you have done what you wanted with little regard for anyone else, including me."

"That is not true."

"It is, otherwise you would have confided in me about your family's finances and the takeover. As well as the real reason for the house party."

He put up his palms in surrender. "You're still angry with me for lying, even though I've apologized and explained why I didn't tell you."

"Yes, but it's more than that." She clasped her elbows and gave a tiny shrug. "It's pushing me when I ask for time to think. It's not listening to me or taking my wishes into consideration. We are not compatible, Harrison. This is doomed to fail."

Wrong. He would not allow them to fail.

Unable to help himself, he closed the distance between them and took her face into his hands. She didn't resist but seemed remote, as if she'd already made up her mind. But he had to try to talk her out of leaving. Prove to her how wrong she was, show how perfect they were for each other.

"What about our wedding night?" he asked softly. "What about those nights since? I'd say we were quite compatible. It could be like that every day for the rest of our lives."

She stepped around him, pulling out of his grip. "Our happiness was fleeting, a honeymoon period full of lust and abandon. I am talking about the way we communicate and make decisions in a marriage."

His ribs felt like they were cracking, the pain inside him ballooning. He stared at her, this woman he'd loved for so long, and he could feel her slipping away, as if he were trying to hold dry sand in his fingers.

But what was the alternative? To let her go?

Everything inside him rebelled at the idea. She was his *wife*. Marrying her was all he'd ever wanted . . and now she wished to leave him.

How would he ever survive it?

Logic. He had to remain calm and use logic.

"You were prepared to marry a duke," he said. "I find it hard to believe you would have expected compatibility and understanding from Lockwood."

"Lockwood never lied to me. And I expected partnership and respect, which I believe he would have readily provided. But that is a moot point because *you are not Lockwood*."

And thank Christ for that. "Meaning you hold me to a different standard."

"I barely knew him. You, on the other hand, were once my closest friend. So yes, I expected more from you. But you've hurt me, Harrison. Again and again since you've returned." She choked on the last few words, a reaction that felt like a punch to his solar plexus.

He imagined more sand slipping through his fingertips. "I never meant to cause you a moment's pain. I just . . . God, Maddie. I only want to protect you."

"I do not need protecting. I am not made of glass. I can learn that my in-laws want to hurt me and still thrash opponents on the tennis court. I can hear of your plans to take over your family's company and still host a house party in your honor. You underestimate me at every turn."

Was that truly what she believed? "I have never underestimated you. You're the smartest and strongest woman I know."

Her expression remained unchanged. "We want different things. Can't you see? I want a true partner and you want to live the life you've always had, answerable to no one and completely independent. Those two things are incongruous, Harrison. We will only make each other miserable."

"I only want you—and I will never be miserable in this marriage."

She closed her eyes briefly, her breathing ragged. "Then I suppose it's me. I am miserable in this marriage. And I deserve better."

His mouth dried out, his ears ringing with finality, as the words sank in. *She wants out.*

Of course she did. She didn't feel the depth of emotion for him that he felt for her. Twice he'd told her that he loved her and she hadn't even hinted that she might love him in return. He was trying to hold on to something that didn't exist, a figment of his imagination, a specter. A ghost of a relationship he'd constructed in his mind in the hopes that it would one day come true.

A pile of dreams built on wishes and faith, not strong enough to withstand the trials a real marriage would need to face. Without equal investment, without love on both sides, the foundation would crumble. Hell, it had already crumbled . . . he just hadn't wanted to face it.

How could he let her go?

He had to find a way, because he couldn't cause her any more pain. While he loved her desperately, completely, he knew it wasn't enough. She'd accused him of never listening to her, never taking her wishes into account. So how could he refuse her this, when it was clear how unhappy he made her?

His pain meant nothing at the prospect of her happiness.

Drawing himself up, he cleared his throat. Twice. "I'll have annulment paperwork drawn up."

She studied him, her brows lowered as if she didn't believe him. "Really?"

"Of course." He thrust his hands in his trouser pockets. "No sense bothering with the trouble of a divorce. We can say we never lived together after the wedding. It's mostly true, anyway."

"Thank you."

He dipped his chin, unable to say more. His chest felt like it had been doused in kerosene and set ablaze. Each inhale a struggle, each exhale pure agony.

Two tears slid down her cheeks and she quickly wiped them away with her fingertips. "Someday, I hope we might be friends again. You and I were clearly much better friends than spouses."

He didn't respond—he couldn't—so she walked to the door, where she paused and looked over her shoulder. "Goodbye, Harrison."

And the door closed behind her with a snap, the final punctuation mark on their relationship. There was nothing more to be said.

He'd lost her.

Chapter Twenty-Six

Dash it. Maddie tossed her hat on the bench and resisted the urge to throw her racket down, as well.

She'd lost. It was the third round, and while the match had been close, she'd given up the lead in the second set and never regained it. Her dreams of winning at her first Nationals tournament were over.

Tears began sliding down her cheeks, the exhaustion and sadness of the past few days catching up with her. She'd lost the match, her husband and her best friend, all in a matter of three days. The weight of her failures sat heavily in her chest, a boulder-sized sense of defeat.

"Now, none of that," Vallie said, coming in right behind her. "You had a great first tournament, Maddie. No one wins their first time out."

Her coach had said this before, likely to manage Maddie's expectations, but it did not ease the disappointment crashing over her in the moment.

Because this isn't just about the tournament.

No, it was about her entire life falling apart.

She hadn't told anyone about her argument with Harrison and the impending annulment, but it was obvious her husband was no longer at the tournament. Her parents were the only ones to inquire after Harrison's whereabouts, so she'd made up a story about pressing business back in New York City. Preston had probably known the truth, his worried gaze tracking her wherever she went, but he said nothing.

Right now, Vallie was staring at her as if he didn't know what to do, like she was this wild creature he'd never encountered before, and she knew she had to pull it together, even if just for a moment or two. "You're right." She forced a smile. "Thank you, Vallie. For everything. I certainly couldn't have done this without you."

His expression grew more confused. "This isn't over. Your days of playing lawn tennis will continue. There are tournaments down South and in Cuba. We'll play over the winter and prepare you to come back next year."

She lifted a shoulder, unable to garner any enthusiasm for future matches at the moment. "I'm sure you're right."

"I know I'm right." He thrust his hands in his pockets. "You are too talented, too smart to let a few setbacks stop you from what you really want. But I understand disappointment. I've had my share." He huffed a laugh. "Believe me, I've had my share. So take the next week off. Don't pick up a racket. Then we'll start making plans. All right?"

Nodding, Maddie said, "All right."

"Good. Your friend is outside and has asked to come in. Miss Young, I believe."

Nellie was here? Maddie hadn't seen her friend in the crowd during the match, but then she'd been a bit preoccupied while losing. "Send her in, if you please."

"I will." Vallie came over and embraced her. "Congratulations, Maddie. I know this doesn't seem like a victory, but I promise you that reaching the third round in your first Nationals is a big achievement."

With her failed marriage so fresh, nothing seemed like a victory. More tears leaked from the corners of her eyes. "Thank you, Vallie."

After a final pat to her back, her coach released her and departed. Not even a minute later, Nellie swept into the room, her bright smile firmly in place as she rushed to hug Maddie. "Madeline Archer, you were brilliant! I've never been so impressed."

Maddie swallowed and nodded, certain the lump in her throat was all that prevented a torrent of emotion from flooding out.

Taking Maddie's shoulders in hand, Nellie leaned away to study her face. "This isn't like you to cry. What's going on?"

Maddie dragged in a deep breath and struggled for composure as she stepped back. There would be time to fall apart later, when she was alone. "Just the stress of the past few days catching up with me."

"Uh-huh," Nellie said absently, her brow furrowed. "I noticed that your husband wasn't here today."

Maddie began collecting her equipment from the box she'd been assigned for the tournament. She tried to give Nellie the same lie she'd told the others but the words wouldn't come.

"Maddie, what's happened? Preston wouldn't tell me, but it's clear something is going on." Nellie's comforting hand landed on Maddie's back. "Did you two have a fight?"

"We've decided to separate." There, she said it.

Nellie gasped and forced Maddie to turn around. "What do you mean, separate? Like, divorce?"

Maddie glanced about, ensuring they were alone. Divorce was more scandalous than being compromised and forced into a marriage. The last thing Maddie needed was to be branded as both a jezebel and a divorcée. "No, we'll file for an annulment." –

"I cannot believe this. What happened? And Harrison agreed?"

Maddie gave her friend a very quick version of the story, from the hat pin to the moment she walked out. "It's for the best. We'd only make each other miserable."

Nellie pursed her lips. "Awfully quick to arrive at such a conclusion, wouldn't you say?"

"I cannot stay in a marriage where decisions concerning my life are made without my input."

"You've been married a minute, Maddie. Goodness, give the sails a bit of time to find some wind before jumping back out into the water."

If only it were that simple. "You don't understand what it's like to feel so helpless, as if your life is spinning out of control."

"Oh, don't I?" Nellie said, an edge to her voice. "Watching my mother wither away and die in front of my eyes doesn't count?"

Maddie instantly deflated. "God, Nellie. Forgive me. I am being selfish."

Nellie waved her hand. "Forgiven. And I realize a marriage is different than losing a parent. You love Harrison and you hate surprises."

Maddie's lip quivered so she sank her teeth into it. "Love isn't enough. There has to be respect and trust, too."

"You know him better than I do, obviously, but I have a hard time believing Harrison doesn't respect or trust you. After all, he had the best of intentions in hiring the guards and not telling you."

"Best intentions or not, that is not permission to hide something from me."

"If you want perfection, then you'll never find it because no one is perfect—not even you," Nellie said with a shake of her head. "You'll be doomed to spend your life alone because no one will ever measure up to your expectations. Is that really what you want?"

"Whose side are you on?"

"Would you rather I lied to you?"

"No, but if you are attempting to comfort me, this effort is falling short."

Nellie winced and gave a light, self-deprecating chuckle. "I'm not known for wrapping things up in a pretty bow, which is probably why you're one of my only friends. So I'll stop trying to make you see reason."

"Thank you," Maddie said, her words laced with sarcasm.

"What happened to the masher, by the way?"

"He was arrested and I had to give a statement. Turns out he wasn't hired by the Archers, which was a relief."

"Meaning he's just another entitled man who thinks women are objects and not human beings."

The way Nellie said it, with such vehemence and resentment, gave Maddie pause. "You sound as if you have some experience in that regard."

"Don't we all?" Nellie muttered. "Now I should let you get changed. We can chat more on the way back to New York."

"I was planning on taking the train with my parents."

"Not anymore. I'm sending them back without you. We'll stop in the hotel bar for a drink first."

"We can't do that!" Most hotel bars were men only, certainly the ones open during the day.

"Of course we can. Stick with me, Maddie. I know all the best places to cause trouble."

A DOOR SLAMMED just before a shout rang out. "What have you done?" The words echoed in the empty Xavier house, the voice sounding a lot like Kit.

Bracing himself, Harrison called out, "Up here!"

Heavy footsteps marched closer, the only sound in the quiet space. In his bedchamber, Harrison excused his valet, the single staff member he'd allowed within these walls, and continued sorting his clothing on the bed.

"I've just had a visit from Preston," Kit said,

now in the doorway. "You and Maddie are separating?"

"Yes."

"Separating?"

Harrison didn't answer because he'd already made himself clear. Why was Kit being so obstinate?

Kit leaned against a bed pole. "Are you going to elaborate or make me pull it out of you?"

Harrison exhaled slowly. "She would like out of the marriage. I have agreed. My lawyer finished the annulment papers yesterday, I signed them, and they've been delivered to her home. I assume she'll deal with them when she returns from Philadelphia."

Scrawling his name on that piece of paper had been the single hardest thing he'd done in his life. If his lawyer hadn't been staring at him, Harrison likely would have bawled like a baby as the ink dried.

"She's back," Kit said.

"Oh?" He tried not to sound interested, but he was dying to know what happened at the tournament. He'd purposely avoided reading the sporting section of the newspapers.

"Lost in the third round. I understand she gave a good fight, though."

She must've been devastated. His heart, already battered and bloody, gave a small squeeze, wishing he could see her and comfort her. Tell her he loved her and that he was proud of her.

She doesn't love you, remember? She wants freedom from you.

Realization dawned, nausea blooming in his

stomach. Their marriage was over. If she had returned, then she'd likely signed the annulment papers already. They'd soon be filed with the city, and it would be like their marriage never happened.

Except in his dreams.

Every time he tried to sleep she was there, smiling and laughing with him, teasing him. He ached for her, his body in constant pain, his mind wailing with the unfairness of it. He wanted her so badly, but he'd ruined it, pushing and maneuvering until he'd driven her away.

His silence must've annoyed Kit because his friend huffed. "Will you tell me why you are just letting her go? And why are you packing?"

Open trunks were half-full on the bedroom floor. Harrison placed a stack of collar boxes into one of them. "I'm leaving for Paris."

"When?"

"Tomorrow." He hadn't been able to book passage sooner, otherwise he'd be halfway across the Atlantic by now.

"Have you considered that your wife might merely require time to cool down? That perhaps you are hastily running away—again?"

"I haven't, actually. Rather, I think I should've ruined the Archers from Paris and never returned to New York. Coming here was a mistake, and I am rectifying that."

"What do you plan to do, go back to your old life and pretend this never happened?"

"That is precisely what I intend to do. I've already cabled Esmée and told her to expect me in a week."

"Jesus Christ, Harrison." Kit dropped onto the bed and put his head in his hands. "You cannot be serious."

He shrugged and opened the crate of Kentucky bourbon he'd bought. Wrapping one of the bottles carefully, he placed it in a trunk, then reached for another bottle. "The marriage never happened. It'll be wiped off the books, nothing but a faint memory for both of us. She's free to become a duchess or a countess or whatever dashed title she desires."

In fact, he'd decided to help that cause along by paying a call this afternoon. Perhaps he could right one wrong before he left this country for good.

"Are you taking that entire case on the boat?" Kit gestured toward the bottles.

"Yes." His plan was to get stinking drunk as America faded in the distance, and then stay stinking drunk the entire journey. At least until he could forget her for any serious length of time.

"What about Archer Industries? What about this house? You are leaving all of it behind?"

None of it mattered without Maddie. "I've turned everything over to my—to Stephen Webster. He's more than capable of handling it in my absence."

"I see." Kit walked around the room and peered inside the trunks. "Were you going to say goodbye, at least?"

"I figured you'd try to talk me out of it. For the record, Preston has already tried and failed."

"He told me. Said you were more stubborn

than a union boss at the negotiation table. What am I supposed to tell her?"

Harrison didn't honestly think Maddie would bother asking after him. She could return to the way things were, back to her plans and parties. Enjoy her perfect world without him mucking it up like he did everything else. "I've already told her what she needed to know." That he was sorry, that he loved her.

That she was all that had ever mattered to him.

"For what it's worth, I think you are making a mistake."

"Well, I've never done anything right, so why would I start now?"

Kit made a scoffing sound in his throat. "Do not let that Archer childhood nonsense into your brain. It's entirely unhelpful."

"Just like you are able to block the Ward childhood nonsense?" Kit's family was no better than the Archers. In some ways, they were worse. There was a reason the two of them became inseparable in college; each man had demons from his youth that refused to let up.

"Touché," Kit said. "I suppose all that's left to say is that I'll miss you. I was looking forward to having you around again."

"You're welcome to visit. It'll be just like it was before. Debauchery at every turn, with more available women than you could ever screw."

"Harrison." Kit paused as if choosing his words carefully. "Nothing will go back to the way it was before. This is not a small thing, losing Maddie. I hope you realize as much."

"You forget that I lost her once before. This will be no different."

"But you weren't married. You hadn't slept with her or—"

"Stop trying to be helpful," Harrison snarled, dragging his hands through his hair. "Fuck, Kit. Just . . . Christ almighty, stop talking."

His friend's expression went blank, devoid of any emotion. "I'll leave you to your packing, then. I've said enough."

Guilt swept across Harrison's skin like needles. "I know you are trying to help, but please stop."

They stared at each other for a long moment. "Good travels, then. Enjoy Paris and Esmée. Drop a line once in a while, will you? Let us know you're still alive." Kit walked out, the sound of his retreating footsteps ringing out in the emptiness.

The guilt didn't ease up, but Harrison pushed it all from his mind. Today, he had to finish packing and pay one visit. Then he could leave for Paris in the morning and forget every minute of his time in New York.

Chapter Twenty-Seven

*T*he knock startled Maddie. She'd been standing at her bedchamber windows and staring off into the gardens. Dusk had fallen, shadows lengthening with the approach of nighttime, the time of day she dreaded the most.

It was when thoughts of Harrison took hold in her mind and wouldn't let go. Every conversation, every moment reenacted and replayed on an extended loop until she thought she'd crumble. It hurt to think she'd never have that again, that he was out of her life forever.

If you want perfection, then you'll never find it because no one is perfect—not even you.

Nellie was wrong. This wasn't about expecting perfection. This was about her life and having a partner by her side, not a husband who lied and took away her choices.

She didn't regret her decision in asking for the annulment. Separating was the best course of action for them both. What other choice did they have when their paths were so completely different? They could never be happy together, not as a couple.

Her gaze swung to the annulment papers sitting on her dressing table. They'd arrived while she was in Philadelphia, with his signature already in place. All that was left was for her to sign and return the document to the lawyers. Then their marriage would be over.

So why couldn't she bring herself to do it?

The knock came again. "Maddie." It was her mother.

"Come in."

Mama's worried face appeared in the doorway. "You have a visitor, my dear. Shall I send him away?"

Maddie's breath caught. Had Harrison come to talk? She wasn't certain whether she wanted to see him.

Something must've shown on her face because her mother quickly added, "It's the Duke of Lockwood."

Lockwood was here to see her? Goodness, whatever for?

Though she was hardly dressed for visitors, she supposed she owed Lockwood an audience after all the aggravation she'd caused him. "I'll come down."

"Perhaps brush your hair first," her mother suggested gently.

Maddie resisted the urge to roll her eyes and settled for a rueful half smile instead. "Mama, I humiliated the man. Publicly. Trust me, he won't care that my hair is a mess."

"Still, he is a duke, Madeline."

She kissed her mother's cheek on the way out the door. "Don't worry. It's safe to say that my chance at becoming his duchess has passed."

The receiving room door was ajar, so Maddie slipped inside. Dressed in a fine navy-blue suit, Lockwood peered at the knickknacks on the mantel. She closed the door behind her. Lord knew there was no need to protect her reputation any longer. "Your Grace, this is a surprise."

"Mrs. Archer." He bowed.

She curtsied, a pang going through her as she realized the name wouldn't apply much longer. Soon, she'd return to Miss Webster. "Shall we sit?"

Nodding, he waited for her to settle on the sofa before relaxing in an armchair. "Forgive the late intrusion. I know you've only just returned from Philadelphia. How did you fare in your tournament?"

"I lost in the third round." It still rankled. The woman hadn't been a better player. If Maddie had played smarter, paid better attention during the match, she would have won.

"That is remarkable for your first time at such a prestigious event, is it not?"

"Undoubtedly, I'll come to see it that way in a few days. Right now, the loss merely smarts."

Lockwood studied her. "I understand that isn't all you lost."

Her tongue thickened as she wondered what to say. Had Lockwood heard about the annulment? That seemed impossible. "Forgive me, but I don't follow."

The duke crossed his long legs and leaned back. He appeared annoyingly comfortable in his own skin. "I had an interesting visit earlier this evening. From your husband."

Harrison had gone to see Lockwood?

Maddie fought to remain still. "Oh?"

"He's informed me that the two of you are separating."

Embarrassment skated along her nape, down her sternum. No use denying it, she supposed, seeing as how Harrison had oh-so-helpfully spread the word. "We are filing for an annulment, which I assume will be granted expeditiously."

"I have to say, I am surprised." Lockwood's gaze narrowed on her. "I thought the two of you were a perfect match when I saw you together at the house party."

"Friendship does not always translate into a marriage," she said vaguely. The details of why it hadn't worked were no one else's concern.

"True, but there was a spark as well, wasn't there?"

She opened her mouth, then closed it. This was quite an odd conversation to have with one's former fiancé. "Yes, I suppose there was," she finally said.

"Which is why I found the reason for your husband's visit tonight both annoying and perplexing."

"The reason?"

His brown gaze glittered in the gaslight. "He has encouraged me to court you again. First, he apologized for compromising you—for which he took the entirety of the blame, by the way—and then tried to tell me how disappointed you were when our betrothal came to an end."

Her face slackened, and she didn't know whether to laugh or cry at the news. How could Harrison have done this? He was manipulating her life once more without telling her. It was both humiliating and utterly absurd. "I don't know what to say."

"There is nothing to say. Even if you hadn't married Harrison, I would have severed the engagement once the two of you were discovered together. It was the only honorable thing to do."

"Of course," she mumbled, wishing the sofa would open up and swallow her whole.

"Your husband tried to convince me the whole episode was a fever dream, that everyone would soon forget you'd even been married. Then he said you and I belonged together."

Oh, my God. A fever dream? That hurt more than she would've thought possible. What was Harrison thinking? He was trying to reconcile her with the duke, but to what end? Was he so anxious to be rid of her? "I am terribly sorry, Your Grace. This is embarrassing, to say the least."

"I can see that you weren't expecting this. Neither was I, to be honest."

"I certainly did not put him up to it, if that's what you were wondering."

"I never thought you did. What I do think is that this is your husband's attempt—albeit a clumsy one—at turning back the clock. Setting everything as it was before he arrived and wreaked havoc on our lives."

That actually made sense, in a strange way, especially when she recalled her very public campaign to become a duchess. Yet there was no erasing this from their minds. Too much had happened to ever forget. She gave the duke a sad smile. "Only we cannot go backward in time."

"Indeed, we cannot. I may not have funds, Mrs. Archer, but I do have my pride."

"Of course. I hope you may forgive me one day."

"I hold no ill will toward you or your husband. I think what he is attempting to do is again clumsy, but sweet in a roundabout way. He wants to see you happy and is willing to sacrifice his future with you to make it happen. Believe me, it killed him to pay me a call." His lips twitched with secret mirth. "And I did not make it easy on him."

She could only imagine how uncomfortable that meeting had been. "I hope he apologized to you."

The duke dipped his chin. "He did, and threw in future shares of Archer Industries, as well."

Men. They solved everything with their fists or their wallets. "I'm happy to hear it."

Lockwood sat forward. "Before I go, I have two requests."

"Of course. I am in your debt."

"First, seek out your husband before he sails for Paris in the morning."

Maddie paused, her lungs unable to function, while her mind turned over the news. Harrison was leaving? Had he planned to let her know or say goodbye? What about the business?

Lockwood cleared his throat delicately. "I apologize if you hadn't been told. I assumed . . ."

"Don't worry. Someone would have shared the news eventually."

"Undoubtedly, but it seems especially cruel to hear it from me. Nevertheless, the man clearly adores you."

Maddie didn't know what to say, her head spinning with all she'd learned. It must have killed Harrison to call on Lockwood with the intention of reconciling her with the duke. Yet he'd done it, trying to undo some of the perceived damage he'd caused. But she didn't want Lockwood.

God help her, she still missed Harrison.

When the duke quieted, she prompted, "And the second request?"

Lockwood stood and pulled his cuffs, straightening them. "I'd be grateful—and this is for both of you, really—if you would lose my direction. As delightful as this experience has been, I'd rather not find myself in the middle of my ex-fiancée's marital squabbles again at any point in the future."

Cheeks hot with mortification, she rose. "Of course, and please accept my apologies."

Ever polite, the duke inclined his head. "I shall be on my way, then, and leave you to your evening."

"I'll show you to the door."

They walked out into the entryway, where he found his top hat and cane. Then he faced her, his expression kind but solemn. "For what it's worth, I assume every marriage is bound to take some knocks in the beginning. Who knows? You may have arrived in England and hated it." He placed his hat on his head and reached for the door. "I wish you every happiness, Mrs. Archer."

"And you as well, Your Grace."

He strolled out into the night, disappearing into a closed carriage, while Maddie shut the door and pondered his words. Had she reacted hastily in asking for the separation? Nellie had said as much earlier, too. Indeed, there had been good days amid the bad in her marriage, but how could she ever trust Harrison not to lie to her again?

Unbelievable that he went to see Lockwood in the first place, but asking the duke to court her once more was downright shocking. Was Harrison so eager to see her paired off with another man? Furthermore, the thought of him sailing back to Paris and probably straight to Esmée made her want to stab *him* with a hat pin.

He wants to see you happy and is willing to sacrifice his future with you to make it happen.

If that were true, she could almost forgive his high-handedness. Almost. Still, she wasn't certain he was ready to be a partner, not a dictator. Could she ever trust him not to hurt her again?

STANDING AT THE steamship's railing, Harrison stared out at the miles of blue ocean, while the waves bounced off the hull and misted his skin. He hardly felt it. He hadn't felt much of anything, really, since leaving Philadelphia.

New York was behind him now. More than half a day's journey existed between him and everything he'd lost, and he was forever stuck inside a prison of his own making, a hell he'd designed with his machinations and stupidity.

Turned out Kit had been right. This wasn't like before; it was much worse. He'd had a small taste of happiness, true happiness, with her, and it had been stripped away. The rest of his life stretched out before him much like this ocean, cold and empty, the prospect more dismal than he could bear. So he had to clear his mind and lock down his emotions, think of nothing. *Be* nothing.

Bourbon certainly helped, he thought as he lifted a silver flask to his lips. Other vices awaited in Paris, ones that could also help him forget, like absinthe and women. Perhaps he'd try the sweet oblivion of the opium pipe. Who cared anymore?

He didn't want to remember her. *Ever.* He left word for Preston and Kit not to visit for several years, needing a clean break. Sort of like cutting off an arm. It was the only manner in which he'd survive.

America held nothing for him any longer. The Archers were ruined, so at least he'd succeeded there. He finished the bourbon in his flask, shaking it to release the remaining drops onto his tongue. There were eleven more bottles packed in his trunks, more than enough to last the week-long journey, which meant he needed to return to his cabin for more spirits.

"Pardon me," a female voice said. "Aren't you Mr. Harrison Archer?"

Christ, could he not escape high society for one damn minute? *I shouldn't have traveled in first class.* These decks were like a floating Delmonico's,

Central Park promenade and the Knickerbocker Club all rolled into one.

Turning, he found an older woman, likely mid-thirties, staring at him from under her parasol. Her gaze held something akin to either curiosity or attraction, but the alcohol had dulled his ability to focus. Probably a gossip, for which he had no patience, or someone looking for a roll in the sheets with a younger man, in which case he had no interest.

Clutching his empty flask, he gave a shake of his head. "No. You're mistaken."

"We met at the Paris Opera last year. I'm certain it was you."

"You're wrong. I'm no one."

Another voice came from behind him. "He's my husband."

Harrison looked over his shoulder and blinked. She was here.

Maddie was *here*.

He had to be hallucinating. Dropping his flask to the deck, he reached out to steady himself with the railing. Was this real?

Dimly, he heard the older woman say, "Then I hope you take better care of him. He looks terrible." He assumed she walked away after that, but he only had eyes for Maddie.

Maddie was on the boat.

Wait, how? Rubbing his eyes, he lost his balance a touch. Suddenly, she was there beside him, her fingers wrapped around his arm. "Please move away from the railing. You're starting to scare me, Harrison."

"Am I dreaming?"

"No, you're not. You are, however, drunk, and I don't want you toppling over the side."

"You don't?"

She began towing him toward the first-class cabins. "Of course not. Come with me, please. Let's get some coffee in you."

He still didn't understand. "Why?"

"Because I wish to talk and it would be nice if you remembered what I said."

Talk? He stopped in his tracks, his body refusing to go an inch farther. "Why?"

She wore an exasperated smile, the one she used to give him every time he suggested some silly idea. "May we go inside and have this conversation in private? I recognize no fewer than six people on deck, and no doubt they are eagerly hoping to overhear us. Please, Harrison." She dragged him along and his feet followed eagerly, as they always did when she was in the vicinity.

He couldn't keep away from her, even when she'd asked to separate.

Wait, what was this about? "Is this regarding the annulment? I won't fight you," he said as they entered the corridor leading to the cabins.

"I know. And yes, it's regarding the annulment."

His stomach sank, nausea rolling in his belly. There must have been a legal loophole or detail he'd missed, and she'd come to sew it up before moving on without him. So why hadn't she cabled him instead?

"Because this is a private conversation best had in person and not over the wire," she answered.

Oh, had he spoken out loud?

Removing a key from her pocket, she unlocked a cabin door, then practically shoved him inside. He stumbled in, his limbs heavy and uncoordinated, shoulders stooped, and he dropped onto a tiny sofa as she closed the door.

She lowered herself into an armchair, unpinned her hat and tossed it onto the side table. Her simple beauty struck him like a fist to the center of his chest, as it always did. He loved looking at her, from the moss green of her eyes to the freckles across her cheeks. The upward turn of her nose and the perfect bow shape of her lips. He struggled to draw air into his lungs, each breath a stark reminder of what he'd never have, his body taunting him with the knowledge that she no longer belonged to him.

He licked his lips. "I already signed the paperwork. Are you here to give me the final copies?"

"I didn't sign—and I don't want to."

"You'd rather *divorce*?"

"I'd rather stay married, actually. That is, if you can forgive me."

His heart lurched, restarting as if it had been frozen, hibernating inside his chest. Suddenly, he felt as sober as a judge. "You've done nothing that warrants apologizing. I'm the one who is dashed sorry, Mads."

"I know, but I do owe you an apology. I shouldn't expect either of us to be perfect. Everyone makes mistakes, myself included. I was just so angry and I felt powerless, but I should've given you the benefit of the doubt. You've earned at least that from me in all the years we've known each other."

He said nothing. There weren't words for what was building in his heart, a sensation terrifyingly close to fragile hope. Speaking might spoil whatever was happening.

She stripped off her gloves. "Do you want a partner, Harrison? An equal? A woman to stand by your side, not linger in the background?"

"Mads, all I've ever wanted was to be yours. You can stand beside me or in front of me, even on top of me, as long as you never let me go."

"Yet you tried to give me to Lockwood like some piece of heirloom china."

"You wanted to be a duchess. I thought you'd be happy if Lockwood courted you again. I up-ended your life when I returned, so I tried to undo a little of my damage."

"That wasn't necessary. And I participated in said damage, so you cannot assume all the blame."

"But I rushed you. I pushed and pushed to get what I wanted."

"True, and you've been two steps ahead of me ever since you returned from Paris. I merely needed time to catch up."

"Have you caught up?"

"I think so, now that the tournament is over and I've had time to think."

"Congratulations, by the way. I am proud of you."

Her cheeks flushed and her smile grew soft. "I only made it to the quarterfinals."

"That's astounding for your first tournament. Just wait until your second year."

"We'll see. That is, if my husband doesn't mind my playing."

Warmth took root in his belly, heat spreading outward like lightning strikes of pure joy. He sported a grin that had nothing to do with bourbon. "He wouldn't dare prevent you from chasing a championship, if that's what you decide."

"It will require a lot of traveling."

"He loves hotels and trains."

"And a lot of standing around in the hot sun."

"He loves a good sweat in the outdoors."

"And a lot of liniment rubs and long baths."

Fuck, he wanted that. Now. He wiggled his fingers. "I've heard he has ludicrously strong hands."

She chuckled. "What a perfect man this is . . ."

That word caused him to frown. "He's not perfect, Mads, but he loves you more than life itself. And if you'll forgive him, he'll spend every day trying to prove it to you."

"I know and I don't need perfection. He's a good man, one who has always watched out for me. My best friend. And I love him madly."

As if pulled by a string, he sat up, his back straight. "What did you say?"

"I said I love him. I probably always have, only it took me this long to realize it."

Harrison was out of his chair and kissing her before she finished speaking. Her mouth was lush and welcoming, and he thought he'd never get enough. He poured every bit of his relief and longing into that kiss. "I love you, Mads," he said when they finally surfaced for air. "It's always been you for me."

"I believe you—and I've come to realize that I can't live without you. As soon as I heard you were sailing for Paris, I knew. No matter what else happens, you are stuck with me."

"Good, because I am never letting you go again. Twice is enough for one lifetime."

"You won't need to. No more hiding from me, though. The truth from now on."

"You have my word. I'll never keep anything from you again."

She pressed a kiss to the tip of his chin. "Now, I think we should put you to bed to sleep off all that alcohol."

"As long as I'm not alone, you can put me wherever you'd like."

Rising, she took his hand and led him toward the large bed. "Oh, don't worry, Mr. Archer. I definitely have plans for you . . ."

And he followed her, as he always had, to wherever she might lead. Together.

Chapter Twenty-Eight

One Year Later

Harrison checked his pocket watch for the time. Again.

He gestured to the stack of paperwork remaining in front of him. "How much more of this do you have, William?"

William Innis, Harrison's right hand at Archer Industries, shifted in the chair, his expression grim. "At least an hour's worth."

"Impossible. My wife's match begins in twenty minutes. I've got to hurry across the street to the club or I'll never make it."

Last year, after an extended honeymoon in Paris, Harrison and Maddie had returned to New York City, where he'd assumed the role of Archer Industries' president. He'd hired William, and together they'd done wonders for the company's bottom line. The company had finally turned a profit last quarter—the first since his father's death. The construction of big ocean liners, along with Stephen Webster's cooperation in transporting lumber, had made all the difference.

The company took up almost all of his time, which Maddie didn't seem to mind. She focused on her lawn tennis game and traveled to tournaments all around the country, which had led to a spot at the U.S. Nationals again this year. He was damn proud of her.

She'd won handily throughout this tournament, advancing to the championship of the All-Comers bracket. If she won, then she would play last year's winner for the overall title. The bookmakers were currently giving odds on her winning the whole dashed thing.

Nothing would keep him from being at her match today.

"Just a few more minutes," William said. "You have been out of the office all week and issues are piling up."

"Feel free to make whatever decisions you deem necessary. I trust you, Innis." Harrison pushed to his feet. "Or the world can wait for one week while my wife plays for the national championship."

He started for the door, but William trailed him. "Wait, one more question before you go. Your brother has accepted your offer of a position at the company, but we don't know where to place him."

Harrison paused at the door and thrust his hands into his pockets. Thomas had come begging for money almost a month ago and Harrison had refused. He had, however, agreed to give Thomas a job at Archer Industries, if his brother wished to truly work like everyone else there. No favoritism, no using the Archer name to jump ahead of others. No taking days off to gallivant around Europe or sail in Newport. Just hard work for an honest wage.

It seemed Thomas was truly serious about providing for his family.

"Start him in the mailroom," Harrison said. "If he succeeds there after an extended period of time, then we'll move him up."

William nodded. "We'll continue this after dinner, I assume?"

"Nope. Win or lose, I'll be busy celebrating with my wife tonight. I'll find you in the morning. And thank you, Innis. I know this week has been a long one for you. Feel free to take the rest of the day. You're welcome to come to the match with me, if you like."

"No, thank you. I'll just catch up on some cables, then head out for dinner. I have family here in Philadelphia that I'd like to see. Wish her luck for me."

"Indeed, I will." Harrison left the room and took the elevator downstairs, where he strode out into the bright June sun. With the hotel directly across from the Philadelphia Cricket Club, he was through the gates in hardly any time at all.

The main court was surrounded by spectators, a heady excitement hanging in the air. Lawn tennis fever had gripped America, and Maddie was one of the reasons for its popularity. She was bold and outspoken, a brash player who took the game seriously. The newspapers loved to quote her, this woman of high society who dared to sweat and struggle in public. She'd become a national celebrity.

While Harrison supported her wholeheartedly, part of him still feared for her safety after what happened last year. They had decided—together—that guards weren't yet necessary, that the masher had been an isolated incident, but Harrison never stopped worrying.

He spotted Preston, that tall bastard, right away at center court, surrounded by their friends and Maddie's parents. Harrison pushed through the crowd to meet them.

Kit slapped him on the shoulder. "About time you arrived. Your wife is already warming up."

The two opponents were on the court, hitting easily to loosen their muscles. "How does she look, Vallie?"

Maddie's coach didn't take his eyes off her as he calmly answered, "Like a champion."

"I'm nervous," Preston admitted, wiping his palms on his trousers. "I cannot fathom how you are all so relaxed."

Harrison was also nervous, but he had faith in Maddie's abilities. Also, no matter what happened today, she'd already won in his book. Hell, she was ranked the third-best female player in the country at the moment. A spectacular achievement if you asked him, especially when one considered that most of the other players weren't even twenty years old. Maddie said she often felt like a tottering old fool next to some of these young gals.

"Is it too much to ask for shade?" Mrs. Webster,

perched on a tiny folding chair, adjusted her parasol. "Only a man would think women wish to sit in the hot sun for two hours to watch a tennis game."

"It's a match, dear." Mr. Webster patted her shoulder. "And I said you could wait inside."

"And miss Maddie's win?" She sniffed. "I think not."

Even Maddie's mother had come around on Maddie's tennis career. Harrison knew that Maddie had been touched by her mother's support in the last year, though it hadn't stopped Mrs. Webster from asking about grandchildren.

They weren't ready yet. Harrison wouldn't expect Maddie to give up playing competitively to raise their children. He'd used condoms in Paris for years and he didn't mind using them again now, though they were harder to procure in the United States thanks to the Comstock laws. The trouble was worth it, however, because he was enjoying having her to himself when their schedules allowed.

"Here we go," Kit exclaimed, and the crowd quieted down.

The match began, with Maddie serving first. Heads moved left and right, back and forth, following the progress of the small round ball as points were traded. On and on it went, the two opponents fairly equal in skill. Vallie stayed quiet, his face stoic, while the rest of them clapped and cheered. Maddie won the first set, but lost the second.

As they changed sides, Maddie walked past them. "Find it," Vallie said, and she nodded.

Then she gave Harrison an exhausted smile, worry shining in her green eyes. *I love you*, he mouthed to her, adding a wink for good measure. Her shoulders relaxed a bit as she went to the other side of the court.

"What does 'find it' mean?" he asked her coach.

"She needs to find her opponent's weakness and exploit it," Vallie said. "As soon as she does, she wins."

In the third set, the other girl played conservatively, staying at the baseline, as if she were scared to play too aggressively. Maddie sensed it and began coming to the net, jumping and diving for balls that seemed impossible, yet she returned them for winners. It was an athletic feat that dazzled the crowd. Everyone seemed to be rooting for her, and she began to pull away as the clear winner of the third set. Even Vallie cracked a smile and clapped.

The next set remained the same, with Maddie controlling the pace and staying ahead, and then it was over. Maddie jumped up in happiness and relief when her opponent's last shot went wide. She'd won the match. As the two women shook hands across the net, Harrison traded handshakes and hugs with the rest of their jubilant group. Finally, his wife came running over and threw herself at him. He held her tightly, propriety be damned. "Well done, Mads. Congratulations."

Quickly, she was pulled away by their impatient friends and family, who all congratulated her with kisses on the cheek and slaps on the back. He'd never seen her look happier as she basked in their attention.

When she made it back over to him again, he put an arm around her shoulder and kissed her sweaty cheek. "You were spectacular."

"It's not over yet." She leaned against him. "There's still the championship game tomorrow."

"No matter what happens, I'm proud of you."

"Even if I lose?"

He heard the teasing in her voice, but he answered with all due seriousness, his lips near her ear. "Win or lose, Madeline Jane Archer, you're still the best thing that has ever happened to me."

She grinned up at him, squinting in the bright sun. "I'll go change and then we can go back to the hotel and celebrate."

That meant taking a bath together and falling into bed naked. He could hardly wait. "Lead the way, champ."

Acknowledgments

Some books come out fully formed and some books take a village. This book took a metropolis. First, I have to thank the super smart and incredibly generous Sarah MacLean, who spent many hours helping me untangle the mess I'd made with this story. In addition, thank you to Sophie Jordan, Diana Quincy and Nisha Sharma for their help along the way. I couldn't have done it without you!

I also couldn't have done it without Tessa Woodward, my fantastic editor at Avon/HarperCollins. This is our seventh book together and she makes me a better writer each time.

The team at Avon/HarperCollins works hard on producing and promoting my books, and I'm extremely grateful for their efforts: Elle Keck, Jessica Lyons, Angela Craft, Pam Jaffee, Guido Caroti and everyone else behind the scenes. Thanks to Jon Paul Ferrara (Jon Paul Studios) for another fantastic cover illustration. Also, thank you to my agent, Laura Bradford, for always looking out for me.

A special thanks to Heather Charron and Joana Vieira Varela, members of my Facebook group, the

Gilded Lilies, who came up with the name for the Websters' Newport cottage when my brain melted near the deadline.

Here are some historical notes for you . . .

Lawn tennis became an organized, competitive sport during the Victorian Era/Gilded Age. I based Maddie on a number of ladies tennis players from the late 19th and early 20th centuries, but mostly Suzanne Lenglen. A Frenchwoman, Lenglen became an international phenomenon in the 1910s and 1920s, and her aggressive style of play revolutionized ladies tennis. (Seriously, research her because she was one unconventional and outspoken woman, and I'd like a biopic now, please.)

Mashers were a serious problem in Gilded Age America, as women gained more independence and went out in public more frequently. Hat pins became a way for women to defend themselves, though many cities looked to regulate the hat pin instead of cracking down on the sexual assault. (Some things never change, I suppose.) Thanks to the "Racing Nellie Bly" blog for the info that started me down this rabbit hole.

Before I forget, thank you to the readers, bloggers, reviewers and lovers of romance. We adore you! Your support allows authors to have the best job in the entire world.

I can't send enough love to the author pals who listen, support and distract me when I need it. There are too many to name here, but you know who you are!

Lastly, thanks to my family. I couldn't continue to do this without their love and patience.

The next enthralling romance
from Joanna Shupe in
the Fifth Avenue Rebels series,

⁂

The Lady Gets Lucky

Debuts Fall 2021

Next month, don't miss these exciting new love stories only from Avon Books

Love of a Cowboy by Jennifer Ryan

Skye Kennedy has always loved the close-knit community of Sunrise Fellowship—but when she witnesses the commune's new leader commit a terrible crime, she flees . . . and finds herself in Montana, on the McGrath ranch, and drawn to the stoic yet kind man determined to help her, Declan McGrath.

Dark Melody by Christine Feehan

Lead guitarist of the Dark Troubadours, Dayan was renowned for his mesmerizing performances. His melodies stilled crowds, beckoned, seduced, tempted. And always, he called to *her*. His lover. His lifemate. Fragile, delicate, vulnerable, Corinne Wentworth had an indomitable faith that made her fiery surrender to Dayan all the more powerful.

Scoundrel of My Heart by Lorraine Heath

Lady Kathryn Lambert must marry a titled gentleman to claim her inheritance. Yet she is unable to forget the scandalous Lord Griffith Stanwick, who aided in her achievement—or his betrayal. But when old passions flare and new desires ignite, she must decide if sacrificing her legacy is worth a lifetime shared with the scoundrel of her heart.

The Wildes of Lindow Castle

Wilde in Love
978-0-06-238947-3

Too Wilde to Wed
978-0-06-269246-7

Born to Be Wilde
978-0-06-269247-4

Say No to the Duke
978-0-06-287782-6

EJ6 0719

*G*ive in to your Impulses!

These unforgettable stories only take a second to buy and give you hours of reading pleasure!

Go to *www.AvonImpulse.com* and see what we have to offer.

Available wherever e-books are sold.

AVONIMPULSE

IMP 0811